FAGIN

HAVISHAM

Fagin & Miss Havisham
by James Thayer
Published by Creative Texts Publishers
PO Box 50
Barto, PA 19504
www.creativetexts.com

Copyright 2024 by James Thayer
All rights reserved

Cover credit: Dan Chosich
Creative Texts ® and Creative Texts Publishers ® are registered Trademarks of Creative Texts Publishers, LLC.

The following is a work of fiction. Any resemblance to actual names, persons, businesses, and incidents is strictly coincidental. Locations are used only in the general sense and do not represent the real place in actuality.

ISBN: 978-1-64738-099-1

FAGIN & MISS HAVISHAM

JAMES THAYER

To my wife Patti and our daughters Alex and Annemarie.

TABLE OF CONTENTS

1 1

2 9

3 20

4 29

5 38

6 49

7 60

8 69

9 77

10 93

11 99

12 110

13 118

14 129

15 137

16 148

17 162

18 170

19 183

20 194

21 203

22 213

23 224

24 239

25 250

26 260

27 269

28 279

1

The pickpocket hid behind the dustman's wagon, and when it lurched forward on the cobblestones—the dustman chanting "Dust ho, dust ho"— the pickpocket moved with it, his eyes always on the mark. The pickpocket's name was Fagin, and if he had a first name no one had ever heard it. He stepped over a pile of brown cabbage leaves dropped by a costermonger who displayed his knife to the pickpocket, maybe as a warning to stay away. Fagin from Field Lane was well-known even here, outside his rookery.

Up the street a hackney coach—its wheel spokes the same shiny green as the carriage—waited for a fare in front of a candle shop. Fagin rose on his toes, peering over the mound of dust on the wagon. The mark pulled a coin from his waistcoat's pocket and held it out to a woman who lowered her basket from her head and allowed the mark to select an orange. The mark playfully tossed the orange into the air, caught it, and tipped his hat to the woman.

Fagin had no interest in coins, not with this mark who the pickpocket had spotted some days ago, and who walked the same route each morning. The mark's greatcoat—with brass buttons the size of half-crowns—was open in front, revealing a waistcoat with patch pockets stitched with thick crimson thread. The waistcoat might as well have had a bull's-eye on it. Fagin smiled.

The mark also wore Blucher boots and a wide-brimmed beaver hat. He stopped in front of a haberdasher's window, then moved on to a draper's shop, his hands behind his back gripping a walking stick with an ebony head. When the dustman's cart halted behind a cheapjack's wagon, Fagin left the cart, closing in on the mark, pushing past a clot of ragged, barefoot children and an apple woman with a basket on her head. The mark stopped in front of a kidney pie stand, and said a few words to the pieman, then moved on.

When Fagin was within ten feet of the mark the bells of St. Giles rang the hour, the hollow sound racing down the street just loud enough to be heard

1

over the vendors' shouts and the jangle of harnesses and wagon wheels. Nobs often pulled out their pocket watches to check the time when church bells rang, and the mark did just that. He stopped in front of a cobbler's shop. From his pocket he lifted his watch, which was secured to his waistcoat with a silver chain.

Pickpockets were called dippers and toolers but Fagin sniffed at these contemptible names. He was a fine wirer, a genius at unburdening a mark of his possessions.

Fagin narrowed his eyes at the mark's watch. The case was gold and enamel and Fagin thought he glimpsed a mother and child and a tree bough on the case, maybe made by John Wright on Red Lion Street in Clerkenwell. The case was intricate, and so the movement would likely be jeweled with a verge escapement, a fine timepiece. As the last of the St. Giles knells rolled down the street, the mark pushed his watch back into the pocket. Fagin removed blacksmith's shears from his coat pocket, and palmed them. The watch chain wouldn't add much difficulty to the lift, not when the bulker stumbled against the mark. The mark's other waistcoat pocket bulged, probably holding a snuff box.

Fifty yards farther up the street the bulker leaned against a lamp pole, his hands gripped in front of him. The bulker's name was Sikes who, leering, tipped his battered top hat to an oyster woman who kept her gaze straight ahead. Mud dappled Sikes's breeches and half boots. His eyes were so close together they pinched his nose, and his low brows were a roof over his eyes, a physiognomy suited to his temperament. A blue and white belcher handkerchief was knotted around his neck. He had the build of a coal heaver. Sikes was a shirkster, and looked comfortable leaning against the post, a comfort borne of experience.

A red wool scarf hung around Fagin's neck, and he waved the end of it at Sikes, the signal for the stall. With his elbow Sikes pushed himself away from the lamppost, and drunkenly staggered toward the mark. At this time of the day the lurching walk was an act. The brewery and the coach office at the end of the street were obscured by gray coal smoke. The sun found its way through the clouds, and the smoke gained an orange tint. Flecks of soot floated along the street. The smell was of coal smoke and brewery malt.

Fagin lifted a dozen silk handkerchiefs each day—he was the main supplier of a shop on Field Lane where the proprietor plucked out the monograms and hung the silk squares in the window —but a Wright repeater pocket watch was ream swag, and so it was worth having to deal with the likes of Bill Sikes, who closed in on the mark. Sikes was a coarse fool but he could bump into a swell on the street well enough.

Wrapped in a greasy shawl, her face hidden under a bonnet, a beggar woman leaned against a water butt, and the mark dropped a coin into her hand,

and then stepped around a vendor who carried a dozen umbrellas under his arm. The mark idled along, and glanced into a baker's shop. He was squared up, positioned between the fine wirer and the bulker. Fagin touched the brim of his cap, the signal for Sikes to close in. The shears dropped lower in Fagin's hand.

The reason Fagin glanced over his shoulder at that moment cannot be known because the fine wirer himself did not know. Maybe it was an odd current in the air, a shift in the tone of the street, some quiver in the unspooling of the day. A hunch, but it had saved him in the past, and when—two steps from catching the mark—Fagin looked behind him two Bow Street Runners were sprinting toward the pickpocket. Blue wool coats with rows of glittering brass buttons, oilskin capes, and tall chimney hats. One of them carried a leather sap likely filled with lead. He dashed forward and reached for Fagin's coat collar.

The fine wirer feinted left and ran right, across the street, pitching himself into a crowd of navvies who carried their suppers wrapped in handkerchiefs. Fagin pushed through them, earning an elbow in the ribs that staggered him. He ran by a shopman in a spruce coat and white neck cloth who swept dust through his doorway into the street, and he passed a dressmaker who was decking his window. He dodged a boy playing with a barrel hoop, and a job man carrying a wicker carpet beater. Fagin glanced across the street. Sikes had disappeared.

Bow Street Runners were policemen, mostly honest and mostly diligent. If they caught Fagin, they would clap ruffles on his wrists and haul him before the court on Bow Street, and from there it'd be on to the Fleet Prison. He yanked from his coat pocket the four handkerchiefs he had lifted that morning and dropped them into a doorway. His foot caught on a hay band but he righted himself and slipped into a lane that led to a warren of courts and alleys.

"You, stop." called one of the runners.

Fagin's bones ground together as he ran and his breath burned in his throat. His coat flapping behind him, he ducked into an alley, a narrow path lined with wretched hovels lit by meager daylight, and he dashed passed a reeking garbage pile, the runners' breaths on his neck.

As he splashed through a puddle an unseen dog snarled at him, and then the Bow Street Runner had him, gripping his shoulder and spinning him around, shaking him so hard his teeth rattled.

One of the runners laughed disagreeably. "Don't squirm or whine, Fagin, or we'll serve you out."

"I have done nothing," Fagin said. "You won't find anything on me."

The taller of the runners—whose nose had been broken and set badly so it pointed to his left—gripped the rope that held up Fagin's trousers, and the other runner seized the pickpocket's collar, and they hauled him deeper into

3

the alley, passing a low gin house where a man in a tattered coat had made it just through the door before collapsing. The second policeman was five and half feet tall, with blunt hands and a knobby chin.

"Gentlemen, please," Fagin said, more a gasp. "May we speak about this?"

The runners dragged and carried the pickpocket, the tops of his shoes scraping along the cobblestones.

Fagin called, "Perhaps some arrangement can be made. I am not without resources." He hung inside his clothes as he was roughly propelled along.

The Bow Street Runners turned down another side alley farther into the maze, passing decaying tenements that leaned out over the alley blocking the sunlight. Dark and forbidding doorways ranged along the alley, and pallid children peered out windows. A three-legged cat hurried alongside a gutter then disappeared into a crack between buildings. Another change of direction revealed daylight ahead: a street, with hansom cabs and a cart carrying chickens in cages.

Fagin tried to rise but the policemen apparently didn't want to afford him this dignity so they pushed and carried him along, Fagin's legs and arms in disarray, all four of the runners' hands gripping him, never allowing his feet to find purchase. They dragged him over a refuse pile and passed an abandoned market cart that had only one wheel.

They emerged from the alley onto a street filled with wagons and carts, and the shouts of hackney coachmen trying to clear their ways along the street. A baked potato man chanted his spiel, and flower girls arrayed their blooms on canvas on the street. A paperboy with broadsheets under his arm called, "*Herald*, ma'am. A curious murder in Lambeth, gentlemen."

The fine wirer tried again. "Gentlemen, let's be reasonable. You can search me. I'm as clean as a dog's tooth."

"Shut your trap, you," the smaller runner said, shaking Fagin so hard the pickpocket's chin bounced off his chest.

The policemen lugged Fagin toward a Berlin carriage parked in front of a tobacconist's shop. High on the box with the reins in his hand, the driver wore a Petersham great coat, and when he looked at the approaching Bow Street Runners and Fagin, he scowled and shook his head. From the box to the spokes to the footboard, the coach was maroon, shellacked and shiny, and it was an airy vehicle with quarter lights and door windows.

"Wait, don't," Fagin called.

When the carriage's door opened from the inside the two runners heaved Fagin into the cab. He grunted as he landed on the deck.

"Prettily done." A woman's voice. Someone on the carriage seat. She passed a cloth purse through the window.

The taller Bow Street Runner dipped his hat to her.

The other said, "Anytime, ma'am. You just call on us."

Fagin tried to rise but his hand slipped on the crinoline of the woman's dress. Still on the deck, he glanced up at her. A hard gaze, a fine necklace and bracelet—Fagin couldn't make out the stones—and a hat with a geranium in the band.

"Get up," the woman ordered.

Fagin put one foot under himself but when he tried to rise to the seat opposite the woman, the carriage jolted forward, and he tumbled onto her.

Her voice crabbed. "Get off me, you oaf."

His hand caught in her dress fabric as he scrambled to right himself.

She pushed him away, then looked at her hands as if touching his clothing might have left grease on them.

"Your pardon, madam." He took off his hat. "I was tossed like dice in a cup."

Harness bells chimed as the carriage moved along the street, passing a milliner's shop and a circle of children playing knucklebones in front of Cadder's Bottle warehouse, identified by a flaking sign above the door.

"You may be wondering," the woman said, "what wind has blown you here."

The fine wirer replied, "Not a good one, is my guess. So now I must beg to take my leave." Fagin reached for the leather strap that would open the carriage door.

"I hope you have a clear head when it comes to the main chance, Mr. Fagin." She waved him to the carriage bench opposite her. "Because I am going to offer it to you. Sit down and hear me out."

Fagin's hand closed around the door strap.

She said, "I intend you no harm."

"I am not persuaded of it, madam." But he lowered himself to the pleated leather seat opposite her.

As the carriage trundled along, he brought his eyes up to her, and it was a grim visage he beheld. Her mouth might have been full and lush but it was pressed into a thin line, and looked comfortable in its severity. Her nose was as narrow as a knife. The bones of her face were finely planed, her cheeks sunken, and her chin was pointed so that her face was a triangle. Her gray eyes had faint lines at their corners that hinted at some life lived. Her hair was not quite blond and not quite gray but rather the color of tarnished silver. Curls hung from under the hat, covering her ears. Hers was a haughty face but without the languid boredom that usually accompanied haughtiness. Her gaze pushed Fagin back in the seat. This woman's countenance was of business, and her business was with the fine wirer.

"I have learned much about you, Mr. Fagin," she said. "As far as can be determined, you are as loathsome as a French comb."

5

He pulled off his hat and smiled, revealing a black lower tooth. "Perhaps you will state your purpose in employing Bow Street Runners to kidnap me."

Window curtains hung from brass rods but they were pulled back, allowing gray daylight into the carriage. A patch of cloth that had been dipped in lilac water hung from a clip near a back window, and filled the interior with sticky scent.

"You are the best pickpocket in London," she said. "At least, that is your reputation. Am I right?"

"You ask me to incriminate myself." Fagin smoothed his trousers. "And you have me at a disadvantage, madam."

"My name is Havisham." The woman's voice was iron. "Miss Havisham."

Her dress was spread on the carriage's seat on both sides of her. The dress was a light blue with needlework roses near the hem. Mother-of-pearl buttons on her red spencer jacket glittered in the half-light inside the carriage. White calf gloves covered her hands, and she gripped a cloth reticule where coins clinked together.

"I've heard you can steal a man's eye teeth from his mouth without him knowing it." She lifted her head so that she looked at him down her nose. "Your hands are as skilled as a cellist's. You are a genius at light-fingering."

"I am a wholesaler of fine imported silk handkerchiefs."

She laughed, a brittle sound. "Decades dedicated to perfecting your art of stealing, and yet your life remains lamentably squalid. Just look at you."

The pickpocket's hair that stuck out from under his cap was matted and a dull red. Liver spots marred his forehead. His nose was long but his ears—as if to compensate—were orderly: small and tight against his head. The hair of his red beard was fine and sparse, and revealed sallow cheeks beneath. Because his green eyes—bright with self interest—were widely set under oddly feminine lashes, and because his cheekbones were high and noble, his face was not entirely disagreeable. Something nameless and yellow had stained Fagin's course checkered shirt on his left arm. His canvas trousers were ragged at the ankle.

Fagin's voice was harsh, the sound of a rusted gate closing. "You will tell me what you want before this carriage gets to Glasgow, I presume."

"I need someone who is good with his hands who can stealthily insert items into pockets and take items out of pockets."

Neighing came from a coach stable at the side of the street, adding to the din of vendors' chants, children's yells, and horseshoes cloppping on stones. The haze had thickened, and a banner above a shop advertising Davies' botanic wax candles was obscured by the smoke though it was only sixty yards away.

Miss Havisham picked at laces to open the reticule, then pulled out five sovereigns. "Have you ever been to the countryside, Mr. Fagin?"

The fine wirer gazed steadily at the glittering coins, and his tone became congenial. "Never in life, madam. Two or three miles from St. Paul's and only on this side of the river is my bailiwick."

"My home is Satis House near Rochester in Kent. I would like you to visit me there in two days' time."

He brought up his eyes. "Leave the city?"

She held out the coins.

"I don't know anything about the country," he said.

"The Nimrod coach leaves from the Clerkenwell office for Rochester every day at ten in the morning. Satis House is only a hundred yards from the stage stop there. After we meet, I may offer you your life's main hope and opportunity."

Fagin brought up his hand but stopped it two inches from the sovereigns. His knobby fingers resembled tree roots. He bit his lower lip.

She added, "Seldom will an offer come along, Mr. Fagin, that will change your life."

The pickpocket rolled his hat in his hands.

"Take this money and appear at Satis House the day after tomorrow. You may of course then decline my offer, and you will have lost nothing but a day of your time."

Fagin took the coins and bounced them in his hand as if testing their weight, then dropped them into a coat pocket. Miss Havisham opened the ceiling hatch and asked the driver to stop the carriage. Market carts lined the street. A fishmonger's wagon from the Billingsgate dock rolled along, the scent of the sea trailing after it. The carriage stopped near a man selling penny magazines from a tray suspended from his neck.

"I will see you in two days then." Fagin returned his hat to his head. "Until then, madam." He pulled the strap to open the carriage's door.

The horse pistol had been on the bench under the folds of her dress. She brought it out and leveled it at the pickpocket's nose. Fagin inhaled so sharply his breath whistled through his teeth. The flintlock was the size of a sheep's leg, and when Miss Havisham pulled back the hammer the sound filled the carriage. The etched metalwork on the stock glittered evilly.

She said, "You must think me a naïf, Mr. Fagin."

His eyes locked on the pistol; Fagin wobbled on the carriage deck. "Madam, please."

"The arm that is holding this pistol—a weapon which may in the next few seconds be the end of you—had a silver and diamond bracelet on it just before you entered my carriage. Now it does not. Perhaps you have an explanation."

He shrugged, the smallest of movements, his gaze still on the weapon. Seconds hung in the air.

She said, "Perhaps something to do with your falling onto me when the carriage lurched."

Fagin's mouth soundlessly worked, and then he pulled the bracelet from an inside pocket of his coat. Diamonds studded the silver band.

"Forgive me, madam." He passed the bracelet to her. "Force of habit."

She lowered the pistol to return the bracelet to her wrist. "Satis House near Rochester in two days."

"Until then." The pickpocket stepped down from the carriage. "Your servant, madam."

"Be there, Mr. Fagin," she said to his back as he walked away. Then in a lower voice, "Much depends on it."

2

"Madam, if you shoot Compeyson when he comes out the door, you'll hang at Newgate," Inspector Bucket whispered, looking at her from under his hat brim. "Put that thing away."

But Miss Havisham held the horse pistol, her arm perfectly steady, the flintlock's barrel pointed down the hallway, the diamond bracelet hanging on her wrist. "I can hear him laughing." She inhaled sharply. "Laughing at what he did to me. He is stock and stone. It would be worth it."

"You'll Morris dance at the end of a rope with ten thousand people watching." Inspector Bucket's whisper was fierce. "The last woman suspended at Newgate was the husband murderer Edith Baker. The hanging of a woman is a rare treat. People came from as far away as Brighton and Bath, and it was a grand holiday. You don't want that. Put it away."

She and Inspector Bucket were hidden by the gloom of the hallway where only an Argand lamp near the stairwell cast a delicate yellow light. The wood floor had squeaked with the slightest of their movements so they were still. Four doors lined each side if the hallway, and the place smelled of tomcat spray. The dingy claret wallpaper had peeled along the door jams.

Inspector Bucket was built like a Thames collier, almost filling the hallway side to side, with Miss Havisham squeezed in beside him. Little of his bulk was in his belly but rather formed from his shoulders and arms which were the size of hawsers, and his neck was as thick as a stump. His clothing was black, from his hat to his greatcoat to his shoes. His only ornaments were the buckles on his shoes.

More laughter came from a room down the hall, then a door lock rattled. The occupants were about to come out. Miss Havisham's pistol was still level.

Mr. Bucket said in a low voice, "And I will hang next to you as an accomplice. You have hired me to protect you and to introduce you to several skillful criminals but you aren't paying me enough to swing at the end of a rope."

The door opened and Samuel Compeyson emerged, backlit from the room, and he stepped into Miss Havisham's line of sight down the pistol barrel. Undoubtedly ignorant of his peril, the man said something in a jocular voice. He was as slender as a gas pipe, and wore a blue tailcoat with a white neckband above the collar. He carried a hat in one hand and a bottle in the other, and with a broad gesture beckoned another man out.

He was joined in the hallway by a bulkier man wearing drab corduroy trousers, a green guernsey sweater, and half-boots. He locked the door with a key, then tested the knob by trying to turn it. They walked to the stairwell. The first man laughed, a hint of inebriation in the sound.

Miss Havisham whispered, "And that's my brother Arthur."

Not until they disappeared down the stairs did Miss Havisham lower the pistol. Her hands trembled and she breathed raggedly.

Bucket peeled her fingers from around the weapon and slipped it under his waistband. "Let's search his room."

She followed him along the hall to the door.

Bucket lifted a key ring from a pocket; skeleton keys but also picks and hooks. He slipped a pick into the keyhole and sprung the lock. "Let's take a look." He pushed open the door.

The odor brought up her head, and she turned away so Bucket would not see her face. The scent was of the perfumed Rowland's macassar oil her one-time fiancé had applied to his hair. When she had playfully run her hand through his hair, her fingers would come away with this cloying scent. She thought the smell charming then but now it was the odor of decay. She winced at how she had tolerated the hair and the smell and his smile, all of it. He was a contemptible artificer, a humbug, and she had fallen for it.

Bucket crossed the room to an oak campaign chest. He first opened the writing slope, then the side drawers, searching with practiced rapidity. The top drawers contained a pin cushion and a thimble, a comb, and a pocket mirror.

"I don't see documents," Bucket said. "Anything he used to swindle you. Letters of introduction. Letters from his invented family he may have shown you. Forged bank statements. Documents that made him appear substantial. Evidence that can be introduced in court."

Miss Havisham lifted a snuff box from a wrought-iron table. "I gave him this. Had his initials engraved on the lid." She laughed bitterly. "He doesn't take snuff, and I never had to brush the crumbs off his shirt. I just thought an elegant man should have an engraved silver snuff box."

Bucket opened a wood box on the table and brought out a feather pen. "You did not tell me he is left-handed, Miss Havisham."

"Is it important?"

"This quill is from the right side of the goose so he is left-handed. True?" She dipped her chin.

"Does he carry a knife?"

"In his boot," she said. "I was surprised the first time I saw it. Maybe I should have learned something from it."

"Should I ever get close to him, I'll know which hand to watch." He placed the quill onto the bed and dug farther into the box.

The two windows in the sitting room looked out upon Barts Hospital and beyond to St. Paul's dome. Flowery chintz curtains hung at the sides of the windows. Embers glowed orange in the fireplace behind a wire screen. A brass coal scuttle was to the side of the fireplace.

Miss Havisham lifted a green coat from a rack and sniffed the collar then brushed wig powder from the shoulders. "He usually doesn't wear a wig. I wonder who he is trying to fool this time."

They stepped through a doorway into the second room. A bow-front sideboard lined a wall on which were four bottles, including one of Sun in the Valley brandy, and along another wall was a chest of drawers decorated with painted red roses. A dozen cologne bottles crowded the top of the chest. A wing-back chair was between a window and the bed.

Bucket lifted a bottle from the sideboard. "This is Pearl's Liquid Blooms of Roses. Does he live with a woman?"

"He was engaged to be married to me." Miss Havisham gripped her hands together.

"There is also talcum powder and three sheets of rouge." He pointed. "And a box of Gentlewoman's Rice Flour Powder, and a tub of Carnation Lip Salve. And here's a silver cachou box for lip rouge. The question remains: was he living with a lady?"

"I do not believe so, Mr. Bucket." Her voice was choppy. "I can't imagine it."

"You couldn't imagine that he would leave you at the altar on your wedding day."

Her hands flew to her mouth and she stepped backwards as if Bucket had shoved her. Her leg caught on a boot jack and she short-stepped to keep herself from falling. "Mr. Bucket, some discretion, please."

"Madam, we are dealing with the basest of swindlers, an infernal scrub. When such a confidence man isn't hiding the truth, he is shading the truth. He names things that are not, and he is silent on things that are. I must be able to speak the truth."

She brushed unseen lint from her sleeves. The room smelled of mildew and mothballs. A washbasin and water pitcher were on a stand near a corner. A towel and a razor strop hung from the stand's rod.

He added, "It will not serve to color our words, Miss Havisham."

"Decorum would be appreciated." Her voice was just above a whisper.

"On your wedding day, your fiancé—this Samuel Compeyson, whose rooms we stand in now—failed to appear at the ceremony, leaving you there in your wedding gown. In the preceding month this Compeyson and your brother Arthur had convinced you and your enfeebled father to sign documents that transferred much of the Havisham wealth—your inheritance—to Compeyson, some of it as a dowry, and the rest just a swindle."

She looked at the hem of her dress as if it might be dragging on the floor as she shrunk under his words.

"I am working with zeal," Bucket said.

"For a guinea a day, I expect no less."

"And I cannot tiptoe around the issue using synonyms and vagaries to guard against bruising your feelings. You were jilted by a confidence man and your brother. Have I cleaned our window of soot?"

"Indeed." Her word was percussive.

Bucket's eyes were far back in his skull, and constantly moving. His remarkably boxy head might have been designed with a carpenter's T-square. His nose was an insignificant protuberance. His thinning dark hair was combed over his head from a part just above an ear.

He picked up a leather valise from a footstool and brought out a sheet of paper. The paper had sharp creases, likely folded and unfolded many times, and what may have been a tea stain colored a corner of it. "Did Compeyson send you love letters?"

Miss Havisham gripped a bed post. Pale under the best of circumstances her face drained to the color of candle wax.

Bucket said, "The letter begins with 'My most beloved,' and then there's no name, just a blank. It continues in the first paragraph, 'Only days have passed since we parted, and yet I still feel you in my presence, an eternal closeness between us.'" He looked up from the page. "Have you received a letter with precisely this wording from Compeyson?"

She cleared her throat but couldn't form the answer.

"This appears to be a form meant for copying again and again," Bucket said. "He apparently has sent the same letter to several women, perhaps many." He looked through the remaining pages, then returned them to the valise. "Miss Havisham, I have known you for a few days now, and I would not presume you to be susceptible to the blandishments of this fearful imposter. What hold did he have on you?"

She gestured despairingly.

"You and most probably other women are the victims of his swindles. Judging from my brief acquaintance with you, Miss Havisham, you are an intelligent and discerning person. What is it about this Compeyson that allowed you to be taken in?"

She covered her mouth with her fingers to deny him her answer but then she spoke through them. "He is beautiful."

"He's handsome?" Bucket said. "Handsome men are in abundance, and I'm sure a number of them have courted you."

"I was as deaf as an adder to other men. They were course and lumpish compared to Samuel Compeyson. And handsome is an insufficient concept. Samuel is beautiful."

Bucket asked, "Were you not free to make wiser decisions?"

"I was not, such was the power of his appearance."

Bucket's expression was without sympathy. He returned the valise to the footstool, and opened a dresser drawer, searched through its contents, then opened another. A kerosene lamp was on the dresser next to a razor. Nacreous gray light came through windows that looked out onto a cobblestone courtyard.

"Was he charming?" Bucket asked. "Witty?"

"If you are beautiful you don't need to be charming or witty. Or humorous or polite or caring. But he was all those things."

Bucket stared at her. "I understand."

"It's unlikely you do." Miss Havisham's head came up at a sound from the door.

The grating was of a key shoved into the door lock. Inspector Bucket seized Miss Havisham's elbow, and fairly lifted her to the wall that separated Compeyson's two rooms. With an arm he pressed her against the wall with such force she grunted, and then he shoved himself as flat against the wall as his bulk would allow. From a pocket he pulled a leather-covered truncheon.

"I forgot it," Compeyson called as he opened the door from the hallway. "Be with you in a moment."

Miss Havisham flinched when Compeyson shoved a chair in the other room, the legs squeaking along the floor. Bucket pressed her harder into the wall.

"Where'd I put it, Arthur?" Compeyson laughed in the other room. "I call it lubrication."

Miss Havisham's breath stilled in her throat as Compeyson stepped into the bedroom, almost brushing her right shoulder. His hair was so yellow it seemed on fire, and the scent of his Cologne water trailed after him. He stepped to the sideboard to snatch the bottle of brandy.

"Got it," he said.

He turned back to the door, and this turn wasn't in Bucket and Miss Havisham's direction but rather to Compeyson's right, and he walked back into the sitting room. He hadn't looked and so he must not have seen them.

At the hallway door, Compeyson asked, "Have we got enough for tonight?"

Arthur Havisham said something from the hallway. The lock was thrown again, and the two men's footsteps receded in the hallway.

When Bucket released his grip on her, Miss Havisham brought her hand to her breastbone. Her voice was as high as a bird's. "That was frightening. What if he had seen us?"

"I would have laid him out." Bucket wiggled the billy at her. "Nothing to be frightened about." He put away the club.

"Still, that was close. All my plans . . . ." Her words trailed off.

"Men's clothing." The inspector was already back at work, looking through other drawers. "No documents in these rooms. No evidence we can use."

"I'll find evidence of his swindles," she said. "I'm already arranging it."

He looked sharply at her. "You are paying me for this to be my job, Miss Havisham. I cannot answer for your doing something dangerous or foolish."

She followed him from the rooms into the hallway. He locked the door with a pick.

At the stairwell she said, "Samuel Compeyson." Her words were said more to the dim hallway than to Bucket. "He disoriented me. There is no other word for it."

* * * *

If Samuel Compeyson knew anything it was perfume. Every morning after careful consideration he applied scents to himself, and he assiduously refreshed them several times a day from bottles he carried in his jacket pockets, which clinked together pleasantly when he walked. He always moved in a cloud of delightful odor, his antidote to London's brown smells.

Rowland's macassar oil for his hair, of course, but also, when the mood struck him, Freshman Cologne from Truefitt & Hill on St. James's Street, smelling of mint and bergamot oil, a favorite of Oxford students. Or it might be Albany Cologne, with its notes of citrus and lavender. Or Mayfair toilet water, which had a rose scent. Sometimes Spanish Leather, an *eau de Cologne* smelling of saddle soap and lily of the valley. Or the costly Sultan Oil, imported from Persia and smelling of nutmeg and patchouli, and available only at Berman and Sons on Piccadilly. And, when he couldn't decide—and, it must be admitted, such decisions are most difficult—splashes of bay rum were always perfectly fine, if rather common.

Samuel Compeyson waited behind a water trough across the street from his lodgings, in an alley between a tinplate shop and a leather dresser's. Carriages and carts passed along the street. His building was made of red brick, and was square and squat, as inviting as a prison but nicely anonymous with nothing distinguished about it. Staring at the building's door, he forced himself to breath evenly.

Yes, Compeyson knew scents, and in his rooms several moments ago he had detected a foreign odor, one that he did not wear; the distinctive sharp smell of lilacs, a treacly, cloying, syrupy smell that he could not abide.

And he instantly had known that Margaret Havisham lurked nearby, maybe even in the room. Lilac was her scent, too much of it, he had once told her to no avail. Walking through his rooms he had not seen her but he had smelled her. Without breaking step, and with his eyes on the floor, he had fled the room, knowing she was somewhere near, and probably with a tough, someone she had hired to extract vengeance from him.

Compeyson leaned forward. A mule-drawn grain wagon rolled by, interrupting his view of the building, and when it had passed she was on the steps holding the door open. Compeyson stepped back farther into the shade of the alley. He tapped the knife in his boot. He disliked violence. It was inelegant, and was a persuasion of the lesser classes, those people for whom he had an intense aversion.

Margaret Havisham said something over her shoulder, and then from the doorway emerged a solid block of a man. He wore a dark coat as wide as a sail, and a black scowl. Undoubtedly a hard knocker, maybe a policeman, someone there to do Miss Havisham's dirty work.

Compeyson inhaled sharply between his teeth, then receded farther into the alley. His pigeons seldom chased after him because the women and their families were too paralyzed with mortification, much less did they hire a professional banger.

He walked toward the street at the far end of the alley. He hadn't figured Margaret—so sweet and so in love with him—as having a backbone but perhaps he had misjudged. He would have to be cautious. He bit down. Sure, he'd have to be careful, but so would Margaret and her hired thug.

* * * *

Mornings are the optimal time to make choices. The previous day's indecisions and postponements have yet to intrude. The mind is clear, the perspective fresh, the energy renewed.

But some decisions do not need the light of a new day because the answer is so patently obvious, and here is one of these: the choice between the arrival of the Four Horsemen of the Apocalypse or the arrival of a lawyer.

Miss Havisham was not offered the choice.

In rank and file like the Horse Guards, marigolds were arrayed in a perfect grid below the parlor windows. Before Samuel Compeyson had deserted Miss Havisham, she had hardly been aware of the flower bed but now she obsessively tended the gold blooms, and woe betide the tiniest of weeds or the wind-blow leaf or the wandering snail that found its way to the marigolds.

Since the wedding day debacle, most of Satis House's rooms and gardens had received Miss Havisham's minute attention and frantic exertion. She had squared the furniture to the walls, aligned the silverware in its drawers, polished the parlor's fireplace andirons until they gleamed, all to the consternation of the cook and maids, whom Miss Havisham asked to let her be. In the Sun Dial Court, she had snipped off faded blooms from a bank of lilac bushes, taking two days, the nonplused gardeners hovering nearby. Each long day she straightened this, dusted that, sorted this, and raked that until she was spent. She was too perceptive not to know what pushed her: on the day she should have been married she had lost control of her life, and so those things she could now control she would control, and that was Satis House and its grounds. It was a futile attempt to rectify the past and she knew it, but she could not help it.

An apron covered her pelisse and frock, and she stabbed the dirt with a trowel. The broad brim of her sennit hat fluttered in the wind. She bent to her work, though the dirt appeared to have been just combed with a dinner fork, and there was little work to do among the precise rows of marigolds.

Such was her concentration on the flower patch that the carriage—squeaking springs, four clattering horses, and ringing harness bells—had stopped at the gate before she was aware of the visitors. She narrowed her eyes, as if she could exclude the intruders by focusing on the pristine dirt.

"May I speak with you, Miss Havisham?"

She flinched, and turned to the voice. Her father's lawyer, calling from the carriage as he stepped to the ground. In prior visits he had just nodded at her, and had displayed what she presumed was a smile, resembling a skull's rictus.

She brushed dirt from her sleeve. "Your voice has a higher pitch than I would have presumed from your size, Mr. Jaggers."

He pushed open the gate and approached her on the brick walkway. "Surely you have heard me speak before."

"You save your conversation for my father."

"My time is the only thing I have to sell," Jaggers said. "Were I to inquire after your garden I would charge your father an extra guinea each visit."

The lawyer's beaver pelt hat threw a shadow, darkening his face which was even in the brightest of lights the color of oak bark. He was squat, built with solidity, with a bald head so large it appeared to be precariously balanced atop his neck. His white neckcloth was wound tightly, perhaps to shore up his neck for its formidable task. His eyes—hidden in dark hollows under wild black eyebrows—seldom rested, moving back and forth, perpetually seizing and dismissing. A gold watch chain crossed his waistcoat, and he wore a Petersham greatcoat with its short cape despite the benign weather.

"I am here on business, Miss Havisham," the lawyer said, "and that business is with you. My journey today is at your ailing father's request."

Miss Havisham brushed aside a wayward strand of hair from her forehead. A nightjar rattled high in the oak tree south of the house. A charwoman beat a rug behind the garden wall, the sound muffled and rhythmic.

"Your father is worried about your health," Jaggers said. "Judging from your appearance he has good reason to be. You have lost—what?—a stone? You are wasting away."

The breeze shifted, and the smell of malted barley was as thick as tar.

"I am perfectly healthy, thank you," she said.

"I take everything on evidence," Jaggers said. "There is no better rule, and the evidence before my eyes is of a woman so slender she resembles a rake handle, whose hands tremble as she holds a garden spade, whose eyes have lost their luster, and who stands there boneless and hunched as if expecting a blow."

She ran her tongue along her lower lip.

"Let me put the case to you, Miss Havisham," Jaggers said. "Your father believes, and I must now concur after seeing you, that you are dying."

Miss Havisham swayed in the breeze like a sapling. "Nonsense."

A sound came from Jaggers' carriage, a dog's whimper or maybe squeaking from a carriage spring. She glanced at the vehicle. Someone else was inside, masked by shadows.

"Your recent misadventure with that infernal scoundrel Samuel Compeyson has left you despondent, and it is working away on you as would consumption." Jaggers removed his hat, revealing more of his vast forehead and brown hair too sparse to be powdered. "You are dwindling away to nothing."

"Kindly allow me to return to my gardening, Mr. Jaggers. It will be more profitable for both of us."

"May I call you Margaret?"

"Please do not." She twisted the trowel in her hand.

"Saving your life is my assignment from your father, one I have undertaken with the utmost gravity," the lawyer said. "We must be alive to the necessity of bold action." He turned to the carriage and his voice rose. "Molly, come here, if you please."

The carriage shifted on its springs, and the door opened. Holding a bundle in one arm, a woman stepped to the ground, her movements cautious and tentative. She looked up at the sky as if unused to daylight and squinted against the sun. With small steps she entered the garden. She was not wearing a bonnet, and though she looked to be in her early thirties her hair was as gray as a gravestone. The skin on her drawn face was so papery that her bones showed beneath. She wore a faded muslin frock that might have once been blue. And her eyes perhaps had been blue, too, but they were as pale as milk glass, and they were damp. Wrapped around both her wrists were bandages covering wounds. Blood stippled the white gauze. That sound came again, soft and mewling. In her arms was a baby.

As the woman drew near, Miss Havisham said, "She is injured, Mr. Jaggers."

"She has had the best of medical care. A physician, mind you, not an apothecary. I have instructed her not to scratch the stitches but it has been unavailing."

Miss Havisham stepped back. "Why does she bring a baby here?"

The child—no more than two months old—was wrapped in a white cotton cloth and wore a red knitted cap.

"Seldom does life offer the perfect joining of two opportunities, Miss Havisham. Here is my handmaid, Molly. She must separate herself from this baby girl for Molly's health and the baby's safety, and you must have a reason to live." His voice took on an amused tone. "And so here we are."

Molly fairly thrust the baby forward in such a way that Miss Havisham would either catch or drop the infant. Keening fiercely, the maid spun away and fled back to the carriage.

"I have friends on the bench in Chancery Lane," Jaggers said, "and they occasionally push through a document for me without the usual piffling delays. You, Miss Havisham, are the legal mother of this child, the papers signed, stamped, taxed, and filed away."

The baby gurgled and kicked against the blanket's constraints.

"Her name is Estella," he said. "I give you joy on your new motherhood."

Her face was slack, the most undignified lack of expression that had ever captured her features. She held the baby so that it did not touch her chest as if it might be contagious. "Mr. Jaggers, surely you cannot mean what you are saying. I know nothing about children."

"Then here is a third opportunity." Jaggers simulated a smile. "You can learn about them." He returned his hat to his head. "You have just been given a reason to return to health and live a long life."

Her voice rose uncontrollably. "I cannot tolerate children."

"Then you may leave the baby at a parish doorstep. It is entirely up to you."

She held out the child. "Mr. Jaggers, please . . . ."

"I must take my leave." He tipped his hat. "Good day to you, Miss Havisham."

Jaggers crossed the gravel driveway to the carriage. Molly could not be seen in the window so perhaps she was slumped back against the seat.

Miss Havisham's breath was rapid in her throat. And only after the carriage had turned around on the driveway and drove off toward London—the driver casting her only the smallest of glances—did she dare look down at the infant's face.

Had Jaggers called her Estella? Round and pink, the baby smiled up at her.

3

Satis House had been built two hundred years earlier, and had been purchased by Miss Havisham's father Hugh two decades ago when the Havisham family came into money and so moved to the mansion from a two-room lodging in Rochester. Miss Havisham's most vivid memory of her childhood home in Rochester was the filthy ditch behind it that drained into the River Medway.

There wasn't a ditch within a mile of Satis House. English bond brickwork covered all sides of the mansion, and three-story wings ranged east and west from the great hall. Kent tile covered the roof. Satis House had rooms Miss Havisham had never visited, and a sitting room where her governess had told her "all the bodies are buried." Miss Havisham scoffed but it was another room she had never entered.

Satis House's butler had been there when Hugh Havisham purchased the home, and had never left. Cranky old Tavers oversaw two liveried footmen, both as tall as grenadiers and who wore ribboned knee breeches and white silk stockings. Working in the mansion were the housekeeper and three housemaids, a cook, a kitchen maid, and a scullery maid. Tavers also captained four, five or six gardeners, it had been impossible for Miss Havisham to determine how many because of the topiary and yew hedge rows. Walls divided Satis House's three acres of grounds into five areas; the Mulberry Garden, the Lilly Pond, the Queen Elizabeth Promenade, the Sun Dial Court, and the Yew Garden. *Satis* meant *enough* in Latin, and her home was so named because whoever lived there would never want for more.

The place was lovely and grand but it suffered an implacable insult to its very existence: the brewery that shared the mansion's west wall, stuck to it like a barnacle to a barge. The brewery had come with the house, and so Hugh Havisham had learned the beer trade. The winds in Kent mostly came from the southwest, which meant the scent at Satis House was of brewing malt—day and night, year round—while the sounds were of cork bungs hammered into wood barrels and the clank and grind of barley wagons and barrel drays on the roadway.

Miss Havisham was no longer aware of the brewing odor at Satis House but she felt its absence whenever she was anywhere else, where the air seemed empty and cold. On her trips to London, she would pause near a brewery, inhale the perfumed air, and so be newly infused with composure and equanimity. She spent six weeks every summer at her Uncle Felix and Aunt Nell's estate near the River Severn, and the air was too fresh for her there, "not enough malt in it," as she liked to tease him and Nell. Felix had been the brother in Havisham Brothers Brewery until he had taken his profits and retired out west.

Carrying the baby as she might a hedgehog, Miss Havisham entered Satis House's foyer where a maid in a blue apron and cap dusted a Chinese vase as tall as she was.

"Mary, do you know anything about babies?" Miss Havisham held the infant out to the maid.

Mary whipped the duster behind her back so her hands were hidden. "Not so you would notice, ma'am." She was a stubby woman, only as high as Miss Havisham's chin. Brown curls stuck out from the sides of her cap.

"How many children have you had? The number escapes me."

The maid's face was doughy and pitted. She stared at the bundle in Miss Havisham's arms. "Seven, madam, and four still among the living. I've had my struggles so I don't claim no special skill with the wee ones. First thing you need, though, is a wet-nurse, I know that much."

Still holding the baby and tapping the banister with a precise tattoo, Miss Havisham climbed the curving stairs to the first floor where she passed in the hallway a gilded, multi-armed Lord Shiva statue her father had purchased somewhere and a Joshua Reynolds portrait of her grandfather Hiram, though Miss Havisham's mother—bitter to her last breath six years ago—had claimed it was not a Reynolds painting nor was it Hiram.

Awkwardly shifting the infant to her other arm, Miss Havisham paused at the door to touch the corner of her eye, making sure it was dry. She forced herself to breathe evenly. She had promised herself she would not again weep in front of her father and his ravaged leg. Two days ago she had broken down at his bedside, bawling out her eternal love for him and her undying gratitude, her hands over her face, bucking with uncontrollable sobs, and finally seizing his bedpost to keep herself from toppling. Minutes had passed before she could control herself, and then she saw that she had terribly frightened her father. He lay there as white as his pillowcase, his eyes wide. He had until that moment met his impending fate with aplomb. She had resolved never to alarm him again. Miss Havisham gathered another breath and knocked on her father's door.

She knew not to wait to be summoned into the room because Hugh Havisham could no longer raise his voice nor could he raise himself from his bed. These were her father's last days, perhaps his last hours. When she pushed the door open and stepped into the room she gasped at the malevolent odor of gangrene. Pitiless putrefication roped her and cinched her chest, and she had to will herself not to flee the room. The smell was so thick it felt as if it were being applied to her with a butter knife, and it lodged in her throat and blurred her vision. She swallowed, and stepped farther into the bedroom, moving against the smell of rot as if wading up a stream. Several times a day the maid poured vinegar on a glowing-red shovel that had just been taken from the fireplace, and the vaporized vinegar would hide the stench for a while but it always rushed back.

Hugh Havisham lay on his bed, his head sunk into a pillow, his pallor ghastly and the wrecked stump of his leg under a damp cloth. Miss Havisham averted her eyes from his leg, instead settling her gaze on his face, which wasn't much better. Her father stared at the ceiling, his eyes so watery and filmed they resembled egg whites. He moved his lips without speaking.

At his bedside she lied, "You look much improved."

He turned his head on the pillow and stared at her vaguely as if trying to place her. His silk-fine hair was pasted to his scalp with sweat. His mouth twitched into a faltering smile.

He asked, "Where is the gunfire?"

"Papa?"

"In the garden. Doesn't your fiancé take target practice most days about now? I've watched him. He's a crack shot. A steadier arm I've never seen."

His words squeezed her, and she gripped the bed post. "Papa, my fiancé is gone. You remember what happened, don't you?"

He blinked several times and silently worked his mouth. Then he said, "Forgive me, Margaret. I'm not thinking clearly. It's this leg." His voice was creaky. "Is that your baby?"

"Her name is Estella."

"I had no idea you were with child." He coughed wetly. "Your mother always said I wasn't observant."

"Your lawyer Jaggers passed this baby to me a few moments ago. I would not have been more surprised had he sprouted wings and flown to the top of a tree. He said it was your idea."

"I asked him to help you." He inhaled, a clattering sound. "I didn't tell him how."

Hugh Havisham's cheeks were so sunken that the bones of his face had become stony promontories. Night and day he trembled as if he had the ague, and the ague would have been a blessing compared to his wicked circumstance as he lay there. Six weeks ago Hugh Havisham's foot had been crushed between a barge and a dock. Gangrene had taken hold, and the surgeon—who also had cut Hugh's hair for years—removed the foot in a procedure involving an ebony-handled amputation saw, a leather bite stick, and four gardeners who pinned Hugh to the table. Not enough was removed. The gangrene had continued its miserable climb up his leg. A second surgery cut off the leg just above the knee. Still not enough. The rot had crawled into his hip, and so for Hugh Havisham there was no escape.

When Estella kicked against the blanket Miss Havisham surprised herself by bringing the baby closer to her chest.

"I must speak of serious matters to you, Margaret," he blinked several times, "while there is still time."

She gripped his wrist. "We still have a lot of time, papa."

The windows' curtains were drawn, and the room was dim. Against the wall was a world globe so old that the western shores of North America were undrawn. Next to the globe, etched walrus tusks and whale teeth given to him over the years by whalers were displayed on a bookshelf. A broad-backed mahogany and horsehair chair was near the bed.

"Our family business, the Havisham Brothers Brewery." He coughed, and his head fell back into the pillow. "I'm leaving it to you, of course, along with Satis House. Jaggers has prepared my last will and testament. Your half-brother Arthur—an abject and worthless villain—inherits nothing."

"Let's not talk about these things." She rocked Estella in her arms.

Her father tried to turn onto his side but groaned with pain. He clamped his jaw together. She kept her gaze away from the Gloucester broadcloth that covered his ruined hip and leg stump, speckled and stained green and brown as it was, where the dreadful stench of corrupted flesh rose in waves.

Hugh Havisham chewed on a lip as if gathering courage. "We have lived a good life here at Satis house, Margaret. Haven't we?"

"The question is unlike you, papa. You are becoming sweeter as you age. Soon you'll be talking of rainbows and leprechauns." She smiled, inviting him to laugh.

With a handkerchief he dabbed saliva at the corner of his mouth. "Our home and our servants and four-in-hand carriage and investments in navy bonds and sending you to France—a nation of dance masters—for your education; these are not supported by the Havisham Brothers Brewery."

"I've learned about your business over the years, father. There's more to it than brewing."

"Between Satis House and London are sixteen breweries, and London is home to a thousand breweries, one on every corner. How does our brewery compete? It doesn't, and. . . ." He bit off his words, his mouth pulled back into a gruesome grimace, and his breath whistled in his throat.

"Where is your elixir?" The baby tucked in her arm, she rounded the bed to the washstand on which were a blue bottle and a spoon.

The bottle's label read *Dr. Holly's Refined Laudanum,* and in smaller print *Tincture of Opium. From the Finest Turkish Poppies.*

She poured half a teaspoon of the brown liquid into the spoon, Estella snug against her chest. "Here you go, papa."

When she moved the spoon to his mouth, her father with surprising strength yanked the bottle from her hand, and put it to his mouth. He gulped greedily; his eyes squeezed shut.

"Too much of that isn't good for you." Her voice was unintentionally as prim as a schoolteacher's so she smiled to lessen the reproach.

He exhaled gratefully. "At this point, Margaret, too much elixir is the least of my concerns."

The baby in her arms cooed happily, sounds as foreign to Miss Havisham as a hieroglyphic.

His voice steadier, he said, "This little enterprise—the brewery—attached to our home has never provided sufficient funds. Listen closely to me, Margaret."

"I always listen closely to you." Maybe she could get him to laugh. "You alone have kept me from a life of invincible ignorance."

He hadn't laughed since the barge had ruined his foot, and he didn't now. "You are aware that the brewery is a deceit, Margaret."

"You told me this several years ago, when I started noticing certain things."

"Havisham Brothers Brewery is chicanery designed to deceive. It makes beer but its main purpose is to misdirect."

Teamsters called to each other out on the road, and one of them laughed coarsely. A mule brayed.

"I have another business, one far more profitable than barley and malt and yeast could ever provide." Her father's voice wavered. "I want to introduce you to my partner in that endeavor."

Miss Havisham smiled. "You don't have a partner any longer, papa. Remember? You bought out Uncle Felix five years ago, and he retired to an estate out west along the Severn. Are you feverish?" She placed her free hand on his forehead.

He shook his head, and he gasped in pain even with this slight movement.

"You're as hot as a cinder," she said. "I'll bring up a new water pitcher."

Half hidden in the room's murk; a movement caught her eye. A man stood next to the Grecian couch, and her breath stopped. She had been so intent on her father that she had not seen him. And no one was allowed into her father's room except her and her father. The maids were forbidden entry, and so had been her mother. Her parents had kept separate bedrooms. A hat in his hand, the fellow stepped toward the bed.

"Margaret, you know Edward Murdstone, my partner."

"A pleasure, after so much time." Murdstone spoke without moving his lips. "How long has it been?" His voice was unctuous, as if he begrudged the need to speak.

"Edward has come from London." Hugh Havisham wheezed. "With my leg like this, more and more he has been running our company."

Murdstone's eyes were so brown they were black, and they were too high on the plane of his face, as if they had just bobbed to the surface from deep in his skull. His perfectly formed eyebrows below a full black head of unpowdered hair, precisely combed, mitigated the queerly malevolent cast to his eyes. The skin of his face was as pale as ashes. His beard was so black it was blue, his nose was Gallic in length, and his flat ears were the size of buttons. These features fell together in a more pleasing way than each would suggest considered alone. He was handsome if viewed from more than ten feet. A lily nosegay was pinned to his black coat, red stripes patterned his waistcoat, and his neckcloth was white.

He smiled, it faltered, and he smiled again, as if it were an effort. "Your father and I have worked together for fifteen years. In business he is as sharp as flint." His voice was so deep it seemed to have its own echo as if he were speaking into a bucket.

Miss Havisham gripped the baby more tightly and stepped back from Murdstone's oily smoothness.

Her father's voice was serrated by pain. "As I leave this life, I am leaving you with a dreadful choice, Margaret. Had I the gift of a few more weeks I would make more careful arrangements for you but now there is nothing to be done."

She glanced at Edward Murdstone. Without the slightest change of expression his face shifted from suggestions of benevolence to those of sly malice then back again. She frowned at herself, allowing her mind to be so fanciful.

"Margaret," her father said, "pay attention to me now. Put that wretch Samuel Compeyson out of your mind for a moment, and that baby as well."

His words braced her. Her father had always been playful around her. It was not until she was nineteen or twenty that she understood that he avoided weighty topics to protect her from the world's harshness and vagaries. In the past few days, she had worked to put aside the uncharitable notion that in shielding her all her life her father had left her without discernment, had left her susceptible to the charms of Samuel Compeyson. But, no, it would not do to lay that disaster at her father's feet. It was her own doing. She had closed her brain when she had opened her heart.

His voice as clear and as forceful as he had expressed anything in recent days, Hugh Havisham said, "Our ship, the *Blessing*, did not come in. It was due at Southampton five weeks ago, and it is presumed lost."

"*Blessing*'s master was here for dinner before she sailed." She grinned. "You were acting as a matchmaker"

Her father shook his head, a small movement. "We had cargo space on the ship, and our cargo has been lost with the ship."

"The Society of Lloyd's doesn't insure our type of cargo," Murdstone said. "Not when it doesn't appear on the ship's manifest, not when it is hidden in the hold."

"I'm fully aware some of our imports are deeply in the hold," Miss Havisham said. "What was the cargo this time?"

"Aubusson tapestries," Murdstone said. "From central France."

"You are a drapery merchant this time, papa?" She was determined to make him smile. "Next it will be American beaver pelts. Any valuable item you can bring into the country without being taxed. Over the years you've told me of your business."

Hugh Havisham said, "Edward and I paid 6,000 pounds for the tapestries. Some of that money was borrowed. The tapestries went down with the ship, and we are in a precarious position." He coughed weakly. "*Desperate* is a better word."

"You've had losses before, and you always even the keel, and . . . ."

He cut her off. "You cannot continue living in Satis House. You will lose it, and everything else."

"Father? Lose our home?"

"You have disliked Edward for many years," Hugh Havisham said, "and perhaps understandably."

Murdstone cleared his throat, perhaps reminding them he was still in the room.

"But unless you join with Edward in the business—you, fully as his partner, you will lose everything after I'm gone. We have another ship coming in. Maybe it will save you and save Satis House." With an effort that made him wince he gripped her hand. "You have always judged my importing business to be sordid. But you have no choice but to join Edward—he gestured to include the room, the entire house—"not if you want to continue living here."

"Your importing is illegal, papa."

"It's given us this house and gardens. It's a good business."

"I may end up in chains in a prison."

He smiled thinly. "Yes, there is that."

* * * *

The wedding was to have been in the Satis House ballroom, over strenuous objections from the parish pastor who thought a place of worship was the proper venue for joining husband and wife but who quieted after receiving a donation from Hugh Havisham to the parish's building fund. The ceremony was to have been followed by the wedding breakfast in the ballroom.

Right after Samuel Compeyson had failed to appear, and before the three hundred guests including the Earl of Narmoor had all left the grounds, Hugh Havisham had ordered the servants to rid the ballroom of the flowers and food and decorations, directing the household staff with vigor, trying to remove the stain of the humiliation. He himself had jettisoned Pastor Smyth from Satis House, as if the reverend had been the source of the trouble.

In her wedding dress, the white veil across her face, Miss Havisham had been heartsick—broken on the wheel—and on an impulse, she had asked the servants to take all the wedding finery to her room upstairs. Then not one more word had escaped her mouth for a month as shame and rage fairly drowned her.

Now her father's room was a sanctuary from bitterness—she could apply herself to someone who needed her attention—but as she carried Baby Estella out of the room—leaving behind this Mr. Murdstone, her father, and the reek—and along the hallway the sorrow and fury returned, and by the time she gripped her door handle her hands were trembling. She and the infant entered her room.

The curtains were drawn, and the room was dusky. Fading flowers filled the place; vases, baskets, and urns of them, losing their color and becoming brittle. Roses symbolized love, ivy fidelity, freesias commitment, violets hope, and each stem was a cruel rebuke to her. The fruit and vegetable garlands that had draped the ballroom's windows were laid out alongside her fireplace, a pile of them that sank lower and lower as they aged, and would soon resemble clippings on the back of the gardeners' cart. The garlands' pears and apples were brown with rot and made the room smell like a swamp. The magnificent beaded reticule that had been part of her trousseau—a gift from their neighbors the Herndons, the shipping family—hung at the corner of a mirror near the door to her dressing room, her wedding gown had been returned to the seamstresses' mannequin at the foot of Miss Havisham's bed, and her satin, beribboned shoes were below the gown.

The wedding cake—sent down from London in a coach hired for that very purpose—rested on a table near the bedroom window. It was brittle, carried a fine layer of dust, and one side had fallen in. The cake's candied roses had fallen to the table. A crystal goblet intended for Hugh's toast was on a sidetable next to the silver bowl still filled with punch that had turned brown and was congealing. Unopened gifts were a jumble in a corner. After breakfast she and her new husband were to have taken a curricle to Dover, then cross to Paris for two months where a home on Rue de Rivoli had been arranged. Never unpacked, the travel trunks were stacked at the end of the table. On a wall, a pendulum clock had stopped at twenty minutes to nine. Filled with the detritus of her humiliation, the bedroom was a monument to her folly.

Miss Havisham lowered herself to a settee near the fireplace, rocking the baby in her arms. The bedroom was as familiar to her as the back of her hand but it was changing, and not to her bidding. A spirit resided in the room. Not a spirit spirit; she scoffed at such falderal and could have easily whistled *The Drunken Sailor* while strolling across a cemetery at midnight. But something else, an ethereal presence in the walls, as slight as a pulse, with no more corporeal substance than a thought. If she turned her head, it diminished, then swelled again. If she narrowed her eyes to focus, there was nothing to be seen.

It was a mere suggestion that she remain in the room and that there was never any reason to leave. Her axis was here. What could be of importance beyond these walls? These thoughts were easy to dismiss. Yet more and more insistently they returned. Two days ago she pressed her ear against a wall trying to detect a whisper, and heard nothing. This notion existed apart from her and could not be attributed to her but rather was in the walls and flooring and in the wedding decorations in the room. The place was always offering itself to her, inviting her to stay. And sometimes, when she was tired, when she had exhausted her dose of astringency and loathing, she succumbed to the idea, at least for a day or two.

"For a long while, up here in this room, I have known nothing about time, nothing of days of the week or weeks of the year." She looked down at the baby. "I have things to do, Estella, so I need a calendar, and I cannot stay in this room long."

The baby gripped one of Miss Havisham's fingers.

She laughed, and it sounded strange and choleric in her ears. Her voice rising, she asked the baby, "What sane person doesn't know the day of the week and never leaves her bedroom?"

4

If a fool is born every minute, then that minute twenty-four years ago saw the birth of Bill Sikes. And in those subsequent twenty-four years he had demonstrated a remarkable ability to avoid learning anything. He could not be taught, certainly not by instruction: his formal education ended at age six in his fourth day of school when he pushed the teacher into a fireplace. Nor by experience: he might accidentally bang his head on the same street sign three days in a row. But he possessed a base cunning, of that there could be no doubt, the same primitive guilefulness that allows a rat to evade the best-laid trap in the pantry.

"Left or right, sir," the woman said. "Nothing could be easier."

Sikes stared at her hands, both of them closed with their knuckles up. He scratched his chin. "Right."

She opened her right hand, and it was empty. Then her left hand opened to reveal the sixpence. She lifted Sikes' sixpenny bit from the table and slipped it into her leather reticule, where it chimed against other coins. "Again, sir? Your luck will turn, I'm sure of it."

Sikes dug into his trousers to produce another tanner. He put it on the table, and said, "Burn my body, do it again."

She pulled out a sixpence from the reticule, cupped her hands together to shake the coin, then held out both hands again. Bill Sikes studied them, his eyes shifting back and forth between the woman's hands.

The public house was on Gray's Inn Lane, and was a low place patronized by scoundrels and felons. The meat was fat, the beer was thin, and civility was scarce. Low over their mugs, men on the chairs and benches spoke out of the sides of their mouths and glanced time and again at the door. A boar's head hung above the fireplace. A rotund man with a red scarf around his shoulders carried mugs back and forth between the patrons and the beer spigot, sweat shining on his forehead. The floor was swept once a month, and he was the one to do it.

When Sikes tapped the woman's left hand she opened it, and it was empty. Then her right hand opened, and there was the sixpence. She snatched Sikes' wager from the table and put it into her reticule.

"I've never seen such terrible luck," the woman said, fairly purring. "I'm sure you'll do better. Let's try it again."

Sikes dug deeply into his pocket to produce a threepence and placed it on the table. "I'd better start winning."

"I'm sure you will." The woman retrieved a threepence from her purse, and then using both hands shook the coin then held out her fists. The skin of her face was as pale as porcelain, and her lips were colored wild red. Her smile was both an invitation and a taunt. At first glance she was pretty. On second, she was as hard as a hammer, with matted hair and a scar pulling down a corner of her mouth. She wore a lace cap and a green muslin dress with embroidered spangles and a brown stain on a sleeve.

Sikes narrowed his eyes at her hands. "Left."

She turned her hand palm up, and it was empty. "Ooh. Too bad." She showed him the coin in her right hand, then plucked his wager from the table. "Two hands, one coin. What could be simpler? Try again?"

Sikes found a tuppence from his pocket and dropped it onto the table. He inched closer to her, his gaze on her hands. The whites of his eyes were red lined and the same color as his nose, courtesy of the prior evening's imbibition.

A fellow near the fireplace broke into a drunken song. He clicked mugs with a man in a striped sailor's shirt who had a peg leg. The woman shook a tuppence in her hands then held out her fists for Sikes to examine.

Fagin came through the door and called out, "There you are, Bill."

Sikes didn't remove his eyes from the woman's hands. He rocked back and forth on his heels, his finger hovering over her fists. His tongue was out as if he were trying to read.

The pickpocket wound his way between chairs and benches to Sikes. He frowned at the woman, and gripped Sikes' arm. "Come along, lad. You don't want anything to do with this cheat."

Sikes shook off his arm and didn't look at him. "Strike you dead, Fagin. It's a game, and I'm losing. I've got to win back my money."

"She's a thimblerigger, Bill. You can't win."

Sikes block-and-tackled his gaze away from the woman's hands to stare at Fagin. "I want to win my money back."

When Fagin again tried to pull him away, Sikes swatted him away as he would a gnat.

"Tush, tush, my dear," Fagin said. "She has cheated you fairly and squarely. Let's go."

The thimblerigging lady stepped back from Sikes.

"Cheated?" Sikes' voice was low and menacing.

"It's an old con," Fagin said. "The coin is always in the other hand. Her hands are quicker than your eye."

"I've been cheated out of my money by a sneaking varmint?" Sikes turned to the woman, his face a mash of imbecilic rage.

"You've had your fun." She glanced at the door. "And you paid a few coins for it."

Sikes growled, then grabbed a chair and placed it in front of her, and then another chair, so that the two chairs separated Sikes and the thimblerigging woman.

"Now it's your turn to choose," Sikes said. "Pick a chair."

The chairs had block-and-turned legs and stretchers, and seats of woven slats.

"What do you mean?" Two deep clefts formed between her eyebrows.

"Bill, come on." Fagin stepped toward the door, then looked back over his shoulder. "It's not worth it, my dear."

"Pick a chair, you white-livered thief," Sikes ordered. "Do it now."

She pointed. "The left one."

"Should've picked the other one." Sikes grabbed the chair and swung it at her, crashing the chair into her shoulder and arm, two broken chair legs sailing into a wall, and sending the woman to the floor. She shrieked and then moaned. She tried to roll over but he stepped on her face, grinding the soul of his boot into her cheek. He ripped her reticule from its cord. He shook it, and the coins chimed.

Sikes followed Fagin toward the door, and said, "My hand is quicker than the eye, too."

* * * *

Hugh Havisham had wanted to see the brewery one last time. He hadn't put it that way but Miss Havisham had known what he meant, and so had the four brewery employees who had transferred him from his bed to a cot then carried the cot next door to the brewery. They placed the cot between a mash tun and a copper where Hugh Havisham could watch the works. Casks were against a wall next to bags of barley. A water wagon arrived, the mule wearing a straw hat with its ears sticking out.

The brewery employees glanced at Hugh Havisham, sometimes nodding encouragement, once in a while knuckling their foreheads, trying to smile. Ernest—Miss Havisham's favorite—turned away from Havisham to wipe his eyes. To the employees of Havisham Brothers Brewery, their boss had always been steady and fair.

Havisham was propped up on three pillows. A towel lay over his rotted stump. Ernest placed a three-legged milking stool next to the cot so Miss Havisham could sit next to her father. Sweat dappled Havisham's forehead. The scents of malt and gangrene rot were about equal.

"You are better today." Miss Havisham gripped his hand.

"You can't fool me. I'm near the end, and I know it." He raggedly cleared his throat. "Tell me a secret."

She looked at him. "Pardon me? A secret? You want to play a parlor game?"

"In a year or two or three, you'll wish you had told me something about yourself, a secret you've been hiding from me, maybe since you were a child. But it'll be too late. So, you should tell me now."

"Such a request is unlike you."

"Gangrene crawling up my leg toward my crotch has changed my perspective."

A muleteer jumped down from his wagon's seat and walked toward the rack of pipes. Another worker emptied a gunny sack of hops into the copper, then added coal to the fire pit under it. With a wood spoon another brewer sampled liquid in the hopback.

"Tell you a secret?" She looked at a wall, touching her chin with a finger. "All right, I will. But you go first."

"I have just revealed to you that I am a smuggler and that our family's fortune is based on criminal activity." He grimaced against pain. "Isn't that enough of a secret?"

"I already knew that and have since I was ten or eleven when I first started figuring it out." She inched her stool closer to the cot and brushed an errant lock of hair from his forehead, tucking it behind his ear. "Any father could be an international smuggler. That's not a notable secret."

He laughed, more a cough, his chest bucking under the blanket.

She closed her eyes. She hadn't heard her father laugh in weeks, and even this raggedy wet laugh made hope for her father surge. She patted his arm. But then a waft of gangrene rot caught her, and the arctic certainty of his fate returned. Blackbirds whistled from trees across the road.

"Then here's a secret." He wet his lips. "The new tuppence you have been finding under your pillow every Sunday evening since you were three years old: that's been me putting the coins there."

"Dad, how can I not know that?" She laughed. "Of course it was you, and I've known it since I was three. That's not a real secret."

"That's my favorite secret, and you knew all along?" He shook his head. "Now it's your turn. What will you wish you had told me after you no longer can do so?"

She stuck out her lower lip, deep in thought.

A worker rolled an empty oak barrel along the aisle, and nodded at Hugh Havisham then may have thought it insufficient so he called, "God protect you, sir."

"Here is a secret I swore you would never learn," she said. "I have visited Rome."

His eyes shifted from the mash tun to her. "In the Papal States? That Rome? Surely not."

"My year in Paris at Mademoiselle Arsenault's school?"

"Your mother and I were proud to be able to send you there." He lifted a hand to cover his mouth, coughing into his palm.

"It was only half a year at Mademoiselle Arsenault's. Bored and wanting adventure, my friend Genevieve Bothell—you've met her when she visited us here at Satis House, remember?—decided we'd had enough of Paris so we took a stage south to Marseille, then a ship to Civitavecchia, then overland to Rome."

"But you wrote us a letter every week from Paris. I saved those letters."

She smiled at him. "I'm a conniver, father. I wrote those letters before I left for Rome, and gave them to a friend at the school to mail once a week."

Hugh Havisham inhaled sharply, and his daughter didn't know if it was due to her revelation or the pain.

He said, "But those things you wrote about: the icicles hanging just outside your Paris lodging, the tree blossoms along the Champs-Élysées. What lovely images, and I still remember them. What about those things?"

"All from my head." She laughed and tapped her temple. "All inventions—my stab at fiction—made before I left on the Rome journey. I've wanted to confess this to you for years and years but never had the courage."

"I've never heard anything so outlandish." He smiled feebly.

She gripped his hand. "Now it's your turn. A secret. Something about yourself I don't already know."

Carrying a maul, the brewery's cooper entered the building from the road. He doffed his cap to Hugh Havisham, then disappeared behind the coal bin on his way to the cooperage.

He exhaled, a long rattle. "I deeply loved your mother."

Miss Havisham's eyebrows climbed her forehead. She had never heard anything like this from her father. She managed with, "I know."

"No, you don't." Havisham squeezed his eyes, pain writ on his face. "You never saw me be affectionate with your mother. I look back now, and I don't think you ever saw me hug or kiss your mother, not once. I did though, an abundance of both."

She hesitated. "That wasn't my business, was it?"

"I loved your mother dearly. Maybe if I had shown it in front of you, my love would have rubbed off on you both, and you and your mother. . . ."

33

FAGIN & MISS HAVISHAM

The words spilled from Miss Havisham. "I loved mother."

A worker with the mash mixer—a wood spatula the size of a shovel—walked past them, stopped abruptly, and blinking back tears extended his hand to Havisham, who generated a smile, and weakly shook the man's hand.

Then Havisham turned his eyes back to his daughter. "I'm not so sure about your love for your mother."

"Of course, I loved her."

"Your mother was bristly; I'll grant you that. But after Peter died, emotion drained away from her and never returned."

The Havishams' second child had succumbed to scarlet fever at age three. Margaret Havisham had been six years old at the time.

Hugh Havisham made a rough noise in his throat. "After Peter passed away your mother never had a happy day, not for the rest of her life. I tried but I just couldn't bring any light or warmth into her life."

"Father, I just . . . ." She stopped herself.

He shook his head, a slight moment. "Your mother tried with you, to bring you close to her, but she just didn't have the strength once Peter was gone." His voice was thin. "I'm sorrier for the trouble between you and your mother more than you will ever know. Maybe I could have found something to do about it, some way to bring you two together. But I could not, and it's my everlasting regret. So, there's my big secret."

Words trapped in her throat, she looked away from him to stare at the copper, where steam rose and drifted along the ceiling.

Hugh Havisham said, "Will you get the laudanum from my room, sweetie? I need some of it. Then I'll lie here awhile and watch beer brewing."

She looked at his pallid, pain-riven face. Again, she gripped his hand, and then left him there on the cot in the middle of the Havisham Brothers Brewery to return to the house. A sound escaped her, a desperate yowl that she bit off as she rushed back into Satis House for the tincture of opium.

* * * *

The whorehouse's name was the Green Park Gentlemen's Club but the regulars referred to it as The Gunroom, a patriotic nod to the navy from the club's patrons, almost none of whom had ever served in the navy but had determined that this nickname was sufficiently close to actual naval service.

The proprietress, Madam Arabella, despised the terms *whorehouse, bawdy house,* and *cathouse,* not even to speak of *house of ill repute.* She called it a gentlemen's club, and if clarity were needed, she might mention under her breath that it was in fact a ladies and gentlemen's club, and those who could not at that point understand her meaning were not welcomed in her establishment in any event.

A guard stood at the door dressed in loose Turkish trousers called *salvar*, a green coat known as a jubba, and a red fez. The fellow weighed twenty stone and was no more a Turk than was the First Lord of the Admiralty but Madam Arabella thought the costume added dash and mystery to her enterprise. If she held up one finger and glanced at a rowdy patron, the Turk threw him through the doors onto the street. If she held up two fingers, the Turk hurt him as he sent him through the doors.

Madam Arabella had been christened Bella Bonds fifty-five years ago, and early in life had found she had a natural bent for business, selling herself and then selling young ladies who appreciated her acumen. Madam Arabella had always been buxom, and now, in her fifth decade her breasts were held up by a bespoke collection of stays, struts, and cantilevers that allowed a fine presentation of her assets. Henna tinted her hair, and the thickness of her makeup allowed no glimpse of actual skin. Her light blue silk frock glimmered, and her emerald and silver bracelet was weighty.

Her desk was on the club's ground floor behind a potted palm. She made entries into a ledger, and sipped barley water. Her eyes were green and large, and despite her years and her profession humor remained in them, and she was quick to smile.

Six gentlemen and seven or eight of her young ladies chatted and laughed, many holding glasses. Madam Arabella's gaze settled on a fellow who had just come through the door, and who handed his frock coat and walking stick to a bewigged valet. Studying him, Madam Arabella pulled one of four cords hanging down the wall to her right. Her desk was from Sweden: blond wood with bright brass handles. Her trash bin was a preserved elephant's foot she had taken in trade from a sailor who had just returned from India. Expensive beeswax—rather than tallow—candles lit the room. Sofas around the room were made of gleaming and pleated leather, and the carpets came from Kermanshah in Persia. Hothouse roses filled half a dozen vases in the room. The Turk shifted back and forth, eyeing the newcomer.

A young woman—also in silk, this the color of a ruby—came down the stairs, passed a serving table on which were bottles of port and brandy, and as several of the patrons stared at her she walked to Madam Arabella's desk.

Her name was Honora Culpepper but at the club she went by Elise. "Yes, madam?"

"The gentleman near the door, do you recognize him?" the proprietress asked.

"In the old-fashioned ribbed waistcoat? That's Arthur Gride, the moneylender. I thought you knew him."

"No, the fellow with the gold hair. The handsome one."

"I have seen him several times, and he was with me once. His name is Samuel."

35

"Yes, Samuel Compeyson," Madam Arabella said. "He visits us every four or five days. He spends money as if it's falling to the ground like snowflakes. And most often he doesn't ask for a girl."

"He told me he loves it here. Beautiful women and fine spirits. But I've heard bad things about him from other girls." Elise was an extraordinary beauty with a long neck and flowing arms, a masterful Gallic nose, a broad forehead, and lush lips above a soft chin. Her flame-colored hair was loose to her shoulders. Madam Arabella charged more for an evening with Elise than she did for any other girl.

Carrying a silver tray of stemmed wine glasses, a waiter wandered among the patrons. Compeyson took a glass then indecorously slipped a coin into the waiter's jacket pocket. Near the fireplace, a violinist and a cellist sawed their instruments, filling the room with pleasant squeaks. A young lady in a pink frock—the fabric so thin it was diaphanous—led a gentleman up the stairs.

"I want you to take care of Samuel Compeyson this evening." Madame Arabella patted Elise's hand. "You are a wonder with the clientele."

Elise's jaw set. "He slapped Florentia last week, and she had a purple cheek."

"Is that why Florentia went missing for several days?"

"Powder couldn't hide the bruise."

Madam Arabella shifted in her chair, eyeing Compeyson.

Elise said, "What happened was, Florentia corrected Compeyson's grammar. When he said, 'I could have went to the river,' she laughed and playfully punched his arm and said, 'It's gone. I could have gone to the river.' And he hauled back and slapped her."

"He struck her because she mentioned he used a wrong word?" Miss Arabella asked.

"I think he's from the poor countryside and despises being reminded of it. But that's not his only problem. He has trouble performing."

Miss Arabella said, "Our house is famous for performance. All men here perform."

Elise shook her head. "He was my customer last week. I tried and tried and tried. And failed."

"I've never heard of such a thing, not with you." Madam Arabella tapped her fingers on the desk, a drumroll. "Did Compeyson talk about it? His failure?"

"He told me not to worry because he usually needed more fireworks than the ladies here could provide."

With one movement Samuel Compeyson drank off his glass, and stepped to the waiter to obtain another. He looked at two of the women, then sidled up to a dazzling brunette wearing a green ribbon choker that matched her eyes. He said a few words to her. Even though they were professionals, the ladies in the room stared at Compeyson, with his golden hair and perfect smile. Compeyson put his arm around the shoulders of the brunette, who went by the name Eve.

The proprietress asked, "Why does he visit us, if we cannot service him?"

"He likes it here." Elise tucked a lock of hair behind her ear. "He told me it is an elegant place where he can buy his way in, which he cannot do at the Pall Mall clubs."

"I'm not going to allow a ruffian to hurt my girls, slapping Florentia like that. He needs a lesson."

By half standing Madam Arabella caught the Turk's attention. With a glance, she directed the Turk to Samuel Compeyson. She held up two fingers. The big man in the fez revealed a stump-toothed smile, then stepped to Compeyson and gripped his elbow hard enough to make the swindler wince.

Compeyson exclaimed, "My good man, remove your hand from me."

The Turk weighed twice what Compeyson did, and he towed the swindler away from Eve as easily as pulling a thread. Then the Turk shoved him to the door, which the doorman opened with apparent eagerness. Subtly but with much force, the Turk sent a blow into Compeyson just below his ribs. The swindler grunted and his legs gave way but the guard gripped his trousers and propelled him through the door.

Smiling, the Turk turned back toward Madam Arabella, who nodded at him. The patrons and most of the young ladies either hadn't seen the ejection or had ignored it.

The madam said to Elise, "A fellow who slaps girls around and whose carnal tastes cannot be determined, we don't need his money."

5

Fagin and Sikes had boarded the coach at the Cross Keys in Wood Street, crossed the Thames at London Bridge, and five hours later approached Satis House. Sikes bounced on the coach bench, his elbows on his knees, head down and eyes closed. He moaned pitiably.

"You're in poor condition, my boy." Fagin sat across from Sikes, their knees almost touching. On the pickpocket's lap was a felted beaver hat he had lifted off a toff at the coach inn. "It's this damned coach, of course. All the bouncing and swaying."

Sikes wet his lips. "Don't talk to me, old man."

"How can I carry on a conversation when you stick you head out the coach window every few moments?"

"I've heard enough talk from you." Sikes didn't raise his head. "Ever since I was your fagger—talk, talk, talk—and I should've quit you then."

The harness leather squeaked, the bells rang, and the iron wheel rims ground on the roadway. The carriage rose and fell on its springs like a boat buffeted by waves. Ten passengers had started the journey from London—six in the cab and four on the roof—and all but Fagin and Sikes had left the carriage at earlier stops. The teamster had sung one bawdy song after another to his horses, and Fagin didn't know whether the only lady passenger had fled the carriage at Dartford because she had reached her destination or to get away from the driver's vulgar lyrics and from Sikes's recurrent retching out the carriage window.

Sikes was a product of the Seven Dials, part of the St. Giles Rookery. Seven streets converged at the Seven Dials, where a cobblestone court had once featured a sun dial, removed half a century ago by the Paving Commission because vagabonds, criminals, and harlots gathered around it as if they all needed to know the time of day. The noble paving commissioners had failed in their purpose, and Seven Dials remained a blighted sinkhole.

"This lady I've told you about," Fagin said, "she is sure to end up at Bedlam. I could see it in her eyes which I had the unfortunate circumstance of viewing along a pistol barrel."

The coach's seats were covered in canvas, and an unlit brass lamp hung from the wall near Fagin's head. The curtains were back, and Fagin glanced at the passing trees. He didn't like trees, particularly when there was no London haze to obscure their more sinister aspects. The roadhouses and inns they passed had distinct edges and sharp corners. And here in the country the sun was a close disc rather than a smear in the sky. Even sounds were more acute, unfiltered by London's thick atmosphere. All this clarity oppressed the spirit.

Sikes wiped spittle from the corner of his mouth. His color was liverish, emphasizing the base malignity of his expression. A coiled rope was at his feet, along with empty gunny sacks and an iron pry bar.

"She wants to meet with me, likely involving some foolery." Fagin ran his fingers through his rust-colored beard. "There'll be little profit in it except that you provide, dear boy. All you need to do is to get into her house."

Sikes squeezed his eyes shut. "I'm ill. All of this moving."

"Perhaps it is only a bit of undigested breakfast," Fagin suggested. "You have always had a lamentable tendency to bloat."

"This is the last time I ever ride in a coach, old man."

It was also the first time Bill Sikes had ever ridden in a coach or been more than five miles from Seven Dials and Clerkenwell, and he only traveled that extreme distance when presented with the glittering opportunity of a residence with an unsecured window or wide chimney or unlocked coal chute. And he always walked, seldom having the few coins needed for a hack, having invested his coins in brandy or a dollymop.

Fagin asked, "Can you do the job, eh, my dear?"

Sikes rubbed his temple. "You do your part and I'll do mine. I'll get into the house."

"I'm gratified to hear it, upon my word and honor. I knew you were the person for me when I first spotted you, and took you in, an act of charity which has never been adequately acknowledged, if I may say."

Fagin had found Sikes in Clerkenwell on Cowcross Street, where cattle were driven through the neighborhood to the Smithfield Market. Sikes had been eighteen years old, and was twelve inches away from being trampled by cows. The pickpocket—protected from the herd in a pinion-cutter's doorway—had snatched the boy to safety, an act of heroism that grew more bold and dangerous each time Fagin reminded Sikes of it.

FAGIN & MISS HAVISHAM

The vehicle slowed, and the coachman called, "Your stop, sirs. You'll be getting off now or it'll be on to Margate with you."

Fagin opened the coach door, gripped the rail, and gingerly stepped to the ground. He, too, was unfamiliar with travel other than that provided by his shoes. Carrying his equipment, Bill Sikes followed him out, the screws and betties jangling in his coat pit. Fagin touched his cap to the driver, who clucked his tongue and snapped the reins. Trailing dust, the coach moved away.

They had been deposited near two sycamore trees whose peeling trunks dropped curled bark on the ground. A split log bench was between the trees for passengers waiting for the stage. Fagin turned a full circle. Lined by buckthorn bushes, a stream paralleled the road for a way, then wandered off. Crabapple trees grew along the road, and some of the roadway was lined by stone fences. Buildings were in the distance. It was a place of large homes and vast grounds. Hauling barrels, a dray pulled by two horses rolled past. The sky was pure blue and limitless.

"There it is. It's called Satis House." Trying to appear employed, Fagin wore an inkhorn in his coat buttonhole. "The brewery and the manse. The gardens, the rooms, the stables, the well-house. I could walk it in my sleep, after all I've learned."

"You've told me enough about the place, Fagin."

"That old Irish footpad Connor McGinty, you've met him?"

"Never when he didn't have a skin full." As if the ground were rolling under him, Sikes spread his feet.

"McGinty had been hired as a gardener at Satis House, and after some weeks was nibbed for trying to hoist the plate. He was released from Horsemonger Lane after four years."

With his teeth Sikes scraped the film off his tongue.

Fagin said, "Last night he and I sat down at the Crown and Glory, and as long as I purchased the wine he gabbled about Satis House. He peached on it good. I left him there at midnight, his face on the table. So you know where to go, and what to look for, am a right?"

"It's me taking all the chance, ain't it, Fagin? While you'll have tea with the quality."

"It's Sunday afternoon. Most of the servants are gone."

"I want more of a cut." Sikes balled a hand into a fist.

"I will meet you back here, my dear, at the stage stop in an hour or so. Get going now, and remember, don't pick up something just because it's shiny." The pickpocket put his hand on Sikes's arm, about to push him toward the house but with his habitual instinct toward self-preservation Fagin caught himself. "Only the ream swag, Bill. Only the ream swag."

* * * *

40

Fagin pulled the bell chain at Satis House's door. Wisteria grew up the door jam and lay across the cornice, another plant he loathed, always climbing and creeping. Vines complicated entry through a window. That's why nowadays he sent in Bill Sikes, always with clear instruction because Sikes was otherwise a bull in a bush. Fagin lifted his nose at the scent of the brewery. Beer was a poor man's libation, and he drank wine when he could afford it or steal it. He pulled his hat from his head.

The door opened, and a voice said, "Fagin. You have appeared."

Fagin knew the voice and knew the stolid man at the door, and he jerked back and tried to spin away but the man grabbed him by the scruff and hauled him through the door into the hallway, then passed the Chinese vase, and into the great hall.

"Bucket, I am carrying nothing untoward."

The detective said, "Such a vow from you isn't worth a farthing, Fagin."

"Search my every pocket. You'll find a half crown, and it was earned by the provenance of hard labor."

Bucket laughed. "Any coin you possess is likely a lead slug. If you are carrying a blade there'll be the devil."

The inspector gripped the pickpocket's collar so tightly Fagin's face was red. Bucket steered him into a drawing room.

Miss Havisham was sitting near a fireplace, and she gestured toward a chair opposite her. The brass andirons were five feet tall, and the fireplace was as wide as a chesterfield. The day's heat had warmed the room, and no fire was burning. Silver candle holders were arrayed on a pianoforte near the windows. The piano had been polished so that it gleamed like a looking glass.

With starched dignity, Fagin plucked at his coat sleeve and rose on his toes. "Had I known this bluebottle was going to be here,"—he flicked a finger at Bucket— "I would've stayed in London."

"I am told you need to be watched closely," Miss Havisham said, "and indeed that is my experience with you." She held up her wrists. "Kindly note I am not wearing jewelry." And she touched her bare neck. "I have even left my tortoise-shell comb in another room, not wanting to have it plucked from my person."

"You flatter me, madam. Why have you brought me here?"

"Every day on London's streets you deal in illusions and deception. Nothing is permanent in your world, Mr. Fagin. It comes and goes. A theft here, a swindle there, you win some, you lose some. Each morning you do not know whether you'll end the day in your own bed or in jail. Everything is transient and fleeting. An evanescent existence."

Fagin said, "Perhaps you will honor me by arriving at your point, madam."

"I have brought you here to introduce you to another world, to show you that some things are permanent and stable. Satis House is such a place. This home endures, and so will I. Some things you can count on as being lasting, as will be my commitment to you should you join my enterprise."

A red and gold Kidderminster carpet covered most of the floor. A round library table was to Miss Havisham's side, and a gilt portrait frame leaned against it, the back of the frame to the room. A mahogany chest ornamented with pilasters took up some of the wall near the fireplace.

When she motioned toward a black lacquer cane chair, Fagin gripped its arms to lower himself into it. The detective moved to the doorway, his hands locked behind his back and his eyes on Fagin. Bucket wore black trousers and a blue wool surtout not quite sufficiently loose to disguise his lead-filled leather neddy. A garden was visible through the drawing room's windows, and a red-flowering trumpet vine hung over some of panes.

She asked, "Do you know one Samuel Compeyson?"

"I've never had the pleasure of an introduction," Fagin said.

From the doorway Bucket said, "Fagin won't admit to knowing his own mother, Miss Havisham."

She said, "If I detect honesty in your answers, there will be payment for them. You may leave Satis House more comfortable than when you arrived." She smiled as if to encourage him.

Fagin's eyes darted left and right. He may have been looking for a purse. "I do not know a Samuel Compeyson, madam."

She stared at him as one does a butcher's thumb too near the scale, then she lifted the gilt frame, and turned it so Fagan could see the painted canvas. "Do you recognize this person?"

The portrait was of a dandy in a black tailcoat with velvet trim and deep notches in the lapels. A diamond stickpin adorned a lapel. The brocaded waistcoat—it appeared to be shimmering silk—had a high stand-up collar. The breeches fit snugly around the subject's thighs and were adorned with black lace. He carried gray gloves in one hand and a top hat in the other. His yellow hair was short on the sides and built up on top in the fashion of the day. Large and languid eyes were under long lashes, something of his mother in his face. The corners of his mouth were turned up, and he stared straight out at the viewer, an expression of insouciance and knowing.

Fagin laughed. "Why that's Harry Beecker, and would you look at him?" The pickpocket swatted his knee. "He looks ready for court."

Miss Havisham's face closed like a cupboard. "Harry Beecker? Are you sure his name isn't Samuel Compeyson?"

"Ay, it's Harry, plain as plain. And he's doing rather well, with a diamond on his coat."

Miss Havisham's voice was as bitter as a bolus. "I gave him that piece of jewelry, an engagement present."

"Diamonds are his weakness," Fagin said. "And he has always had sublime success in obtaining them."

"Can you tell me anything about this Harry Beecker?" Her yellow cotton dress was ornamented with bands of brown satin. A white cashmere shawl covered her shoulders.

"He is no friend of mine, madam. I see him here and there but he doesn't brush shoulders with the likes of me."

"Would he recognize you?" she asked.

"He couldn't tell me apart from Adam. He prefers the fancy." He showed his palms in a gesture of aplomb. "Harry prefers the wealthy, and all their trappings. He won't wear cotton if silk is to be had, and he won't speak to a baron if an earl is at hand."

"He is well situated, then?"

"For a month or two he is as rich as Croesus, dancing a quadrille in Mayfair and attending the Royal Ascot but he is susceptible to games of chance. He can lose more money on a hand of cards than I will see in five years. After a spell of spectacular spending and gambling he'll be found in a dubious flat at the docklands and as poor as a shorn sheep, having a cruel time of it, one step from a sponging-house."

"He is a profligate with money then, Mr. Fagin?"

"He earns it and he spends it as he will, madam. It is not up to me to judge."

Near the wall Mr. Bucket raised his nose as would a dog on a scent. His gaze went to the hammered tin ceiling. His focus seemed to be beyond the tin. When he shifted toward the door, the ruffle clicked on his belt under his coat.

She pulled at a strand of hair over her ear. "How does he earn it?"

"I hear only rumors. I would not slate the man based on third-hand stuff."

"Humor me, Mr. Fagin."

The pickpocket glanced over his shoulder at Bucket, who seemed preoccupied with the ceiling. "Far be it from me to blow on a fellow in the trade, miss."

"Consider yourself on wages, if you will." She pulled her shawl more tightly around her shoulders. Olive-colored crescents were under her eyes, and her lips were pressed together with force.

Fagin said, "It is believed—perhaps as an article of faith in Harry's audacity—that he was betrothed to Gwendolyn Barris thirteen or fourteen months ago, and then Harry disappeared a day or two before the ceremony. He was going by the name George Wolford at the time. He arrived back in the city and lived like a bishop. For several weeks he owned a coupe pulled by two grays, and he dined every night on turtle at the Adelphi."

Blushing like the bride she never was, Miss Havisham asked, "Whatever happened to Miss Wolford?"

"She fled to Vienna with her mother and several household servants, and has not been seen since. She is likely in a nunnery."

"I have a proposition for you, Mr. Fagin. It will earn you as much as any of Harry Beecker's swindles."

"Set out the particulars, if you will."

Bucket asked, "Miss Havisham, may I go up to the next floor?"

She switched her gaze to the policeman. "What could possibly be up there of interest to you?"

Fagin half rose from the chair but then, gripping the armrests with more force than required, sank back down.

"But, yes, of course, Mr. Bucket," she said. "My security is in your hands."

Bucket stepped across the carpet to the fireplace to lift the silver tinderbox, which glittered brightly in the window light. The box was etched with flower patterns, and on top was a socket holding a beeswax candle. He opened the lid to check the tinder.

The detective held up the box. "And may I borrow this for a few moments?"

His requests were surely a puzzle to Miss Havisham but her confidence in him was reflected in her narrow smile, and she dipped her chin. As he walked to the drawing room door, Fagin raised a hand, perhaps about to voice an objection, but he desisted, shaking his head. Bucket disappeared into the great hall.

She turned back to the pickpocket. "Open your ears and your imagination, Mr. Fagin. You will find it profitable. Here is what I want you to do."

* * * *

"Bill?" Fagin called. "I don't see you, my boy. Come on out. The danger is past." He had assumed Sikes—never one to stand if there were a horizontal surface nearby—would be waiting for him on the stage bench. He stepped around the sycamores, and said in a loud voice, "I have guided our ship safely past the shoals, Bill."

A cart sped by on the road, the driver speaking nonsense syllables to the horse. A goat bleated from the other side of a stone fence. A small breeze shifted the sycamore leaves.

"Can you hear me there?" Fagin turned his head at a sound. "Where are you?"

A noise came, a low burble from the buckthorn bushes that grew under the far reaches of the sycamore boughs. The sound echoed the nearby brook but there was a primal quality to it out of place in the peaceful countryside. Something of Bill Sikes in it.

Fagin pushed branches out of his way, startled that they snapped back after his passing, as he was unused to foliage. "Bill, you there? This woman might not be as daft as I had thought. She has a plan."

Fagin stepped around a moss-laden stump to find Sikes face down on the ground amid fescue and cock's-foot. Sikes groaned and clenched his fists. He tried to rise but squealed like a hog in a gate and fell back flat on the dirt. He appeared to have been toasted on a fork. His shoes were gone. Blisters and seeping wounds covered his feet. His trousers had been burned off up to his thighs, and evidence of a scorching was on his legs, too, angry red swirls of skin and blisters. Where his pants still existed, they were blackened tatters.

"Can you get up, my dear? We need to return to the city straightaway."

Sikes unclenched his eyes. His mouth moved wordlessly. Those portions of him not roasted were covered in chimney soot, thick smears of black. Soot matted the hair on the back of his head. Smudges covered his nose and cheeks. His hands looked as if he worked in a blacking factory. He slid a hand under himself and groaned as he levered himself to all fours.

"I can't get up," Sikes croaked. "My feet. . . ."

"Can you move at all, Bill? The coach stop is just over there."

"My legs. They put a fire under me."

Fagin surveyed him. "It does look it, doesn't it?"

"I was halfway down the chimney." Sikes coughed raggedly. "It hurts too much. My knees and hands. I can't even crawl."

"Can you roll?" Fagin asked. "The coach bench is right over there. I can't carry you."

Sikes inhaled hugely. "Help me up."

Fagin hooked Sikes's arm with his own, and Sikes—panting, his grimace stretched to the snapping point—climbed Fagin like a rope. The pickpocket stumbled under the weight but braced himself mightily, and helped Sikes stand upright.

"My feet." Sikes whistled in apparent agony.

"You are in a doleful state, Bill, but take one step at a time, just over to the coach stop, and then we ride to London."

Sikes moved a foot and grunted. Another step, another grunt. Legs and back bowed and creaking, Fagin propped him up, having to right his hat when it threatened to topple. The smell was of singed meat. They neared the coach bench.

Sikes walked on the edges of his feet, mouthing "Ow, ow, ow, ow," with his steps.

Huffing with effort, Fagin helped Sikes onto the bench. Fagin tried to brush soot smears from his coat but only succeeded in transferring it to his hands. Sweat beaded on Sikes's brow. His mouth sagged open.

"This Havisham woman has laid out a path to our fortune, Bill." Fagin wiped his hands on his trousers. "No more of these contemptible burglaries for us. Have you ever met Harry Beecker? Thanks to Harry, lady luck has found us."

His face twisted with pain; Sikes lifted a foot so Fagin could better see it. It was a crimson, charred wreck. "Don't talk to me about luck, old man."

* * * *

Samuel Compeyson had taken the coach to Rochester, and then walked to Satis House as he didn't want to be seen getting off the coach near the residence. Wooing Margaret Havisham, he had visited the home a dozen times. He knew the place as well as he knew anywhere, and he had thought he had known Margaret, too, but it appeared that she had more fortitude than he had guessed, with her finding his flat and going through his rooms accompanied by that bodyguard or policeman.

Crouching, the pistol in his belt slapping his thigh, Compeyson moved along a stone fence then sprinted across road into the Yew Garden on the east side of the mansion, where he hid behind a bush clipped to resemble an African lion. That the Havishams would name their gardens was another indication that they had too much money and had deserved to be relieved of some of it.

He walked through a bed of white calla lilies toward Satis House's east wall. No one looked out from the windows. The sound of a hedge clipper came from the gardens behind the house. Compeyson moved along the mansion's wall, ducking below windows. The bricks radiated the sun's heat. He peered around the corner toward the front door. The porch and driveway were empty.

He lifted the knife from his boot. He was going to hurt her, to slash her. She had undoubtedly longed to see him again, and she was about to. She needed a lesson regarding interfering with his new plans.

Those plans—involving the wealthy Wilkinson family, the carriage manufacturers —simply could not be fouled by the meddling of one of his former fiancés. Compeyson disliked violence, not because he was squeamish but because it was coarse and callow. Fisticuffs and firearms were inelegant. They were of the milieu which he desperately wanted to avoid. And there was no pleasure gained from violence. Rather, fulfilment was found when a woman and her family voluntarily surrendered to his beauty and charm.

Still, no one came from the house. Margaret rode her horse at this time every day. She would leave Satis House's front door and walk to the stables on the other side of the brewery. He had traveled that route with her many times.

He swatted at a horsefly. Margaret had told him that he would become accustomed to the smell of the brewery but he never had. It thickened the air.

Distant hammering came from the brewery's cooperage. A swallow flitted past, and the sun drifted out from behind a cloud.

Who would have thought Margaret Havisham would try to strike back? She had been besotted with him, couldn't stop staring at him, could hardly form sentences when he was near, so in love was she. She was smart enough, he supposed—better read than most of his marks—but love and credulity are partners in the human mind, and Compeyson made a living because of it. Margaret Havisham had been just another chump.

Satis House's door opened, and a woman came out. It wasn't Margaret Havisham but rather a maid carrying a basket. She walked along the gravel driveway toward the brewery. Perspiration slid down Compeyson's cheek.

Compeyson's victims usually disappeared after they learned the extent of their gullibility, after the family had given him the money and after he had vanished. The women fled the disgrace, usually at the urging of their families. The jilted bride almost invariably went to the continent, often with her mother. The family would invent a story in an attempt to salvage honor, such as the groom succumbing to typhus just before the wedding day. Beatrice Carmody, daughter of Ethan Carmody who owned copper mines in Cornwall, was sent to Philadelphia in America, which was the record distance for his jilted fiancés. Compeyson kept a list of his fiancés and where they had fled after he had jilted them. It offered much amusement.

As a wagon passed on the road, its wheels grinding on the gravel, Compeyson lowered himself behind a yew hedge near a Satis House corner. A muffled conversation came through the window, Margaret Havisham's voice and someone else's. Across the road a goat bleated.

Compeyson's father Ephraim had been a legendary mace cove, and had told his boy Samuel that only fools went down into a mine or scraped hides in a tanning yard. The senior Compeyson's specialty was selling plots of farmland on the island of Eylenda, promising fertile soil and a temperate climate, and even going so far as chartering a brig and crew to transport the marks to the island. Eylenda was the Icelandic name for Iceland, and the vessel would appear at a dock at the tiny village of Reykjavik, greeted by baffled Icelanders. Ephraim had made several fortunes with his land swindle, and had lost them at cards and dice, a trait his son Samuel had unfortunately inherited. Selling land seemed like work to Samuel, so he had settled on wooing and winning wealthy young women. He was a confidence man, a good one, and he was proud of it.

The conversation in the room on the other side of the window ended. Compeyson twisted the knife in his hand. He gazed along the plane of the mansion's south wall toward the porch.

The door opened, and Margaret Havisham stepped onto the porch. She wore a blue riding dress he had seen before. Knife in hand, he stepped along the front wall on a flower bed toward her. He would not hurt her badly. A slice or two. She frightened easily, and this would do it. She would stop pursuing him, stop her meddling in his business.

She turned away from his direction to face the brewery. The planting bed's soft soil muted Compeyson's footfalls. Then that wagon-wide fellow emerged from house to stand next to Margaret, the same man Compeyson had seen come out of his building in London, who looked as hard as an anvil. He said something to Margaret, and she gestured toward the brewery.

Compeyson grimaced with frustration, and pulled his pistol from his belt but he did not draw back the hammer. He backstepped along the wall, returning across the flower bed the way he had come, tulip stems snapping under his shoes. With Margaret Havisham and her big bodyguard still looking to the west, Compeyson reached a corner of Satis House. He stepped alongside the east wall, and returned the knife to his boot and the flintlock to his belt. Cursing under his breath, he walked east, away from the mansion.

He could not take on Margaret and this big fellow by himself. He needed help, and he knew where to find it. He would visit London's most notorious precinct.

6

Fog lay over the river, hiding everything more than a few yards from shore. Ropes of it coiled and uncoiled along the water's edge, curling around trees then retreating, enfolding the dock then revealing it again. The haze was smothering but low over the river, and stars above filled the limitless sky. The moon was nowhere to be seen. Water lapped against the pebbled shore and ships' fog bells rang out in the murk. The dank air had a weight, and surrounded Miss Havisham, reaching through her coat to chill her.

A leather-lunged crewman out in the fog yelled, "A brig here, outward bound. Clear the way." The fog muffled his call.

Thick patches of reeds grew at the water's edge, and horse chestnut and lime trees hung out over the shoreline. A rutted dirt road led from a dock onto land and through red maple trees. A horse and wagon waited on the road. The horse—a blue roan—flicked its ears.

"Why is the boat out in this weather?" Miss Havisham asked. "It isn't safe. I can't see anything out there."

"That is the point." Edward Murdstone carried a lantern that had a red-tinted horn window and closed blinders. "We can't see and can't be seen. And I implore you to keep your voice down. Lurkers are out on the water and on the land."

Jutting into the river fifty feet, the dock was less a dock than it was a jumble of rotted wood covered in moss. Rusted iron bolts stuck out from pylons where the timbers had fallen away. Pylons leaned drunkenly.

"My father loves everything about the river," she said. "Not me. It always smells of boiled cabbage."

Hugh Havisham had often chided his daughter for her nose, which he claimed was as acute as a hound's, and she always commented on the smells of things.

Murdstone held up his hand for silence. He peered upriver into the fog.

"What's the matter?" Miss Havisham followed his gaze but could see only diaphanous haze.

The smallest of sounds came from the fog, the lapping of water, but it was rhythmic—a cadence—and nothing the river would produce on its own.

Murdstone whispered, "Rowers." He grabbed Miss Havisham's elbow. "Hurry. Into the trees."

She frowned at his hand on her elbow which was too presumptuous even in his haste. Glancing over his shoulder he hauled her away from the river until they were surrounded by branches and leaves thirty yards from the shore. The horse nickered. Murdstone stopped near a beach tree, and angled his head so he could view the river through the foliage. The ground was soft from earlier rain. Fog swirled and eddied. The sound from the river was louder, repeated splashing then creaking. The tar black night and viscous fog were as revealing as a wall.

"Deadhead on your right, there. Push us away." Out in the fog, a fierce whisper.

Murdstone cocked an ear.

The sound grew louder, and it was deliberate and orderly, a repeated splashing that gave Miss Havisham the impression of stealth. When she was young her father had taken her on Sunday excursions on the River Medway in his rowboat, and she knew the sound of oars dipped into the water and of leather oarlocks.

Just above a whisper, a voice came from the night and fog. "A pier. Nothing on it. Keep clear. They're here somewhere."

At first the boat was only a suggestion, a flickering glimpse of something more solid than fog. Then it gathered together and formed up as it slid closer to the dock. It was a lapstrake dory with three rowers on three thwarts. A man in the bow pushed a spar against a submerged log, and the dory veered away from it. At the stern one man held a flintlock and another gripped the tiller. The gunner's gaze swept the shore, the stock hard against his shoulder. The oar blades were in the air as the current pushed along the boat. It passed the derelict pier.

"No one," the gunner said. "Get us away from the shore."

The rudder was put hard over and the oars dropped into the water. One of the men called a cadence and the crew put their backs into the work. The dory became less and less corporeal, then blinked out, leaving only ghostly swirls of fog.

"Who were they?" Miss Havisham asked.

"A tide waiter or tide surveyor," Murdstone said. "Hard to tell along the river. Out here they are free to follow their own devices, and are in it for themselves, grabbing whatever they can."

Miss Havisham stared after the dory but not a trace of it could be seen.

Murdstone said, "They are the king's men but when the king is far away and the night is dark they become nothing more than highwaymen afloat. The world around, customs officers are dunder-headed and grasping."

Carrying the blinkered lantern he stepped out of the brush. Shoreside mud sucked at his boots.

"There are thirteen customs ports on our grand island." He laughed in an affected way, the unnatural sound of one who didn't laugh much. "This moldering dock isn't one of those thirteen and so it answers our purpose."

Gorse branches left traces of moisture on her shawl as she moved from the brush to the water's edge. They were near Gravesend, five miles from Satis House. The River Thames swept by ceaselessly below the layer of fog. Something flickered by her head, a bat or an owl, gone in an instant.

"Follow me." Murdstone stepped onto the dock.

"You will fall through the planks," she said. "And the river will take you away."

"This dock is sturdier than it appears. Walk in my footsteps."

She kept to the upriver edge of the pier, testing each step before settling her weight, moss squishing under her shoes. Fog tendrils wove around the pylons.

"My schooner is out there." A breeze plucked at the tail of Murdstone's coat. "Two masts, fore and aft rigged. A hundred fifty tons. It's been anchored since dusk, ostensibly waiting for the tide to turn to push it up the river but in truth it has sent out a crew in a tender, which is waiting for my signal."

"I didn't know you owned a ship, Mr. Murdstone," she said.

"I misspoke." He glanced at her. "I own half the schooner. Your father owns the other half. And with his passing—and may that day be far in the future—you will own his half. Its name is *Emma Grace*. Did he never mention the *Emma Grace?*"

She shook her head. "Father never spoke of it. And I know nothing about schooners, and wouldn't be able to distinguish one from a brig or a frigate or whatever else is out there."

"You will not be called upon to take hoist a jib. We own it, we don't sail it."

Murdstone pulled a fire steel from his coat pocket and opened the lantern. He put the tip of the steel to the charcloth, and squeezed the handles together. Sparks flew, and fire sputtered to life on the charcloth, and then the flame jumped to the wick. He returned the lid to its place. The blinders were closed, and the lantern's light came only through thin cracks in the brass casing.

"Have the tide waiters searched the schooner?" She placed her hand on a pylon to steady herself, and shivered against the damp air.

"Probably. But a double hull is below the sail locker. The hatch to the compartment is invisible, courtesy of Havisham Brothers Brewery's Ernest Blythe."

"The brewery's Ernest?" Miss Havisham asked. "He makes the best barrels in southeast England." And he had taught her to play cat's cradle with twine when she was little.

"Blythe is more than a cooper." Murdstone stared into the fog. "As you will see momentarily."

Distant calls and the rings of bells came from the water as mariners warned each other of their presences in the ether. Miss Havisham turned her head to another sound from the river, a clicking. Iron against iron. Three clicks, then two. Then the pattern came again. When Murdstone opened the lantern red light suffused the fog, seeming to bring the haze closer. He opened and closed the blinders in the same sequence, thrice followed by twice.

A boat drifted out of the haze fifty yards upstream, coils of fog trailing after it. The man on the stern seat tapped the rower's shoulder and pointed at the dock. Murdstone doused the lantern and lowered it to the pier.

A wood box the size of a bushel basket rested on the burden boards in front of the rower. A coiled painter was attached to a metal ring below the breasthook. Miss Havisham didn't recognize the rower who guided the boat to the decayed pier. He wore a pea jacket and a wool cap. River current carried the rowboat to the dock.

The man at the stern knuckled his forehead at Murdstone, then said. "Hello, Missy."

"Ernest?" Miss Havisham exclaimed. "What in the world are you doing out in a boat in the middle of the night?"

Blythe said, "Nothing I hope to ever explain to a judge."

A waxed canvas cape covered his bulk, and he had the dimensions of a barrel. His heroic belly was the result of imbibing in Havisham Brothers Brewery product at work, as was his roseate, veined complexion which glowed even in this darkest of nights. His cap was low over his forehead, almost hiding his eyes, which Miss Havisham knew to be lively, seldom missing anything. Blythe's gloves were fingerless, and he had only four fingers on his left hand, an asymmetry that had fascinated her as a child during cat's cradle. He claimed he had lost the finger to a French musket ball at Waterloo but her father had said he had whacked it off at the brewery simultaneously swinging an axe and sneezing.

Blythe tossed the painter to Murdstone as the rower benched the oars. Murdstone looped the line around a pylon. Blythe and the rower lifted the box from the boat, and slid it onto the pier. *Blackstrap molasses* was stenciled on the top.

"The third refining of sugar syrup produces blackstrap," Murdstone said.

"You and my father import molasses?" she asked. "At night in a fog hiding from the king's customs agents?"

Blythe laughed, a surprising trill for a man of his size. He passed a claw hammer to Murdstone.

"This crate is worth its weight in gold," Murdstone said.

The fog hid the river, and it hid the land along the river, too, and all of its perils. Staring at the mysterious box Miss Havisham did not hear a brush snap and a horse nicker, hard to discern at a distance when masked by the sound of lapping water but still there to be heard for those paying attention, which Miss Havisham and Murdstone were not, Miss Havisham in her curiosity and Murdstone in his apparent greed and delight.

A deputy of the Commissioner of Customs and Excise—termed a riding officer—approached the river accompanied by two dragoons, all three on horses. Usually, they were intent on capturing wool owlers, but any smuggler would do, and this derelict dock was known to receive contraband. They came toward the dock as quietly as their three horses could walk, the riding officer with a pistol in his hand and the dragoons with flintlocks under their arms.

Murdstone hooked the claw under a slat and reefed open the box. A tarpaulin hid the box's contents. He levered away another slat then lifted a corner of the tarp.

Margaret Havisham bent closer. It was nothing she had ever seen before. A waxy, grayish, pinkish lump. It quivered and pulsed like a living thing, but that might've been pure fancy. She shivered.

He said, "It was found on a beach in Maldives, sold to an Arab trader, and then was purchased by our agent in Agadir, the port in the Moroccan sultanate."

She reached toward the lump then thought better of touching it and withdrew her hand.

"Your father and I have brought it here on *Emma Grace* without the taxes and bribes to king's officials that bleed away the profit. And no fractious guilds to deal with, and without having to pay Portsmouth smugglers."

"What is it?'

"A sperm whale vomited it out or otherwise passed it out—nobody really knows how it gets out of the whale—and it floated to shore."

Miss Havisham stepped back. "It's vomit? Or something worse?"

"It's ambergris."

She gathered her nerve to touch it. It was a combination of chalky and clammy, and all repulsive.

"Any perfumer in Paris or Rome will purchase it," Murdstone said.

"They'll buy this ugly lump?"

"For three thousand sovereigns."

She gasped.

Murdstone's voice was compelling. "Just like I said: it's worth its weight in gold."

Miss Havisham's head turned inland. "I hear something."

Murdstone followed her gaze. "You are imagining it."

"I hear it," Blythe said. "Someone is coming. We're going back into the river." He motioned to the oarsman.

From the pier the boat slipped downstream, then the rower turned it into the fog where it disappeared.

"Help me move the box," Miss Havisham whispered. "Hurry. Over there."

She and Murdstone carried the ambergris's crate two dozen steps into the woods—their feet sinking in the soft ground, their coats brushed by branches—and placed it behind a tree. Then they moved away from the river toward the blue roan and wagon. An owl sounded, mournful and distant.

Halt," came from down the road, a rough voice filled with authority. "Stop there."

The riding officer and dragoons put their horses into gallops.

Miss Havisham seized Murdstone's arm, and squeezed against him. She called, "It's my father. Hide." Her voice rising, she cried, "He's found us."

"Halt in the name of the king." The riding officer appeared out of the night, approaching the roan and wagon on his horse.

The dragoons were just behind him, their weapons raised to their chests. The riding officer wore civilian clothes: a blue wool coat and knee-high boots. His ears were large enough to catch the wind, and his lower jaw was undershot. The dragoons were of the 3rd Dragoon Guards on assignment to the Customs and Excise Office, and wore red coats. One of them was as slender as a bed slat, and the other wore a mustache that hid his mouth. Dragoons were mounted infantry.

Miss Havisham clung to Murdstone. She laughed so hard she bent over, releasing him. "My God, you aren't my father. I thought he'd found us."

The riding officer touched the brim of his hat. "Madam, we are looking for smugglers."

Again, she laughed. "My friend here . . . ."

The slender dragoon lowered his firearm. "He looks to be more than your friend."

"My friend Barton here smuggled me out to the river tonight." Her words tumbled out, vast relief in every syllable. "The window at home is still open. I'm so relieved. I thought you were papa. He would have killed Barton right here at the river, had he found us."

The thin dragoon laughed, and he was joined by the other.

"Papa suspects we have plans to marry," she said. "He says Barton is 'unacceptable.' That's his word for him."

Murdstone put his arm around Miss Havisham's shoulders. "I'm saving money. We'll get away from here, and he'll never find us."

The riding officer scowled. "Consider staying away from the river at night, miss. It's dangerous. Smugglers and owlers, armed and desperate."

The riding officer kicked his horse, passing Murdstone's roan and wagon, and the dragoons followed him west on the road.

The thin dragoon called over his shoulder. "Next time try an inn." He cackled in a suggestive manner. "Too many stinging nettles and pine cones on the ground out here."

* * * *

Two men stepped to the chalk lines drawn on the floor. Both their heads had been shaved to the scalp because yanking hair was allowed but otherwise they were as dissimilar as dirt and diamonds. One was as squat as a hogshead, his height and width about the same. His chest was massive, and his arms were muscle laid over muscle. His eyes were small, suspicious, and guarded by thick cheekbones and heavy brows. He wore only tights, and his hands were bare. His name was Abel Magwitch, and he stared without blinking at the man at the other line.

If the Honorable Josiah Talbot—third son of the Earl of Shrewsbury— were concerned about Magwitch he did not reveal it in his expression as he stood behind the chalk. The bridge of his nose had a bump on it, and perhaps it had been broken in the past. His eyes were widely placed though his face was narrow. His cheeks and jaw were covered with stubble—likely a week without having been shaved—to protect the skin from being torn by a fist but even so his was a cultured face, evident in the cast of his eyes and the lift of his chin. He was a foot taller than his opponent, and slender but with thick biceps and a flat, corded stomach, surely an athlete. He would have the reach on his opponent. Talbot, too, wore only tights.

His friends hooted encouragement. Talbot and his group had arrived in a glistening red barouche pulled by four horses with a coachman on the seat and two guards on the footstep behind the cab, fowling pieces in racks near their knees. The hall was on Jacob's Island in Bermondsey, an isle only when the ebbing tide emptied the stinking, trash-strewn ditches that surrounded it. Jacob's Island was a place of hovels and rubbish, pestilence and penury, and rogues and rascals, as wretched a place as a bird ever flew over. The police never visited the island.

The match was being held in an abandoned public house, a tumble-down building with walls leaning at peculiar angles and a sagging ceiling. The only light came through the windows where most of the panes had been smashed out, and glass shards littered the floor. The smell was of creosote and dead fish.

The island's dreariness was of no consequence to the boxing fancy who had gathered there. They held fistfuls of currency and coins, waving them at other sportsmen, placing wagers. Some made bets with bookmakers down from the city who used quill pens to enter wagers on ledgers, grabbing the money and stuffing it into their jackets. Some of the fancy—mostly congregated behind Josiah Talbot—wore top hats, silk breeches, and shoes with silver buckles. Many carried jeweled walking sticks. Their accents placed them as being from Mayfair and Belgravia, and their jollity was loud and fierce, companions out on a lark and engaged in the wealthy Englishman's passion for visiting slums.

"He won't last fifteen minutes, Josh" called a young man who held up a pocket watch. "Ten guineas will say so." He moved in the crowd toward a bookmaker.

Other dapper young men—gold watch chains, silver nosegay pins, calfskin boots—gathered around the tall boxer, who was probably their St. James Street club's ring champion who had made a reputation by batting around his club mates before dinner, a little push and shove, a few lucky roundhouses and some dancing footwork, all before turtle soup and truffles up in the club's dining room. Then after dinner: cards, cigars, and Madeira.

One of the young men—in Hessian boots with tassels—vigorously rubbed Talbot's shoulders. Another, who had a blue handkerchief artfully arrayed from a jacket pocket, held a canvas bucket of water, and lifted a ladle so their champion could sip from it. Yet another leaned close to whisper words of advice, punching the air with his hands. There wasn't a callus among the young sports, and the scents of their colognes and hair oils drifted across the floor to the other chalk line, where Abel Magwitch sniffed the air. A mean grin slid across his face.

"Would you have a moment, sir?" a man asked Abel Magwitch, right at Magwitch's ear.

"Be gone with you." Magwitch's voice was as gruff as his appearance.

"I may place a wager on you, if you can give me some assurance of your bottom."

"As I give you to understand, I'm thinking deep about that fellow over there, wondering how long he will be standing upright, and it don't appear long." Magwitch wiped his mouth with the back of his hand. "Lookee here, take to your heels and leave me be." His hands were bare, without gloves or a wrap.

"Can you last thirty minutes? Be frank with me." Spectacles hung from a ribbon pinned to this inquisitive fellow's coat. He held up a wad of currency. "Much will be at stake."

With what appeared to be considerable effort, Magwitch removed his gaze from Josiah Talbot, and turned to the fellow at his elbow. "What's your name, punter?"

The fellow smiled. "Today it's Harry Beecker. Sometimes it's Compeyson, sometimes Franks, whatever name seems appropriate for the occasion."

Magwitch surveyed him up and down. "You're a toff, like them others. Go over and join your chums."

Beecker laughed. "I'm nothing like them, despite appearances."

Most of the boxing fancy in the room were a rougher sort than Talbot's acolytes. Men had come from Thames colliers for the match, and coal dust covered their clothes and blackened their hands and faces. Tenant farmers wore straw hats their wives had likely woven. Factory boys in ragged clothing rose on tiptoes or tried to squirm between the men for a better look. Sail makers and biscuit bakers were there, as were a Strand tea dealer and a Southwark linen dresser. With his hands stained deep red, an annatto maker had arrived from the Coleman Stairs. A seedsman and a corn chandler placed their wagers. A Somerset cheese monger sold slices of cheddar on brown bread from a tray hung from his neck. A salt merchant was there, his hands—which clutched coins—forever shriveled from handling his merchandise. A blacksmith hadn't bothered to take off his leather apron.

The room was loud and tense, last minute wagers being made, handfuls of money shoved at the bookmakers, men shaking hands after betting with each other, earnest glances at the two boxers as the spectators decided which man to back. Josiah Talbot's club friends whooped and hollered, swigging from pewter pocket flasks, laying down wagers with the bookmakers, patting their hero again and again, a fine old time.

Harry Beecker asked Magwitch, "I should put my money on you, do you think?" Beecker wore a crimson vest and Wellington boots. His curly hair was silver in the thin light. His vast smile poured forth benevolence and good cheer.

Staring again at Josiah Talbot, Magwitch waved a hand toward Beecker as he might to shoo away a fly. "I'll thankee to hold your noise. I'm busy."

Each round would last until one of the boxers collapsed to the floor. He would be given one minute to rise and make scratch. After half an hour the boxer's hand would be swollen to the size of pillows. A typical match might last an hour, maybe two. No stools were provided for rest between rounds. Biting and eye gouging were not allowed but anything else was fair, including kidney and groin punches and blows to the back of the head. When one of the pugilists could no longer rise to his feet the match was over.

Beecker waved the bills in front of the boxer. "I'd be grateful for any whiff of a prediction you might care to offer, the slightest news about your stamina and spirits at the moment."

"I'm going to lay that chap out in ten seconds." Magwitch sucked loudly on a tooth. "And he'll be pissing blood for a month."

"You are confident?"

Magwitch held up his fist, the size of a ham hock. "Him going down today and the sun coming up tomorrow, same odds."

"Have you money on yourself?"

"Every farthing I could beg or steal. When I put that sod down, I'll be in food for a month, and I'm a heavy grubber."

"Then I'll drink to your opponent's confusion." Beecker hurried away toward a bookmaker.

A fellow wearing a cropped riding coat and strapped trousers stepped between the boxers, and held up a hand. "Gentlemen, you are at the marks." He looked at one boxer then the other. "Are you ready?"

Josiah Talbot nodded, and perhaps for the first time closely espied his opponent. He blinked, then wet his lips. If this were hesitation his friends were having none of it: they hurrahed and whooped and slapped his back. Behind his own chalk line Magwitch moved no more than would a portrait.

The man in the riding coat dropped his hand. "Gentlemen, begin."

The St. James Street sports pushed Talbot forward, and he raised his fists. Magwitch moved forward, a low shuffle.

The match took less time than the telling of it. Magwitch closed in. Talbot's fist glanced off Magwitch's temple to the cheers of the fancy, and then Magwitch sunk his fist so far into Talbot's belly that it bounced off his backbone. As Talbot folded like a hinge Magwitch sent a vicious uppercut into his forehead. The sound was of a barrel stave snapping. Talbot dropped to the floor, his eyes rolling back in his head. Blood gushed from his mouth because he had bitten into his tongue.

For five beats the crowd was church quiet, and then came shouts of outrage from wager losers and cries of glee from the winners who rushed the bookmakers, grinning, with hands out.

Talbot's friends approached their blacked-out champion, staring down at him and glancing at each other, perhaps afraid to discover the extent of the damage.

One of them knelt next to the prostrate form. "Josiah, can you hear me?"

"Don't be a fool," another said, grabbing Talbot's wrists to slide him away from the chalk. "He couldn't hear the Bow Bells if he were in the tower with them. He might not come around for a week."

They dragged Talbot toward a door, leaving smears of blood.

One of the young men lamented, "I just lost my month's allowance. What'll I tell father?"

None too gently they pulled the limp Talbot over the threshold and out to the alley where the barouche waited.

Abel Magwitch plucked his shirt from a nail in the wall. Perhaps he was too forbidding and glowering for any of the fancy to approach him for congratulations. Except for Harry Beecker, who appeared at Magwitch's elbow stuffing currency into his own vest pocket.

Beecker asked, "Are you employed, my good man?"

"I just employed that chappie to the floor." Magwitch grunted, and it might've been his version of a laugh.

"I have an opportunity for you, a chance to earn ready money."

Magwitch buttoned his shirt. "There's them that listens, and I'm one of them."

"I must advise, though," Beecker said, "that it might not have the full approbation of the constabulary and adjudicators."

"This is England," Magwitch said. "Speak English."

"It's illegal as hell, and I need a minder, a bodyguard."

Magwitch's bony face was one clearly unaccustomed to smiling but he worked it into a grin. "I'm still listening."

7

The Theater Royal in Drury Lane was treating its patrons—3,000 of them every evening—to *Cataract of the Ganges,* replete with a horseback ride through a waterfall surrounded by fire. A real horse, real water, and real fire, all on the magnificent stage. And the lead actress was Baroness Eva Watersham, whom the posters claimed was the most beautiful woman in England, and who was no more a baroness than a Spitalfields Market flower girl but who was frequently seen in Earl Stratford's carriage, which was close enough.

The Skipjack Building Theater in Cheapside was far removed from the Theater Royal if not in miles certainly in cachet and dignity, and not just because the building was named after a fish for reasons long forgotten. The building had been home to many enterprises over the decades, one succeeding another in a parade of bankruptcies and abandonments, the most recent being a leather tannery which explained the odor that still lingered about the place. The theater contained 350 seats and a curtain that had been mended so many times it was more patch than curtain.

Vincent Crummles had leased the building, installed the seats and stage, and this evening he had posted himself on the footpath in front of the door hoping to deflect pedestrians off their courses and through the theater doors. He was adept at stepping sideways, shifting his hip, extending an arm, and announcing with his chronically hoarse voice, "A profound theatrical experience is at hand," or "A most thrilling exhibition of the theatrical arts, just through these doors," or some such. Crummles was proprietor of Crummles Family Troupe, which had been leasing smaller and smaller venues, and if this production failed would have to change its name to Crummles Family Traveling Troupe, and stage its productions in barns out in the country.

This was indeed a nagging prospect but Crummles was of a fine feather standing on the Cheapside walkway, the proximity to a stage always having that effect. A poster tacked to the theater's wall announced that evening's production, *How She Has Fallen* by *The Estimable Playwright Bronson Sloane, great grandnephew of*—then in enormous letters—*The Bard William Shakespeare.* The name of the play's author and the relationship to Shakespeare had as much basis in reality as did the Hammersmith hobgoblin.

Crummles dipped his chin to a man in a top hat too small for his head and thin woman walking arm in arm, and said, "May I introduce you to a theater production for the ages?" He gestured widely to the door. "*How She Has Fallen* is destined for Drury Lane within the month."

"Thank you, no," the man in the top hat said. "We're leaving town yet this very night, sir. To Plymouth, where something will turn up."

The couple dodged him without breaking steps. Crummles' cheeks were shiny red apples that required a tuppence of foundation whenever he played a serious role. With Falstaff, he didn't need makeup. His face was over-featured, with large eyes—rolling his big eyes in mock exasperation always drew a laugh from an audience—and a nose that flared so that it was almost as wide as his mouth. He wore breeches with black ribbons, a cream-colored waistcoat, and a green coat with wide lapels. In his coat pocket was a cramp-bone, the polished kneecap of a sheep which warded off leg cramps.

Many of the shops on Cheapside had closed for the day but the street was still crowded with carts, drays, and wagons transporting goods, and gigs, landaus, and hacks carrying passengers. Horses drank from watermen's troughs. A knife grinder pushed his cart along the street, a vendor of cough tablets right behind him.

A child emerged from the theater doors. She was four or five years of age but dressed in an infant's smock and was bare of foot. She rushed to Crummles' leg to seize it, laughing.

Vincent Crummles said, "Where is your mother, the redoubtable Mother Crummles, object of my adoration? She should be here to peel you off my leg, should she not?"

The girl laughed again and tried to grip Crummles' wrists but he pulled her hands away, grinning.

"Be off with you, poppet" he said in the court's plumbstone accent. "The shepherd's costume for you this evening, if you please."

The child's name was Dorothy—Dotty to all—and she was billed as the Infant Phenomenon, who could pass as a two-year-old in the right clothing, and who knew how to shrink herself and walk with roll and sway like a toddler, and coo and burble as would a tot, already a fine actress. Crummles had taken Andrew Foyles—owner of the Foyles Tent Spectacular—to law when Foyles publicly accused Crummles of feeding Dotty only ginger water to stunt her growth so that she could continue as the Infant Phenomenon. It was an outrageous slander—as far from the truth as a Frenchman is to bath day—and the court had awarded Crummles twenty guineas, an exquisite victory over a scabrous charlatan.

Vincent Crummles pushed his daughter back through the doors. "Go tell your mother to give you a chicken leg or some oatmeal. Anything to keep you from trouble."

Across Cheapside from the theater three wall workers rested on a bench in front of a public house. These elderly gentlemen hung wood advertising boards on fences in the morning and took them down at night. Holding pewter mugs, all three had clay pipes hanging from their lips. Smoke blurred their faces. A water cart rolled by the theater, followed by a rag and bone wagon, the horse's iron shoe sparking against the cobblestones and drains. A boardman passed Crummles on the walkway, advertising Dr. Benjamin's Female Pills on his front and Dr. Farnham's Nerve Syrup on the back. The scent of formaldehyde drifted along the street, courtesy of the undertaker's establishment two doors from the theater. A hearse—a gleaming black four-in-hand with black trappings, two elegant brass lanterns mounted near the driver's seat, and black Egyptian velvet covering the windows—was parked at the curb.

Vincent Crummles' watch chain was adorned with letter seals that pleasantly clinked together as he lifted the watch from his pocket. Fifteen minutes to raising the curtain, and the house was only a third full.

He redoubled his efforts inveigling potential patrons. "The finest show for miles around," and "A world-renown extravaganza, just through these doors."

Pedestrians flowed around him as if he were a boulder in a stream.

Until one stopped. "You are the owner of this theater company?" came from Vincent's left.

"Indeed." He turned to the fellow. "Owner, stage manager, director, prop supervisor, and often the principal actor, at your service."

The man said, "I knew at once you were an actor, sir, from the cut of your hair."

Crummles ran his hand along his pate. His dark hair was short with scalp visible beneath, the better to allow the fitting of wigs.

"Allow me to introduce myself. I am Ambrose Franks."

Vincent Crummles was amiable to his bones. Smiling, he gripped Ambrose's hand. "May I interest you in a ticket to our new show, *How She Has Fallen*? Too scandalous for Drury Lane. Three shillings, and cheap at the price. Step to the ticket table, just inside the door."

Franks said, "Perhaps in a moment. I'm waiting for a friend, and maybe I can convince her to watch your show with me."

Crummles took snuff from a screw of paper and inserted it behind a cheek. "Do you happen to be a writer, Mr. Ambrose? The troupe's playwright walked out this morning." It was a random snippet of conversations designed to keep Franks on the footway beside him. Few things were as pathetic as a stage manager standing alone outside a theater desperately trying to induce passersby into his establishment, and Crummles felt it keenly. This fellow—even this stranger—was a reinforcement.

"I am a fair hand with the language, sir," Ambrose's waistcoat was appliqued with silver lace. "Though steady employment is a peevish prospect."

"I tell the troupe's playwright to draft a play that fits with whatever scenery we find when we arrive at the theater. If there are painted hay bales behind the curtain, the fellow writes a rustic romance. If a painted village is the backdrop we find, he writes a tragedy set in town."

"Your writers must be versatile," Ambrose said.

"Writing is like juggling; it is a small skill, though one that eludes me. My writers must be quick. No one should take longer than three hours to compose a play." Crummles smiled at two young men about to enter the theater. "Excuse me, gentlemen. May I have a word with you?"

The two prospective theatergoers were sixteen or seventeen years old, and dressed in long coats, one brown and one gray, both of wool. They turned to Crummles, and glanced at each other. One of them bit his lip and then the other stared at the ground.

Crummles stepped to them. "Your wardrobes are too lumpish, are they not?" He gripped one of the boy's shoulders, then slipped his hand to the fellow's short ribs, and squeezed. The boy flinched. Then Crummles grabbed the fabric covering the pocket, and crushed it. The coat's wool acted as a wick, pulling fluid to the surface. The coat turned black in spots.

"This is a theater, gentlemen, not a greengrocer. Be off with you lest I call upon a sheriff."

The two lads hurried away, and disappeared in the drift of pedestrians.

"Spoiled tomatoes and rotten squash, most likely tossed aside at Covent Garden," Crummles said. "Louts buy tickets not to see a fine play but rather for the amusement of hurling produce at the actors. My production of *Not for Naught* in Bristol last year was halted by these projectiles, and the riot in the theater lasted two hours bringing ruination to the place, and my troupe had to flee the city before the landlord discovered the damage, and . . . ."

Crummles brought himself up. This was too much confidence to place in a stranger, this fellow Ambrose Franks, with his expensive set of clothes and winning smile. "I beg your pardon. I bore you with details about the theater."

"Not at all," Ambrose said. "I value any insight into the human condition. Often a profit can be made from the knowledge."

A bootblack tried to set up his box in front of the tailor's shop next to the theater but the tailor had not as yet closed for the day, and he rushed out to chase away the boy with a broom, apparently not wanting passersby to be distracted from the frock coats in the window. A donkey-drawn wagon rolled by the theater, its load of case bottles clattering together.

Vincent Crummles looked anew at Ambrose. Crummles adjudged himself an authority on actors, most of whom were shiftless and needy, flaws in their characters that required a stage manager's constant attention in the form of flattery and cajolery. The aspect Crummles searched for in his actors—and when he discovered it Crummles could forgive much else—was magnetism, that property that gripped the audience's attention. He had discovered three such actors during his career, youngsters bound for greater glory than the Crummles troupe could provide, and they had lasted two or three months with the troupe until they were discovered—*stolen* was more accurate—by scouts for the Adelphi or the Royal Coburg. These new actors had that effervescence that turned eyes toward them whether entering stage left or walking into a room or strolling in a park. It was a mysterious quality beyond mere beauty.

Crummles had seen Sarah Siddons as Lady Macbeth at Covent Garden, and had no memory of the production other than her exquisite face, willowy form, languorous movements, and how she drew the light to her, casting all else on the stage into dusk. A thousand people were in the audience, and she appeared to be looking at each one of them in the eyes. The young Vincent Crummles could not remove his gaze from her for the entire ninety-minute production, and he wasn't the only one. Patrons—both men and women—left the Royal wearing dazed expressions and shaking their heads in disbelief at the power Sarah Siddons had had over them. They had been in the presence of an actress touched by otherworldly powers, something beyond the ken of mortals.

Crummles narrowed his eyes at this fellow next to him and, yes, Ambrose Franks had that same aspect as had Sarah Siddons, a singularly rare handsomeness combined with the compliment of paying one close attention. Franks did not wear a wig, and his hair was in tight ringlets that appeared haphazard but may have been carefully coiffed to lend him an air of insouciance. The hair was not so much blond as it was golden and drew passersby's glances on the gray street.

Franks's mouth was wide and peaked, and along with his brilliantly white teeth allowed his smile to be both puckish and sympathetic, accented by dimples. His eyes were crystalline blue. His ears were hidden by the gold hair. Under lofty cheekbones, his chin tapered elegantly to a mischievous cleft, and his nose was slender and straight. Nothing was lopsided on Franks's face. The symmetry was perfect. He was as tall as Crummles—six feet even— but weighed three stone less. His clothes—a dark blue dreadnought coat and blue silk cravat, trousers rather than ribboned breeches, and laced patent leather shoes—were the latest in fashion, perhaps straight from Paris. He carried a folded black umbrella with a stag horn handle.

The sum of all these parts was an enchantment even there on the street. Men and women stared at him as they passed the theater, and young ladies brazenly glanced back over their shoulders at him as they continued on, a few grinning wickedly.

"Are you an actor, Mr. Franks?" Crummles asked.

"Not on the stage." He grinned slyly.

"No other profession offers a young man such as yourself exemplary advantages as does the stage."

"I have never studied acting." He laughed. "I don't know a stage curtain from a stage door."

"The entirety of acting as a profession can be learned in an hour, with enough time remaining for a cup of tea." Crummles pulled at his waistcoat to straighten it. "I detect genteel comedy in your manner and in your voice, tragedy in your eye, and farce in your laugh. Your name could be on the lips of theater enthusiasts from Land's End to Margate within half a year."

Franks dipped his head, as if accepting the high regard as his due. "I am meeting someone here, sir. Her name is Anna Wilkinson. Do you know of the family?"

"The Wilkinsons are the carriage makers over in Lambeth. The streets are filled with Wilkinson carriages. Why do you ask?"

Wings piping, pigeons flew close overhead. A gut wagon rolled past the theater, followed by two dogs, one missing an ear. The sun was lowering, and the light striking aslant cast the smoke in the air in bronze.

"Anna Wilkinson is attending your theater this evening," Franks said.

Crummles' eyebrows rose on his head. "One of the Wilkinson family? Here this evening?" He brushed flakes from his sleeves. Londoners called soot falling from the air *blacks*. "How do you know?"

"People tell me things."

Curtain time neared, and a few more folks entered the theater. Others stared at the troupe's bills pasted to the boards, likely trying to determine if *How She Has Fallen* was worth three shillings. It was Friday evening, and Crummles hoped for a good house.

He tipped his hat to Ambrose Franks, and returned to coaxing pedestrians toward the theater door, smiling, gesturing, pointing at the posters, and saying, "The finest production in the city," and "Acclaimed throughout the land." Of his many duties, touting out on the street was the most burdensome because it was pitiable.

"You there," came a call. "Pull aside."

It was the driver of a barouche, high on the box, who held the reins in one hand and a whip in the other, and he attempted to wave away a gig in front of the theater. The spokes of the barouche's wheels were painted gold, and the rims were green, the Wilkinson Carriage Works colors. The black hood had been folded down, and four horses pulled the vehicle, two more than were necessary other than as a matter of presentation.

Three young people and one elderly scowling woman rode in the barouche on seats that faced each other. The two males—in their early twenties—wore top hats and white gloves, and the young woman of about the same age were dressed in evening finery consisting of yards of wildly colorful cloth that filled the barouche's cab as roiling clouds fill the sky. Much laughter and wisecracks and squeals came from the barouche as it pulled to the curb after the gig pulled away. Green leather trappings squeaked as the matching bay roans stopped in front of Vincent Crummles and his theater.

The older woman's clothing was plain, including a prim green bonnet and black gloves. She wore her decades on her face, with harsh features, and so wrinkled it resembled a cracked window. She was likely a chaperone, maybe a governess. A mere glance at her revealed she was a woman with a formidable stolidity of mind, and that whatever benevolent aspect she might possess was left at home on these outing.

Ambrose Franks smiled again. "This is Anna, I believe. The one with the dark hair pulled back in a chignon. I don't suppose you would make the introduction."

"An introduction presumes an acquaintance," Crummles said. "I don't know her and I don't know you." He may have been wondering why a Wilkinson would come to his theater rather than to the elegant establishments over in the West End. As proud as he was of his troupe, it was not a premier English theater company. Nowhere near it, in truth. Maybe these young people were in search of adventure, of funny and snooty stories to tell friends at their next amusement.

"I will introduce myself to her," Franks said. "I'm good at this."

With badinage flying back and forth and laughter the order of the day, the party stepped down from the barouche, the lady careful to keep her dress hem from the curbside muck. Vincent Crummles smiled at them and gestured toward the theater door.

One of the men—wearing white gloves and with a red feather in his hat band—called out, "*How She Has Fallen?* Whose idea was this?"

This was met with much laughter.

He added, "I could be at White's enjoying a sherry."

The young lady said, "As if White's would let you through the door."

More laughs.

Following her charges, the chaperone climbed down from the barouche and gazed at the *How She Has Fallen* poster, her mouth pulled back as if she had just tasted a tamarind. She made a production of shaking her head. Her jaw was the size of a mule's hoof.

"Welcome, one and all," called Crummles. "You are about to experience the show that has all of London talking, and you will leave the theater flaccid in your admiration of the acting skills about to be displayed just through these doors."

They ignored him, still bantering and laughing, moving toward the theater door. The young lady opened her reticule and retrieved a tint strip that she wiped across her lips, reddening them. Her brown eyes were set at an angle that gave her face a persistently merry expression. Her yellow velvet frock—the very latest—was cinched at the waist, accenting her figure, unlike the high-waisted dresses still worn by parents. Her yellow jacket matched the dress.

Clutching his umbrella Ambrose Franks drifted away from Crummles as if to stand in line. As he reached Anna Wilkinson, who was searching for something else in her purse, his umbrella opened, apparently unaccountably, and one of its ribs caught on Miss Wilkinson's arm.

Ambrose tugged at umbrella, jerking her arm, and then turned to her, his eyes widening. "Miss, are you hooked there? Forgive me. This old umbrella, I should have left it behind."

"Release me, if you will," Anna Wilkinson said, grabbing for the umbrella's canopy. "This instant."

"You oaf," cried one of the young men escorting her.

Frowning mightily, Anna Wilkinson tugged at the umbrella but then her eyes found the face of the malefactor, and all efforts to free herself ceased. As still as a hitching post, she stared at him

"I should watch where I'm going," Franks said. "My evening at the theater has turned into an assault on a young lady with my umbrella. It was unintentional, I assure you." He increased the measure of his smile. He folded the umbrella, taking more time than necessary.

Crummles shook his head. This had been a fine performance.

Anna Wilkinson unabashedly stared at him, her face assuming the expression of one hit by a carp.

"Anna," the chaperone said in an iron voice, one in strict conformity with her countenance. "Mind your manners."

"It is all my fault, madam." Franks addressed the chaperone. "I will be on my way into the theater."

Anna's voice was the ghost of a whisper. "Are you alone, sir?"

"Regrettably, I am. I was going to bring my mother to the show this evening but she is out of sorts. She blames yesterday's mutton."

"Will you join my friends and me?" she asked.

"Anna." A bark from the chaperone.

One of the Anna's escorts—a young man wearing a howling red cravat and matching waistcoat—squared himself to Franks, perhaps about to issue a challenge.

Franks replied, "I couldn't possibly. It would be untoward, with you and your friends here."

"I insist, sir," Anna Wilkinson still had not removed her gaze from his face.

Franks stepped nearer to her. "You are someone of sublime compassion, miss. If you insist."

The chaperone huffing and the two young men looking at each other in apparent disbelief, they all passed through the theater doors.

Vincent Crummles had watched Ambrose's production. A young fellow had arranged an encounter with a girl for whom he had a fancy, a timeless bit of guile, usually harmless even as it shocked the chaperone. Crummles had seen it before a dozen times.

But perhaps not in this permutation. Much ignorance had been on the street that evening, and not just the carriage horses' unfamiliarity with long division. Ambrose Franks's name entered at the parish registry a few days after his birth had been Harold Beecker. At Satis House courting Miss Havisham Franks had been known as Samuel Compeyson. He went by a score of names. His moniker depended on the nature of his endeavor. He changed his name as easily as he changed his linen, and it seldom boded well for those who heard that day's alias. Because of its nature, ignorance cannot be precisely tallied but suffice it to say there was much outside the Skipjack Building Theater that evening.

Crummles watched Ambrose Franks and the others disappear into the theater, then he turned back to his task. "A production for the ages, ladies and gentlemen and bound for Drury Lane in one week, just through these theater doors."

8

"I would loan you my nosegay." Murdstone flicked the reins with one hand and held a linen handkerchief over his mouth and nose with the other. "But a flower is defenseless here."

Miss Havisham breathed through her mouth, which her governess had warned her against daily since a time before memory served.

The putrid odor invaded from every angle and through every aperture, a corrosive presence. The air was so laden with toxic smells that it appeared to hang in front of Miss Havisham.

She leaned to the side to view the roadway. "Will we be walking?"

Offal and ordure, rotted hay and decayed grain, bits of leather and fur and wool, pig ears and oxen tails, sinew and foam; the lane was covered with a brown pudding of reeking foulness.

Murdstone said, "If you decamp this wagon, your footwear will avail you nothing because the muck is deeper than your shoes are high."

Attached to Miss Havisham's shoes were pattens, wood stilts that kept her shoes two inches above rainwater and dung in normal streets but the excrescence on this street was likely up to her calves. The wagon squished along.

"You are not afraid of the customs police?" Miss Havisham asked. "The sentence for smuggling is death, is it not?"

"Seldom enforced in that extreme but if those fool officers catch us cheating the exchequer we may be sent to Millbank or a hulk out in the river."

Murdstone wore a felted beaver hat and kid gloves. His oddly flat eyes restlessly moved left and right. He snapped the reins against one of the horse's flanks, turning the two horses. "They usually don't search wagons headed into the market, only those travelling away from it, mostly looking for wool being smuggled to France without giving the crown its share."

FAGIN & MISS HAVISHAM

As the wagon rolled over broken hay bands farther into the Smithfield Market the cacophony grew. Sheep mewled, cattle bawled, pigs squealed, dogs barked, bull bells rang. Shepherds cursed, drovers whistled, traders quarreled, hawkers called. The market was half a mile north of St. Paul's. Its six acres were bordered on the north by St. John Street and on the south by Giltspur Street. The market had been there 600 years, and the French had called the English *roast beefs* for 600 years.

Murdstone said above the din, "And gangs of highwaymen lurk just outside the city. They have taken to wearing gray smocks and calling themselves the Grays. They would steal the nails from a coffin. But they won't search this cart when we get done with it."

They passed a gut-scrapery, a shack where two men, blades in hands, bent over a cow's carcass.

When the wagon rolled over a nameless lump hidden in the street's detritus the crate rattled on the bed. Murdstone's hand went to his coat pocket where doubtless there was a pistol. He glanced back the crate. "This place is a notorious cesspool of thieves."

Swinging his goad a drover moved steers across the lane, and the wagon waited until they had passed, then it moved forward again, passing through a cloud of steam drifting from a bone-boiling house. To the regret of most Londoners, the Great Fire had spared the market, and it was lined with dirty residences, slaughterhouses, and shops. Narrow, perilous alleys branched off from the place.

"Where is the baby?" Murdstone asked. "I presume your household staff is looking after her."

"I am looking after her," Miss Havisham shouted, partly to be heard above the market's clangor and partly at the effrontery of the question. "I spend much of each day with Estella. Right now, she is with a nurse. Do not worry about her."

"I do not worry about children as a matter of principle and sound judgment," he said. "They have the capacity to look after themselves."

The market was a writhing mass of cattle, hogs, and sheep. Some of the livestock were in pens and some tied to rails. Most of the stock had come from the north counties, and had entered the market along St. John Road. Drovers with sticks propelled the animals along, and the sound of the animals being smacked was so constant it was a drone. The sheep were almost always silent as they were herded toward their doom while the pigs squealed, their heads frantically darting left and right as they sought escapes but there were none to be had. Manure mountains were as high as men's heads. Smithfield Market was a vast expanse of unrelieved wretchedness.

"Only cash works here," Murdstone said. "Letters of credit and bank drafts will not do. I always carry a heavy purse. But not because I'm dealing in livestock."

When he jiggled his coat Miss Havisham heard the clinks of coins just above the bawl of the cattle.

She said, "It sounds as if you have a fortune in your pocket."

"Most men can be bribed for a sum equal to one quarter of their annual wages," Murdstone said. "I always carry thirteen gold sovereigns, and I advise you to do the same."

"Why not carry folding money?" she asked.

"It is a perplexing but universal truth that anyone low enough to take a bribe is deeply suspicious of Bank of England notes." He flicked the reins. "But do not be concerned about the details of the business, Miss Havisham. I will take care of them. Do not trouble yourself."

She looked at him, her face hardening. Fifty butcher shops lined the market's perimeter, where tightly packed carcasses hung from ceiling hooks. Counting houses were above the shops.

Murdstone pulled the reins, and the wagon stopped in front of a triperie. A dirt-colored dog with pronounced ribs watched from the shack's corner. Gripping a pry bar, a man emerged through the triperie's gate.

Miss Havisham called, "Ernest, is that you again?"

"None other." Blythe smiled up at her. Sweat stained his shirt and mire dappled his boots. "I never thought I'd see the daughter of Hugh Havisham at the Smithfield Market, missy."

Blythe climbed up onto the wagon bed and jammed the pry bar into the crate. He was as skillful with the prybar as he was with a stave hammer. Within seconds the crate had been torn apart, exposing the ambergris. Miss Havisham cringed at the renewed sight of it, a raw pink wad both slimy and chalky that resembled a giant beating heart.

Blythe tossed the crate slats onto the cobblestones, leaped down from the cart, disappeared into the triperie, and returned pulling a cart and carrying a shovel. He plucked something from the cart and tossed it toward to the dog, who caught it before it hit the ground, and took off between two buildings.

"That same cur always appears when you do." Blythe laughed. "Maybe he recognizes you, Mr. Murdstone."

"Get on with it, Blythe. We are exposed."

Miss Havisham leaned over the edge of the wagon for a better look. She shuddered. Blythe's cart contained dregs from the tripe shop; beef hearts, sheep guts, hog snouts and tails, goat ears, hooves and knuckles, animal parts so distinct that they could not be disguised by grinding them into sausage.

Ernest Blythe shoveled with purpose, unloading the cart of the offal and loading Murdstone's wagon with the same, throwing the animal parts onto the ambergris. He worked until the ambergris was covered in animal pieces. Carrying a pole a man ushered steers by the wagon, heading for a pen.

Murdstone said, "No customs agent or thieving vagabond—and I speak as if there were a difference between the two—will ever search through a rotting pile of animal organs. But this is more than you need to know." He shrugged. "These details of business are tedious."

She shifted on the seat.

He nodded at Blythe then flipped the reins. The wagon rattled forward.

"Constables have sometimes stabbed the pile with pitchforks," he said, "searching for contraband and fugitives. Pitchfork punctures do not harm the ambergris. And even if one of the constables held his breath and swatted aside the offal, all they would find would be a reddish lump which looks precisely like the rest of it. The plan is perfect."

The wagon rolled toward St. John Street, passing a slaughter pen where a fellow shot a pole between the horns of a steer, which collapsed to the ground as if through a trapdoor.

A note of satisfaction in his voice, Murdstone said, "You wanted to see our entire operation, including this dreadful place, and now you have."

"Indeed," she said.

"How is your stomach? After I first came here, I could not eat meat for a month."

She grinned artfully. "I'm not as delicate as you are, Mr. Murdstone."

* * * *

Fagin dipped his head so the brim of his slouch hat hid his face. He carried a slice of currant pudding, chewing with exaggeration to look occupied. Perhaps he might not be recognized. He approached the street peddler whose cart was piled with medicines, some helpful, some benign, and some dangerous.

An umbrella mounted on a pole above the cart kept the drizzle from the bottles and tins. The vendor wore a double-breasted green jacket. His ears stuck out like handles on a tankard. Braces kept up his trousers. He enticingly waved a bottle at passersby, smiling widely at them. His teeth were so green they might've been covered with moss. A poster tacked to the cart advertised Dr. Gurdy's Gout Lozenges featuring a drawing of a red, grotesque human toe. Hanging from the umbrella's ribs was a sign promoting Roman Burn Salve that included a depiction of the Venus de Milo.

Fagin cast his gaze at a barber's window then at a donkey pulling a cabbage wagon, and the pickpocket appeared fascinated by the street bustle. He neared the vendor, still hiding his face under his hat. The pickpocket flexed his fingers, and stepped toward the vendor's cart without looking at it, just strolling along, the perfect portrait of innocence.

It didn't work.

The vendor lifted a dagger from behind a stack of tins and held it up. "You are known around here, mutcher." He lifted the weapon higher. "You get your thieving fingers close to my merchandise, I'll cut them off."

Fagin grunted at the insult, an affront to his profession of lightening persons and households of their possessions. A mutcher was a thief who stole from drunks, a carbuncle on the posterior of humanity. Fagin didn't stop to confront the peddler because he was disinclined to argue with a dagger.

Carrying the pudding, he cut across the roadway. He dodged a mason's wagon that carried bricks and a hod. Avoiding street slime he stepped on the apex of each cobblestone as he moved around a mule hitched to a glazer's wagon. He approached a candle shop which was next to a linen drapery. He bit off a piece of pudding. Two soldiers in red coats strolled by, stopped to peer into a shoe shop, then moved on. On the pavement at the corner children played tip-cat.

Fagin needed medicated salve, and as he chewed, he pondered how to get it. A whelk seller rolled his cart along the walkway, the smell of low tide drifting along behind him. On the street in front of the candle shop a locksmith had set up shop, his tools on a folding bench. Only when Fagin leaned against a lamp post did he notice the child huddled in the doorway of a boarded-up shop. The boy was eight or nine and dressed in tatters and wearing only one shoe. He sat on the bricks, his knees under his chin and his arms wrapped around his legs. Dirt smudged his face, and his cheeks were sunken. His wool cap was so filthy its original color was impossible to determine. The boy wiped his nose with his sleeve.

The pickpocket's eyes went between the pudding and the boy. "You hungry, boy?"

The child might not have heard the words. His gaze seemed on the middle distance, perhaps seeing nothing.

Fagin nudged the boy's shoulder. "You are welcomed to this pudding, young man. I've had my fill."

The boy turned his head toward Fagin but slowly, as if unused to being addressed. Fagin opened the boy's hand and placed the pudding into it.

"Those black things are called currants. It's a desert." Fagin rubbed his own belly. "It's tasty."

The boy tore off a piece and shoved it into his mouth. He appeared to swallow it without chewing, and he instantly ripped off another chunk and jammed it into his mouth

"And good luck to you, boy. You look like you could use some." Fagin turned away to peer at the medicine vendor and his cart. He scratched his chin.

"My name is Luke," the boy said around the mashed pudding in his mouth.

73

"You go on home, boy." Fagin continued to survey the medicine vendor's cart. "Night is coming. Your mum will be worried about you."

"She's dead."

"Your father, then. He'll be waiting for you. Better get on home."

Luke pushed the last of the pudding into his mouth and pushed himself up to standing. "What're you looking at?"

"I need some medicine from that cart. I'm figuring out how to get it."

The boy rose on his toes. "Just go over there and give him some money."

"I never pay for anything, boy." Fagin pulled his scarf more tightly around his neck. "There's a lesson you can profit from."

"Then how did you get the pudding I just ate?"

"Piemen and bakers don't have eyes in the backs of their heads. Nobody does. I figured that out long ago."

"What about that man over at the medicine cart?" Luke pointed. "Does he have eyes in the back of his head?"

"He has a dagger."

Luke said, "Daggers don't scare me."

"Then you've never been sliced by one." Fagin pushed up the sleeve of his coat and sweater. "See this red scar from my elbow almost to my wrist? A hatter on Holborn Hill took offense to my method of exchange, that being, I tried to take the topper from the counter without recompense. I sewed this up myself using fishing line." The puckered line of red skin was crosshatched with thinner scars.

"Did it hurt?"

"Where's your other shoe?"

"Somebody took it when I was asleep. I don't know why he didn't take both."

Fagin said, "Young man, I try to profit from everything I do, and I see no profit in conversing with a boy on the street. You go on home to your dad."

"He went away," Luke said. The hair sticking out from his cap was matted, and pink eye colored his left eye. "I'll get the medicine for you. Which one do you want?"

"Where did your father go?"

The boy shrugged. "Last time I saw him he hit me with a fire iron."

The pickpocket inhaled through his teeth. "You and he didn't get along?"

"Not when he was hitting me with a fire iron. An Irish family has moved into our room. Seven of them. The lady said there was no room for me but she gave me a biscuit."

"How do you propose to get the medicine, eh?" Fagin asked.

"Same way I got an apple yesterday." The boy's eyes were locked on the medicine cart. "Which medicine do you want?"

74

Fagin wiped his mouth with his hand. "The white can with the red markings on it, about as big as my hand. There's a stack of them just at the edge of the cart. See them?"

"How many do you want?" the boy asked.

Fagin's eyes shifted between the boy and the cart. "Two. I'll meet you down there." He gestured. "In front of the mercer's shop, the one with the carved dog hanging above the door."

The boy crossed the street toward the medicine cart, his hands behind his back, his mouth puckered as if whistling, likely his version of profound innocence. A hackney coach veered around him, the driver cursing. In his one shoe the boy walked up the street fifty yards, then turned back, paralleling the footway and passing a type foundry and an engraver's shop. The boy's chest puffed out like a partridge, more innocence on display. The medicine vendor pitched his product to a woman with an ostrich feather in her hat.

Ten feet from the cart the boy broke into a sprint, and as he passed the stacks of medicinal boxes and bottles he grabbed two salve tins. He was there and gone before the vendor's eyes had left the customer. Then the peddler yelled an oath, and chased after the boy.

The vendor took only five steps before he rushed backed to his cart, undoubtedly knowing that thieves would snatch away his inventory were he gone from the cart more than a heartbeat. He glared down the street but the boy had already disappeared among the pedestrians.

Fagin hurried after Luke on the opposite side of the street, then crossed the roadway toward the mercer's shop. He skirted two women looking into a dressmaker's window and a fellow carrying an empty canary cage. Stepping around a perambulator pushed by a young lady he met the boy on the corner.

"Here they are." Luke held out his hand. "Two, just like you said."

"If I could run as fast as you, I wouldn't have to rely so heavily on my wits." Fagin pocketed the tins. "Thankye, young sir. You are the greatest of all time. A clever dog and a fine fellow." He touched his hat brim. "I am in your debt. And good day to you."

The pickpocket pivoted on his heels and walked east along the street, nodding at a screwsman he had employed several times, who was leaning against the brick front of a tobacconist's store. The screwsman's skeleton keys were likely hidden in a jacket pocket, each wrapped in cloth so they wouldn't clink together. Fagin turned down Woodworkers Street, then dashed into an alley that opened on a court so filled with coal smoke that the wretched hovels that lined the square were blurred. He moved speedily.

Fagin had different routes to his rooms, and on each route were locations where he always turned around to view who might be following him. The police bedeviled him whenever they caught him. Sometimes they smacked him with batons, sometimes they threw him onto a garbage pile, whatever fit their moods. As far he could determine, they didn't know where he resided, and he worked hard to keep it that way. He turned left through a decrepit gate, then along another foul alley. He stopped at a pile of discarded bricks to look to the rear.

The boy had followed Fagin, and stood twenty feet behind him. Luke held up his palms, a gesture inviting understanding and sympathy.

Fagin said, "Lifting two salve tins for me doesn't get you a new pa, boy."

Luke smiled.

The pickpocket took off again, and so did the boy, right on his heels.

9

Fagin bent low at his door, squinting at the keyhole, trying to locate it in the dimness of the hallway. He changed residences every few months, hardly long enough to learn a place. He stabbed the key at the door several times before it found the lock. He turned the key, pushed open the door, and entered his chambers. The boy followed him in.

Though it was daytime oil lamps on the walls illuminated the parlor, as Fagin called the room which had once stored barrels of tar. Narrow, grimy windows looked out on an alley. Shelves lined one wall, and silk handkerchiefs of many colors hung from a line that crossed the back of the room. A washstand and towels on a rack were in a corner near a coal cooking stove on which was an iron pot. Due to a turpentine distillery in the building's ground floor, the room had the smell of a pine forest but not in a nice way.

Bill Sikes lay on a straw pallet wearing only his small clothes. Pink burn blisters and leaking charred skin covered much of his legs and feet. His eyes were closed, and he held an empty gin bottle. His lips were pulled back exposing disreputable teeth.

"I have returned, Bill." Fagin held up the tins. "Help is at hand."

Grimacing, Sikes raised his head. "Strike me blind, who's the brat?"

Luke walked to the bookshelves and lifted a porcelain inkwell. He held it up to the light, then returned it to the row of inkwells, which included a silver traveling inkwell, a bronze Nautilus inkwell, a marble Grand Tour inkwell, a red griotte marble inkwell, and a dozen others.

"Sir, do you write a lot of letters?" the boy asked. "You sure have a lot of inkwells."

"I never put anything in writing, boy. I've never written a letter. There's another lesson for you." Fagin opened one of the salve tins. "This may sting, Bill."

77

"I hate jackanapes, always under foot." Sikes threw the gin bottle at Luke but his aim was wide, and it shattered against a wall.

The boy glanced at the bottle's glass shards. "You're like my father."

"Now, now, Bill," Fagin said. "Let's be charitable. I'm here to provide relief, and soon your burns will be under the genial influence of this balm." He wagged a tin in front of Sikes's eyes, then dug his fingers into the paste.

When he dabbed the salve onto an ankle burn, Sikes yelped, then said, "Careful, Fagin. Don't do me more damage than the chimney fire did."

"Ay, I'll be as tender as a rose petal."

Sikes flinched and whimpered as Fagin applied more salve to his burned legs.

"What's this, mister?" Luke held up another shiny item.

Fagin looked over his shoulder. "A silver needle case made in France, made to resemble a marshal's baton."

"And this?"

"A nutmeg grater made of silver, one of my prized possessions."

"You have a lot of stuff." The boy stepped along the shelf, peering at the items and handling some of them, turning them over and rubbing his thumb along them.

The shelves contained French perfume bottles, inlaid silver trinket boxes, glittering snuff boxes, silver pin cushions in the shapes of dogs, swans, and pigs, brass tobacco boxes, silver table bells and silver wine funnels, pewter salt boxes, silver toothpick cases, a dozen scrimshawed whale teeth and walrus tusks, and sixteen matching silver spoons with engraved Zs on their handles. These items were arrayed in precise rows on the shelves in a manner allowing a frequent and loving inventory.

Fagin beamed at the lad. "You will observe, young Luke, that my collections consist entirely of items that can be hidden under a coat."

When the pickpocket layered more salve, Sikes squirmed. "Easy, Fagin. That hurts."

Fagin said, "Luke, I dispense these lessons to you in the spirit of amity, and I tend to Bill's injuries with a physician's dedication and skill. You both receive the benevolence of a benign, indeed, a charitable and humane nature."

"You talk too much," Sikes said.

"These are pretty." Luke held up a pocket watch.

Fagin said, "That's a George Graham cylindrical escapement watch, and I narrowly escaped with it, a dog the size of a steer chasing me, and then its fangs caught in my coat, and I only lost the dog when I crawled under a moving wagon, and the wheel rolled over the monster's tail. That watch brings back fond memories so be careful with it."

"It's nice and round," Luke said.

"Pay attention, Fagin." Sikes's voice was stormy. "You're putting that stuff on my knees, the only place that ain't burned."

The pickpocket spread the ointment on Sikes's oozing ankles, tossed the tin aside, and opened the second can. "I have put your trousers to soak."

"If I ever catch the cove who lit the fire in that chimney, I'm going to scrag him, you mark my word. He ain't going to have the laugh at me." His club— a stout branch whittled and sanded to a shine with a polished knot at the end—was under the pallet. Sikes brought it out and menacingly chopped it in the direction of the boy.

"You trouble my mind with your sad gabble, Bill."

"To hell with your mind. Get me another bottle."

Fagin closed the tin and wiped his hands on his pants. "I'm old enough to remember, Luke, when watches were square and hung from pendants around men's necks. That was before waistcoats became the fashion. Now the watches are round so they can slide in and out of tight vest pockets."

"You have ten of them," the boy said, lifting a second pocket watch, this one with a polished piece of amber in a silver setting at the end of the gold watch chain. "You must like to know the time of day."

"Because vest pockets are tight those watches are difficult to liberate from their owners, and it requires a certain dexterity of which I possess, I don't mind saying, straying from my usual modesty regarding my profession."

The boy swung the pocket watch on its chain and looked at Fagin. "I could lift one of these from a pocket."

"Could you now, lad?"

"Get me that bottle, Fagin." Sikes's words were a growl. "And stop using big words. Liberate. Dexterity. What do those words even mean? They don't mean nothing."

"Luke, daily I deal with invincible ignorance. My lot has been cast and there is no escape."

"What's this?" Luke held up a palm-sized silver box that did not have a lid.

"A playing card holder, the pinnacle of elegance in the better gentlemen's clubs."

"You must play cards a lot," the boy said. "You have ten or a dozen decks all lined up here."

"Life is a sufficient gamble without wagering on cards, Luke. So, when I play cards I'm not gambling. I cheat, and I'm good at it." Fagin held up both his hands and wiggled the fingers. "Here is where the skill lies. The hands. Had I any integrity I would have been a surgeon, with these proficient digits."

"How do you cheat playing cards?"

"Peek at the second card or the bottom card. Deal the second card or the bottom card faster than the eye can see. If you insist on keeping me company, Luke, which would be against my better judgment, I will teach you."

Fagin's door lock was sturdy as befits a fellow who thoroughly knew locks, but few locks could successfully resist a policeman's ram, and this was the case with Fagin's. The door burst open, splinters flying. Inspector Bucket dropped the ram—rope handles on a two-foot-long length of tree trunk with an iron cap on the battering end—and it thumped on the floor. Lantern flames guttered in the air pushed by the swinging door.

Bucket rushed into the room, moving so quickly his coat tails flapped behind him. His face filled with menace and his gaze swept the room.

"A peeler," Bill Sikes barked. With his elbows he pushed himself backwards on the pallet.

Bucket's nightstick dropped from his sleeve into his hand. "I'm the fellow who charred your legs in the chimney over in Rochester."

"When I get out of this bed," Sikes shook his fist, "I'll put an end to. . . ."

The policeman swung the stick, and it glanced off Sikes's temple, an expert blow that instantly blacked him out. Sikes collapsed to the bedding.

With the baton Bucket pointed at the recumbent Sikes. "Fagin, when your friend wakes up tell him to mind his manners." He nodded at Luke. "Who is the boy?"

"I haven't a single notion as to that." Fagin was so slender he appeared lost in his clothes. "He was hungry, and he followed me home because he doesn't have one of his own."

"That true, boy?"

Luke nodded.

"I came here to deliver a message, Fagin." Bucket pushed the nightstick up his sleeve. His hat was low, shading his eyes. "My client, Miss Havisham, has hired you to help her with some foolishness. She has refused my advice to have nothing to do with you, and I cannot talk sense into her."

"When she isn't pointing a pistol at me," Fagin said. "she can be quite pleasant."

"So, my only recourse is to talk sense into you."

"With your nightstick?"

"My duty is to protect Miss Havisham."

"I found her a touch daft, myself," Fagin said.

"She has been swindled by this fellow Compeyson, and for some reason has turned to you for help, figuring if anyone knows swindlers and thieves, it's you." Bucket gestured at the pickpocket. "I've known you for ten years, Fagin."

"Ten years? It seems longer?' Fagin smiled, but his gaze was on the sleeve hiding the baton.

80

"She invited you to Satis House, and you used the occasion to send this moron"—Bucket pointed at the inert Bill Sikes—"down the chimney to burgle the place."

Fagin said nothing.

"Nothing is ever as it seems with you but I'm telling you here and now, Miss Havisham has endured her last swindle. The moment I catch a scent of you doing anything outside of her best interests I'm going to find you again, and you won't like my visit. Am I clear?"

"I have never had a proposition so lucidly placed before me."

The policeman moved toward the door, then looked at Luke. "You can do better than tying up with these scoundrels, boy. You hear me?"

Bucket stepped through the door and disappeared down the hallway.

"What did he say?" Luke asked Fagin. "I didn't hear him."

* * * *

"Margaret Havisham?" the doctor exclaimed. "My lord, you've changed." He gripped her hand. "If I may offer my professional opinion, you've filled out. Your hair is a shade darker. And what a beauty."

She squeezed his hand. "Your spectacles are new but you aren't a day older."

The doctor's white linen waistcoat was striped in pale green. He lowered his brows. "May I be so bold as to ask to see your arms?"

"I wore this dress especially for the purpose."

Miss Havisham's walking dress was made of lilac sarsenet with a twill weave and trimmed on the bosom and wrists with darker lace. At an angle on her head was a French hat made of lilac silk topped with flowering baby's breath, and on her feet were lilac kid slippers. The dress's sleeves were fastened with silk cord, and she removed her white gloves, then untied the cord on her left wrist.

Sliding her sleeve up her arm, Miss Havisham said, "See? Nothing new."

The doctor gripped her arm and turned it left and right, bending for a better look. "The old scars never went away. Too bad." He lowered his head for a better look. "But there is indeed nothing new. My heartiest compliments and congratulations."

Three white, pulpy scars—each about an inch and a half long—marred the inside of her forearm. Pink crosshatches left by the stitches crossed the scars. They gave her arm the aspect of a garden trellis.

She lowered her sleeve and pushed up the other one. The skin there was pale with no scars.

"Lovely," the doctor said. "As clear as a new day. Come into my office, Margaret."

81

Steven Roberts was the founder of the Roberts Institute near St. Bartholomew's, not far from the city wall. He was a physician, and he was careful never to label his establishment a lunatic asylum lest it bring forth images of the notorious Bedlam. Rather, it was a temporary home for girls and women who had "fallen out of themselves," Dr. Roberts's phrase. The windows had no bars, the attendants were almost unfailingly polite, and the straightjackets were kept out of sight and used only in dire circumstances. The institute was little known outside of England's affluent families and was a bracing reminder that money didn't exclude madness. It was notable, too, because the Roberts Institute, unlike other asylums, did not admit women solely on the grounds that their husbands or fathers found them disagreeable.

Miss Havisham followed the doctor along a carpeted hallway lined on one side with windows that looked out on lilac bushes. A young woman in a white smock stood near a potted mother-in-law's tongue, running both hands through her hair again and again. Another patient—no more than eighteen years old and also wearing a smock—sat on a leather chair chewing as if at a meal, staring at the opposite wall, and she didn't spare a glance at Miss Havisham and the doctor as they passed. Carrying a tray of food, an attendant in green shirt and trousers nodded at the doctor as he walked by them. A patient sang *A Soldier's Widow* at the top of her voice from somewhere farther into the building.

Doctor Roberts unlocked his office door, and stepped aside so Miss Havisham could enter. Except for the sculpture above the fireplace, the office was just as she remembered, with the heavy maroon curtains and the bookshelves bowed under the weight of all the volumes. The massive desk was made of dark walnut on which a collection of Dutch tobacco pipes was arrayed in a glass case, along with paperweights and a quill stand. The doctor never sat behind the desk when talking with a patient. Instead, he always pulled up a cane-back chair and waved the patient into the overstuffed settee. He did so now with Miss Havisham. The new addition to the office was a deep-relief sculpture on a tablet of a horse and rider, and it was as large as the fireplace under it.

Dr. Roberts had served as a surgeon with the 2nd Union Cavalry Brigade at Waterloo, where he determined he had his full of others' blood, and so returned to London for more training, qualifying as a physician. He founded his Roberts Institute with a loan from Georgiana FitzRoy Ponsonby, widow of Major General Sir William Ponsonby, who had been attacked by French Lancers at Waterloo, and who was dead by the time Roberts got to him, but Mrs. Ponsonby was nevertheless grateful, and later willing to lend Roberts the funds, saying she had had a sister who was "as crazy as a fly against a window," and who might have benefited from the institute Roberts proposed.

He said to Miss Havisham, "I heard about your wedding day, Margaret. Is that why you are here?"

"No," she blurted. "Not really." She looked out a window, then back to him. "Maybe a little."

"Have you had thoughts of harming yourself?"

"Certainly not," she said. "Nothing could be farther from my mind."

Doctor Roberts was a wisp of a man with the dimensions of a fencepost. His neck was slender, his wrists were so thin they appeared fragile, and his height was little more than five feet two, but what he lacked in dimensions he made up for in allurement. His nose was narrow, his teeth large and white, and his hair was auburn and full.

He said, "Perhaps I should have admitted this to you and your parents." His voice was oddly orotund for a small man. It filled his office. "But you were the first person I had ever seen with your specific . . . needs."

"I needed someone to yank the knife away from me, and you did so."

Doctor Roberts rubbed his hands together, a gesture she remembered as a prelude to the heart of the matter. "In my medical practice, Margaret, before your father delivered you to my door, I had never come across a person who cut herself, who took a knife and deliberately wounded herself. I was at a loss as to what I might do for you."

"You cured me. I've never done anything to myself since I left this institute."

He shook his head. "I didn't know enough to cure you. You grew out of it. When you left my care, I could only hope you were better but I didn't know whether you were. I've since seen two other young ladies with the malady."

"I should have written to thank you."

Dr. Roberts pointed toward the fireplace. "Your father thought I did some good. He sent me this frieze to thank me. I was astonished to receive it."

The frieze above the fireplace was a rectangle, though a lower corner—perhaps an eighth of it—was missing below a jagged fracture line, looking as if the missing part could tightly fit back into the frieze if it could be found.

Miss Havisham rose from the settee and crossed the room to peer at the sculpture.

"It's a Greek cavalryman on horseback," the doctor said. "You can see the man's armor and the horse's bridle. And look how beautiful the horse's mane is, and it's all in marble. It was part of the entablature high on the Parthenon in Athens. It's the ancient building there, thousands of years old." Roberts laughed. "How your father found it, and how he managed to have it cross the continent and the Channel to deliver it to me is a mystery."

Miss Havisham remained standing. "Does it belong to you now?"

"It's in my office, and I don't see anyone else claiming it." He spread his hands, as if casting understanding around the room.

"There is much more to my father than I had ever imagined." She put her hand on the door handle.

The doctor rose from the chair.

"I came here to ask you something, doctor." She wet her lips.

"And you didn't generate the courage to ask me until you were almost out the door?"

She smiled in a small way. "I wonder if . . . ." Her voice trailed off. Her gaze fell to the floor.

"You know me too well to be nervous, Margaret. What are you wondering about? Maybe I can help." He leaned toward her as if he might hear her thoughts.

She inhaled between her teeth. "Can one condition lead to another?"

"Be more specific."

"Does someone who harms herself, might she later hear things that aren't there, maybe feel things more intensely than she should?"

Doctor Roberts opened his hands as if to invite more information.

She said, "Can a person feel as if a room—a certain room in her home— never wants her to leave?"

"A room at Satis House? How is it enticing you not to leave it?"

"It just seems to invite me to stay. It makes me comfortable. With all my things."

"The room does this?" His expression was professionally impassive. "The walls and floor?"

"The room. I think it wants to trap me there."

"What does the room do?"

Her lips moved as if she were speaking but no sound escaped her. She brought a hand to her mouth. Her gaze swept the room.

"Can you sit down again, Margaret?" He indicated the settee. "We can chat about this."

"I've said too much, Doctor Roberts. It doesn't want me to talk about it."

"The room doesn't want you to? I'd like to hear more."

Her words tumbled over each other. "I'm not comfortable talking about it, not even with you, and . . . ." She couldn't manage even a few more words, not even goodbye.

She opened the door and fled down the hall, passing the woman who was still chewing on nothing.

* * * *

Fagin pulled a yarmulke from his pocket and slipped it onto his head. He entered the synagogue on Goswell Street, the boy following him. They sat on a bench near the door.

"Do I need a hat like yours?" Luke asked.

84

"I only have one," Fagin whispered. "You are fine."

On the eastern wall was the holy ark behind an embroidered parroket. The room was lit by lanterns but was dim. Conversation and the clinking of a spoon against a cup came through an office door on the west wall.

"What do you do here?" Luke asked.

Fagin rubbed his chin. "I think."

"Is this a church?"

"As I'm a living man, no," Fagin said.

"What are you thinking about?"

"About how fine it would be to sit here in solitude."

"Are you praying? My ma used to pray in front of a candle, down on her knees. Why aren't you on your knees?"

Fagin sighed heavily, then rose from the bench. Luke followed him to the charity box which was made of pewter with enameled flowers in front and an iron lock on the back. Voices still came from the office, then light laughter. Fagin dropped a penny through the slot.

"Was that a penny?" Luke asked. "Who is going to get it?"

"Whoever needs it most, I hope." Fagin rested his fingers on the box. "It will purchase a quarter loaf for someone. I visited this synagogue with my father many times."

"A quarter loaf won't fill up anyone," Luke said. "It never has me. If I had a guinea, I'd put a guinea into the box."

"That's the only coin I have, young man."

"If I had a pocket watch I'd put it into the box. That would buy a lot of loafs."

"I do not have a pocket watch." Fagin turned away from the box.

The boy remained where he was, and he tapped the slot. "What about the watch in your pocket? I saw you lift it from that fellow in the yellow coat in front of the greengrocer. It would buy a whole loaf."

Fagin felt his coat pocket. "It would buy a whole banquet."

"Why don't you put it into the box?"

"Technically the fellow from whom I took this watch twenty minutes ago still owns it until I cross the threshold of my home. Those are the rules." Fagin glanced down at Luke. "So, I can't drop this watch into the box. It's not mine to put there. Come along, lad." Again, Fagin motioned toward the door.

"If I had a watch, I'd put it into this box." Luke smiled.

"I am not going to let a . . . . How old are you?"

"Nine."

"I'm not going to allow a nine-year-old boy to be my conscience."

"What's a conscience? Is it the same as a banquet?"

"I have enough things weighing me down, boy, and you need not be among them." Fagin glanced at Luke, then at the door to the offices. "If I want an anchor I'll go to a shipyard, eh?"

Luke gripped the charity box, and it apparently would be a struggle to pull him away from it. "I know what it's like to be hungry," the boy said. "If I had something in my pocket, I'd drop it into this box."

Fagin winced. His gaze dashed around the synagogue as if he were searching for help. Sighing again, he withdrew the watch from his pocket and stared dismally at it. It was a Joseph Johnson gold watch with a white enamel dial and black hands, a lovely piece made in Liverpool. He wrapped it tightly in a linen handkerchief to protect it, then dropped it into the charity box.

Luke released his grip on the box and followed the pickpocket toward the door.

As they stepped into the street, Fagin removed his yarmulke and said, "And if I want a nag, I'll go to a horse race."

* * * *

Inspector Bucket said, "I will be a fearful fraud at this event."

"Then you won't be the only imposter." Miss Havisham adjusted his cravat. "Fagin will be here."

"You are tempting the devil, are you not?"

"I'm going to see if I can trust him," she replied. "Never in his life has he had the opportunity for theft that will be presented to him this evening. The jewelry, the pocket watches, the silver. They will all be dangling in front of him like apples in an orchard in August. Let's see if he falls for the temptation."

"Of course, he will," Bucket said. "He's a lifelong criminal. It's in his nature."

She said, "And there's another reason I'm here: it would be an act of supreme cowardice to hide myself from this event."

"Cowards often live to see another day."

"And I am anticipating my reception. If I cannot be amused by what is surely to come this evening then I am indeed dead to the world."

They stood under the entrance arc to the Pulteney Hotel on Piccadilly near Green Park. Tsar Alexander and his widowed sister Grand Duchess Catherina had resided there during their London sojourns. The hotel had been named after the former owner of the building, William Pulteney, the Earl of Bath.

Down the street a watchman carrying a staff called, "Nine o'clock and all's well." He tried the handle of a jeweler's door to insure it was locked, then moved on.

A porterhouse cart rolled by, its pewter pots clinking together.

Inspector Bucket wore white breeches and white silk stockings. His stiff neckband rose almost to his chin. Tails hung from the back of his riding coat. "Do you take my arm?"

She put her hand into the crook of his elbow. "If you are ready, let's go in."

A man in green livery held the doors open for them. Inspector Bucket and Miss Havisham walked along a hallway lined with plush sofas and gloomy oil portraits. Two clerks worked at the reception desk at the end of the hall. A circular stairway wound up to the first floor. Ivy with red berries had been wound around the balusters. Kerosene lamps on the walls gave the place a golden glow. They entered the ballroom through a double-door that was framed with an ivy garland bedecked with red and blue bows. Miss Havisham's fern green gown clung to her enticingly.

Hundreds of candles lit the ballroom, most high above the revelers in crystal chandeliers, others on floor stands, wall sconces, and candelabras. Gas lighting had been installed at Drury Lane and Covent Garden but gas had yet to come to this ballroom. An orchestra tuned up at the far end of the room, musicians pitching their violins and violas to the pianoforte, notes that sounded like birds in a tree. The place was awash in scent: from rose and lilac perfumes and *eau de citron*—used to whiten women's faces and breasts—and from vast arrays of glasshouse roses and freesias, from hair oil, boot leather, perspiration, pine bough garlands, caviar served on quails' eggs, and the city's inescapable coal smoke that worked its way into the room through the thinnest of apertures. The air was thick with smells.

The gala's hostess was Countess Eugenia Stonecraft, stationed just inside the ballroom's door with her husband by her side. When her eyes settled on Miss Havisham, they blinked like an owl's. She cried, "Margaret Havisham, what in the world . . . ?" With an effort that contorted her face, she bit off the rest of the words.

"How kind of you to invite me, Lady Stonecraft." Miss Havisham extended a gloved hand.

"I was not expecting you, Margaret, with your father's health travails, and your . . . other difficulties."

"But here I am, ready to have my spirits lifted regarding my father's health and my . . . other difficulties." Miss Havisham's cadences mimicked the countess's.

Miss Havisham said, "May I introduce my beau for the evening, Police Inspector Lewis Bucket."

The count, who wore a blue sash across his coat and whose face was a map of capillaries brought to the surface by drink, bowed stiffly.

The countess stepped back. "You have brought a policeman to my affair, Margaret? A policeman? Who walks around at night with one of those sticks?"

Bucket smiled at the countess. "I wore out my first nightstick several years ago, knocking heads. I had to purchase a new one."

Lady Stonecraft glared at the detective, her mouth moving, her words not quite audible. She stepped toward the door to welcome the next couple.

Bucket said, "I doubt whatever the countess was murmuring was flattering."

"I know precisely what she said," Miss Havisham replied. "'A brewer's daughter and a policeman. What next? An organ grinder and a monkey?'"

Bucket asked, "How is a brewer's daughter admitted to this soiree, filled with grandees, as it is?"

"My father loaned Count Stonecraft thousands of pounds when the count's investment in the Midlands Fire Assurance Company was lost, and Stonecraft was on the verge of losing his estate and lands. The count was able to keep his property, and I suppose he felt he was duty-bound to elevate father into his circle. I'm confident it was grudging."

"And now his wife can't find a way to strike you from the invitation list?" Bucket asked.

"She is wily, and she'll figure it out one of these days." She gripped his arm more tightly, and whispered, "Mr. Bucket, it has become so quiet in here I can hear your shoes squeak."

Three hundred people were in the room, and most of them were looking at Miss Havisham. A graveyard stillness had fallen upon the revelers. Mouths were open and eyes were wide. Not one of the revelers moved nor spoke. Only the orchestra, still tuning, made noise.

Miss Havisham said in a low voice, "Steady, Mr. Bucket. I've prepared myself for this, but you have not had time to do so. I don't want you to flee."

"You underestimate me, madam."

On Bucket's arm, she moved farther into the ballroom. "Why, Mrs. Spender, how is your daughter? Last I heard she was in the middle of her grand tour. Vienna, was it?"

Mrs. Spender put her face together. Her gown was of light blue chiffon. Filled with powder, smallpox scars dappled her neck under her ears, and a patch covered the deepest of them. "Miss Havisham. Margaret. I'm a trifle surprised, if I may be so bold to admit."

"My father continues to breathe, and he insisted I come to London for this gala."

"But your wedding." Mrs. Spender's expression was as if someone were stepping on her toes. "I was in attendance and . . . ."

"I'm grateful you and Mr. Spender came to the event."

The massive Mr. Spender—who had two double chins, one below the other, and who resembled a frog in other particulars, too—attempted a bow but he was known to wear a corset, and his dip in her direction was shallow.

Mrs. Spender wasn't done. "And I had assumed that should you attend this event you would be with your new husband, and for appearance's sake I would have thought . . . ."

"A new husband wasn't to be, Mrs. Spender. And if the hostess sent a note retracting the invitation, I never received it."

"Lady Stonecraft would never do such a thing," Mrs. Spender said, "but perhaps she thought it was unnecessary."

"Turns out it was." Miss Havisham's smile carried much meaning. "Good day to you, madam." She tugged the policeman along.

The guests regained modicums of decorum, and most broke their stares from Miss Havisham but her appearance at this event was likely the most bizarre and titillating breach of decorum they had ever witnessed, and word of it would spread across the land as quickly as tongues could wag and Royal Mail horses could run. Miss Havisham was, after all, the beautiful and stately daughter of a brewer who had somehow entered the ranks of London and Kent society—a *brewer*, no less: one who deals in malt and grain and barrels and such—and this audacious and grasping condition had become bafflingly acceptable to society. In truth, a number of the men in the ballroom—braced by rum punch and out of earshot of their wives—would admit, "I like Hugh Havisham, and he has done me a favor or two over the years." But even so, Hugh Havisham's daughter being deserted at the altar was an exquisite, irresistible news item traded back and forth in music salons, cardrooms, and parlors.

"Not one other guest has braved catching my eye," Miss Havisham said. "Spineless, the lot of them."

The room gleamed with the army and navy officers' scarlet and gold and blue uniforms, and plumes, epaulettes, and gold-worked scabbards. Dragoons, Jaegers, Highlanders, and Foot Guards. Jewel-encrusted stars and bright silk sashes decorated the coats of the nobility and senior officers. The floor fairly sank under the weight of the necklaces, bracelets, rings, and brooches. This year pastels were the fashion for gowns, and the diaphanous fabrics revealed the women's curves in a manner that would have shocked an earlier generation, and if blame were to be had for the décolletage it must be laid at the feet of the French, of course. Turbans, tiaras, and bandeaux adorned the women's heads, and some of the older men wore powdered wigs despite Pitt's tax on hair powder. The conductor sprinkled sand on the parquet dance floor.

Miss Havisham tugged the policeman's arm, guiding them toward the refreshments tables. "I don't see Fagin yet." She turned a full circle, searching for the pickpocket. "Maybe I've made a mistake."

"May I inquire, miss," Bucket said, "how it is that you have found the wherewithal to come here this evening. Prior to tonight I had supposed you were touching upon madness."

"Are all police investigators so blunt?"

"You have stocked a cupboard with lunatic behavior, what with your pistol aimed at Samuel Compeyson, and your engaging that reprehensible pickpocket, and your isolating yourself in your room with the wedding cake and decorations for hours at a time. And just now at the mention of Compeyson's name you didn't flinch, as have you every time in the past when his name has escaped my mouth."

They walked toward the orchestra, the guests parting in front of them like the bow wave of a boat.

Bucket's head came up. "There's Fagin, by God."

Miss Havisham's gaze found the pickpocket, then she closed her eyes a moment. "I don't know whether I should be relieved."

"And he has bathed and shaved."

Miss Havisham said, "I hired a hairdresser, and the tailor and bootmaker, too. And so there he is, crystal goblet in hand, which he may or may not steal at the end of the evening. What if he fails this test, and steals something? I'm nervous. But he looks splendid, don't you think?"

The pickpocket Fagin chatted with Beverly Hamsbury of the iron foundry family. Her necklace was a swatch of diamonds positioned across her chest in a blinding array but this display had nothing on Fagin, who positively gleamed in a melon yellow waistcoat with brass buttons, a daring white tailcoat, and a spectacularly knotted blue cravat with a gold pin. An emerald the size of a penny in a gold setting graced a finger of his left hand. His burnt orange hair was parted and pomaded, and his face was bereft of whiskers.

The orchestra finished tuning and then arranged sheet music on their stands. The conductor's tails almost reached the floor. No expanse of wall had been left bare, draped with the flags of England and Scotland. Greece being all the rage, Zeus, Athena, and Aphrodite shimmered on the walls, ghostly apparitions thrown up by magic lanterns. Red, blue, and white silk banners hung from the ceiling.

She again spotted Fagin. "So far, so good. His pockets don't appear to be filled with stolen items. Maybe he is passing my test."

The orchestra struck up *Bonnie Highland Laddie,* and some in the crowd put their goblets and glasses on serving tables and moved toward the dance floor. Women in gowns and men in tails moved by Miss Havisham but at a distance, most casting the smallest of glances at her, close enough to look but not so close as to tempt Miss Havisham to converse. A few *tsk tsk*ed loud enough for her to hear. A lady in a vast purple garment who was built like a Dutch barge glanced at Miss Havisham, then frowned in a manner suggesting regrettable banishment, the expression used when depositing a loved one at Bedlam. An attendant raked coals through a fireplace's lower grates, sending sparks up the chimney.

Miss Havisham said, "On the chair near the fire is Earl Cathcart, and he is speaking with Prince d'Arenberg from Brussels. Behind him is Lord Hill, who served with Wellington at Vittoria. And with that group of officers near the banquet room door is the Duke of Brunswick, whose father was killed at Quatre Bras. He's a handsome brute, and every time I see him he tries to charm me into a liaison."

"Has he been successful?"

She laughed. "Such a question."

"I'm a professional detective."

"A professional gossip monger, it sounds like." She smiled at him. "But, no, let me assure you the Duke of Brunswick's wiles have availed him nothing, at least with me. And though he favors me, he and the other men here will likely oblige the social edict that I am not to be consorted with."

"Does a broken romance deserve this shunning?" Bucket asked.

The grin fled her face. "My mother and father—father, a lowly tradesman—assiduously worked their way into the *haut monde* with years of precise and expensive cultivating, tactically ignoring slights, groveling when required, being ever useful and accommodating to anyone who might assist their advancement. Scraping and begging, father called it. Over the years mother and father were accepted into more and more homes in Kent and even in London."

A fellow with a cane limped along like a three-legged dog, and he tentatively smiled at Miss Havisham but his wife pulled him away, almost toppling him, her chin magnificently in the air.

"And so the Havishams' silk stocking friends appeared at our home to celebrate my wedding, and when my fiancé didn't show up it was an unforgiveable affront to those who had daringly come to Satis House for the ceremony."

"How was it daring?" Bucket asked.

"They had taken in a family of brewers. The calamity of my wedding day was a blow to their high regard of their own judgment."

When the tune ended, the conductor announced *Roger de Coverley*. Couples on the floor formed lines, and the orchestra struck up the lively reel.

"And my appearance at this ball is shocking," Miss Havisham said. "Had I been sufficiently contrite I would have traveled to Switzerland to join a convent. Yet here I am tonight, mud in the punchbowl."

Fagin laughed at something Mrs. Hamsbury said, and when her husband— rotund, short, and as bald as a peeled egg—joined them Fagin shook his hand, and leaned toward Hamsbury, nodding and smiling, and apparently in complete ambrosial comity with the world and all its inhabitants, and there are some movements only a professional can see.

Bucket was staring at Fagin, and in a sour voice he said, "Your pickpocket just lifted that old gentleman's pocket watch."

Miss Havisham spun toward Fagin. "Oh Lord." She narrowed her eyes. "I don't see the watch."

"He has palmed it. He'll slip it into his own pocket in a minute."

Miss Havisham exhaled slowly, her breath whistling. "What a mistake I've made. I thought I could trust him. I'm paying him enough."

Wearing a burgundy gown, a woman so slender she resembled a fistful of sticks harrumphed as she passed Miss Havisham.

"I'm not leaving the room without arresting Fagin," Bucket said. "I saw him in the act of stealing the watch. He is clever and fast but I saw him take it." He stepped toward the pickpocket.

Miss Havisham caught his arm. "You'd cause a spectacle. Wait a while."

Three violinists stood from their chairs to take the reel's lead. The bouncy music and the flowing liquor prompted the dancers to promenade with boldness.

Fagin looked at Miss Havisham, and his right eyelid flicked—the slightest suggestion of a wink, as if trying to catch her attention, and then he displayed the pocket watch to her in the palm of his hand in a manner so that none of his new friends could see it.

Miss Havisham's voice rose like a wind and blood rushed to her face. "He is showing me the watch, flaunting his thievery. He's making fun of me."

Fagin turned back to the Hamsburys. They were joined by Sir Jeremy Bolton, who extended his hand to Fagin, and Hamsbury and Bolton politely laughed at a comment by Mrs. Hamsbury but Fagin almost doubled over with a guffaw and Mr. Hamsbury seized Fagin's arm to steady him. Fagin's hand moved.

Bucket said, "He just returned the watch to the fellow's pocket."

"He put it back into Mr. Hamsbury's pocket?" Miss Havisham asked. "I didn't see him do it."

"You have to know what to look for, and I do," Bucket said.

The smallest of smiles in place, Fagin again glanced at Miss Havisham. "He's showing off for me." Miss Havisham laughed. "I am so relieved."

Bucket said, "I still don't trust him."

"Must you be so suspicious?" Miss Havisham asked. "He is now in my employ."

"Fagin has never made an honest shilling in his life."

Miss Havisham laughed again. "And he isn't going to start with me."

10

Hugh Havisham's eyes had filmed over, and his gaze was fixed on the blue ceiling, but Miss Havisham did not know whether he saw anything. He had not spoken for half an hour.

Holding his hand, she was sitting in a chair next to his bed, and she had been ceaselessly chatting about anything that came to her mind; about Boots the black dog with white feet whose ribs showed and who rudely walked through Satis House's front door when Miss Havisham was eleven, and who adamantly refused to leave, and who turned out to be the best dog who ever lived; about Miss Havisham's tapping the stairway banister precisely seven times whenever she went up or down the stairs, an unbreakable habit from her girlhood; about anything, a torrent of words manifestly unlike her, a woman who treasured being in a room alone with the accompanying silence, and one of the more detestable memories of Samuel Compeyson is that he could make her giggle. Giggle and mewl and flutter her eyelashes. Even gripping her beloved dying father's hand, even awash in the odor of gangrene rot, she reddened at the memory.

She wondered if her father knew she was holding his hand. Estella tutted happily from her bassinet, a gift from the brewers. The bassinet design had been passionately argued among the brewers with many votes taken. The bassinet's oak had been sawed, planed, drilled, turned, lathed, sanded, hammered, bolted, and painted. It is likely that none of the brewers had ever before seen a bassinet, given that when completed it had nobs, scrolls, handles, buttresses, a drawer, an iron hook, and a mounted compass, and that it took three men to lift. It had been topped off with a pink blanket. The bassinet's delivery by the brewers to Satis House had been a joyous moment for them and for Miss Havisham. She released her father's hand to tuck the blanket more tightly around the baby.

Hugh Havisham gasped, and his exhalation clattered. His words were just on the edge of perception. "I haven't done enough."

She rose from her chair. "Father, can you hear me?"

His milky eyes were locked on the ceiling. "Margaret isn't ready." He ran his tongue along his lower lip. "I'm afraid for her."

"Papa, it's me, Margaret."

He pulled back the corners of his mouth. "I should have done better for her."

She rubbed his arm. "You did fine, papa."

Hugh Havisham's head didn't move, nor did his eyes. His words were ragged. "I'm sorry for my daughter."

Without knocking, Edward Murdstone entered the room. His top hat was in his hand, and his dark hair was combed back with strict precision, the striations left the track of the comb's tines visible. His blue trousers were tucked into riding boots.

"Miss Havisham," he said, "may I speak privately with you?"

"It's not a good time, sir. My father. . . ."

"Your father might like to hear this." His grin brought neither humor nor happiness to his face. "I have a proposition for you. Of a personal nature."

Estella looked at Murdstone but her eyes quickly found Miss Havisham again.

"I cannot put a gloss on my proposition as we hardly know each other." His voice was oily and compelling. "But it would be a way to insure Havisham and Murdstone continues on to the next generation, if I may be so bold."

"Papa?" She knelt next to her father on the bed. "Are you here?"

Hugh Havisham's last breath had left him. His chest was still. His phlegmatic eyes were open but the life force had wafted away, and under the blanket he seemed to sink into the mattress.

Her hands at her mouth and her eyes white all around she backed away from the bed.

Murdstone gripped Hugh Havisham's wrist. "No pulse. He is gone." He lowered the dead man's wrist, and searched his own pockets, producing two half guineas. He made to close Havisham's eyelids to place the coins on them.

Miss Havisham shouted, "Don't do that. Don't touch him."

"Madam, he is beyond caring if he is touched. And the coins are an old tradition."

"The coins . . . they seem so final."

Murdstone surveyed the body, including the damp, spongy, odiferous cloth that covered the stump of Havisham's leg. "Madam, I have never before seen anyone who looked more final."

* * * *

Held over the fire with iron pincers, the needle glowed red. The perfumer's eyes squinted against the fire light, never leaving the needle as it hovered above the licks of flame. The rest of the room was lost in the contrast. The presses and vats were just suggestions in the dark room, though the guard at the door—who rhythmically slapped his palm with an axe handle—could be heard well enough. The fire was in a brick-lined pit on the floor. A tin ventilator hood was above it, its shaft rising to the ceiling. Nearby was a coal bin.

Edward Murdstone said, "It is ambergris, I assure you,"

"I never believe anything anyone tells me." The perfumer pulled the needle from the fire. "Though sometimes I believe they believe it." Gripping the pincers, he stepped to the bench.

"You are going to burn it?" Miss Havisham asked. "It's too valuable to destroy even a bit of it."

"A negligible puncture." The perfumer glanced at Miss Havisham then at Murdstone, perhaps wondering who would make the decision.

The perfumer's name was Ezra Livingston, and wire-framed spectacles rested on his nose reflecting the flames and hiding the cunning behind them. A cotton apron covered him from neck to calves, and was stippled with reds, purples, and yellows. His eyebrows grew together over his nose. A horseshoe of hair went from one ear around back to the other below his glabrous pate. His chin receded as did his forehead so his nose always arrived at a destination in advance of the rest of him.

Livingston said, "Let's determine what you have for sale."

The perfumer inserted the tip of the needle into the ambergris. Liquid beads of it formed instantly, and a gray wisp of smoke rose.

The perfumer inhaled deeply through his nose. "A hint of the sea, a touch of musk, and an intimation of fecal matter."

"It is genuine?" Miss Havisham asked.

"I rarely see ambergris, and I've never come across a piece even a fifth as large as yours. Most perfumers would be moved to tears by the sight of your huge specimen." He lowered the needle to the bench. "But I am made of sterner stuff."

"Give us a price. We are in a hurry." Brass buttons ornamented Murdstone's black coat. The ring on the little finger of his left hand was amber set in silver. His dark hair was swept back so severely he looked as if he were facing a gale. Miss Havisham found his eyes to be peculiar. The pupils were dark, more black than brown, and his eyeballs appeared to be spheroids, wider than they were high. And lusterless, as if they absorbed all light rather than reflecting it. There was no sparkle. Newton would have written about Murdstone's eyes in his book on optics.

"I am not a Paris perfumer." Livingston swept his arm to encompass the room. "Mine is of a smaller scale, much smaller."

Miss Havisham said, "You have the advantages of operating an illegal business."

"*Illegal* is a harsh term, madam."

"Your perfumery is entirely *sub rosa,*" she said.

Murdstone waved away her comment. "Mr. Livingston does not need an education on his own business."

She would not be deterred. "You do not pay the window tax, the workman's tax, the spoon tax, the vat tax, the walkway tax, the coal tax, the sewer rate, and if you owned a dog, you wouldn't pay the collar tax. Your imports never stop at a customs house. You are the only perfumer in London because your expenses are low and so your profits are high."

Livingston pointed. "The glass sheets on that rack, on which I spread flowers for *enfluerage* are half an inch thick and are leaded, and three sheets of it cost more than a fine stallion."

Miss Havisham said, "Kindly don't play the pauper, Mr. Livingston."

Murdstone held up a hand in her direction.

"Simply name your price," she said, "and I'll determine if it is sufficient."

Her gray jacket was unbuttoned, revealing a cream-colored frock with a twining vine pattern.

"And these presses," Livingston went on, "are made of the heart of oak just as was Nelson's *Victory.* Getting oak away from the navy is costly."

The two machines—each of size of a bed—had handles on top with which to tighten the jaws to squeeze out plant oils. Tin gutters bordered the presses.

The perfumer gestured toward a bank of equipment against a wall. "A steam distiller from Manchester, and a solvent extractor from Amsterdam. All that glass and gleam is pricey, I'm here to testify. And the roses, violets, jasmine, magnolia, lilac: most often imported from Grasse in southern France. And on those shelves are bottles of deer musk from Asia and beaver castor from Canada. My expenses are shocking."

Miss Havisham asked, "What is the ambergris for?"

Murdstone cleared his throat, a message to her.

"Why, it is a fixative." Livingstone may have sensed an advantage in her ignorance. "It makes the scent last. Without a fixative a flower's oil will stop emitting a smell within a few moments. Coal tar will also work but it adds an industrial note that a good nose can detect."

The guard at the door stopped smacking his palm with the axe handle but his eyes never left Murdstone and Miss Havisham.

"And then there are the payments to the policemen and the magistrate, and even the nosey beadle. I am bound for the workhouse, madam."

Miss Havisham rubbed her thumb on the lump of ambergris. "Make an offer, Mr. Livingstone."

"As you say, I am the only perfumer in the city. So I can make my own price."

She smiled. "Then do so."

"Two thousand," Livingston said. "Three hundred in cash right now, and the balance with a draft on the Bank of England."

Murdstone rose to his full height. "Two thousand five hundred, and we will have a deal."

Livingstone extended his hand to shake Murdstone's.

"No, we won't," Miss Havisham cut in. "It's three thousand or nothing."

Livingstone grimaced.

Murdstone reached for her arm, then stopped, perhaps thinking better of it. "I have made the offer, Miss Havisham."

"Nothing of the sort." She slipped her hands under the ambergris, and then with an effort that made her grunt in an unladylike manner lifted it from the table. She looked at the jeweler. "Mr. Murdstone made his offer without consulting me." She carried the waxy lump to the fire pit, where flames crackled and smoke rose to the hood. "I propose to drop the ambergris into the fire. It means nothing to me."

When Murdstone's eyes were wide open they were even more odd. He stepped toward her. "Put that back on the table."

She said, "You have misjudged our partnership, sir."

"I have worked with your father for years. We understand each other." Murdstone moved closer. "You are standing near a fire with a flammable fortune."

She said, "The Havishams have all the money we could ever want." The flames threw shadows behind her as she inched closer to the pit. "A little more means nothing to me. I would as soon toss this gob of whale expulsion into a fire as I would sip lemon water on a sunny day."

Livingston's hands were knotted together, and his eyes went back and forth between Murdstone and Miss Havisham as if they were following a shuttlecock. His mouth opened but no sound escaped him.

Murdstone asked, "What do you want?"

"From Mr. Livingston I want three thousand sovereigns for the ambergris."

"Done," the jeweler fairly gasped.

"And from you, Mr. Murdstone, I want an understanding. You are to undertake no negotiations without my knowledge and make no deals without my approval."

Murdstone's face gained a pink hue. "You do not know this business."

97

The ambergris began to slip, so she bobbed herself to gain a better grip, and she moved even nearer the fire. A sheen arose on the ambergris surface as it warmed.

Miss Havisham said, "I may not understand the business but I understand you, Mr. Murdstone, and that is enough for now."

"It's going to melt." Livingstone's voice rose. "Each drip is worth . . ." His voice trailed away.

She locked up Murdstone with her gaze. "And our partnership will do without your sniveling condescension. Agreed?"

Murdstone inhaled so fiercely through his nose it whistled. Glaring at her, he nodded.

She stepped away from the fire pit. "Here is your purchase, Mr. Livingstone."

The ambergris thudded to the table. The jeweler glowered, perhaps trying to determine if his deal had been a good one.

"I have an accord with you, Mr. Livingston." She brushed her hands together as if the ambergris had been dusty. She turned to Murdstone. "And also with you, sir."

11

"Kindly do not pick your teeth at the table." Miss Havisham rearranged the napkin on her lap.

"How else will I clean them?" Fagin put the toothpick behind his ear. "A blacksmith near Charterhouse Square has pulled two of my teeth over the years. He is quick, just as we hope the hangman will be. My teeth are in fine fettle due to my diligence."

"There are practitioners of the dental arts in the city. Why don't you visit them?"

"The blacksmith will take in payment anything I snatch on my walk to his shop." Fagin leaned back in his chair. "A soup pot, a sterling fork, a scarf, a dog collar. It hardly matters."

"You would take the collar from a dog?" she asked.

"And the bridle from a horse. They seldom object."

"Do not lean back in your chair, Mr. Fagin. It is not considered polite. And do not store your toothpick behind your ear."

"Madam, I thought I had passed your examination at the Stonecraft ball, wearing those fine clothes and chatting with my betters."

"That was simply to determine whether you are a moron."

Fagin lifted a spoon from the table.

"That you were not thrown through the Pulteney Hotel's door onto the street was encouraging." She smiled. "You have the ability to converse with people who would scrape off their own skins had they known with whom they were speaking." She wore a cream half dress with puffy sleeves and a neckline of yellow silk Van Dyke points. "I was immeasurably relieved."

"What is in this soup?" Fagin asked. "Shouldn't soup be brown, eh?"

"It is *potage a la Reine*, also called *white soup.*" Her words had gained a parson's primness but she couldn't help it. *"Chicken, veal, and almonds in a cream sauce, and those red dots are pomegranate seeds."*

"How I love pomegranate seeds." He dipped the spoon into the soup.

"Not that way." She picked up her spoon. "Now, watch. As the ships sail to sea, I move my spoon away from me."

The pickpocket pulled at an ear.

"And then you sip the spoon from its side, not from the tip." She showed him the proper way.

"Why don't I drink the soup from the bowl? It would save a lot of time."

"At this restaurant, were you to lift your soup bowl to your mouth English civilization would collapse." She smiled again at him. "Mr. Fagin, are you blushing?"

"I am incapable of embarrassment, madam."

"Your face is red."

"This week it has been shaved for the first time in years. The razor blade burned my skin. And these clothes,"—he plucked at a lapel—"are so new they itch." Silver buttons adorned his maroon jacket.

A touch of coyness in her voice, she said, "You are presentable to the point of being handsome."

Their table was near the fireplace of Stone's Chophouse which was around the corner from Shepherd Market. A waiter hovered nearby. All twelve tables were occupied, including the one nearest the door where Inspector Lewis Bucket finished his venison soup.

"The doorman smiled at you," Fagin said. "You have been here before?"

"When my Uncle Felix and Aunt Nell are in the city I meet them at St. Paul's then we come here in their coach with matching bays. Everything is big and grand with them. You should see their estate. St. James Park is nothing to it."

Fagin stabbed the air with his fork in Bucket's direction. "Must you travel with that police officer? He would just as soon throw me into the clink as look at me."

"Are you familiar with . . . clinks?"

"Bridewell, Clerkenwell, Horsemonger." He shrugged. "A few weeks here and there, maybe a few months, depending on how the magistrate's dinner was sitting. If horseradish is repeating on the judge, I might be sent off for six months."

A waiter lifted the claret bottle from their table but neither Miss Havisham nor Fagin had touched their glasses so he returned it to the coaster.

"Have you ever been to school, Mr. Fagin?"

"Clerkenwell Jail is a school, of sorts. I was sent there when I was twelve, and I learned a prodigious amount."

"Can you read and write?"

"I own a Shakespeare folio published by Chetwinde, and I have thumbed it well."

She said, "It must have cost you a fortune."

"The previous owner paid handsomely for it, I'm sure." He turned a palm up. "It didn't cost me a thing."

It took her a moment. "You stole it?"

"How can something that is destined for the ages belong to anyone? In this life we are only stewards. I might as well curate Shakespeare's priceless folds of paper as anyone else."

"So that's how you justify thievery?"

"I am a caretaker. A bailee."

A waiter placed roast beef in a mushroom sauce in front of her.

Fagin said, "It follows, then, that one cannot steal at item that cannot be owned."

"Your folio is well-thumbed but so is a pack of playing cards," Miss Havisham said. "Are you dodging my question regarding whether you can read and write?"

"My father sent me to the Twelve Patriarchs School for Young Gentlemen when I was seven years old. I was a student there until I was twelve. By then I had learned to read English well enough, plus a touch of Greek and Latin."

The waiter placed Fagin's serving of roast beef on the table. Peas and carrot slices were artfully arranged on the plate.

The pickpocket said, "One Saturday the Twelve Patriarchs' headmaster pushed me out the door and threw my trunk after me. Took me two days to find my home near Golden Square but by then it wasn't my home. Another family lived there, six children and a mother who brooked no insolence from me when I dragged my trunk up to the door. She grabbed my shoulders, turned me around, and put her foot to my backside. I landed in the gutter and the door slammed behind me."

"Where were your mother and father?"

"Have you ever heard of the Woolwich ferry disaster? A Belgian bark—filled with radishes and turnips, as it turned out—rammed the ferry, and two dozen passengers drowned. I believe my parents were among them."

"You don't know for sure?"

"My father had a business in Woolwich. He often traveled there. I recall him speaking about selling things to the royal armory in Woolwich but I have no idea what he sold. He would be gone for two or three days, and sometimes my mother went with him."

"Were their bodies recovered?"

"A few bodies were pulled from the river but not those of my parents. All of these things I found out later, piecing together information. I don't know if it's true but it's my best guess as to why my parents vanished. And vanish, they did. I was tossed out of school when the headmaster no longer received tuition from my parents because they were dead. This was two months after the ferry sank."

"You had nowhere to go?" Miss Havisham asked

"And I was hungry so I lifted a quarter of bread from a vendor's tray and ate it while running from him. Fortunately, his pursuit of me was impeded by his wooden leg. A few minutes later I plucked a tin of butter from another peddler. I learned it was easy to fill my belly, and it was an intimation of a special talent." Fagin lifted a horn-handled blade from his boot.

"Allow me to advise," she said, "that at a fine restaurant one does not produce a dagger from one's footwear."

"How else should I cut this meat?"

"A table knife is near your wine glass, as you can plainly see. It may not be as sharp as your weapon but it won't frighten our fellow diners."

The dagger disappeared. He lifted the dainty knife from the tablecloth, eyeing it suspiciously.

"Mr. Fagin, this evening, with you sitting across the table from me, I am attempting to polish a brick, as it were." She lowered her voice. "So will you kindly stop glancing at that gentleman at the next table? It's rude."

"Do you know him?"

Miss Havisham whispered, "He is Jeffrey Beals, owner of a rope factory near the Fresh Wharf, and he is sitting with his wife Charlotte. They are pretending they don't know I'm in the room."

Jeffrey Beals's napkin was tucked into his collar. His eyes were watery and his noes was large and shapeless. The Bealses may have sensed they were the topic of Margaret Havisham's conversation. Charlotte sniffed loudly and lifted her nose so abruptly the feathers in her hat vibrated. Beals cast a poisonous glance at her.

Miss Havisham leaned over the table toward Fagin. "Years ago, when I was five or six, my father owed Jeffry Beals thirty pounds. Some business deal turned sour, I suppose. Dad tried to get Beals to extend the terms but he would not. There must have been some other way, some forbearance by Beals but none was offered. No understanding, no compassion. Beals took the debt to law, and dad was imprisoned as a debtor at Marshalsea."

"That's one London prison I've never been inside, I'm proud to say," Fagin said. "The diamond in his ring is the size of a grape."

"Mother and I often traveled to London to visit dad at the prison, bringing food and clothes. Dad was locked up for six months until the debt was paid. Most children have dreams about monsters under their beds but I had nightmares about Jeffrey Beals for years. Still do, in fact."

"And he is wearing it on his little finger," Fagin said, "which indicates he is slimy and conniving. Such a person does not deserve to possess such a stone."

"As skilled you are, you will never remove a ring from someone else's finger."

Fagin lifted the corners of his mouth. "Would you care to make a wager on that, Miss Havisham? A gold sovereign?"

She said with exaggerated propriety, "Your life has been a compendium of crime, and I am not here to tempt you farther astray."

"Except for the crime I will commit for you."

She smiled. "Yes, there is that."

* * * *

Oh, but Bill Sikes was a hard-hearted, sullen, and nasty young scoundrel. He was a bruiser and a rakehell. Larceny coursed through his veins and calluses covered his heart. He would rather spend two months in jail for stealing three shillings than work a day to earn the same amount. If he could lift it he would steal it. A kind word never passed his lips and a smile never marred his countenance. Anger was a fire always roaring in him and tenderness was as alien as Timbuktu. He existed in a perfect penumbra of rancor. Each day life presented Sikes with the chance to make three good choices or three bad choices, and he always made five bad choices. He was as generous as a shark and as welcomed as a tick. When he passed a milk pail, the milk curdled. If he walked by a clock, the pendulum stilled. Dogs cowered, flowers wilted, and streetlamps dimmed. Sikes was as covered in villainy as a wolf was in fur, a reprobate in deed and thought. And he was about to prove it again.

Jeffrey Beals walked with a folded umbrella, stabbing the ferule into the cobblestones with each step. When he glanced over his shoulder, Sikes ducked into a doorway, kicking a cat out of his way. Warehouses and mills lined Westferry Road. The Thames flowed by a hundred yards west of the buildings. Smoke softened the buildings and dimmed the sun. Horse-drawn drays filled the street, hooves clapping the cobblestones. Teamsters cursed and horses whickered. Once or twice Beals's diamond pinkie ring flashed with sunlight.

Sikes took off down the street again, limping. He leaned sideways as he walked as if bracing against a nor'wester off the starboard quarter, and he winced with each step. White salve covered burns on his ankles. He pushed between two women with baskets of potatoes on their heads. The belcher handkerchief circled his neck as tightly as a noose, and his brown hat was too small, topping his head precariously, causing him to right it with a hand every few steps.

FAGIN & MISS HAVISHAM

He followed Jeffrey Beals past a boneyard where dozens of carrion crows pulled sinew from cattle and pig skeletons. Nearer a chemical plant the bones—picked clean—were whiter, a vast field of them reflecting the daylight. Horned steer skulls and oxen thigh bones filled the yard. Pig ribs looked like cages, and cow backbones resembled centipedes. Pickers in aprons sorted the bones, tossing some aside for combs and handles and the others into a wagon that would be sent into the mill as grist for fertilizer.

As he walked Sikes tapped the club against his thigh. Fagin always sent him on these errands. The pickpocket thought he owned Sikes, and how that came about remained a fog in Sikes's mind, along with much else. On Dudley Street two years ago Sikes had been leaning against a post and sucking on a tooth. A Bow Street Runner had seized Fagin by the scarf and trousers and propelled him toward jail. In an unprecedented burst of energy and enthusiasm Sikes had smashed the Bow Street Runner's shoulder with the club, probably breaking the collarbone. The runner howled, dropped Fagin, and fled.

Sikes had never before laid eyes on Fagin, and had clubbed the policeman merely as a matter of principle. Adjusting his pants and scarf, Fagin had started jabbering at Sikes that day, following him along the street, and had somehow let on that Sikes was now in Fagin's debt, not the other way around. Sikes had tried swatting Fagin away but the fellow had stuck to him like a limpet, gesturing widely and ceaselessly talking. Only when Fagin pulled out a silver hip flask and offered it had Sikes paused on the street. By the time Sikes had emptied the flask Fagin had proposed a brawns and brain arrangement. Sometimes, Fagin had said, he needed more persuasion than argument could provide. And once in a while perhaps Sikes could help him liberate an item from its owner by bulking him. And so Sikes had become the pickpocket's errand boy.

In those two years Fagin had once in a while slipped Sikes a few coins but always begrudgingly, seldom enough for a proper night on the town, always with the promise of more soon. Fagin hadn't as yet asked Sikes to club anyone but Sikes was good at kicking open a home's door, and it turned out that Sikes had a talent for bracing Fagin's marks, the victim so affronted or worried about the hulking, jug-jawed Sikes jostling him that he didn't notice Fagin's hands. Fagin had let Sikes bed down in a corner of Fagin's diggings. From cock's crow to the lamplighter's "All's well," Fagin never stopped talking, always some big windy scheme.

Sikes tolerated it because a man must set a candle before the devil, and sometimes there was a strike. The silver plate taken from Sir Roderick Bruce's home on York Street near St. James Park. The leather pouch of sovereigns found in a barrister's pantry near Gray's Inn. The Argonaut moon-phase repeater lifted from a coxcomb's pocket on the Strand, a particularly skillful stall by Sikes.

JAMES THAYER

The old man always gave Sikes a cut but there were loans to be repaid to Fagin, fees for room and board, and roundings and estimations and calculations, Fagin flicking the beads on his heathen abacus before sliding a few coins to Sikes across the table along with a bottle of sailors' rum. Sikes risked much but gained little in these endeavors. This would stop soon enough, he vowed, slapping his own leg with his billy.

Buoyed along by base malignancy and implacable ignorance, Sikes quickened his pace, closing in on Jeffrey Beals. Mountains of coconut husks lined the street, as tall as first story windows. A mule pulled a wagon piled with coconuts toward the crushing mill's dock. The coconuts—covered in fiber and the size of skulls—were as strange a sight as Sikes had ever come across. This was Beals's rope and mat plant.

Sikes looked over his shoulder. Down the street workers unloaded sacks from a cart, hollering back and forth and laughing. Beyond them two swells in top hats leaned toward each other, talking earnestly. No one seemed to pay attention to Sikes.

At the clerk's entrance to the factory, Jeffrey Beals withdrew a key from his trousers pocket. With one more survey of the street Bill Sikes raised his club and was on him.

* * * *

Actor-manager-director-playwright Vincent Crummles peered around the curtain at the audience filing into the theater. It was a sizable crowd, at least 150 people on the benches and more coming in. He waved to a repeat patron in the front row, a fellow who sat next to an empty space on the bench, and who with a husky voice addressed that empty space as Mrs. Harris, and then appeared to listen to the invisible Mrs. Harris's comment. Madman or not, he was a welcomed paying customer.

Crummles glanced at Ambrose Franks. "Word has spread across town."

Franks—known to his mother as Harry Beecker, to Miss Havisham as Samuel Compeyson and to yet others as Ronald Farquhar, Cecil Anton, and Giles Stoddard—grinned as he looked through a slit in the curtain at the audience. "Your play is bringing them in, Mr. Crummles."

Crummles' costume was of a chimney sweep: a black mourning coat and a top hat because sweeps were known to obtain their clothing from undertakers' cast-offs. His face was dramatically smudged and he held a long-handled brush.

Franks was dressed as an English duke, with leather boots up to his knees, a sword in a silver scabbard, gold braid hanging from the shoulders, and a blue sash. A dashing red velvet cape had been added to the costume because audiences loved capes, and the manager believed in giving his patrons what they wanted.

105

"Your play is a success, sir," Franks said.

Crummles pushed out his chest by way of accepting the compliment. He had taken the Beaumarchais play *The Barber of Seville* and had changed the title to the *The Sweep of Salisbury*. He had added a dog, Sweetlips, played by the Infant Phenomenon in a costume made of rabbit fur. A dance number had been added, also featuring the Phenomenon, and she would be dancing to a tambourine as the troupe did not have an orchestra. Miss Snevellicci—seventeen-years old and new to the troupe, who had nice ankles and all her teeth, would play the Rosine role, except that Crummles had changed Beaumarchais's Rosine to Roz, and had made her a Billingsgate oyster shucker.

Crummles fashioned himself a student of human nature, and he didn't wonder that Ambrose Franks had readily agreed to become an actor in the troupe. Some folks cannot resist the urge to display themselves like courting pheasants, and Compeyson was one of those. These people enjoyed a delicious pleasure when others looked at them. Crummles didn't suffer from the same deficiency. He was an actor and theater manager because the stage was the only thing he knew about.

Miss Snevellicci's mother was also with the troupe, a consummate gossip who could transform the whiff of a scandalous rumor into a ruinous certainty with a few barbed phrases. As tireless as Mrs. Snevellicci was at oral defamation when off stage she could not utter a word when behind the foot lamps, and so had been given a silent role in *The Sweep of Salisbury*, cast as an elephant in the hallucination scene involving Hannibal crossing the Alps.

"There she is," Franks said from the side of his mouth. He might have been speaking to himself or to Vincent Crummles. "It has taken her three days to arrange another visit to the theater." He laughed. "I knew she would."

Three days ago, after their meeting on the pavement outside the theater, Franks had asked Crummles for an acting job, and had been hired instantly. With his dazzling handsomeness and dapper manner, Franks was born for the stage.

Crummles peered out at the audience. The young lady who Ambrose Franks had approached at the theater entrance three days ago was settling onto a bench in the pit two rows behind the stage. Her chaperone—the older woman with the face hewn from a log—fidgeted in her seat, glancing at other patrons in the pit: the soap makers, slop sellers, tallow workers, ironmongers, and meat packers who the Lord had fated to work with their hands. Smelly, loud creatures, the lot of them, and the governess clearly disliked sitting among the rabble in the cheap seats.

The young lady had said her name was Anna Wilkinson. If Vincent Crummles knew anything it was makeup: his second role of the evening was as Tomrando the Troll, which would mean applying vivid splashes of rouge, false eyebrows, and a putty forehead bulge. Miss Wilkinson was wearing more makeup than during her first visit to the theater.

Not that she needed it, as she was fine featured, with full lips, a slender nose, and a dainty chin. But her cheekbones were accented by loud rouge, her lips were two shades darker than three days earlier, and her eyes were thickly drawn with liner. Her dress was of yellow silk, and pearls hung around her neck.

Nymphs of the pavement occupied pit benches, there to find customers among the boisterous bucks seated near the stage, and several were in Crummles' audience that evening, wearing gaudy feathers and too much color. Not that Miss Wilkinson approached them in her presentation of herself, but it was clear to Crummles—standing at the screen espying her—that she was in earnest this evening. She was there to catch someone's eye, and Crummles knew who it was.

He asked, "Mr. Franks, how did you know this young woman would return to our theater?"

"The other day—when I introduced myself to her—I told her I was an actor in your production. Pardon my presumption but you had a few minutes earlier offered me a role."

"And you knew she would come another evening?"

Franks tugged at the hem of his jacket, straightening it. "I have that effect on people."

Compeyson glanced at Franks. Yes, he could see it, that illusive quality, more than mere pulchritudinous—of which Franks was blessed abundantly—but he also had an aspect of the mesmerist. These past few days Misses Snevellicci and Gazingi had hardly removed their gazes from him.

The theater manager looked again at Anna Wilkinson, whose head was bent toward her governess who gestured widely and spoke without moving her lips, likely condemning everything and everyone in sight. Miss Wilkinson's eyes were on the stage curtain where Ambrose Franks would appear. The newest actress to join the company, Miss Lafontaine, was not behind the curtain and was known to slip away to any nearby coffee house to flirt with whomever she found there.

Franks left the curtain peephole to take his mark in the center of the stage. He inhaled deeply and narrowed his eyes, maybe concentrating on his opening lines.

The chandeliers had been raised to the roof. The candles would remain ablaze during the performance so folks in the audience could watch each other, which Crummles believed was the main reason people went to the theater. The latest trend from Italy—dousing the audience lights just before the curtain was raised so the audience would focus on the actors—wouldn't catch on.

In her dog costume the Infant Phenomenon warmed up with pirouettes, the ears and tail horizontal as she spun. Other troupe members included Thomas Lenville, whose pale face and airy mannerisms made him perfectly cast as Gryffudd the Ghost, a part Crummles added to *The Sweep of Salisbury* to emphasize the lack of society found in graveyards after sunset, a theme Crummles thought missing from *The Barber of Seville.*

Crummles's sons Charles and Percy worked as stagehands. Charles would throw pebbles at a board imitating rain on a roof and Percy was skilled at shaking a piece of tin, sounding like thunder in *The Sweep of Salisbury's* cyclone scene just before the intermission. Because his wife, the exemplary Mrs. Crummles, was unavailable that evening the prompter Mrs. Grudden would play the witch in the *The Sweep*'s closing scene. Crummles had named the witch Mamie to avoid confusion with Hecate, the witch in Shakespeare's *Macbeth,* a play that had inspired Crummles as he wrote *The Sweep of Salisbury,* such as in the first act's powerful line, "Twice upon twice, hard work and toil. Flames alight, and the pot will boil."

Actor-manager-director-playwright Crummles knew that two subjects always drew patrons; trolls and the Paris sewer system. He had included both in the *The Sweep of Salisbury*. The Infant Phenomenon would play a troll after changing out of her dog costume. Crummles was proud of the Paris sewer scene he had incorporated into the script, a clever bit of writing in that the play takes place in Salisbury.

He scanned the stage. All was ready. The curtain was a patchwork expanse of mended and re-mended cloth that the troupe carried with them when they traveled, useful when the venue was a dining hall or a barn. Crummles signaled Charles and Percy, who pulled the curtain ropes.

Ambrose Franks opened the first scene, and he was the only player on the stage, lit by oil lamps in the foot boxes. His first line was to be "Of Paris I am dreaming, the city I want to embrace."

Instead, Franks stared right at Anna Wilkinson, and veered from the script. "Of you I am dreaming, and you I want to embrace." He gestured toward her as if gathering her in.

Frowning so deeply the corners of her mouth were down to her jawbone, the governess's head snapped to her charge, who smiled up at Franks so broadly she appeared to be emanating light. Franks continued with the opening scene, mostly keeping to the script but always looking at Anna Wilkinson.

Franks was up to chicanery, probably trying to breast the fearsome rampart of the governess, and so to arrange a meeting with Anna. Crummles brushed his jacket with his hands, readying for his entrance. Once again, he glanced at Franks and then at Anna Wilkinson.

They were plotting for each other. There was much at work here between those two young people, some of it in plain sight and some of it hidden. Crummles shook his head, then stepped to back of the stage to prepare for his cue.

12

Inspector Bucket had been following Compeyson for two hours. The swindler had taken a hackney cab to the tower, then walked along the Limehouse Reach and the docklands where he headed toward the West India dock, moving briskly.

Masts, yards, and ratlines webbed the sky ahead. Derricks unloaded crates while stevedores moved up and down gangplanks. Horses at their wagons snuffed and clopped, and ships creaked against their bumpers. Dockside agents and ship chandlers huddled with vessel owners and masters doing business with handshakes and nods. Black-backed gulls circled overhead. The dockland smelled of tar and bilge water.

Compeyson moved along a row of warehouses, walking in an exaggerated manner, firmly planting his walking stick in rhythm to his steps, his chin lifted high, his top hat at a rakish angle, perhaps imitating the financiers in the city. Bucket hurried to keep pace with him, and dodged a donkey pulling a cart of oakum.

Then Compeyson darted right, disappearing into an alley between warehouses. Bucket sprinted after him, intent on finding the swindler's destination. Compeyson had deserted his rooms in the city, and Bucket wanted to search his new place. The detective turned sharply into the passageway; a garbage-strewn damp alley lost in shadow.

A brutal blow to the head toppled Bucket.

He bounced off the stones. Pain coursed from his skull into the rest of him. He groaned and tried to find his feet but another strike to his head flattened him in the alley. His thoughts flickered.

In his life Lewis Bucket had been hit with a barrel stave, the stock of a shotgun, a table leg, a codfish, and dozens of fists. The detective invariably and painfully taught these assailants the errors of their ways. Bucket knew fists, and as he tried to scramble away from another blow—his vision white at the edges—he was dimly aware that a fist had knocked him down but it was not a fist as his experience had taught him a fist should be. It was not a balled hand as Dr. Johnson defined a hand. Rather the blow had felt like being struck with a ham hock shot from a cannon. It had been a devastating jolt, the worst of Bucket's life, and he was reduced to trying to squirm away from the attacker on the wet cobblestones, his mind blurry.

From above him came, "I don't like this any more than you, chappie, but a man such as me has got to make a wage."

Hands seized Bucket's collar and lifted him toward standing, holding him upright. Bucket's legs swayed uncontrollably. The attacker was a square and solid fellow, and Bucket had been hefted from the street as easily as a daisy from a meadow.

The assailant was thick-chested man who held him up by the shirt front. Bucket blinked and his mouth sagged open. He moaned and started to go limp.

But it was a feint. The detective savagely rammed a knee up at the assailant's groin but the man had twisted sideways protecting himself, and the detective's knee brushed the man's thigh.

The mugger laughed—a sound so deep it seemed to come from the ground—and slapped his palm against Bucket's ear so ferociously that a gong went off in the detective's head, and he collapsed once again to the ground. Bucket's head was a vast expanse of agony. The time the moan was genuine. He rolled onto his back, and his hand found something on the stones, a board or a post on a trash pile, maybe ship refitting debris. He swung it savagely up at the assailant.

The board snapped into two pieces as it smashed into the assailant's arm. The man grunted and stumbled back. On his back Bucket lashed out with his foot, catching the man's knee and sending him to the ground.

Bucket's thoughts were murky and pain rattled around in his head but he instinctively knew the attacker was not the usual dipper he had handled for years, miscreants on which finger jabs at the chest would make them fold and drop. This fellow was a henge. Bucket crawled toward the man, intent on grabbing his head and smashing it into the ground.

"Now don't be fighting," the fellow said in the tone of a teacher. "This here is a lesson, not a fight." He pushed himself away from Bucket.

Dizzy, the detective tried to stand, his hand sliding in the muck in the alleyway. The assailant rose, using a brick wall for balance and favoring a leg, and his fist found Bucket's temple again. Pain blossomed in Bucket's head.

Then the attacker bent low over Bucket, as his voice was close as he said, "The lesson is this."

The words slipped around in Bucket's head as blackness came and went.

111

"Don't follow a fellow who don't like it." The attacker laughed, a low, grating noise. "And that gent you were following don't like it."

Standing above Bucket, the attacker seemed to fill the alleyway with his girth and his blocky head. His face was backlit by the slice of sky between the warehouses. Low brows and a big chin. The last blow had rung bells in Bucket's head but he could hear plainly enough what came next.

"Leave him to me, Magwitch." A second voice, a higher timbre and more cultured, evident in just those few words.

A walking stick struck the detective's shoulder, then again. Not great blows, hardly enough to make it through the suffering already in Bucket's head. The detective tried to rise to his elbows but fell back. He croaked feebly.

Then the second man said, "Here's a brick. You hold him down. We can finish this now."

The assailant's voice—the rougher voice—was sharp. "Lay off there, cullie. I weren't hired to scrag the man."

The second fellow: "Get out of my way, Magwitch. You've done your job, and you've been paid, now leave me to my own devices."

The man named Magwitch—the assailant with the deeper voice—apparently shoved the second man, Bucket could not be sure but it sounded like a scuffle.

Magwitch said, "Drop the brick, Beecker. Or Compeyson, or whatever you're calling yourself today."

"How dare you touch me." The second man's voice was reedy. 'Release my arm."

'You'll not snuff this bloke's candle, Beecker. You've paid me a few coins and I've dented him some for you, and that's where it lights."

His head throbbing, the detective managed to push himself to sitting. He sagged against a water-butt. He couldn't focus his eyes. The two men in front of him were blurs. Despite the ringing in his head Bucket could hear them well enough.

"Magwitch, you will not be telling me my business."

"Drop the brick or I'll drop you."

Bucket tried his legs again but sank back onto a sodden pile of debris. The brick landed on the stones near his leg.

"Leave him here and let's go," Magwitch said, his voice retreating.

Beecker followed, saying, "I hired you to do what I tell you."

The last thing Bucket heard them say was from the fellow Magwitch, the one who had felled him. "And you'll thank me in the light of a new day."

The detective was left alone in the alleyway, clothes sodden, head pulsing with pain. Once again, he tried to rise, and once again he fell back to the cobblestones and trash.

Two thoughts somehow emerged from the suffering inhabiting Bucket's head. The first was that he would have to remain down on the cobblestones and the muck for many minutes before he would be able to gather the strength to stand.

The second was that the man who had laid him out knew how to do it and was dangerous beyond all bounds.

* * * *

Guy Fawkes' mouth was contorted in agony, his eyes bulging as if they might pop out of his skull, and the veins on his neck were red and raised. Chains secured his wrists and ankles to the axles, and he was flat on the rack. Bones in his dislocated shoulders stood out at odd angles, and his white shirt was mottled with old blood. Wearing black hoods and stained leather breeches, two torturers cranked the rack's axle handles.

"That looks like it hurts." Luke edged closer to the rack. "Are they ever going to let him go?"

"He was pulled apart on the rack, and hung by the neck from a crossbeam, and his belly was opened with a knife but I don't recall the order of these misfortunes," Fagin said. "Fawkes was thoroughly done in, have no doubt."

Fagin had lit candles in wall sconces but the room was poorly lit, more dark than light, with spectral flickering shadows.

Luke walked to the next tableau, and pointed at the woman whose hands were bound behind her and whose head rested on a wood block. "Who is that?"

"Mary, the Queen of the Scots."

"Her hair is redder than yours. Is she going to be killed by that fat man with the axe? He's wearing a hood, too."

"There'll be a good distance between her head and her shoulders when the executioner finishes his task." Fagin rubbed his hands together. "We didn't come here for your education in history, the little I know of it. Let's return to work."

Luke's hair was clean and combed with a part in the center. His cheeks were no longer hollow, and his smile was quick as he stepped to Queen Elizabeth, who wore a beaded, sequined, bejeweled, laced, pearled and embroidered blue gown, and whose crown was as large as her head.

"Her eyes aren't right," Luke said. "One looks at me, and the other looks over my shoulder."

"The sculptor was likely genial with gin and had more sail than ballast."

"Like Mr. Sikes? He can't even lie down without holding on."

"Now, now, young man. If judgment must be passed, I'll do the passing, with my superior ability to judge character." Fagin signaled the boy to follow him. "Don't bump your head on the gibbet."

FAGIN & MISS HAVISHAM

Hung from the ceiling, an iron cage contained a wax likeness of the highwayman Jack Wills. The eyes had been plucked out, and the skull was patchy with rotting skin. His hands were twisted into horrifying knots of decomposing tissue and bone, and his breeches and blouse were ragged. Two crows hung from the iron bars, reaching through the cage to pick at the body. The real Wills had been short-dropped from the Tyburn gallows and his gibbet had hung at Aldgate for a year.

Fagin gestured with a thumb. "Let's start with the admiral."

Admiral Nelson's jacket was adorned with gold epaulettes and the brilliantly polished insignia of the Order of the Bath and three other orders. Pinned across the front of the jacket, the right sleeve was empty. Beneath the jacket was a white cotton waistcoat. Nelson's lips were pressed together.

Fagin said. "The admiral doubtless kept a repeater in his pocket. Let's see if you can take it, eh? Don't rattle him, Luke. The slightest touch, and I'll be able to tell because he'll wiggle. In and out, your hand should go as if coated with the finest Persian oil."

"Take the watch from him?" Luke asked. "He only has one arm. It doesn't seem fair."

"A lad with a conscience. How delightful. The French couldn't defeat Admiral Nelson, and apparently neither can we." Fagin stepped toward Queen Elizabeth. "We'll try lifting a reticule from her. Turn your back while I hide the purse. You'll need to find it first, then lift it."

Meersman's House of History, Felons, and Freaks on Long Street near Covent Garden was closed for the night but the night watchman had let Fagin in through the back door in return for a shilling and a promise he wouldn't take anything from the place, backed by the watchman's pledge to hunt him down should anything go missing. Fagin had visited the wax museum a dozen times, always after closing.

Meersman gave his patrons what they wanted: glamor and horror in equal measure. Beautiful Marie Antoinette was displayed at the guillotine, her lovely eyes raised to heaven. The dastardly Yorkshire witch Mary Bateman emptied a vial of poison onto a pudding. The assassin John Bellingham held a pistol at the Prime Minister Spencer Perceval's chest, cotton smoke rising from the barrel.

Luke pointed at Queen Elizabeth. "That's a big dress and some of it is on the floor behind her. How will I find it?"

"Deftly and silently, I'm sure."

A hesitant knock came from the back door. Fagin stepped around William Shakespeare and the Two-Headed Man from Borneo to unlatch the door. Miss Havisham entered the museum, glancing at the South Sea mermaid suspended from the ceiling, a remora attached to her scaly thigh, perhaps a pet.

She asked, "Why are you here and why did you ask me to come here, and. ..." She halted in front of another wax figure. "To frighten me? I don't scare this easily. Who is this poor miserable person?"

"He is known as Luther Leper," Fagin replied. "And he is a stellar attraction, the watchman tells me, with a crowd around him during business hours."

The sculptor had left nothing to the imagination. With the skin sluffing off the face, a rotting eye socket, and missing his upper lip, Luther had been known to set adults to whimpering and children to howling.

"This is where I practice, madam. If a gold coin can be removed from Henry VIII's codpiece it can be removed from anywhere."

She asked, "Who is this child?"

"His name is Luke." Fagin affectionately cuffed the boy, raising strands of hair on the back of his head.

Luke bowed to Miss Havisham.

Fagin said, "Luke is my new apprentice, articled to me for seven years, so he says, though I would prefer two years. He has a mind of his own, a significant drawback.'"

"You are teaching him to pick pockets?" she asked.

"And cut purses," Luke said.

"Yesterday he lifted eight shillings and ninepence worth of wipes," Fagin said.

"Today I'm learning to lift pocket watches." Luke wore a laborer's wool cap and short pants. His coat came down to his knees but was rolled up at the sleeves. He held out the coat's collar for her study. "This is new, made of tweed."

Fagin said. "Luke here was in and out of the clothing emporium in eight seconds, more blur than boy. The clerk may not have even seen him."

Miss Havisham said, "You are leading this child into a life of crime."

"A banker on the 'Change leads a life of crime when he calls the note on homes, and thus those unfortunates no longer have a roof over their heads to avoid getting wet in the rain. It is a permanent, eradicable crime from which the family will likely never recover. Anyone from whom I liberate a pocket watch can certainly afford another, and he will be inconvenienced only as long as it takes his carriage driver to take him to a watchmaker."

"You always have an answer, do you not, Mr. Fagin?"

"To your small questions, indeed. To the questions posed by Socrates, not so often."

The patterned shawl around Miss Havisham's shoulders came from Scotland, where oats are eaten not only by horses but also by the people. Her rose-colored walking dress was under a fur-lined green pelisse which matched the green of her bonnet.

"Luke is a precocious wirer, madam," Fagin said. "Turning him into to a pushcart vendor or an iron monger would be to deny his destiny."

"Always an answer, Mr. Fagin."

"And I'm teaching him that, too," Fagin said, "a skill that helps when in front of a magistrate."

Luke bowed to Miss Havisham again, perhaps thinking the first one insufficiently low.

Fagin said, "You are smiling, madam."

"Involuntarily, I assure you. Why did you ask me to meet you here?"

"To test your discernment, to see if you can make the correct choice."

"I'm here with you," she said. "So I've already failed your test."

Fagin led Miss Havisham and Luke to Henry VIII, whose magisterial girth filled a corner of the museum. The king's collar was a believable ermine imitation, and across his chest were golden chains. Faux diamonds and emeralds dangled from assorted devices. His scowl was majestic and his cheeks were so plump they seemed to be filled with dinner. His staff was planted on the floor, and in his other hand he held a silver ball, being the ball of state or the ball of justice. Rings adorned seven of his fingers; glass imitations of rubies and sapphires and diamonds set in pewter mounts painted to look like gold.

"I presume you know about jewelry, Miss Havisham, what with you having cornered the jewelry market in Kent." Fagin rose grandly at this dose of wisdom.

Luke imitated him, pushing himself up to tiptoes.

"I am much amused," Miss Havisham replied.

"Do you have a shilling on your person, madam?"

"I do, not that I would reveal its location to anyone in your profession." She seemed to be suppressing a smile.

"All of Henry's rings are glass. And the settings are iron or pewter painted in gold."

"Of course."

"Except one. I placed an authentic ring on one of his fingers just before you arrived. Can you detect which one is real?"

She glanced at him, an eyebrow raised, then she studied the rings.

"I know which one," Luke said, pride in his voice.

Fagin said, "I'll give you a hint. You are acquainted with this ring."

"I am at a loss," she said.

"Luke, show her the real ring."

The boy sprang forward and plucked a diamond ring from a finger of the king's wax hand. He passed it to Fagin.

The master pickpocket wiggled the ring in front of her. "This is genuine, both the stone and the gold setting." He held out his other hand. "And you owe me a shilling."

"I know the ring?" she asked.

"You last saw it at Pulteney Hotel. You will recall our wager."

She shook her head but then she bent closer to the ring, and her mouth opened.

"It was on Jeffrey Beals's finger." Fagin slid it onto one of his own fingers. "Now it is on mine." Then he held out his hand, palm up. "The shilling, if you please."

13

A chilled fog drifted in from the Thames, and Miss Havisham shoved her hands deeply into her coat pockets. Across the street a fluttering pink light came through a window of Ezra Livingston's perfumery. The light flickered, changed shades, and disappeared only to come again.

She asked, "What's your man's name?"

"Emmanuel," Edward Murdstone replied. "I once asked his last name, and he shook his head. He's from France."

"Does he speak English?"

"All Frenchmen understand English if you yell it at them."

She asked, "What's he doing in there?"

"He's doing our business."

A black horse—as dark as the night that surrounded it—was harnessed to the cabriolet. Sitting next to Miss Havisham, Murdstone idly flicked a rawhide switch, the tip swishing the air above them, his gaze on the building. The brim of his felt top hat almost hid his planate eyes. His cravat was the same color as his coat, a dark blue that blended with the night.

A dung cart had passed them five minutes earlier but now the street was empty. In a lot north of the perfumery a massive salt-white bull tethered to a post stared at them. Its horns were each a foot long.

He turned to her. "Why are you not married, Miss Havisham? You are of an age."

She jerked away from him and inhaled sharply. "Are you not familiar with my circumstances?"

"I am familiar with your father's circumstances, and they were dire, with the rot eating up his leg."

"If we are to be partners let us remain business partners only," Miss Havisham said. "My personal life will remain personal." She disliked the sniffing tone in her own voice.

"As you wish, madam."

"You haven't revealed why you have brought me here."

Murdstone said, "So you can see how I earn a living, and how your father did so."

"We earn it by sitting out in the damp night so late that all the lamplighters have retired? And it involves a Frenchman with no last name?"

The sound of fracturing glass came from the perfume factory, then of blows on wood, perhaps by an axe or maul. Then more glass. A light in a window flared brightly.

"You might as well learn the full of it." Murdstone held the reins in his hands.

"We delivered the ambergris and were paid for it," she said. "Our dealing with Mr. Livingston is finished, is it not?"

"Your naivety is endearing."

She balled her hands, hidden in her pockets. "I am harder than I may appear to you, Mr. Murdstone."

"Then you shouldn't mind practicing on the susceptibility of a perfumer."

A gout of flame shot up from the building's roof. It rolled and receded, and was replaced by another lash of fire, higher and fiercer. Glass panes shattered, and fire reached through the windows toward the street. The blaze crawled along the roofline, and the black smoke twisted up into the sky. The perfumery popped and crackled. The air filled with the scents of roofing tar, and then of rose petals and wisteria blossoms, then of musk.

Its gaze on the fire, the bull—with twelve inches between its eyes—pawed the ground in the lot next to the perfumery. A stake and rope held the animal, which was twelve-hundred pounds if it was an ounce. A wood water trough was near the stake.

"Did the Frenchman start that fire?" Miss Havisham asked. "Is he still inside the building?"

"He works for us." Murdstone smiled in a way that wasn't a smile, as lipless as a skull. "And so, the law of agency says you and I started the fire."

The breeze carried a wave of glowing embers toward the bull, and when it yanked the rope the post quivered. The animal bellowed and twisted, its eyes rolling in its head.

"Do you carry a knife?" Miss Havisham asked. "Let me use it."

Murdstone pulled a dagger from his boot and passed it handle-first to her. The blade was seven inches long, and a silver knob capped the stag horn handle.

119

"Keep a knife on you from now on," he said. "In this business you may need it."

When part of the roof collapsed a flume of sparks rushed skyward. Cracking came from deep within the building. And popping, maybe overheated vials and beakers. More glass shattered. Flame burst out the ground floor windows and coiled and curled up the brickwork. The building howled and snapped. Tongues of flame rose in the night sky. A fire bell sounded from another street.

Blade in hand Miss Havisham stepped down from the cabriolet's seat. She held her dress up as she walked through bindweed and lamb's ear, and she moved around a derelict axle with a spoked wheel on one end. She stopped twenty feet from the bull, who stamped at the ground and who might've had flame coming from its nostrils. Its eyes were on the perfumery fire. The bull twisted and bucked but could not dislodge the post that held it too near the fire.

A gust of wind carried heat across the lot, rushing over Miss Havisham. She glanced over her shoulder. A wall collapsed inward, sending a wave of sparks soaring over her head. A long hiss came from the building, maybe from a steaming barrel. Fire splashed to the ground, embers bouncing and flaring. The walls rippled with flames.

Miss Havisham swallowed and stared at the bull. She hid the knife behind her dress and forced herself to move toward the animal. Rain had fallen that afternoon and the damp ground sucked at her shoes. Her back was hot from the fire, and her front was chilled. Her knife hand trembled.

"Good bull," she said. "That's a good boy." She stepped closer. "And that's silly, isn't it, me talking to you?" Yet closer. "Those are big horns, aren't they?"

The bull may not have seen her. Its eyes rolled in its head, its rear hooves threw up dirt clods, and its horns sliced the air as it yanked against the line that held it. Miss Havisham inched to the post and placed the blade on the rope. The knife bounced off the rope when the bull jerked backward. She leaned against the post and pressed the knife down and sawed the rope. As the blade dug in, strands snapped apart. She worked the blade, eyes going back and forth between the rope and the animal.

Then the rope severed, and the massive bull sprang away, bucking and blowing. The ground trembled beneath Miss Havisham's feet. Hooves pounding, the bull dashed away from the fire and into the foggy night.

She smiled. "Ingrate."

As she turned back toward the blazing perfumery, a man passed along the building, backlit by the fire. He walked leaning backward to counter the weight of the box he carried in both hands, and he appeared to be struggling, shifting his hands on his box and taking uneven steps. He was far enough from the flames so that he wasn't parboiled, and he made his way toward Murdstone's carriage.

Miss Havisham hurried across the lot, weeds slapping at her dress's hem. A vortex of wind and heat surrounded her, and she coughed against the bitter smoke. When her eyes teared over she wiped her cheeks with the back of her hand. Still holding the knife, she crossed the cobblestones, arriving at the cabriolet at the same time as the fellow who carried the box. Flames spiraled into the sky.

"This is Emmanuel," Murdstone said above the fire's roar.

The man moved to the rear of the cabriolet to place the wood box on the footman's step. Miss Havisham peered into the box: it contained the ambergris she and Murdstone had sold to the perfumer.

Emmanuel pulled a cord from his pocket to secure the box to the carriage. He wore a brimmed workman's cap and a canvas coat down to his ankles. He was small, no higher than to Miss Havisham's chin. He lifted his head to smile at her, and his grin was a ghastly thing. He was missing his top front teeth and the bottom teeth were rotted black stumps. His skin was sallow and his nose was short and turned up, and she could see through his nostrils into his skull. Below the cap, his left ear was missing, and she could have peered into his skull there, too, had she cared to. Light from the fire lit one side of his face.

He might not have weighed more than 110 pounds but danger hung about him as plainly as his canvas coat. Miss Havisham knew with certainty that Emanuel would not be trifled with. He moved away from the cabriolet, still smiling at her.

"Climb aboard, Miss Havisham," Murdstone called from the seat.

"What about your man here?"

"Emmanuel will vanish into the night," Murdstone said. "He is skilled at it."

"So after Mr. Livingston paid us three thousand sovereigns for the ambergris, we have stolen it back from him?"

He extended a hand to help her to the seat but she ignored it and used a rail to pull herself up. Crimson and gold sparks showered the roadway, and they sizzled when they landed in puddles among the cobblestones. She swatted a spark from her shoulder.

He gestured toward the ruined perfumery. "The perfumer will think the fire melted the ambergris away to nothing so we leave no evidence of a theft."

She coughed against the smoke.

Murdstone said, "I seldom sell an item such as this ambergris once when I can retrieve it and sell it again."

The fire's red light flashed from his shoes' silver buckles. When he flicked the whip, the horse lurched forward and the cabriolet went with it.

The full scope of Murdstone's actions settling on her and making her head light, she gripped her hands together. Murdstone was gallows bait, a desperate criminal, worse than the highwaymen James Hind and Dick Turpin. That her father would be involved with such a man was sickening. But it simply could not be so. Her father—who had insisted she take flute lessons and learn to sail on the River Medway and attend Mrs. Wallingford's School where she was taught geometry and geology rather than the usual girl's education in setting of a table—could not have been involved in all of this.

Her voice was small. "You are a desperate criminal, Mr. Murdstone. This is theft and arson."

He grinned in his mean way. "I learned them from your father."

* * * *

Old Nichol hadn't seen a policeman in a decade. The neighborhood in Shoreditch, only a half hour walk to the Exchange, was too dangerous, and had been ceded to the criminals and thugs, to the depraved and the poor, to the dog carcasses and rats. Because derelict buildings leaned together, little sunlight made it to the street to trouble the gloom. Centuries of soot had blackened brick walls. Most windows were broken. All was grey and brown and black. A cloud of flies worked on something dead next to a doorstep. This alley was little wider than a cart, and it was muddy and strewn with dross and dreck.

Vestrymen didn't enter Old Nichol to collect the poor rate. Dustmen and nightsoil men stayed clear. The ague and putrid fever never departed. Squatters abounded because landlords were afraid to visit Old Nichol to roust them. Of hope and charity, there were none. Of bedbugs and lice, there were plenty. Gloom and despair lay over Old Nichol like a casket lid.

The place was perfect.

Samuel Compeyson—or perhaps on this day he was Ambrose Franks or Harry Beecker or Lord Brimwell, eighth laird of Brimwell—strolled through Old Nichol with a confident step, grandly swinging his ebony-capped walking stick, apparently not aware of the greedy looks he drew from the riff-raff peering out windows.

Compeyson wore tan calfskin gloves and matching boots and a dove gray wool coat. The jewel on his stick-pin was in truth glass. He wore trousers in the new fashion rather than breeches. Compeyson acted as if he had not a care in the world, walking through a wretched neighborhood stuffed with a surfeit of scoundrels.

He called over his shoulder, "Are you still there, Magwitch?"

"As close as a tail, your worship."

"Are you sufficient?"

"Scum and misfeasors, sir." Magwitch laughed under his breath. His pantaloons had a button fall front, and mud covered his boots to the ankles. "I'm quite at home."

Magwitch was twice as wide as Compeyson, and while Compeyson's hands were made to hold a violin's bow Magwitch's were anvils. A disinterested observer would conclude Magwitch had no neck, and that his blunt head was an iron plug attached to his shoulders with bolts. But Magwitch was a hard man to observe as he always blended into a background. His bulk was his distinguishing feature but even daylight seemed to strike him aslant, unable to pick out his features, whereas Compeyson seemed to glow as if lit from within. With his dapper gait, uplifted chin, glittering jewelry, and exquisite face, Compeyson was a beacon. Ten yards behind him Magwitch might not have been there.

Compeyson's walk through Old Nichol was simply too much. It was a poke in the eye of this neighborhood, a dreadfully verminous place but still a home to many, and this dandified intruder was an affront, a jarring reminder of what had been lost or never possessed.

From a doorway came, "Look, it's his lordship, the prince of toffs." The fellow emerged into the dim light. A wool cap was far back on his head, and his face resembled a gnawed bone. "You're dancing down the wrong street, your highness."

Compeyson slowed and smiled. "Your servant, sir."

A second man stepped out from behind a drainpipe. "What's that on your coat, mate? Something shiny, looks like." He wore a crusty wool sweater. His left hand was withered, resembling a chicken's foot, and his good hand was around a piece of cobblestone.

"You've lost your way, you and your cane." The first man stepped sideways to block Compeyson. "What say we have a look at your dunnage." He reached for the bauble on Compeyson's collar.

Compeyson said, "Allow me to name my associate, Mr. Magwitch."

The big man emerged from the dim light, and with speed that belied his size he seized both men by their necks, stuck his thumbs far enough into the skin below their Adam's apples that their tongues protruded in unison, and then smacked their heads together, sounding like a bung driven into a beer barrel.

He held both of them off the cobblestones as if they were dangling from ropes. "Where are your manners, lads?"

Magwitch released them, and they fell to the dirt, as insensate as oysters on a plate. Magwitch dusted his hands. "There's another ten guineas you owe me, sir."

"Our deal is that I pay you five guineas each time you save my life," Compeyson said.

"Five guineas each time but just now was twice. You can count them down there on the dirt."

Compeyson glanced at Magwitch's face which settled the issue. "Done and done."

"I'm not fond of waiting on payment."

Compeyson pulled a purse from a pocket, and passed coins to Magwitch, who pleasantly rattled them in his hand before slipping them inside his clothing.

"We can't be too far," Compeyson said.

"Must be just there." Magwitch pointed at a door on the other side of an open umbrella that had no cloth on its ribs. A pile of rotting rags was next to it.

They stayed to the side of the alley, away from the open sewer down the middle. The door was made of massive slabs of wood, nothing a shoulder or boot could ever stove in. Muck covered the doorstep. A finely-carved stone keystone that topped a brick arch over the door indicated the alleyway was once a better place.

When Compeyson removed his kid gloves and knocked daintily on the door, Magwitch laughed, nudged him aside, and pounded on the door with his fist. One of the men on the cobblestones groaned, tried to push himself aright with an arm, but fell back to the stones.

The door cracked open, revealing an eye under a handkerchief tied around a head and worn as a cap. A guard, whose voice was abrupt. "Who are you?"

"Customers."

"I ain't seen you before. Get lost."

When Compeyson flicked a finger, Magwitch launched himself at the door. The door shot back on its hinges and smashed into the fellow who lurched backward and fell to the floor. Magwitch rushed over the threshold and into the room, Compeyson laughing lightly as he followed him.

A man as bald as a buzzard rose from a drafting table, his mouth making a perfect zero, and his gaze dashing between the fallen doorman and Magwitch. His hand moved toward a drawer.

Magwitch said in his pavement voice, "Don't you touch that drawer."

The man's hand stopped, indecision on his face.

"If you open that drawer,"— Magwitch crossed the room toward him— "I'll turn your hand to kindling."

The man wore wire-rimmed spectacles and an ink-stained white cravat. His shirt sleeves were stained so deeply that the cloth—white at his shoulders—was India blue at the cuffs, the blue fading farther up the sleeves. He had the face of an amanuensis; narrow with a weak chin, lips that formed an uncertain line, and a high, blank forehead. The skin on his face was as white as flax. Leather braces held up his trousers. A blue-stained Newmarket coat was draped over the back of his chair.

He said in a voice as high as nature ever allowed, "If you are here to rob me, you are more foolish than you look. Nothing here is worth more than a farthing."

The fellow on the floor rolled to his knees, one hand at his nose, which bled profusely, dappling his arm and the floor. He groaned, then sat heavily on the floor, fingers pinching his nose to stop the flow.

"You misjudge my intention, sir," Samuel Compeyson said.

"My door has been flung open, a beast has charged in, and my man has been sent to the floor with a shattered nose, and I misjudge your intentions?"

Compeyson said, "Had I tipped the civil at your doorway, I would have been turned away."

Stained brown from smoke, an intricately carved plaster ceiling was overhead. A wrought-iron candelabra hosting fifty lit candles hung low over the drafting table, leaving just enough clearance between it and the table for a human head. The table was awash in light. Against a wall a cabinet contained stacks of paper.

"The reason for your visit, then," the man said. "Be concise, and then be off with you." He retrieved a wig from a drawer and placed it on his head. One side of it was singed where he may have bent too near a candle.

"I need a baptismal record."

"You have confused me with a priest, sir."

Bottles of ink cluttered a side table, and on a bench near a back window was a cast iron book press and a long-handled perforating machine. Printers' boxes with wood spacers were stacked in a corner. Punches, dies, bodkins, and tweezers filled a display rack, and a composing stick and distribution box contained lead and wood types. Dozens of quill pens were aligned on the top of a galley cabinet.

Compeyson stepped to an iron printing press and turned the handwheel which rose on the central screw bringing up the platen. "Mr. Tilley, I also need a letter of introduction signed by Baron Montrose.

"The baron is often at the Travelers' Club on Pall Mall. Why don't you inquire of him there?"

"And a passport and several other documents."

The man—Tilley—cast a gaze at Magwitch, then at the drawer, where doubtless he stored a weapon. "How is it you know my name?"

"Not many people do." Compeyson nodded at his own words. "Am I right? It's Tilley."

Blood still flowing from his nose, the guard managed to rise to his knees. His stare was vacant, and he may not have yet gathered his wits.

A piratical grin on his face, Magwitch placed a boot on the guard's shoulder, and shoved him over. "Stay down there."

"We have the same profession," Compeyson said, "though your circle of acquaintances is more rarified than is mine. And I require four other documents, all of them foolproof to discerning eyes." Compeyson withdrew a folded piece of paper from his coat pocket and passed it to Tilley. "Kindly read this message."

A draft passed through the room, and the candles guttered. Magwitch lifted an engraving burin from a shelf, and appeared to study the point but flicked his eyes toward the guard as if he hoped the man would try again to rise from the floor.

Tilley looked up from the paper. "You know Simon the Quill?"

"I count him among my close friends."

"How many fingers does he have?"

Compeyson smiled. "He is missing two fingers on his left hand."

"How do you know him?" Tilley asked.

"We occasionally engage in a hand of cards."

Tilley snorted. "Simon the Quill would wager his mother on a game of piquet."

"He and I share an affection for the cards, I must admit."

"And Simon the Quill is a penniless fool as a result. I hope you fare better at the tables."

Compeyson brushed a shoulder of his coat.

"Simon was my cellmate for three years at Millbank just after it opened." Tilley withdrew a rag from a drawer and tossed it to his guard.

The guard sniffed loudly and held the cloth to his nose.

"Simon the Quill says you are the best artist in England," Compeyson said.

Tilley lowered himself to the rush-bottomed chair behind the drafting desk. "If by artist you mean *forger,* he is correct. The next time I'm nicked I'll be sent to New Holland."

"He said you can ink the Magna Carta on a grain of rice."

The forger pulled a bank note from a drawer and handed it to Compeyson, who brought it up to his eyes, turning so the candelabra light caught it in full.

"A five-pound note from the Town and County of Poole Bank." Compeyson gripped the bill with his fingers to loudly snap it. "You created this?"

"I carved the seal this past week, and yesterday that note was a blank piece of paper, and the inks were in those bottles over there."

Compeyson whistled. "You could walk right up to a Threadneedle clerk with this note and ask for change. I hope I may hire you, sir."

"My place of work is located in this festering pesthole because the law does not visit these streets." Tilley spread his hands. "I'm as safe here as if I were on the moon. But my presence in this feculent neighborhood should not lead you think that I work on the cheap."

Compeyson lifted a leather pouch from a pocket and pushed it across the drafting table.

Tilley shook the pouch, his ear cocked toward it. Then he loosened the string to peer inside. "For those documents, this is a fraction of my fee. There isn't even enough for earnest money here. The very best is dear, whether we are speaking of a beaver hat or documents I create."

Magwitch found a chair, placed it next to the guard—whose nose had stopped bleeding—and lowered himself into it.

Compeyson smoothed an eyebrow with a finger. "I will toss dice with you for the fee. Double or nothing. A game of hazard."

"Life among Old Nichol's squalor is a sufficient gamble for me. I do not touch cards or dice." Tilley adjusted his wig. "You come here asking for my products but without the funds to pay for them. Kindly remove yourself from my place of business, sir." He waved his ink-stained hand toward Magwitch. "And take your escort with you."

His lower lip caught in his teeth, Compeyson stared at an iron press. Then his eyes found the forger again. "I'll make you a partner. Twenty percent of my gain in return for your work."

"What is your name?" Tilley asked.

"Samuel Compeyson. Sometimes it's Beecker. Or Randolph. And it could be Farquhar. Depends on what the wind blows in."

"Compeyson?" The forger leaned forward in his chair. "You were involved with the brewer in Kent, I've heard. Havisham Brothers Brewery, and the daughter of the place. That was you?"

"Six thousand pounds in my pocket before they knew the time of day." Compeyson's smile was wintry. "A fine piece of business, if I may say."

"You left the young lady at the altar on her wedding day?"

"For six thousand, I'd leave Joan of Arc tied to her post."

"And where is that six thousand? With that kind of money, you should have come to my office and placed cash on the nail. None of this trifling with a few coins in a pouch."

"Money does not stay with me for any length of time."

Tilley asked, "Aaron Jockle up in Newcastle created your paperwork, is that what I heard? Why aren't you working with him again?"

Compeyson looked toward the ceiling, as if searching for words. "He and I had difficulties."

"Jockle is a friend of mine, and I'll tell you what happened." Tilley leaned forward in his chair. "You cheated him. You paid him with a note, and after your success with the Havishams, you refused to pay the debt."

127

"By the time I saw Jockle again, I had lost the money, all 6,000 pounds. I didn't have it to pay him."

"You lost it?"

"Some at cards, some at the track," Compeyson said. "You know how it is."

"I know nothing of the sort. Life is a sufficient gamble, without fooling with cards or the horses. I never touch cards, and I wouldn't know a horse from a mule. The fact remains: you didn't pay Jockle for the forgeries he created for you."

Compeyson shrugged.

Tilley surveyed Compeyson, up and down. "Who is your new pigeon?"

"The Wilkinson family. I'm already in with one of the daughters."

Tilley smiled. "And why not aim high?" He moved his fingers as if calculating on them. "Twenty five percent, sir. And listen closely. Aaron Jockle is a meek soul but I am not. You have my promise that should you fail to pay me my share, I will hunt you down, and you'll never have another day of peace, with me after you. And your thug here,"—he motioned toward Magwitch—"won't be able to save you."

Compeyson rubbed his chin. Then he nodded.

The forger pointed at another chair. "Sit down and tell me precisely what you require

14

"It was a desperate struggle, sir," Jeffrey Beals said. "And precarious, with a doubtful outcome, and I don't mind admitting to a touch of fear during the skirmish." Beals sat in a leather chair, and with manifest satisfaction brushed invisible crumbs from his trousers.

"But you bettered him?" Sir Clarence Keegan asked.

A red cravat highlighted Beals's black velvet jacket. He held up his right hand. Dressing covered the stump of the little finger. "I paid a price for my actions, as you can see. A dire price as I had been considering taking up the violin. Now I must consign that ambition to the dustbin. And the bruise on my forehead"—he pointed—"was acquired just before I served him out."

Sir Clarence asked, "The woman didn't see the attacker coming up behind her?"

A withered old husk almost entirely hidden under the buggy blanket kept by the club for his use, Sir Clarence shivered even on hot days. The chair's leather wings framed his head, above which wisps of his gray hair floated like gnats. The mottled skin of his face had shrunk, leaving him with a crow's beak for a nose and ovoid eyes. Sir Clarence's profound frailty suggested that were he to sneeze he would launch himself into eternity.

"She was oblivious to her pending doom, sir, with the footpad stalking her from behind, his club upraised, about to smash in her skull. And this was in front of my place of business, mind you."

Clyde Stuyvesant was a member in good standing of the Herald Club despite his suspiciously Dutch heritage. He leaned toward Beals. "And you ran toward him?"

Beals shuddered as if remembering the moment. "What else would an Englishman do, a subject of his majesty George IV? I will remind you that earlier in my life I was close to purchasing a commission in the 7th Dragoon

129

Guards. Yes, I dashed across the cobblestones, yelling a warning, and swinging my umbrella, charging at the hoodlum."

Stuyvesant nodded. "Indeed, any Englishman would have done the same. It is our duty to womankind." His dark hair had been scraped back along his head and kept in place with glistening pomade. His face was round and yellow, resembling the moon. Lost in the flesh of his face, his eyes were pinpricks, and his rosebud mouth appeared always about to dribble spit.

"The spirit of King Arthur's Round Table filled me as I rushed the ruffian." Beals balled his hands. "And remember, I was armed only with a folded umbrella, not an axe or halberd."

Beals's listeners stared fixedly at him, Sir Clarence swinging his hand as if he himself wielded the umbrella.

"The villain was a giant, at least six-feet five, with a coal miner's huge arms, and black beady eyes. He was only two yards from his lady victim when he heard me shout, and he turned my direction, and withdrew a dagger from his trousers."

"I thought you said he had a club," Stuyvesant said.

"He had both, a dagger in one hand and a club in another." Beals inhaled deeply, apparently trying to calm himself as he related the tale. "Two weapons notwithstanding, he hadn't foreseen the storm of violence that was about to descend on him."

The Herald Club had been on St. James since the English court spoke French, it was believed. The club was a hideout from the cares of the world, a place where one could go when troubled that one's eldest sibling was going to inherit or that the vessel *Hampshire* was two months late and so Lloyd's might call names, or that one might not have sufficient time to draft a toast for Lady Oulander's dinner Friday evening. The club's oak paneled library— where Jeffrey Beals relayed his encounter—contained a gimbaled globe, a monstrously tall pendulum clock, oil portraits of racing horses, chairs covered in Cadiz leather, and carpets so thick that shoes disappeared. The library had everything except books.

"And I was on him, savagely swinging my umbrella, it singing through the air, but he parried it with his club, and tried to stab me with the dagger." Beals lifted his hands so that they framed the scene. "But I dodged the blade, and thrust the umbrella point at his sternum then pounded his face with my fist, and I'm confident my ring knocked out several of his teeth."

"What about the poor woman?"

"She cowered against the building's wall, pleading, 'Help me, sir. Help me,' which urged me on to a transcendent effort. I swung my fists, one after another, a veritable cannonade." Beals swung at the air.

Other men in the room drifted closer from the newspaper rack and trays of nuts and olives. One carried a crystal tumbler and another a copy of the *Morning Chronicle.*

"I pummeled him—pow, pow—again and again. His nose snapped beneath my blows. And he whimpered and cried, a disgraceful display, something you'd hear in Ireland."

"Bravo," Stuyvesant said, "Just what I would have done."

"And your finger?" Sir Clarence asked.

Beals majestically raised his wounded hand. "I now possess on this hand only as many fingers as a fox has toes on a foot, which is to say, four. And I am reluctant to receive a hero's acclaim, as anyone would have done what I did." He firmed his jaw and lifted his chin, Wellington at Waterloo. "Almost unconscious, beaten and humiliated, the blackguard swung the dagger—a huge hissing blade—at the woman in an act of desperate revenge."

The gentlemen leaned toward Beals, nodding, mouths pursed, vast approval and admiration writ in their expressions.

The fellow with the tumbler said, "Nothing less than manly, Beals."

"I saw instantly that her time on earth was about to expire." Beals held his maimed hand high. "And that this hideous creature was going to exact revenge on this poor woman who—let me add—was the very picture of feminine frailty and submissiveness, an exemplar for women across our isle."

"And then?" Stuyvesant asked.

"You drag the story out of me, sir." Beals closed his eyes a moment in submission to the will of his friends. "The dagger came down, aimed at her heart, and I thrust out my hand to intercede, and the blade slashed through skin and tendon and bone, and my finger fell to the ground."

"It must have hurt," Sir Clarence said.

"A sagacious observation, sir," Beals said. "Indeed, it was a considerable sting. And the villain—wobbly, contusions on his face purpling, gasping for air, desperate to escape my wrath—snatched up my severed finger and the five-carat diamond ring that graced it and fled, howling in fear and pain."

"Hear, hear, Beals," Clyde Stuyvesant said.

A murmur of admiration filled the library, and Beals leaned back in his chair as it washed over him.

He said, "The stone in that ring was a gift from the sultan of Madrass to my parents. Marie Antoinette herself would have been envious of it."

"Why, there you are, sir." A voice from the door. A woman's voice. "Your doorman tried to stop me and then so did a fellow in a fancy green coat but here I am." A voice both alluring and vulgar.

She swept into the room, a young lady whose lips were as red as poppies and with so much rouge on her cheeks they looked bruised. Her eyes were held in place by eyeliner of a quantity suggesting it had been applied with a trowel. Her bust line was low and her dress revealed her ankles, an unspeakable breach had she been a lady of quality, though there was no suggestion of that about her.

Jaws dropped and eyes widened. Then the men who had gathered around Beals stepped back, turning their faces away, making themselves smaller, perhaps trying not to be recognized. Faces burned, gazes were averted, throats were cleared. A deathly pall swept into the library.

Any woman—much less a tart—in the Herald Club's library was outrageous, an unprecedented slap in John Bull's face. This woman's appearance at this august gentlemen's club represented the receding tide and the waning of the moon. The English had been invaded by the Normans and the Vikings and the Saxons, well and good, but this woman's presence at the club simply could not be accommodated. Two millennia of civilization tossed aside because the doorman could not keep this wretched spectacle from entering the club. It was the end of times. There would be no suet for the pudding.

"Jeffrey," she said with a volume sufficient to carry her words to every corner of the library, "I was told you are here every afternoon, and Madam Arabella wanted me to return your ring to you as soon as possible." With a flourish, she held up Jeffrey Beals's diamond ring.

Beal violently shook his head. "No, I . . . ."

"I'm Nancy," she said. "Nancy Argyle? You remember me, I'm sure. Three nights ago?" Her accent revealed she had been born close to the Bow Bells.

Jeffrey Beals's face turned the color of a beetroot. "Who are you?" He had lowered his voice but it was amplified by contrast with the dead still room. "For the love of God, I don't know you."

She patted his shoulder. "Sure, you do, big fellow. And here is your ring." She held it up for all to see—a massive diamond set in gold—then lowered it to his palm. "Madam Arabella asks you to forgive Abbas, our guard. He thought you were leaving our house without settling your account."

"What are you talking about?" Beals tried to rise from his chair but fell back, perhaps burdened by her sheer impudence.

"And he is wild with the dagger, him being Arabian and everything."

A butler in tails rushed into the room. "Young lady, please . . . ."

Nancy added, "And Madam Arabella never thought of keeping the ring, you being such a good patron. We had a little trouble pulling the severed finger out of the ring but then we used a leather punch."

The butler grabbed Nancy's elbow, and a waiter hurried into the library to help.

"I tried to save the finger to return it to you, too, but Maxey got it. Usually, we keep him chained up outside the front door. You know how he is. Dogs can't be trusted."

"You will leave immediately." The butler's words were drenched in strychnine.

He and the waiter pulled Nancy toward the door, none too gently, her scent of roses following her, so thick it was putrid. She winked at a club member who was fleeing the library. Nancy and her escorts disappeared through the door.

Jeffrey Beals placed his hands on the chair arms, and made to rise. He fell back. He tried again, and this time could come to his full height. Sir Clarence stared up at Beals, having bunched much of his blanket in his hands. Stuyvesant wiggled against the back of his chair as if attempting to merge with it.

Beals gripped his chair. "This is a disgrace." His voice was fogged. "I have no idea who that . . . that person was. I have never seen her before." He looked around the room, turning a circle like a capstan. "I don't know her, I tell you."

He was speaking mostly to himself. Stuyvesant rose from his chair to help Sir Clarence, and they too left the room. The library had emptied. Beals's only company was the grainy light that made it through the heavy curtains.

He rubbed his face with his good hand, then sank back into the chair.

* * * *

Miss Havisham laughed, and then caught herself. Standing on the pavement guffawing at someone else's humiliation was unseemly, certainly. She laughed again. "What did he look like when you handed him the ring?"

Nancy Argyle said, "He was all a-fluster. And all his friends looked at him as if he had the pox—your pardon—and then they scooted away, leaving the room as fast as if it were on fire."

Fagin shook his head. "What nonsense, Miss Havisham." He glanced around, perhaps searching for the police. His coat was so big he could almost disappear in it. He had shaved again that morning and had run a comb through his brick-colored hair.

"It was well-deserved and long overdue," Miss Havisham said. "The Bealses have been snubbing the Havishams for a generation. We are nothing but brewers, after all, which is somewhere below rope makers in the universal order of things." She laughed again. "And I've discovered I have a taste for vengeance."

A breeze moved along the street, ruffling the swansdown that trimmed her neckline. On Fagin's advice she had left her diamond bracelet at home. "Too many toolers on the street near a whorehouse, waiting for wealthy drunks to come out, Miss Havisham."

Fagin, Nancy, and Miss Havisham stood in front of Madam Arabella's place of business, the Green Park Gentleman's Club, a pleasant walk from the Herald Club. Corinthian columns fronted the club's four-story building, and above the door was a leaded glass fanlight. Hackney coaches were parked at the curb. Leather harnesses creaked and horses whinnied. A basket balanced on her head, a flower girl walked by, offering carnations. A meat pie salesman with a wood box hanging from his neck called out for customers. The fog was lifting, and a gauzy moon was revealed. The sound of a bottle shattering came from down the street, along with men's laughter. An ash-gray dog hurried past.

Miss Havisham gave the girl several coins. "Here you are, Nancy. A job superbly done."

Nancy's rouge and eyeliner were less pronounced in the night, and she was more alluring and less hard. Her lips were full and her smile gentle and free of the trade. And despite the slashes of eyeliner her canted blue eyes hinted at humor and sympathy.

Miss Havisham asked, "How old are you?"

"Fifteen or sixteen. I'm from Dorset."

"How did you . . . .? Miss Havisham wanted to learn how Nancy had found herself as a prostitute on the street but could not find the words. She managed with, "How did you end up here?'

"Why, I walked." The girl smiled. "It only took me a week, not too bad for being barefoot."

"But your parents?"

"I have three brothers and two sisters. My mother couldn't feed us all so the eldest had to go, and I'm the oldest. She wanted to buy a pair of shoes for me but didn't have the money. I made it here fine, though. Dust in my hair, is all."

"Your father?"

Nancy shrugged.

Miss Havisham gestured toward the women sauntering up and down the sidewalk, moving their hips more than was required for propulsion. "But why this?

"I was hungry, missus."

"Why do you work outside instead of a place like Madam Arabella's?"

"I ain't fine enough."

"That's ridiculous." Miss Havisham said. "My Lord, you are very pretty."

"Not for long, though," Fagin said. "She won't be recognizable in five years."

Miss Havisham elbowed Fagin. "Hush, you."

"What should I do, sir? Become a barrister?" Nancy laughed. Her smile was large and bright, with more teeth than most. "I know: I'll get elected to parliament."

Fagin turned away, and his gaze followed two laughing and swaying stags in top hats as they climbed the steps to Miss Arabella's door. One gestured grandly, inviting the other to enter first. An immense guard in Turkish dress opened the door from the inside, and the two young men went into the club. Cigar smoke and string quartet music drifted out.

"How does a girl out here . . . invite a customer?" Miss Havisham asked, then added with haste, "Out of curiosity and nothing else."

"Like this." Nancy gripped her frock at the thigh and lifted the hem a foot off the pavement. "It can mean only one thing."

"I must have been raised in a convent." Miss Havisham took out a calling card from her reticule and handed it to the girl. "This is my name and where I live, Satis House near Rochester in Kent."

"Why would you give me this, missus?"

Miss Havisham hesitated. "I don't know. Keep it. Maybe we'll meet again."

Nancy asked, "Mr. Fagin, do you know Bill who found me and brought me to the Herald Club?"

Fagin looked at the girl, half closing one eye as if siting down a muzzle loader's barrel. "My dear, you stay away from Bill Sikes."

"He seemed nice."

"I gave him half a guinea to find such a person as you, and you are the one he found, and that's all there is to it, and other than doing errands for me he is a worthless drunk and bruiser, and will visit only ruination on any women who becomes acquainted with him. Bill even made his mother suffer, as she died giving him birth."

Nancy said, "He's handsome, isn't he?"

Fagin stared at her as if she'd grown another nose. "Are we speaking of the same Bill Sikes? He washes his face once a month but it's usually covered in so much grime I can't detect his features. That grubby fellow?"

"As we walked along, he smiled and took my arm."

Fagin shook his head so fiercely his cheeks flapped. "That slight amount of civility shouldn't deceive you. He is a rogue and there is no help for him."

She spread her hands. "I thought maybe . . . ."

"There are better men out there, even for a working girl."

Miss Havisham put a hand on Nancy's arm. "Goodbye. Take care of yourself."

The girl curtsied, and turned away, drifting off down the street, looking left and right, perhaps for patrons.

Miss Havisham said, "I feel sorry for her."

"Hundreds of those girls arrive in London every day. Feeling sorry for one doesn't change her lot or that of any of the others."

He guided Miss Havisham around a young man in a green tailcoat who counted the gold sovereigns in his hand and glanced at Madam Arabella's. Then they walked around a fellow prone on the walkway, his limbs arrayed as he were on the rack, vomit on his cravat and his top hat beside him.

Miss Havisham asked, "Are you taking me to dinner, Mr. Fagin?"

The pickpocket stopped as if caught in a snare. "Taking you to dinner?"

"It's dinner time, and here we are together." Perhaps there was a message in her smile.

Fagin cleared his throat. "Well, of course." He rubbed his hands together as if washing them. "Here we are. Together."

"Bitts' Coffee House is around the corner. Venison and a glass of port would do nicely."

They resumed walking, Miss Havisham gripping Fagin's elbow.

"And do not be concerned, sir." Her voice carried much amusement. "You've said you never pay for anything. I will take care of the bill of fare."

He moved more assuredly.

She added, "Provided you promise not to steal the silverware."

15

"Kindly do not accost me daily with these failures," Vincent Crummles said in his foggy voice, always so hoarse it would scarcely answer his call. "I am not a carpenter or a painter."

"I cannot go on without the Roman column behind me." Thomas Lenville was in the costume of a Roman senator with a flowing white robe, gold belt, and crimson sash. Too small, the crown precariously balanced on his head. The troupe did not possess Roman sandals so straps had been painted on his bare feet. He said, "The audience must sink into the dream, and with no column, no Rome, no play."

Crummles' intonation was of vast and pained patience. "You will recall, Thomas, that the column was painted over for our production of *Virtue Forgotten* when we needed that canvas for the depiction of the guillotine. You played the doomed Monsieur LeBeaux yourself, and it was just two days ago."

Lenville's magisterially large nose dominated his face, hiding his mouth in shadow. He seldom removed all his stage makeup, and so his face suffered a sickly pallor. The troupe's seamstress had to take in all his costumes, and he was so remarkably thin he was occasionally mistaken for a harbinger of famine.

He rose to his full height. "I cannot work under these conditions."

"So you've said." Crummles pointed at the actor's neck. "You still have black paint behind your ear from last night. You were superb. *Old Scratch and the Hounds* has never had a better kennel."

Lenville sniffed. "I do not like playing a dog."

"Your voice has the ideal timbre for barking." Crummles patted the actor's shoulder. "Next week you'll be Father Time, with a dramatic entrance and many lines, and a gray beard and a scepter. The role will send you to Drury Lane."

Even though it was late in the afternoon and London's allotment of sunlight tried its hardest, darkness suffused the theater. The curtain was open but little was visible beyond the stage apron. Kerosene lamps threw uncertain yellow light across the stage. At the side of the stage the wig rack was stored next to a ship's wheel, a prop for *On Deck with the Captain and the Countess.*

"Father Time calls for no more acting skill than is required from a barnyard gate," Lenville said. "At least, do we have a scepter?"

"Use a curtain rod. Paint it gold." Crummles was a skilled mollifier, and spent much of his day at the task. He nodded toward the side of the stage. "When did she get here?"

"Several minutes ago."

Crummles drew his hand along his mouth. He crossed the stage to the wing where his new actor, Ambrose Franks, grinned at the heiress Anna Wilkinson, and leaned toward her, gesturing in a manner Crummles recognized from last evening's performance, when Franks had played a harlequin in *The Queen's Blush,* one of Crummles' better efforts at playwriting. Franks must've been showing her his stage gestures. She laughed and playfully tapped his arm.

In a rector's voice Crummles said, "You have taken to the theater, Miss Wilkinson. Here you are again."

"I don't know much about the stage." She smiled. "I'm learning."

"I'm confident Mr. Ambrose here"—Crummles gestured toward Ambrose as if he needed identifying, standing two feet from her—"can teach you much about the stage, having been an actor for two days now."

Ambrose said, "You yourself, sir, have told me I have a flair for it." Mother of pearl buttons dotted his green waistcoat, and his shining top boots had been newly blackened.

Crummles smiled crookedly. "Miss Wilkinson, your governess usually accompanies you. Where is she this afternoon?"

The young lady gestured in a small way. "She is at Providence Milliners near the Monument."

"Does she know you are here?"

She replied, "She does not, sir."

"Does she suspect you are here?" Crummles asked.

"Forgive me, Mr. Crummles, but you are not my minder." Her voice carried the authority of inherited wealth and position.

Crummles' face hardened. "Very well, then."

"All my life my chaperones have been vigilant and clever." She laughed from the back of her throat. "But not this time."

Her hair was the color of chocolate, a few curls showing but most hidden under a satin bonnet held in place with a red ribbon tied under her chin. Her eyes were the same hue as her hair and were cheerfully angled in her skull so that they would always contradict a frown. Her chin was notched below lips that had a delightful Cupid's bow. Black velvet bindings and gold lace trim adorned her green Polanese coat. Diamonds on her silver bracelet flickered. Her ear studs were rubies, and not small ones.

Stage manager Crummles clasped his hands behind his back. "May I offer you advice, then. Watch yourself carefully in this neighborhood and . . . indeed in this theater."

She smiled at him. "I will be as alert as the King's Guards, sir."

Crummles turned away, straightening his spine to make his retreat as dignified as possible. In his performance costume of silk tights and a checkered shirt, the Polish mime Bronislaw Pukowsliski entertained the Infant Phenomenon—in her spotted leopard costume—by pretending to pull a rope. The mime's first name couldn't be separated from his last name by anyone in the troupe so they all called him Puck.

The Phenomenon was the only female in the troupe who didn't unabashedly stare at Ambrose Franks. Near the backdrop for *Havoc in the Harem* Mrs. Snevellicci pretended to darn a stocking, her eyes riveted on the fellow. Her daughter, the fine actress Miss Snevellicci, had begun to assemble the breakaway wall for tonight's performance of *Earthquake in Lisbon* but she too gaped at the fellow. In her beaver bonnet and brown pelisse, and sitting on a stool near the Venice backdrop for *The Doge's Daughter*, Mrs. Grudden thumbed a prompt book, her gaze locked on Franks.

A contumacious power was loose here, the work of a mesmerist. Crummles had never before clapped his eyes on the likes of Ambrose Franks, a fellow who could turn women's heads so fast that the bones in their necks crackled. And women never left a room as long as Franks was still in it. Any feeble pretext would do to remain, and often they circled closer and closer. These past two nights the audience had to be ushered out at the end of the performance, Crummles and Lenville fairly shoving the anchored ladies toward the door.

It was more than Franks's handsomeness. The tragedian Thomas Lenville was handsome provided he shaved twice a day and so wasn't overcome by swarthiness. The troupe's magician, the Inimitable Irish Aengus—whose most inimitable trick was coughing up a writhing eel—drew admiring glances from females. And, yes. Crummles contentedly admitted, no mirror wailed in agony when he himself stood before it. But all of this was on a different plane than Ambrose Franks.

Beauty is power. Crummles eyed Franks and Anna Wilkinson as they leaned toward each other: Franks's ash-blond hair—a tightly curled crop of it—his scimitar nose, skin as flawless as chamois, the shockingly blue eyes, the perfectly shaped head. His pulchritudinous made him glow, an irresistible target for feminine gazes, the intensity of which verged on lunatic gawking.

And there was more. Franks paid a woman utter attention, as if everyone else had fallen off the edge of the world, and as if he alone could understand her feelings. Nothing was more flattering. He lavished this attention on the Wilkinson girl. She was nineteen years old, an age where many young women have not learned by cruel elicitation to arm themselves. Pretending to study the pulleys and blocks on the rafters, Crummles drifted closer to them.

"I couldn't possibly introduce you to my parents," Anna said. "An actor? Father would have a seizure, and mother has a plan to introduce me to Baron Gillam's eldest son. And, besides, father is in Hamburg purchasing a boiler for his mill."

"I am acting in this theater simply to amuse myself. I'm not really an actor." Franks touched the back of her hand. "My dad wants me to return to Southampton to learn to manage the yard. I'm putting it off as long as I can."

"What sort of a yard?

"Our shipyard. Nothing fancy, nothing for the navy. We build coast traders. The Norwegians are our largest customers, so they can service the fiord towns." Compeyson smiled. "I said 'we,' as if I had much to do with the firm now. I'm travelling and enjoying myself when I can. But father wants me to get involved. Once a week dad tells me, 'Someday it'll be yours.'"

"You'll return to Southampton?" she asked.

"You are here in London." He shrugged. "Why would I return to Hampshire?"

She demurely lowered her head without losing sight of him. "Oh, you."

Vincent Crummles studied the stage's spike marks; his ear turned toward Franks. Perhaps Crummles' stealth wasn't needed. Franks spoke in a voice he used on stage, one meant to be heard. Not loudly but rather with penetration, an actor's skill. Crummles easily heard him, as likely so did Mrs. Grudden and the other women on the stage. Near the side wall Puck the Pole was teaching the Infant Phenomenon how to juggle. Thomas Lenville stared into a hand-held looking glass, moving his lips, practicing the gamut of his expressions.

"And just look at this." Franks pulled a letter from his pocket and unfolded it. "It's from my father, and it announces that he is reducing my monthly allowance from 300 to 250 pounds." He gave her the letter.

Anna rubbed the letter between her thumb and finger, perchance assessing the paper's crasis, then held it up to catch the light from a wall sconce. "Elegant handwriting."

"My father doesn't write his own letters. He has a scrivener for such things. Father talks, and it gets written."

She pursed her lips. "How will you live on 250 pounds a month?"

"How does anyone?"

In her painting apron Miss Gazingi appeared next to the canvas backdrop for *The Reckoning of the Venetian Vixen.* She nodded at Franks's question. Crummles grimaced. The Crummles family made do with fifteen pounds a month, and those were the good months.

"Maybe you should sell a few of your ponies," Anna suggested to Franks. "You can only ride one of them at once."

"Anna, where are you?" The voice from the front of the theater sounded like steam escaping. "Is that you?"

Anna's hand shot to her mouth. "It's my governess, Mrs. Truly." She turned as if to flee but stopped, and brought her shoulders back. "She's a dog on a scent, and will hunt me down, doesn't matter where I go."

The so-named Mrs. Truly rushed between benches toward the stage. 'What would your mother say, you alone in this tawdry place." As she reached the stage, she glanced at Crummles and then at Mrs. Snevellicci. "And among these people. Miscreants and knaves, one and all."

She wore gray gloves, a faded green bonnet, and an umber coat. A woman of a magnificent circumference, she pushed the air creating a draft as she charged toward her ward.

Her voice sounded like two stones grinding together. "Your father is going to push me into one of his boilers if he hears about this." She grabbed Anna's wrist. "And you, Anna, are the reason he gets up each morning, and you bringing shame on the family by traipsing around with . . . with actors, the lowest of the low and the basest of the base."

"Mrs. Truly, please." Anna glanced at Franks, whose face was carefully deadpan.

"Please, nothing." She dragged Anna down the steps and along the aisle toward the theater's front door. "Among all of these wicked devils, Anna. How could you possibly do worse?"

As she was hustled out, Anna threw a kiss at Ambrose Franks, a wide grin on her face. He sent a kiss back.

Mrs. Grudden hurried over to Mrs. Snevellicci perhaps to discuss what they had just witnessed. Likely knowing he would be their topic. Franks excused himself with a half-bow, and stepped around the backdrops toward the theater's rear door.

"Thomas, let's read your lines," Crummles said.

"I have very few lines in this production," Lenville said. "A paltry few."

"I have enough to think about without entertaining your grievances, young man." Crummles smiled to take the sting out of the words. He looked again toward the theater's front door through which Anna Wilkinson and her governess had just disappeared. "Much to think about."

* * * *

FAGIN & MISS HAVISHAM

Samuel Compeyson-Ambrose Franks on this day was in the guise of Giles Stoddard, wearing a gas blue coat, double-milled kersey pantaloons, brilliantly white neckerchief, and glittering pumps. Suspended from his fob were a dazzling array of seals and gewgaws, and a ruby stickpin adorned his lapel. His silk top hat could not be faulted.

He stepped down from the hackney-coach and tumbled over a bootblack boy who was plying his services at the curb. Stoddard missed the pavement with his foot, and caught the boy as a counterbalance, tipping over the blacking box. The boy cried out and seized Stoddard's coat. Stoddard grunted but grabbed the boy by the shirt collar, and the little fellow didn't fall to the ground. They both straightened themselves. Stoddard vigorously dusted his coat as if he had skidded along the pavement.

"Beg your pardon, your honor." The boy touched the brim of his cap. He came up to Stoddard's breastbone, and wore a dingy wool sweater. His hair stuck out from under the cap, making him resemble a sweep's brush.

'Nothing to it, boy." Stoddard shot his cuffs. "I have survived."

"Put the gleam on your trotters for you, sir?"

"I never allow them to become scuffed, and if this is your way of obtaining customers— feigned clumsiness as your victim alights from a coach—you have failed." Stoddard left the lad, walking toward the track's gate.

A line of coaches and gigs unburdened themselves of passengers. Armorial flags rippled in the wind above the track's tack room. Muffin-men peddled their goods, and blue ruin was sold in corked bottles. High clouds drifted overhead, casting the track in shadow and then sunlight, and a breeze carried the scent of the stables. Gravel sounding under his feet, Stoddard crossed the yard, nodding at two women under a parasol and passing sailors in their clubbed pigtails and blue frock coats. He went through the gate and made his way past bookmakers—bent over their pencils and paper pads—and their punters. Owners and trainers led horses from the stables toward the track. Laughter and chatter came from all directions.

Compeyson-Franks-Stoddard entered the tack room through the door wide enough to accommodate jockeys carrying saddles. The room was the center of the track's conviviality. Horse owners bragged about lineage and placed wagers. Some owners would ride their own mounts, and others had hired jockeys who milled about in the tack room, talking with each other about their duties for the day. Friends and spongers loitered near the buffet table, provided by the coal magnate Sir Alfred Fuller whose horse *Sussex Sire* would run that day. Saddles, bridles, bits, harnesses, and stirrups hung from wall pegs and racks and stands. The room smelled of leather and tobacco and was boisterous.

But less so in the back of the tack room where card players were arranged around two Pembroke tables near a door that led to the grain room. The game was always here on race days, and was often attended by those who had

142

nothing to do with horse racing. These men were in earnest, and the jollity in the rest of the room was absent. Stoddard smiled at the gentlemen at a table with an empty chair.

"Back for more?" asked a fellow who sat so erectly he might have had a fireplace poker for a spine. He laughed. "Have we taught you nothing?"

"My losses at this table may have seemed significant to you, sir." Stoddard settled onto a chair. "You, a half-pay captain without a ship."

"We'll see how deep your pockets are today, Mr. Stoddard," the captain replied. "I suspect I'll find the bottoms of them."

As a lieutenant Claude Dalton had served under John Talbot in *HMS Victorious* when it took the French battleship *Rivoli*. Dalton had been ferocious on navy cutting out expeditions, and as a result wore a saber scar— an angry ridge of purple flesh—diagonally across his forehead. His jaw was large and uncompromising, and the skin on his face had been tanned to leather in the Mediterranean. His head looked as hard as a door knocker. His waistcoat was the color of mustard and his navy-blue cravat was tied precisely. He was the eldest son of Baron Dalton, whose estate in Somerset a bird could not fly over in a day were it inclined to try.

"Gentleman, I didn't come here today to talk," said a man with the figure of an apple, his epic belly pushing against the table. "Had I wanted conversation I would have stayed at home. My wife can talk the wool off a sheep." Lawrence Alder's face was so crimson it appeared he shaved with a wood plane. His red adipose nose was the shape of a cricket ball and looked about to burst, which along with his fat red cheeks lent him a jovial appearance entirely at odds with his merciless handling of those businesses that had challenged his Alder & Sons Ship Chandlery. His warehouses in London and Portsmouth provided Alder a gusher of Royal Navy and East India Company money.

Green wood markers were in front of each card player. Outside the tack room a horse neighed.

Alder made a display of flexing his fingers as if to loosen them to rake in the wagers that might come his way, then nimbly shuffled the cards. Yellow and red court jesters danced on the cards' backs.

He announced grandly, "My markers are good and my money is ready to back them."

The captain smiled narrowly. "You sound fond of your money and markers, Mr. Alder. It will be difficult for you to part with them today."

The fourth gambler at the table was a gentleman not known in horse circles but who had played in the tack room several times, his wins and losses about even but he was a skilled player and bold with his wagers. He was as heavily bearded as a Dutch bargeman, with squirrel tail eyebrows and gray hair as wild as if had been caught in a thresher. He had an interrogative nose and dark eyes but he was mostly hair, which took up a generous amount of the tack room. At their first game he had given his name as Reuben Turner and said his business was milling. His coat pockets were haphazardly stuffed with bank bills, a coarseness among this society but tolerated if he were going to surrender the currency at the loo table.

Turner said, "Don't let those playing cards gather dust in your hands, Mr. Alder." His accent did not place him.

Giles Stoddard seemed unmindful of the women in the room who had varying successes at concealing their stares at him. "We have been playing for picayune amounts, gentlemen."

"Fifty pounds each into the pool is a picayune amount?" Alder asked.

"What do you say that we increase the wager?" Stoddard said. "Two hundred each round."

Alder said, "That amount is out of bounds, sir."

"Perhaps for you." Franks looked at Captain Dalton. "You, sir? Did you bring your fortitude with you today?"

The captain leaned back in his chair. "Mr. Stoddard, you have an infallible way of making a small loss a large loss. From our earlier games I have already deposited in my bank two thousand pounds that once belonged to you."

"A few lucky draws."

"I normally do not caution card players from whom I harvest money but you should show restraint."

"Are you questioning whether I can honor my markers?"

"I'm questioning your skill at cards, sir," the captain said. "I have seen none so far. Were you an Irishman or a Scot I would not say anything but I am honor-bound to offer a warning from one Englishman to another. In our prior loo games, relieving you of your money has been a job for my left hand."

Stoddard placed his palms flatly on the black felt that covered the table. "Kindly do not attempt to disguise your lack of pluck with remarks about my card playing."

The captain's scar appeared to glow. "Deal the cards, Mr. Alder, if you please."

"I'm going to be a spectator." Alder passed the cards to Reuben Turner.

"I have a few coins for the pool in my pocket," Turner said. "Do you need to see it?"

Captain Dalton said, "This is a gentleman's game, Mr. Turner. We accept the word for the deed."

"I am in." Turner placed four green wood markers into the middle of the table. "Each is fifty pounds, then."

The captain and Stoddard dropped their markers next to it.

Reuben Turner passed around cards face-down, three to each of the other players and three to himself, then turned another card over for trump, a ten of diamonds, placing it on the pack on the table. This was loo, a trick-taking game where the pams—the knaves of clubs—could be the top trump cards or could fill a flush which would take all tricks.

A wave of cheers from out at the track swept through the room. Lawrence Alder leaned back in his chair; his fingers entwined across his paunch.

The captain looked at his cards. "I'll play."

Giles Stoddard said. "So will I."

Reuben pursed his lips as tightly as a drawstring, holding his cards against his chest. "I'm out this round." He threw his cards onto the table.

Captain Dalton said, "New cards, please."

When Dalton tossed aside his cards for fresh ones, Turner dealt him a new hand. Dalton brought them up for study.

The captain was to the left of the dealer so it was his opening. He placed a jack of diamonds face up in the center of the table. "Your play, Mr. Stoddard. Can you trump it?"

"Indeed, I can." Stoddard cackled, an unbecoming sound, then spun a queen of diamonds onto the table.

Several people in the tack room stepped closer to the table.

"My luck has turned, Captain." Stoddard leaned forward over the table to take one-third of the pool, four chips. "You should retreat before my bayonet charge, sir. Perhaps you have made such a retreat in your career already."

Captain Dalton chewed on nothing. From his pile he tossed four markers more into the pool. Then he reached for the deck for it was his turn to deal.

Reuben Turner held up a hand. "I pray that I am in error, Mr. Stoddard. I believe I have spotted a vagary in your play."

Stoddard had been stacking and unstacking his markers. He looked up. "Sir?"

Turner pointed. "Your jacket pocket. When you leaned forward to take in the pool you just won, I saw playing cards in your inside pocket."

"That can't be." Stoddard gripped his lapel to pull away his jacket front. He stared down into his own inside pocket.

Captain Dalton leaped from his chair, seized Stoddard by the collar, and yanked him up which toppled his chair backward. The crowd in the tack room turned to look. Dalton stabbed his hand into Stoddard's inside pocket and pulled out playing cards. Still gripping Stoddard's coat, he fanned the cards, three of them including the pam, the wild card. These three cards had the same colorful jesters on the reverse sides as those on the table.

"I have no idea how they got there." Frank's voice was as high as a child's.

Dalton said, "You are a cheat, sir."

"Never in life." Stoddard spread his arms widely. "Those cards belong to someone else." His words tumbled over each other. "How could they be in my pocket?"

Dead silence in the room.

"We can settle this in a gentleman's manner," Lawrence Alder said. "Sit down, both of you."

Turner nodded. "A wiser word never spoken, captain. Let's not be hasty."

Dalton said in iron tones, "Cards were in your pocket, Mr. Stoddard, and my markers are in your stack because you are a card cheat. A low charlatan, sir, and a disgrace."

Stoddard swung from his hip, a blow that caught the captain's cheek, sounding loudly but glancing off. Gasps and cries filled the room.

Dalton released Stoddard and stepped back. He touched his own cheek, then squared his shoulders. "Saturday at six in the morning, sir. At the Holcomb Green near the bridge."

"Sir?" Stoddard said.

"I will bring a matching pair of pistols and a pair of cutlasses, and you may select which weapon. You may also want to procure a second and a surgeon." The captain turned to the table. "Good day, gentlemen."

As Captain Dalton strode away the tack room throng parted for him.

Stoddard lowered himself to the chair. For a man who had just been challenged to a duel with a soldier of Captain Dalton's reputation, Stoddard was preternaturally calm. He smoothed his jacket.

"If you do not appear Saturday morning you will be ruined," Reuben Turner said. "You will have to flee to France."

Stoddard said, "My concern is getting a card game. The duel is a small thing."

"You are more sanguine than I would be," Alder said. "What with Captain Dalton intent on staring down a pistol barrel at you."

"In my life three men have challenged me to duels," Stoddard said, "and yet here I sit today. I will of course appear at the green Saturday morning." He reached for the cards. "Will anyone play me?"

"Not after seeing cards in your pocket, sir." Lawrence Alder rose from the table. "Good day, gentlemen."

Turner also got up from his chair. "I lose enough money with an honest player, Mr. Stoddard."

The man calling himself Giles Stoddard leaned back in his chair and looked around the room. No one would meet his eye. His carefully constructed persona as a wealthy gambler—and those opportunities offered by such a creation—was ruined, and by someone who knew how to do it.

Compeyson-Franks-Beecker-Stoddard now knew he had enemies but he did not know that the bearded player at Stoddard's card table who had introduced himself as Reuben Turner was in truth a notorious pickpocket known as Fagin, and that the young bootblack who had collided with Stoddard as he had exited the hackney coach was a boy named Luke who, to Fagin's delight, had turned out to be a prodigy not only at picking pockets but also at putting items—such as playing cards—into pockets.

The moniker today being Giles Stoddard, he gathered himself, rose from the table, and said in a loud voice as a goodbye to this wealthy crowd, "But I'll have my pleasure Saturday morning."

16

"It is our finest casket, madam. No expense has been spared. Oak on the outside and silk within." The undertaker grandly ran his palm along the wood. "Observe the oak's mirror shine."

His face was as long as a horse's, and his eyes were red and watery, and it was thought that before meeting patrons he squirted lemon juice into them so that he could be suitably morose. The scent of his rose nosegay was sickeningly sweet. "And notice this down-filled pillow for the deceased's comfort, and if dreams are to be had in a coffin, surely his will be benign, with his head on such a fine cushion."

The empty coffin rested on sawhorses in Satis House's parlor. Brass pallbearers' handles glinted with window light, and the top of the casket was curved like a sarcophagus.

"Was the pillow an additional charge?" Miss Havisham asked.

She held the infant Estella in her arms. The baby was wrapped in a white knitted blanket with red and yellow roses embroidered at the edges. Estella's little face was pink, and she stared up at Miss Havisham, smiling and gurgling, an arm waving. Miss Havisham's growing love of the baby had been a surprise. She hadn't known the capacity to love had been left to her after the wedding disaster. The wet nurse—the wife of a Havisham Brothers Brewery cooper—lingered in the hallway.

The undertaker showed his palms. "A trifling amount for the pillow, given the august nature of the occasion."

His name was Albert Mayberry, and his card read *Mayberry's Mortuary: A Haven in Your Time of Grief.* His fingernails were buffed to brilliance and he was shaved so closely that his cheeks and chin glowed. A quizzing-glass hung on a ribbon from his lapel. He had placed a black leather bag on the floor near his feet.

Three bouquets of roses and white lilies were in the parlor, a paltry number given the Havishams' prominence. But then, of course, the better circles had to account for Miss Havisham's wedding day disaster, a dreadful rattling of the social order. Such a thing didn't happen to people of character.

Undertaker Mayberry's voice was suitably sepulchral. "Let me recommend that you take precautions, Miss Havisham. There is a chance that your father is still alive, and is only in a coma."

"How can that be? I witnessed his final moments, and they appeared entirely final." She kissed Estella's forehead as a counter to the thought of the gangrene that had eaten away her dad.

"It is a small chance, to be sure, but we must prepare for all possibilities. Allow me to introduce our Mayberry Mortuary breathing appurtenance, which attaches right to the casket."

From the bag he withdrew a black lacquered tube which he twisted into a slot on the casket roof. "This allows the allegedly deceased to breathe if he emerges from unconsciousness." He reached into the bag again. "This bell attaches to the top, with a cord through the tube down to the casket. Should your father—and may he rest in peace if he has indeed left his mortal coil—regain his wits, he will ring the bell, alerting you that he has come around."

Miss Havisham wrinkled her nose.

"Two years ago the Baron of Hudsfield's coffin was dug up two weeks after the funeral because his son decided he wanted the ruby ring that had been buried with his father." The undertaker nodded sagely. "Imagine the horror when the son discovered his father's body with the fingers raked to the bone as the baron had tried to scratch away the coffin lid to escape. I am told the baron's face was twisted into a horrible rictus as his fate—buried alive—must have registered on him as he lay there."

Miss Havisham touched her mouth with her hand, her eyes wide.

Mayberry's smile was both condescending and ingratiating. "This tube and bell is only an additional fifteen shillings, an inexpensive investment for your peace of mind."

"My father could not possibly still be alive."

The undertaker said, "I confess the tube and bell are a tad pricey. But your sanguinity will be of incalculable value."

She glanced upward as if she could see through the ceiling into the room where her father's body lay. Outside, a buggy clacked and jangled as it came to a stop. She ran a finger along Estella's head, through a ruff of the baby's dark hair, still thin and sparse. The baby smiled and kicked her feet in the blanket.

"For those of my customers who want to trim expenses, Mayberry Mortuary offers a second solution." From the bag the undertaker pulled out an eighteen-inch-long spike and held it in front of Miss Havisham's eyes.

"This is our Golden Lance. Note the lovely gilding, and the point which is as sharp as a headmaster's tongue. And only five shillings, a bargain if ever there was one, given the distress of worrying you might suffer without it."

She rocked the baby, whose gaze was locked on Miss Havisham's eyes.

The undertaker pushed open the coffin's lid and pointed to the socket on the underside of the casket's roof. "This is a Mayberry Mortuary original here in Kent, though I must credit the Poles for the invention. I screw the lance into the casket roof on its underside, right into this socket." He twisted the spike into the coffin lid.

The maid opened Satis House's door. Jaggers' piercing voice filled the ground floor, and could have been heard at the far end of the brewery. He greeted the maid perfunctorily and asked for Miss Havisham.

"And note," Mortician Mayberry said, beaming, "that the lance would be right over the body's heart. When the lid is closed, if there was a chance the deceased was not dead then the lance piercing his chest as the lid closes insures that he will indeed join our ancestors with the heavenly host." He lowered and raised the coffin lid, the lance descending and rising. "And you will not have to worry at all about your father regaining consciousness buried six feet in the ground."

The scent of his soap arrived before Jaggers did. He carried a leather briefcase, and said, "Miss Havisham, I visited your father's room this morning, and he is as dead as I've ever seen anyone. I have gazed upon an abundance of corpses. A few were my clients where my arguments were a shade less than required for acquittal." Then he addressed the undertaker. "Miss Havisham is not interested in your gadgets, sir. You have already made your fortune with this exorbitantly priced coffin. Be off with you."

The mortician stared at Jaggers, and perhaps the lawyer's daunting visage kept him from replying. Mayberry bowed to Miss Havisham, lifted his bag, then hurried away, up the stairs to prepare the body for the coffin.

"You are not my nanny, Mr. Jaggers," she said. "I can make these decisions on my own."

The lawyer followed Miss Havisham to an octagonal table inlaid with turtle stone and burl near a window where the garden view was obscured by purple wisteria blossoms.

'You may indeed require a nanny." He placed the case on the table and pulled out a sheaf of papers. "My clerk, the indefatigable Mr. Wemmick, has proven it. He has tallied your losses to this Mr. Compeyson."

She lifted the baby against her chin, then lowered herself to a chair at the table. He sat next to her, spreading the documents. His bulk overflowed the chair, and the seat entirely disappeared.

"Wemmick is a superb investigator," Jaggers said. "Someday I may tell him so. Now the first loss was . . . ."

She cut in. "I'll look at the paperwork later, Mr. Jaggers."

"I am here for your father's funeral but it would also be a good time to raise an alarm. He asked me to look after you."

Miss Havisham patted Estella's back, burping her as the wet nurse had taught her.

"Will you kindly be brief?" She stroked the baby's hair. "Thinking of Samuel Compeyson . . . ." She stared at the garden through the window and the wisteria. "Thinking of him makes me ill, physically ill."

Jaggers' face was so dark that it was whispered among his club associates—the Alfred Club on Albermarle—that his ancestry was Portuguese, those fine if incitable people who had for centuries built fishing camps in Cornwall. "Then I shall be as concise as my duty to you allows. Samuel Compeyson defrauded you and your father of 6,000 pounds."

Miss Havisham's face acquired the color of parchment. "That much?"

"He did so with his promise of marriage to you, and five documents forged by a fellow named Jockle, a well-known counterfeiter and coiner in Newcastle, including a post-dated grant of dowry payments drawn on the Chatham Bank, the Jersey Bank, and the Exchange. The forger Jockle created the promissory notes and bank notes and forged the required name of the payee—your father—and the cashiers' signatures."

"The money doesn't mean anything to me," she said.

He smiled unpleasantly. "An airy bit of nonsense espoused entirely by the wealthy, a sentiment beneath you."

"Mr. Jaggers, please . . . ."

"You are much reduced. Compeyson's swindle and also your father's trading losses have been significant. You are in a delicate position."

"Mr. Murdstone and I have just imported . . . ."

The lawyer held up his hand. "I want to know no more than I know. I have had nothing to do with that part of your father's life, and it must remain so with you."

A child's voice came from the garden door. "I've finished, Miss Havisham. Ain't a mistake on the whole slate."

Miss Havisham turned to the door. "That would be a first, Luke."

The boy wore a red gingham shirt and blue trousers. He placed the slate into her hand, then rubbed Estella's head, maybe for good luck. He only glanced at Jaggers before skipping off to the hallway.

The lawyer stared after the boy, then said to Miss Havisham, "You have gone from no children to two children in a remarkably short time."

"I'm teaching him how to read and write."

"Where did you find him?"

"He is my business partner's apprentice."

As if to clarify her answer, Fagin came through the garden door into the parlor. When his gaze found Jaggers he stopped abruptly.

Jaggers' eyes narrowed under his shaggy brows. The solicitor splendidly cleared his throat, perhaps to disguise his surprise. "I have seldom seen you without shackles, Fagin. Without them you look almost innocent."

"If it isn't my Myrmidon of justice.' Fagin wore corduroys and a blue wool jacket.

Jaggers' grin was ill-favored. "I had planned to have a cast of your head and neck—rope burns visible—mounted on my wall along with the other death masks of my less fortunate clients."

Fagin said, "But here I am, breathing the same air as you, eh, counsellor?"

"You had a singular genius for saying the wrong thing before the jury. And, of course, the evidence that you stole the diamond pendant from the Duchess of Wharton's neck was compelling."

Estella's head under her chin, Miss Havisham rose from the chair.

"Such an offense merited the gallows," Jaggers said, "and even with me as your defense lawyer your acquittal was a shocking moment. My duty to Mr. Fagin has ended, but you, Miss Havisham, are my client today. I give you my advice as clearly as I can see it. If Fagin is this partner you just spoke of, you are in league with a base criminal."

Miss Havisham stepped back, turning the baby away from Fagin.

"And, worse," Jaggers added, "he still owes me part of my fee, fifteen pounds."

* * * *

"This place looks dangerous," Miss Havisham said. "Are we safe?"

"Safer here than out on the street." Fagin moved to a table and pulled out a bench. "Sit here and don't stare at anyone."

A rough plank served as a bench, and Miss Havisham lowered herself onto it. She lifted her wrap higher on her shoulders so that it covered her neck. She wore a ruby-colored pelisse and matching gloves. She avoided looking at the half dozen patrons but they were not so civil. They stared at her out of countenance.

Fagin said, "That fellow over there, the one with the floppy green hat: his name is Peachy Pickering and he won the Barton Prize."

From the corner of her eye she peered at the man, whose cheeks were as red as raw beef.

"Jeremiah Barton is a locksmith on Regent Street. He invented a pin tumbler lock and displayed it in his shop's window with a sign announcing that anyone who could pick the lock in two hours would be awarded twenty pounds. Peachy opened it in nine minutes and took the prize."

Miss Havisham touched the tip of her chin. "Maybe you should have tried for the twenty pounds."

Fagin shook his head. "I can pick a lock but Peachy is a genius at it, far better than I'll ever be."

The Tub and Gutter was a frowzy public house with low beams, timeworn benches, and potent ale. The place smelled of damp wool. Opaque grime covered the windows. The publican—a white-haired fellow with an eye patch whose remaining eye was narrowed at Miss Havisham—wiped the bar with a rag. His dog was the same size and color as a wharf rat, and it slept on a straw mat alongside a beer barrel.

Fagin nodded in the direction of another patron who was sitting on a bench leaning back against the wall, who wore a gray surtout. His eyes were widely-set and amused.

"That's Chadwick Miles. Once a month he sneaks into Lambeth Palace—he cracks a door or finds an unlocked window or coal chute—and tours the place while the Archbishop of Canterbury sleeps."

"He steals things?" Miss Havisham asked. "From the archbishop? That's tempting the Lord's revenge, isn't it?"

"Miles takes nothing. He says he walks the halls of Lambeth Palace at night for the same reason a dog lifts his leg on a tree."

"Why have you brought me to this place?" Miss Havisham asked.

Fagin lifted his ale. "Because I was thirsty."

For as long as memory served the Tub and Gutter had been a refuge for the underworld, a place to catch a breath and have a drink, where one needn't look over one's shoulder every half a minute. It wasn't as if the place were hidden, next to a wholesale feather dealer's warehouse on Earlham Street, not far from Seven Dials. Through a battered door, down two steps, turn left, through another door, and there was the Tub and Gutter, not truly hidden but—for reasons that were endlessly speculated upon by patrons—beyond the law's reach. To say that the police simply weren't interested was an affront to the customers who were London's finest pickpockets, cut-purses, area-sneaks, footpads, and burglars. All were welcome, from the high to the low, from skilled forgers to milk can thieves. The publican, One-Eye Smitty, may have been greasing the police but he never let on, and the patrons didn't ask because that was his business, and at the Tub and Gutter one's vocation was a delicate topic. One-Eye told his customers that his establishment was protected by "historic emanations," and the patrons were left to puzzle with the meaning of the phrase.

Miss Havisham boldly surveyed the room. "I didn't know a place like this existed. It's a den of thieves."

"We refer to it as a guild." Fagin sipped his ale. "Of thieves."

FAGIN & MISS HAVISHAM

"Your friend Luke is too young to be here, isn't he? Who is he speaking with?"

"Her name is Ruth Willow. She's the best bulker I've ever seen. She stalls a mark with an extravagant display of confusion and irritation and apology."

Ruth Willow made an exaggerated face of mock innocence, and Luke laughed. They were in a corner, under a yellowed pencil drawing of Jerry Abershawe, known as the Laughing Highwayman, the last English highway robber to be publicly gibbetted after hanging.

Ruth Willow crossed her arms under her chest, lifted her chin regally, and spoke again, and Luke laughed so hard he clutched his belly.

"How did she learn to be a bulker?" Miss Havisham asked.

Fagin swallowed ale. "Her husband taught her before he was transported to New Holland. It's hard to tell now—what with her missing teeth and pockmarks—but she was quite the beauty in her younger days. And the marks would spend a few seconds too long looking at her."

"Does one need to be beautiful to be a bulker?"

"Lord, no," he replied. "Look at Bill Sikes."

Fagin's maroon corduroy coat was still stiff with newness, and the collar was flat and sharp. Miss Havisham had purchased the coat for him, saying he should own one thing in his life that he hadn't stolen. He objected, saying it was against his principles but she wouldn't relent. The pickpocket's cap was on the table.

Miss Havisham hadn't touched her stoup of ale. "Did you know that most of my education has been in dancing, drawing, and comportment? I know a bouillon spoon from a citrus spoon from a chocolate spoon. And am capable dancing the cotillon and the scotch reel."

"Why are you telling me this?

"I'd like to learn something useful." She grinned. "Maybe I can help you. If Ruth Willow can do it I can do it."

Fagin's face congealed. "You want to learn to stall a mark?"

"How difficult can it be? The bulker bumps into the victim."

"Picking a pocket is an art. There's more to it than sorting spoons."

She straightened her backbone. "You underestimate me."

"I work in a team. I'm the wirer, and there's the bulker and the Adam Tyler." Fagin twisted his flagon, leaving a ring of moisture on the table. "An Adam Tyler is the person who is handed the wallet or wristwatch right after it is lifted, and he carries it away to safety."

"Where did the name Adam Tyler come from?"

"Nobody knows." Fagin sipped his ale. "Luke is good at it. He's young, he looks naive and innocent, and he can talk his way out of a corner."

"He won't be naïve and innocent long, associating with you." She cleared her throat pleasantly. "What can Ruth Willow over there do that I cannot?"

154

"We'll find out." Fagin rose from the bench. "Follow me."

Kerosene lamps in the Tub and Gutter left much of the place in murk, and the dimness and odors seemed to have a weight. Miss Havisham pushed her way along, following the pickpocket Fagin. A few patrons followed Miss Havisham with their eyes. Fagin greeted Ruth Willow.

She held out her hand to him. "I'm telling Luke here all I know about the trade."

"I'll be your bulker before long, Mr. Fagin." The boy brushed a lock of hair from his forehead. "Bill Sikes will have to look for another job."

Fagin introduced Miss Havisham, and said, "Will you show my friend here how to stall a mark? I'll be the mark."

Ruth Willow rose from the bench. She was exaggerated in every dimension, with wide hips, a wasp's waist, and a magnificent chest, all covered in cream-colored muslin that flowed around her as she moved. A red ribbon circled the crown of her straw hat, and hung over the brim and down her back, swaying as she moved. Her lips had been painted a glowing red, and crimson rouge emphasized her cheeks. She was womanly beyond measure but an element of crust was visible to a discerning eye. Luke smiled up at her.

She curtsied as if Miss Havisham were the Fair Maid of Kent. "Madam, you are likely too well-mannered to be a bulker."

Luke said, "For sure Miss Havisham is well-mannered."

Fagin raised a finger in the boy's direction, perhaps fearing Luke would add, "if nothing else." Then the pickpocket moved backwards six steps, stopping when he bumped into a table. "I'll be the mark, Ruth. I'll walk toward you as if we were on the street, and you stall me. Watch closely, Miss Havisham."

Ruth Willow plucked a handkerchief from her sleeve. When Fagin stepped forward, she dabbed at the corner of her eye, and whimpered pitiably, and then the handkerchief fell from her hand. She tried to snatch it from the air as it dropped, but missed, and bent to retrieve it from the floor, all of her muslin rustling.

She plucked the handkerchief from the floor, and when she attempted to right herself she bumped into Fagin, and then for five seconds she was all apology, fluster, keening, and confusion, her hands outstretched, her hips swaying. "Pardon me, sir. My fault, of course. I'll watch where I'm going. My poor daughter. I must hurry to her. Forgive me there, sir." She was a churning mass of abasement, flurry, and dithering.

"Watch where you are going, woman," Fagin said, straightening the lay of his coat.

"Of course, your worship, sir." Fanning herself with a hand, Ruth Willow stepped aside as if to allow the mark to pass.

Luke clapped, and Peachy Pickering nodded at the performance.

"And that's how it's done," Fagin said. "Forgive me for being blunt, Miss Havisham, but I do not think you have the constitution for it."

Miss Havisham captured her lower lip between her teeth. "Do I have to touch you?"

Ruth Willow chortled. "Hard to stall someone without touching him. You can do it, dearie."

"It's done so the mark won't feel the pickpocket's hand," Fagin said. "The stall brushes him with her hip, hands flying around, fingers curling and uncurling, all the while in a lather."

Miss Havisham looked around as if she had gotten off the stage at the wrong stop. "We Havishams don't touch."

Luke asked, "How do you pick up your pie?"

"My family has never been . . . tactile."

"What's that mean?" the boy asked.

"We aren't touchers in my family. Nor in my milieu."

"What's that mean?" Luke asked again. "You sometimes use big words."

Miss Havisham said, "My friends. The people I associate with. It's considered common, touching all the time."

"Forgive me, your majesty." Ruth Willow glanced at Fagin, her eyebrows up.

"And we don't use 'dearie,' either," Miss Havisham said. "You make me feel deprived."

"Here's another way to stall." Ruth stepped closer to Fagin and raised her nose and brought up her hand and loudly sneezed. When she picked the handkerchief from her sleeve, she brushed Fagin, then turned in apparent surprise and bumped into him. Her voice rose, "Beat it, you. Pushing a lady around. Trying for a feel."

Fagin again played the mark. "I beg your pardon, madam."

She planted her palms on Fagin's chest, looked him in the eye, and said, "Feeling up a woman on the street." She shoved Fagin away. "What is the empire coming to?"

The boy laughed.

Ruth turned to Miss Havisham. "See how it's done? The mark doesn't feel his watch leaving his pocket. Now you try it, dearie."

Miss Havisham's gaze went from Ruth to Fagin. "I can't."

"You aren't being asked to apply leeches to my piles," Fagin said. "Pretend to sneeze, shift into me, be outraged, plant your hands on my chest, and shove me away."

Miss Havisham said, "My cousin served with the Durham Regiment of Foot at the Battle of Vitoria."

His face blank, Fagin stared at her.

"Touching your chest would be worse," she said with a touch of a smile.

"I'll show you how," Luke said.

"Thank you." Miss Havisham's words were dry. "But I'll manage." With much melodrama she brought her hands to her mouth and pretended to sneeze. Fagin stepped toward her.

Miss Havisham moved her hips in his direction but not far enough to bump him. She said, "This is so wayward and shameless." Her voice was drenched in distaste, but an element of falseness was in it.

"Not sufficiently wayward and shameless," Fagin said. "A bulker must carom off the mark."

She half-stepped and shoved into him, her hip ramming him.

Her tone one of much affectation, she said, "Sir, you are impudent. Pawing a woman on the street. I shall call a sheriff." She placed her hands on his chest. "Begone with you." But then she abandoned the script by laughing. "I've never been so appalled. My hands are upon the chest of a London pickpocket. I am destroyed."

Fagin said, "Pretending to be outraged, you are now supposed to shove me."

Miss Havisham held her hands against his chest, her gaze on his eyes.

"Go ahead and push him." Luke held out his palms in the proper manner.

"You have more muscle than I would have guessed," Miss Havisham said.

Ruth Willow shook her head.

"Despite appearances, I'm not contagious." Fagin leaned toward her as if to help her push. "You aren't applying yourself."

Her voice low, she said, "I don't know what to do. My hands are on your chest. It's disorienting."

"Shove," Luke yelled, even though he was only four feet from them.

Miss Havisham's lips parted. Her breath fluttered his collar. She stared up at him.

"Do the same thing I do when confronted with blood pudding," Fagin said. "Shove away."

Miss Havisham flexed her fingers, rumpling Fagin waistcoat. "Are my hands in the right place?"

"You'll never be a bulker, dearie," Ruth Willow said.

Still, her hands were on his chest.

"You see, there is indeed more to it than you thought," Fagin said.

Miss Havisham blinked as if waking, and jerked her hands away from him. Droplets of sweat had appeared on her upper lip. "You are importune, sir."

"Another big word," Luke said.

"I was just standing here," Fagin countered, "with my hands at my side."

"I should have expected no less," Miss Havisham half smiled. "I shall have to watch you closely from now on."

157

FAGIN & MISS HAVISHAM

* * * *

A month ago, Miss Havisham would never have dared this, galloping on Hyde Park's *La Route du Roi,* which most folks called *Rotten Row.* Her horse—a spirited buckskin from Garner Stables in Knightsbridge—may have sensed the day was his, for he pranced sideways, lifted his hooves high, and snorted. Miss Havisham laughed as she patted the horse's neck. The animal's name was Copenhagen—after Nelson's famous victory—and when she tapped his flanks with her heels, he sped off down the road.

A fine sun beamed overhead, London's yellow haze had been lifted by a small wind, and the sky was limitless. Even the august towers of Westminster could be seen on such a day. London's best society—the Ton—promenaded on the roadway which connected the under-construction Wellington Arc with the Serpentine. Hacks weren't allowed on Rotten Row, nor were Punch and Judy puppeteers, street doctors or shoeblacks, though ice cream vendors could push their carts along even though most were Italians.

It was a shocking thing, a woman riding as if she were a jockey on a huge horse. Galloping, no less. Men on horseback and women in carriages followed her with their gazes, and some of the more tender women had their hands to their mouths. Propriety was offended by the sight. And this lady was astride the horse as if she were a man, not side-saddle as might be acceptable at a distant summer home accompanied by a chaperone. And her hair trailed behind her as if it were a pennant on a mainmast instead of up in pins and combs as made *au courant* by the unerring Countess of Carlisle. And—may the sun never set on the Empire—was this woman wearing trousers? This was an unpardonable horror, and onlookers in their carriages turned away, and some of the women furiously fanned themselves with handkerchiefs. Others clutched their pearls.

Miss Havisham reined in the horse and leaned closer to its ears. "Are you a jumper, Copenhagen? Want to try a stone fence?"

The horse didn't deign to respond, other than shaking his mane which whipped her face. She wore a green redingote open at the front to reveal a cotton blouse.

"How forgetful I am, out here." She laughed again. "I should have brought you a carrot, Copenhagen. Perhaps I'll purchase you. We have stables at Satis House, you know." She stroked the stallion's neck. "And you make more sense than most people I listen to, with your silence."

She flicked the reigns, and the horse cantered on the grass parallel to Rotten Row, and she rode through a glade of silver birch, and then so close to a crab apple tree that she leaned over the pommel so a bough wouldn't slap her off the horse. She was attuned to the horse, riding in perfect rhythm with its movements.

A long line of equipage rolled along Rotten Row including high-perch phaetons, where young ladies in white silks sat atop benches elevated ten feet on spidery suspensions, the better to see and be seen. Viscount Ashford—the notorious libertine suspected of fathering twenty children scattered across four nations—rode along in his blindingly-white coach pulled by four white horses.

Countess Sprinerfield and her black poodle rode in her carriage, her two powdered and liveried footmen high on the backstep, their expressions ones of severe superiority. Family crests were painted on the carriages. Landaus carried entire families, the girls in straw hats and the older women in turbans and feathers. The Earl of Barnum's oldest son Bertram drifted along in his two-wheeled chaise, driving himself, the reins likely pipe-clayed so his white gloves would remain spotless.

And there was Sir Horace Pursham in his barouche with the crimson spokes, sitting with his three beribboned and bejeweled daughters. Sir Horace suffered an ugliness so profound it could dissolve a peaceable assembly but his daughters were finely-crafted, and it was widely believed Sir Horace had nothing to do with their conceptions but was well-satisfied with the situation, given the girls' loveliness.

Hundreds of vehicles travelled along the row, moving by each other in a great out-and-back between the Arc and the Serpentine, their occupants acknowledging some passers-by, snubbing others, gossiping and laughing and waving. Other people strolled along the edge of the lane, women in satins and silks with lilacs and hyacinths on their bonnets and the men in striped waistcoats and top hats.

Miss Havisham's father had brought her from Satis House to London for the Rotten Row promenade several times when she was fifteen, thinking it a necessary introduction to the Ton, but she had finally generated the courage to tell him she simply couldn't tolerate it, and he had replied, "I should have known," and had never asked her to go again. Instead, she had made herself a horsewoman, racing along the River Medway paths, and sometimes her father would accompany her on his bay, though he could never keep up. She had never worn a bonnet when she rode, and her hair—platinum even back then— had flapped behind her like a flag.

Miss Havisham nudged Copenhagen, aiming the horse toward a trough. She waved at her school friend Sophie Stratham who rode in a carriage with her parents. Sophie smiled widely and rose from the carriage seat but her mother—gall and wormwood on her face as she glared at Miss Havisham— ferociously yanked Sophie back down.

"Miss Havisham, I was told I'd find you here." The voice came from behind her, punctuated by the sound of hooves.

She looked over her shoulder. Edward Murdstone approached on a cream-colored horse as spotted as a leopard. He tipped his hat to her, and presented what she supposed was his smile.

"The Lambeth wool broker Lionel Short told me he saw you galloping along the row, and I hoped to catch you."

"I thought we were next meeting on Wednesday."

"I have a proposition for you, Miss Havisham. Let me ask again, may I call you Margaret?"

He must have taken her silence for consent.

"Margaret, we are business partners, are we not? And we have done well together. You inherited your father's acumen in trade." Murdstone's white shirt was so starched it resembled a board. The blue cravat at his neck was perfectly executed. Pads in his coat's shoulders made his waist appear attractively narrow.

"But I think we can do better." His peculiar black eyes never left her face. "There is advantage in combining assets."

Copenhagen struck the ground with a hoof as if impatient with conversation. This was his time to dash across the park. Playing bulldog in a pasture next to the lane, lines of boys ran back and forth, hollering and laughing. In a plane tree a jackdaw cawed, scolding a mottled brown dog that sniffed the trunk. The carriages ceaselessly moved along the road, out and back, the great engines of society.

Murdstone rose on his stirrups. "I have had a long and wandering bachelorhood, Margaret. It is time for more substance, and my thoughts turned to you."

She said, "I do not have the honor of understanding you, sir."

He smiled, revealing his small, perfect teeth. "I am proposing to you, Margaret. Will you marry me?"

She stared at him, her horse plucking grass from the ground.

"We would make a strong partnership," he said. "The houses of Havisham and Murdstone would be merged. Think of the possibilities."

Gazing at him as if he had just formed out of the ground, it took her a moment. "I can't marry you, Mr. Murdstone. Edward."

His face, most often the color of old milk, flamed red. "Is there a reason?"

She glanced at the line of carriages on the row, then turned back to him. "You have heard of my recent disaster?"

"On your wedding day? It means nothing to me."

"But it does to me," she said. "I'm done with thoughts of matrimony. I have expelled them from my mind." She bit down. "You have no idea how . . . ." Her voice trailed off.

"I do not make this offer of marriage lightly," he said.

"And I do not turn it aside lightly."

"This,"— he silently moved his mouth, maybe searching for words—"this is unprecedented. I am a man of substance, someone of importance in the City, and you are . . . what?"

Miss Havisham became as calm as a pond. "Mr. Murdstone, you have a singular genius for hitting the wrong note."

"You are a woman approaching middle age and well on your way to spinsterhood." His words were a drum tattoo. "You'll be a dried-up, miserable old lady living by yourself."

His spotted horse whickered and flapped air through its nostrils.

"And there is another reason I will not marry you." She lifted the reins, about to urge Copenhagen forward. "I cannot tolerate you."

Murdstone's mouth pulled back into a ghoulish grimace He kicked his horse so that it sidled up next to Copenhagen, and Murdstone gripped Miss Havisham's arm and yanked her to him. She gasped and made to pull away but he released the reins to grip her with both hands, pressing her into his chest. Perhaps her eyes should have been wide with shock but instead they grew small and dangerous.

Rage serrated his voice. "I will not be turned aside by a country brewer's daughter."

Her hand moved.

He screeched and spasmodically released her and teetered on his horse. His hand dabbed at his chest. Blood wet his fingers.

Miss Havisham said, "You advised me to carry a knife because our business often requires it." She held up a six-inch blade. A drop of blood ran down the gutter. "I took your advice."

His voice was a stormy wind. "You have knifed me." He stared down at his chest, where his shirt reddened.

"Half an inch, an inch. You'll live."

He held his hand up. Fingertips were crimson. "I'm hurt."

"I've been hurt worse playing piquet with my father." She tucked the knife back into her skirt.

His voice was ugly. "You have stabbed me."

"That was more a lesson than a stabbing."

He jabbed his heels at his horse, and when it rushed to her he gripped her arm, and yanked her off balance. He jerked her arm again, and she fell forward over the horse's withers, somersaulting to the ground, where her arm landed at a contrary angle. She yelled in pain. Copenhagen danced away from her. She rose to her knees, and when she gripped her shoulder pain flashed through her.

Murdstone said, "See what happens when you forget your station?" He clicked his tongue, and his horse carried him away from her.

17

Holcomb Green was notorious. More men arrived alive than left in that same condition as it was a preferred London location for gaining satisfaction. In the early mornings fog drifted in from the river hiding the trees, the bridge over Mill Creek, and steeples in the distance, making the world small and focused as if nothing of import could possibly be occurring beyond the confines of the fog, and for duelers the sentiment was appropriate because one of them was likely to be carried from the green with his blood dappling the grass.

Captain Claude Dalton pulled his repeater from a pocket. Five minutes to six. He looked at his second. "Maybe someone who cheats at cards would never appear at Holcomb Green." The purple saber scar on his forehead was the most colorful thing on him, as he was wearing tan trousers, an off-white shirt open at the neck with no cravat. No sense emblazoning a target with red or blue garments.

His second, Lieutenant Amos Wilbur, said, "Be a shame if he doesn't appear, captain. Us up so early and all."

"If you like to sleep late, lieutenant," Dalton said, "you should have joined the army."

Wilbur leaned over the pistol box to again check the flints and pans. He had served with Dalton for a decade, since Wilbur had been a midshipman. He was short in stature and ferocious in temperament, and comments on his height or lack of it invariably resulted in wounds but not to Wilbur. His grin was sly, and the Samoan tattoo on his left forearm was of a porpoise.

Rain had fallen that night. The grass was slick, and dewy cobwebs were draped over bushes at the edges of the clearing. Water dripped off ash and dogwood leaves. In the distance Mill Creek burbled and soughed.

The captain stepped to a folding table. The matching pair inside the box had silver wire inlaid on the stocks, and filigree covered the barrels. These pistols and the presentation box had been manufactured by the esteemed R.L. Quarry of Mount Street, Lambeth, and no finer pair could be had at any price. Dalton ran a finger along one of the weapon's barrels. He had boarded the French frigate *Infatigable* with such a weapon, pistol in one hand and cutlass in the other.

Parliament had outlawed dueling but the law was honored mostly in its breech. An insult or a blow to a gentleman had to be accounted for. The ledger had to be put right. Failure to issue the challenge after a provocation and failure to answer it were scandalous and shameful, the English law on this subject as weightless as the wind.

The third fellow on the green was the surgeon from *HMS Lauder,* which was moored at the Pool of London. Gil Redfern's face was deeply lined, and one of his eyes was milky. He had claimed before the Naval Board when interviewing for his warrant that having vision in only one eye allowed him to focus better on his patients. He had received the warrant anyway because the navy desperately needed surgeons.

A canvas bag at his feet contained his medical supplies. He pushed his floppy felt hat back on his head, and tisked loudly. Duels were both childish and deadly, and a navy surgeon had enough to do without watching someone become a patient by catching a bullet. But Dalton was an old friend, and his request to attend this business on Holcomb Green could not be turned aside. And, of course, a captain in his majesty's navy often did not countenance even rational opposition from a ship's surgeon, friend or not.

Captain Dalton locked his hands behind his back and walked to the surgeon, pivoted, and walked to the lieutenant. Showing nerves would never do and perhaps the captain had none to show but he stopped the pacing and again pulled his watch from his pocket. Then he peered toward the bridge over Mill Creek where his opponent would likely appear. Fog hid the bridge.

"Not even a shiftless gambler is so cowardly that . . . ." Dalton didn't finish the sentence, perhaps thinking that such comments might signal anxiety.

The bell of St. Ives Church tolled, the long and dolorous sound lowering the clouds and thickening the haze. And when the bell completed its work, and the last low note had fled across the green and into the woods, Captain Dalton looked again toward the bridge.

Nothing in the haze. No sound on the path, no rustling of leaves. No one.

* * * *

But time is not a constant, moving inexorably away from the past and into the future. It speeds and slows, stalls and skips. Seconds rush by for a man in his lover's embrace. Not so for a man with a toothache. Time can double back to repeat itself, not having during the first pass visited enough joy on the deserving or suffering on the wicked, or, in its callous vicissitude, the other way around.

Here time has doubled back, for the bell of St. Ives Church is still ringing the six o'clock hour as Samuel Compeyson—in his guise as Giles Stoddard the gambler—rushed along the footpath toward the bridge to Holcomb Green. He was late to the duel, thanks to a wherryman who interrupted his propulsion every few strokes for a pull at a bottle. Being a few minutes late to an affair such as this would be to Compeyson's advantage because his opponent would be puzzled and elated when he didn't appear, and then chagrined and flustered when he did.

He briskly stepped along—and his cloud of orange blossom cologne moved with him, several tiny perfume bottles chiming together in his pocket—avoiding nettles that leaned onto the path. He stared through the brush. The green was just ahead, over the bridge. For a fellow walking to a duel, Samuel Compeyson was remarkably calm, hardly thinking about the match to come.

Compeyson earned his living by reading his dupes' strengths and weaknesses, and he was a genius at this skill. Those who prided themselves on being clever were the easiest to fleece, particularly those who named their colleges within two sentences of an introduction. Windbags and braggarts could be relieved of their money almost effortlessly.

But spinsters approaching twenty-five were where Compeyson made his fortunes, among them poor Margaret Havisham. Compeyson grinned. My lord, she had been ready.

Margaret was lovely and her family was moneyed, and so she had been intensely sought after by the families of marriageable young men but she had a brittle way about her with too many opinions and a sharp tongue, and she wouldn't suffer gadabouts or boors (which is to say: many who came calling), and on occasion she displayed her intelligence in too evident a manner—who can tolerate someone quoting Alexander Pope?—and so she drove her suitors away, and happy they were to escape, though their parents were far less so.

And these suitors had usually brought to her door a black tooth or a wall eye or a turned-in foot or scrofula pocks, these familiar afflictions. Compeyson was perfect. He gleamed. He was irresistible, and he knew it. His targets—the daughters of the wealthy—simply could not help themselves. He had received his beauty from his mother, and a grand investiture it was.

From his father, Compeyson had learned his wiles. The father had once cheated the Marquess of Torquey out of three thousand acres of cropland and the Baroness Lairen out of her Star of Ceylon diamond ring, but hubris had caught up with the father when he had tried to swindle an iron foundry owner out of his plant. The outraged foundrymen threw Compeyson's father into the furnace where he sizzled like bacon before disappearing in the molten metal. But by the time of this unfortunate incident the son had learned the trade well enough so that not once in his life had Samuel Compeyson been forced to earn an honest living. Such a prospect—working—was anathema, a surrender to the contemptible. Where is the pleasure and amusement in labor?

Lady Justice's scales must be in balance, and when she grants a bestowment such as beauty, she also exacts a cost. With Compeyson it was the desperate desire to wager on cards. Or dice. Or dogs or cocks or horses. Or the toss of a coin or a game of draughts. Or which window a fly will exit a room. The list of activities on which Compeyson would place a wager disappeared over the horizon.

And he was dreadful at it. He would make one wagering blunder after another, and he lost and lost and lost. Perhaps the portion of his mind that gave him an instinct for the swindle had crowded out that portion that should have recognized the odds at a card table. He had gained fortunes through his confidence games and he had lost them through his card games. Compeyson was certainly aware of his poor ability—who can lose a hundred pounds on the turn of a card and remain unaware of it?—but it could not be helped. And so this was his curse, and this was how Lady Justice balanced her scale regarding Samuel Compeyson.

He saw the park through the tree boughs, and the three men and their table on which was a box. He didn't miss a step on the path toward the bridge.

Samuel Compeyson could shoot the ace of spades from the center of a playing card thrown in the air. And the same calmness he brought to presenting a stock scheme to a baron he brought to leveling a pistol at a target. This Captain Dalton fancied himself a warrior, and perhaps he was indeed with scores of his armed men alongside him, but out here in the indifferent gray dawn it would be one on one. Compeyson would fire first and accurately, and the captain would sink to the ground with the life force fleeing him, of which there could be no doubt.

Compeyson walked onto the stone bridge that approached the green, and he was as calm as a clock. He had a date with Anna Wilkinson later in the day. He was tempting Anna along, step by step, just as he had Margaret Havisham.

He cared less about honor—to be precise: he cared nothing about it, such being the heart of a swindler—but wanted to have seats at the high-wager loo and hazard tables, and a duel would expunge the calamitous occurrence at the race trace. A duel would erase history, and that was the reason Compeyson was about to step onto the green to select a pistol from Captain Dalton's matched pair. That Compeyson had brought neither a second nor a doctor would further unnerve the captain, which was to the good, of course.

Serene and satisfied and walking along, Compeyson thought he might only wing the captain, which in the unwritten tenants of dueling was as good as killing him.

"In a hurry, chum?"

The question seemed to come from a tree near the path on the other side of the bridge, or maybe from the bridge abutment. The tone was threatening. Compeyson stopped.

His granite brows, beer-barrel chin, and fleshy red nose creating the perfect portrait of unalterable stupidity, Bill Sikes stepped from a shadow onto the bridge, squarely in front of Compeyson, blocking his way. Sikes's rumpled top hat was angled on his head, and his blue and white handkerchief circled his neck.

Sikes said, "Let's you and me have a chat, what say?"

"I don't converse with denizens of the gutter," Compeyson replied. "Step aside."

The swindler knew flintlock pistols and fraudulent wills and testaments but he did not know a fist from a fistula. When Sikes's fist slammed into his forehead with the force of a shipyard maul, Compeyson collapsed to the bridge deck, where he splayed out and was still.

Sikes chuckled. Even his chuckles were brainless. "Guess you won't be going to no gunfight today, eh, chappie?"

Compeyson responded as would a boulder, which is to say, not at all. Sikes gripped him by his collar and dragged him back across the bridge, the tops of the swindler's shoes scraping the bridge deck.

* * * *

Captain Dalton held up his repeater. "Fifteen minutes after six. How much grace time is customary?"

The surgeon replied, "You don't owe him extra time, captain."

Lieutenant Wilbur closed the pistol box and secured the hasps. "I never thought I would live so long as to see an Englishman fail to defend his honor. Maybe he is an American."

"I knew this Giles Stoddard was a cheat," the captain said, "and I learned just now he is a coward."

"You didn't shoot someone this morning, Captain Dalton, so the day has begun well," the surgeon said. "I dislike this foolishness, out here on this wet grass in the fog. I have a sufficient quantity of patients without having to worry about you becoming the next one. I am relieved."

Dalton pulled at his chin. "Something isn't right."

"There were no pistol shots this morning." The surgeon lifted his bag. "Seems right to me."

"At the racetrack, Stoddard hadn't seemed perturbed at the prospect of a duel." Captain Dalton walked toward the entrance to the park.

The lieutenant and surgeon followed the captain. The fog was lifting, the sky changing from gray to silver.

Dalton went on, "Stoddard was enraged that he had been accused of dishonesty at the card table but the prospect of a duel didn't appear to trouble him."

"Maybe he learned your history," the lieutenant said, carrying the pistol box.

Walking between oak trees, they approached the roadway and their carriage, a black hackney with a driver high on the seat and a rufous horse in harness.

Dalton shook his head. "I've never heard of someone not appearing at an affair on honor. Utter cowardice." He opened the carriage door. "He'll never be able to show his face in the city again."

* * * *

Among certain Londoners—those best avoided—the prison wagon was well known but less well regarded. It was a fearsome apparatus, and for its occupants nothing good ever came from a journey in it. The origin of wagon's name—*the Midnight Flyer*—was lost to memory, and was a puzzle as it seldom travelled at night because the crown favored its dampening effect on the criminal spirit, and of course prison wagons don't in fact fly, that activity mostly limited to winged creatures and time.

The Midnight Flyer weighed three thousand pounds. Riveted iron sheets covered all sides, the roof, and the undercarriage Hung on massive hinges, the iron door was secured by a lock the size of a goat's head. Barred windows allowed prisoners a narrow view of the street. The prison wagon was a grubby gray as were the four horses in harness in front of it. The Midnight Flyer was as sobering as a tomb.

On the seat with his foot on the brake, the driver was a malevolent thumper named Finn Legbar whose command of profanity was unparalleled and who was constitutionally incapable of conversation that didn't make the listener blush. Legbar had no front teeth and so appeared to be chewing on his chin. A lead-filled sap hung on his belt.

The other fellow on the Midnight Flyer was a guard who roosted on a seat high and behind the prisoners' compartment. His name was Simon Welt, a simpleton who carried a fowling piece and who spent his days without having to tolerate even the dimmest of thoughts. His gray wool coat was spotted with grime—some from the roads and some from the prisoners—and his face was as blank as a slate.

FAGIN & MISS HAVISHAM

The Midnight Flyer was parked outside the New Prison in Clerkenwell. Pedestrians stayed well away from the wagon because proximity to such a thing might bode ill, and carts and coaches veered widely around it. Pedestrians averted their gazes lest a prisoner leer at them through the bars. Even the smoke from the Jones Tar Plant across St. John Street from the jail stayed away from the Midnight Flyer, coiling and rising in another direction.

The New Prison's oak and iron door opened, and three jailors carried a prisoner onto the road toward the Midnight Flyer. The prisoner writhed and yelled and cursed, and the jailors hauled him along without allowing his feet to touch the cobblestones. He wore ankle irons and a blue cotton shirt. One leg of his trousers was missing up to his thigh. He was about twenty years old, and his beard was scruffy.

Cursing, Finn Legbar climbed down from seat, and pulled a keyring from his pocket. He jangled the keys until the jailors and their burden arrived at the Midnight Flyer's door. The prisoner strained against the jailors, twisting and bucking.

Legbar issued several more execrations, and ended with, "Drop him."

The prisoner fell to the cobblestones. The young man yelled something unintelligible, and his eyes were wide and wild.

Legbar's foot might have been shot from a seventy-four's gun. It soared into the prisoner's head, and the young man stilled instantly.

"That usually calms them," Legbar said. He turned a key in the lock and removed it from the door.

The door creaked as it was opened. A shrill voice came from within the wagon, and then rusty red hair and a face appeared at the wagon's door.

Legbar brought up his hand and cupped the inside prisoner's face as if he were gripping a melon, and savagely shoved the face back into the darkness. Legbar said, "Toss him in and be done with him."

The jailors roughly shoved the young man into the wagon as if he were a sail into a locker, and the prisoner likely landed on the fellow already inside. Legbar locked the door, waved the jailors away, then hauled himself back up to the driver's seat, and snapped the reins. The Midnight Flyer lurched forward in the direction of the police magistrate's office.

Whether the guard, Simon Welt, was asleep at his post on the wagon's rear seat cannot be known but his expression did not change withal.

But half a block behind the prison wagon, young Luke's face registered sufficient emotion for all of them. Breathing in huge quaffs, the boy had hidden behind a water trough and the mules drinking there. His hands were on his knees and the wind rattled in his throat. He had followed the Midnight Flyer for a mile through the city streets, dodging dogs, perambulators, umbrellas, cabbage carts, carriages, eelmen, boardmen, flower girls, and

168

fellow street urchins. His lungs still pumping, Luke stepped from behind the trough toward the prison wagon.

The Midnight Flyer rolled forward, the horse hooves grating on the street's stones, and the harnesses squeaking.

Luke ran after it again. His tone one of utter helplessness, he cried out, "Mr. Fagin."

18

"Nothing is broken." Doctor Hardin's black bag was on a lamp table. "Your shoulder is wrenched and your arm with it, and you will be in pain for two weeks, maybe three, but it will heal."

The doctor was a round little man with the shape of an apple. His red nose shone like a beacon. His pate was bald and appeared to be waxed, and the only hair on his head were white tufts that stuck out from behind his ears. Every few seconds he pushed back the spectacles on his nose. He always chewed mint leaves before seeing a patient, and the sharp scent surrounded Miss Havisham.

"I do not like to complain, doctor," Miss Havisham said, "but I was in pain last night. I couldn't sleep."

"Falling off a horse will do that."

"I didn't fall off a horse." Her tone was sour. "I was yanked off a horse. Should I wear a sling?"

"You do not need one." Doctor Hardin helped her roll down her frock's sleeve. "Your recovery should be like drinking from a cup of tea that has a spoon in it. If the spoon pokes your eye as you sip, don't do that. Regarding your arm and shoulder: if it hurts don't do it."

As Miss Havisham rose from the parlor bench she winced and gripped her sore arm with a hand.

The doctor brought out a bottle from the bag. "I want you to swallow three tablespoons of laudanum. It will help with the pain."

"The tincture of opium? It sometimes made my father say outlandish things."

The doctor shook his head. "Toward his end your father desperately required it, and you shouldn't judge him by his need to escape the pain."

170

She stared at the brown bottle. "I don't know what it will do to me. I've only been tipsy once in my life, when I was seventeen, and my girlfriend and I imbibed in a bucket of dad's beer. I vomited all over mother's Belgian carpet, which she reminded me of once a week for the rest of her life. I haven't been tipsy since."

He produced a cup from his bag and poured the amber liquid into it. "A marvelous aspect of this libation is that you will receive from it what you expect. I take a good swallow before I give physic to a certain one of my patients, an abrasive and whiney hypochondriac. Every time I meet with her she has a list of five things she is dying from that day. That swallow of laudanum magically makes her tolerable. This will reduce your pain, as that is what you require from it."

Miss Havisham stared into the cup, then brought it to her mouth. She downed the drink like a sailor on leave, and the taste made her grimace and shake her head.

The doctor asked, "Now that wasn't too bad, was it?

"I've tasted worse." She inhaled. "Though not in my adulthood."

"I'll leave the rest of the bottle." He placed it on the table. "Two tablespoons before bedtime."

"My tongue is tingling. Is that normal?"

"That's in your head, Margaret. I will return in two days to see how you are doing. Good day to you now."

The doctor left the parlor, and she heard his footfalls as he walked along the hallway and through Satis House's door to his carriage. Miss Havisham's arm and shoulder still ached. She lifted the bottle and swallowed two more mouthfuls of the laudanum. She grimaced again at the taste.

"That ought to do it." She returned the bottle to the table.

Miss Havisham slid her hands along her legs, straightening her frock's pale orange fabric. She moved her injured arm again. Less pain, certainly. She was surprised the medicine had worked so rapidly, or maybe that was in her head, too.

"Mr. Jaggers is in the Sun Dial Court, madam," the butler Old Tavers said from the hallway.

Miss Havisham walked past the hallway's giant blue and white vases and the bouquet of roses on a side table, then to the rear door where the leaded glass cast prisms of light against a wall. She had never before seen such an effect in the hallway. The shimmering light was delightful. She touched the colors on the wall and laughed. How could she have missed something like this right in her own home?

She opened the door and stepped into the garden, moving under a trellis covered in wisteria. The blossoms' scent—so strong it seemed sticky—surrounded her, squeezing her. She lifted her nose, taking in as much of the smell as she could get into herself. Perhaps it lifted her off the ground. She was weightless and timeless. She blinked away the sensation.

"There you are, Miss Havisham." Jaggers lifted himself from a wrought iron chair. "I charge as much for waiting as I do for consulting so in the interests of your economy I am pleased to finally see you."

His briefcase was on a table near the chairs. The Sun Dial Court had been designed by Miss Havisham's mother. The sun dial on the ground was formed by lavender bushes lined with primroses. Numbers one through twelve were artfully arranged white and pink alyssum. In the center the gnomon was a statue of King Richard I holding up a sword. Years ago, a sunken ha-ha wall had been constructed on the east edge of the gardens to keep out the deer but Hugh Havisham hadn't liked the perpetual mud at the bottom of the trench so he had abandoned the project after completing only the east wall. "The deer can have their share," he had announced, a favorite memory of Miss Havisham's.

Jagger rattled his watch chain. "Exemplary has been my investigation. I anticipate hosannas from you, Miss Havisham. It has been a life of toil but once in a while I am rewarded with the unbridled satisfaction of having done a superior job." He gestured toward the chair next to his. "Sit down, please."

"I am sitting down, sir."

He stared up at her. "Forgive me for stating the perfectly obvious—for which I must charge my clients despite the ready discernment available to them—but you remain standing."

"I do appear to be higher than you, Mr. Jaggers, which provides an unwelcome view of the entirety of your hairless head. I have never before been allowed such a glimpse. I wonder why it has occurred now. It means something about the world, do you think?"

He leaned her direction and sniffed the air. "Have you imbibed in a morning cordial, Miss Havisham? Perhaps several?"

"Alcohol?" She shook her head. "Heaven forbid."

"Heaven forbidding is pious but not to the purpose."

"As you know, I live my life as if it were in a corset." She laughed gaily. "Though not so much lately." She settled into a chair. "Have you studied Rousseau, Mr. Jaggers?"

"Just enough to learn he was nonsensical. To business, and we will keep to the record. I have exceeded my brief for you, young lady. Your gratitude will be munificent, I'm confident."

"Did you shave this morning, Mr. Jaggers? Your beard appears to be growing in front of my eyes."

"I will ask you to focus on the subject at hand, and that subject is finding you a suitable husband."

"A husband?" She sat back. "I need a husband like I need a . . . like I need something I don't really need."

"Metaphoric thinking is not accurate thinking, and I'm pleased you have leached yourself of the ability regarding it." Jaggers removed sheets of paper from his leather case. A white rose was attached to his lapel as if to make him appear benevolent. "Have you heard of the Primson family of Cornwall near the English Channel?"

"I have heard of the English Channel." Miss Havisham fanned herself with a hand. "Is it hot in here, Mr. Jaggers?"

"We are not in here. We are out here, as made evident by the grass under your feet and the lilac bushes behind your chair." Jaggers' waistcoat was striped with blue, and his neckcloth squeezed his throat so that the flesh of his neck extruded above the cloth. "Are you sure you are attending, Miss Havisham?"

"Inside or outside. It is all the same."

"Their third son, Waverly, is a widow, his wife having succumbed to dropsy."

"Ah, that Primson family. I danced with Waverly at Baroness Ackerley's ball when I was fourteen or fifteen. He came up to my chin and his hair smelled of turpentine, which meant he was trying to rid himself of head lice, and so I danced with him with my arms extended as far as they would go."

"The Primsons would not require a substantial dowry."

"Mr. Jaggers, have you ever been a cutie?"

"I beg your pardon."

"We all deserve to be cuties at some point in our lives, don't you think? It's only fair."

"The word *cutie*—if it is indeed a word—can hardly form on my lips." Jaggers squared his papers. "I have journeyed here from the city to speak with you about your future, as your father directed me before his passing, not to engage in palaver about being a cutie."

Miss Havisham stretched out her legs, the frock's fabric tight between her knees. "I went from being a reasonably attractive infant to being a gangly young woman, and I never was a cutie. I missed that chapter."

"That is something for me to ponder at a later time. The Cathams in Fulham have a son with five thousand a year. Barnabas is his name."

"Why isn't he married?"

"He had an intermission in his life but he has entirely recovered, I'm told."

She smiled vacantly at Jaggers, and he may have taken it as a further inquiry.

"He spent eighteen months at Bedlam." The lawyer dusted his hands. "A full cure. Barnabas has returned home and is as passive as a lamb."

"I'm not suited for marriage, a lesson inflicted on me recently." She stared at distant clouds in the east. "Do you like rainbows, Mr. Jaggers?"

"It is a sunny day, madam. There are no rainbows between here and the Hebrides. How is your shoulder this morning?"

"My shoulder?" she asked.

"If you will kindly look to your left and then glance down, you will see your shoulder. You were toppled from a horse and your shoulder and arm were damaged. Your physician was just here."

"I can't feel my shoulder."

"Or anything else below your neck, is my guess. What in the world did the doctor give you?"

"Mr. Jaggers, is it? Papa's lawyer? How do you do?"

"Knowing of your recent distress I came here today to offer guidance outside the usual nature of my legal practice, as your confidential agent," Jaggers said, "but it is apparent my time would have been better spent dancing around a maypole." He gathered his papers. "Maybe another day, when you are more closely acquainted with reality."

"I have found it," a fellow called from the door to Satis House's hallway. "As clear as clear can be."

"My confidential clerk." Jaggers waved the man over. "I introduced you to Wemmick earlier this morning, though you may not remember him, given your airy state."

She said, "The man who has a square face resembling a block of wood and who wears his cap far back on his head so that it is always about to fall off."

"I'm relieved," the lawyer said. "You aren't as addled as I had supposed."

She held out a hand toward the arbor on the other side of the sun dial, and sang, "'What's this dull town to me? Robin's not near.'"

Jaggers rose from his chair. "Irish ditties are not in my line, Miss Havisham."

She said, "When I was younger, I had ambitions for the stage. I've been told I have a pleasing contralto voice." Again, she sang, "What was't I wish't to see. What wish't to hear?'"

"Perhaps you will call at my office when you are next in the city." He pulled on the hem of his waistcoat to straighten it. "I beg my leave to absent myself."

He tried to wave away Wemmick but the clerk approached briskly, holding up a ledger. Wemmick was short in stature and intense in purpose. His face had the appearance of being unfinished in its sculpting, a rough visage, with a large nose and blocky cheekbones. His eyes, though, were a sparkling blue and they were restless, of a nature to miss nothing. He walked on his toes as if sneaking along. He held up the account book high as if to ward off evil.

He exclaimed, "Here it is in black and white."

Jaggers switched to his courtroom voice. "Mr. Wemmick, the afternoon coach will not wait for us. Let us repair to the stop to wait for it."

"I cannot be dismissed so readily today, Mr. Jaggers, having discovered the foundation of a vast deception. I pray to inform you that it is a big one."

Miss Havisham asked, "Is it bigger than Denmark?"

"Can it wait, Mr. Wemmick?" Jaggers jut his chin in Miss Havisham's direction. "One of us is feeling merry today."

She asked, "Did you just infer that I am a dunder-headed queen of the noodles, Mr. Jagger?"

"Never in life, my dear. It was simply an observation that a gala ball is occurring in your head."

She said, "If a correlation exists between head size and intelligence, Mr. Jaggers, you are indeed smart."

Wemmick said, "I have made important discoveries, and both of you should turn your minds to them."

"Miss Havisham's mind isn't at the moment able to turn," Jaggers said. "It is gaseous and floating. What can be observed from her current altitude can only be imagined but not by me. You and I would look tiny from up where she is, Mr. Wemmick, despite the size of my head."

She said, "A career at chancellery has made you cryptic and obscure, Mr. Jaggers. I do not have a notion of what you just said. Have you just asked me to dance?"

"I have spent eight hours bent over a table with a magnifying glass in my hand," Wemmick said, "a martyr to your instruction, Mr. Jaggers. Examining this book of accounts, and three others, and inspecting Hugh Havisham's papers."

Miss Havisham leaned in her chair to pick at the red furbelow on her hem. She flicked away an errant bit of thread.

Jaggers glanced at his client. "If your information cannot wait, will you offer me a truncated version?"

His face reflecting the benevolence of superior knowledge, Wemmick said, "Through diligence and attention to detail, through the unabated power to bring my mind to bear . . . ."

"All due credit to you," Jaggers said. "Get on with it."

Wemmick formed one of his hands into a claw, a depiction of grasping crookedness. "Miss Havisham here does not own Satis House or the brewery."

The lawyer's eyes narrowed. "Of course, she does. I have seen her father's last will and testament. She is his only heir."

"Just before his death Hugh Havisham transferred fee simple in the property for an undisclosed reason. At the time of his death, Mr. Havisham did not own Satis House. One cannot bequeath in a last will and testament what one does not own."

Miss Havisham's head came up. Had there been prancing unicorns and twinkling fairies in her vision, they had abruptly vanished.

Jaggers pulled his mouth into a ferocious scowl. This news was an indictment of the lawyer's stewardship of the Havisham family.

"Under terms of the document," Wemmick said, "Miss Havisham here has two weeks from today to vacate Satis House."

His voice low and ominous, Jaggers asked, "Who owns Satis House today?"

"A name I'm not familiar with," Wemmick said. "A fellow by the name Murdstone. Edward Murdstone."

* * * *

Perhaps later in life young Luke would view this day with charity and fondness. Time blurs events too painful to recollect in grim detail. The passing years are a balm. Memories become less hurtful. But sometimes time is also strawberry marmalade, and no matter how much of it is spread on an onion, the onion remains an onion, and so this day was for Luke an onion, never to gain a sweeter taste or a rosier glow or a duller edge or whatever other amelioration the passing of the years might offer to a less dreadful day, and such is the nature of a day filled with bullies, thieves, and hogs.

The Margate coach—this one named Blue Streak—departed from the Red Stag Inn on Old Bond Street every morning at seven, and the assigned moment approached. The coachman's wooden-soled shoes echoed between the buildings as he moved along, attending to his horses and passengers. With eight gilt buttons on his coat, the Blue Streak's guard climbed aboard. His smooth-bore piece was passed up to him. Porters stowed carpet bags and wood trunks on top of the coach and also on the rear board, securing them with rope. Aided by a porter who placed a wood step on the cobblestone, a woman wearing a green travelling shawl climbed into the cab, followed by three men in long coats and half-boots.

Several people studied the stage schedule posted to the side of the booking office's door, and folks rushed up the steps into the office, and others sped back down. A line of stages formed behind the Margate coach, waiting turns to load passengers and freight.

The driver called, "Let them go, Willy. Give them their heads."

The stable hand released the lead horse's collar, and the Blue Streak jolted forward. Luke sprinted from a wine merchant's door, and gripped rope on the back of the stage, hoisting himself onto freight platform and wedging between carpet bags.

The stage picked up speed. The Blue Streak had been manufactured by John Bessant, and featured Obadiah Elliot's spring suspension but even so it bounced wildly over the street stones and drains. Luke fiercely gripped the ropes, the freight plank threatening to bounce him off as the street retreated behind him.

A boy's burdens should be a boy's, not a man's. In this were a world of justice, a yoke would fit the shoulders on which it sat rather than being a cruel weight strapped to a thin frame. But of course, justice was airy and rare, and it seldom alighted on a street waif such as Luke. In his young life he had already been burdened with cold and hunger, and now—with justice distracted and distant—Luke's burden increased tenfold. He possessed desperate news, and it had to be delivered at all costs.

The stage passed civilian and military tailor shops, bootmakers, dairies, fishmonger stands, china and carpet dealers, printers, art studios, and upholsterer shops. The driver bawled at pedestrians and drivers, and cracked his whip in their directions, attempting to get them out of the way. The Blue Streak negotiated passages between barouches, hackneys, beer wagons, salt carts, curricles, gigs, landaus, horses, mules, and donkeys.

After the stage had traveled by the shops of saddlers, watchmakers, cutlers, tobacconists, dress makers, parfumiers, and jewelers, the town became sparser. The Blue Streak crossed London Bridge toward Southwark. The air smelled of the clammy riverbanks.

As the stage rolled off the bridge onto the river's south bank and turned southeast onto Tooley Street, the driver called, "Hiddap, you. Never seen such a lazy troupe. Get going there."

The vehicle gained speed. Luke glanced down at the roadway. He could make nothing of the road surface, the stage was moving so quickly. He had never before ridden a vehicle. The fastest Luke had ever traveled was the speed with which his legs could carry him. His fingers were around the fright rope so tightly his knuckles were white.

"Go on with you, brat," came from above him. "No free rides on the Blue Streak, you hear me?"

The guard had crawled back along on the carriage's roof, and peered over the ledge down at the freight boot. His chin was large enough to throw shade. He jabbed the barrel of his weapon down at the boy, poking him in the shoulder and then on the hands that gripped the ropes, not too hard at first but then in earnest, stabbing the muzzle into Luke's shoulder and the back of his neck and his hands. Luke grimaced with pain and released the rope to ward of the blows.

When the man thrust the muzzle into Luke's chin, the boy could no longer hold on, and he slipped off the baggage ledge and fell to the roadway. He rolled and rolled, scuffing and scraping himself.

The guard laughed and called out, "No spongers on this route, boy."

The Blue Streak rattled away. One of Luke's knees bled through his trouser leg. He rolled up his pant leg and picked out sand from the wound then squeezed his eyes closed against the pain as he stood. Luke dodged a horse and rider heading toward the city, and then a wheat wagon and then a royal mail coach where the driver wore a scarlet coat trimmed in gold braid. Dust rose from the vehicles' wheels as they passed.

Luke lifted his wool cap from the road and snapped it across his good knee to rid it of dust, and returned the cap to his head. He limped along in the direction the stage had travelled.

"This here's a toll road, MacDougal." A boy of about fourteen years old had appeared from behind a stone fence.

Luke checked behind himself. Nobody else there. This fellow was speaking to him.

"My name isn't MacDougal," Luke said.

"It is until I'm done talking to you. We was speaking about this here being a toll road, and I happen to be the toll collector. I'm a road rate man standing right in front of you, waiting for the coins."

The young man's hair was the color of the thatch on the roof of the nearby hut where he must have lived. A mangy brown goat was tethered to a corner of the hut, and black and white chickens hurried about, stabbing the ground. The fellow's face was the color of a dead leaf, and his ears stuck out like wind vanes. His jaw was wider than his forehead, making his head appear upside down. His filthy wool jacket had bone buttons and ragged pockets. He was barefoot. He stepped closer to Luke and crossed his arms. The goat bleated.

Luke pulled coins from his pocket. "I've only got four pence."

"This is your lucky day, MacDougal, because the toll on this here road happens to be four pence, and not one farthing less." The fellow held out his hand.

"This is my money for bread and cheese."

"Now it's my money for bread and cheese. Hand it over."

"You aren't a real toll collector," Luke declared. "You just stand out here with your stupid goat and pick on people littler than you, and I don't like it."

The fellow lifted Luke off the ground by his jacket front, and held his face right in front of his own, not two inches apart, their chests bumping each other.

"Don't make me bang your head on the ground, MacDougal. You'll be crying for your ma and pa."

"Let me go," Luke said, a squeak. He swatted at the bigger boy's arms.

When the young man shook Luke like a rug Luke's teeth clattered together.

"Here they are." Luke held out the pennies.

The toll-taker grabbed the coins and dropped them into a pocket. He shook Luke again, then shoved him away. Luke tumbled backward over roadway stones but kept his feet under him.

"And don't forget the toll on the way back." The young man scowled in a way he may have thought ferocious. "I'll be here." He jumped over the stone fence, likely to wait for the next child to come by.

Luke stepped along the road, then opened his hand. In his palm were his four pennies, and two more pennies that had belonged to the toll taker, along with a lead slug, half of a chewed pencil, a bit of twine, and a polished agate the size of a knuckle. He laughed. The toll taker hadn't felt a thing as he had been light-fingered. Mr. Fagin was a good teacher.

Luke would come to wish that Mr. Fagin had taught him about pigs. A mammoth hog waited for the boy. At least, it appeared the hog was waiting because the animal was on his haunches just sitting there, partly hidden in a bank of gorse alongside a hawthorn tree, its eyes following wagons and horses as they passed. The pig wore a rope collar and notches in one of its ears.

The boy strolled past the pig without seeing it. If pigs are capable of wondering, perhaps this pig wondered about Luke because it pushed himself to standing, crossed a ditch to gain the road, and followed Luke about ten feet behind the boy.

Luke soon realized he was being shadowed porcinely. An oink—more a deep-throated rumble—gave away the animal. Luke spun to the sound to find not just a pig—many times he'd seen pigs ushered along London streets, and he had thought he knew of pigs—but this wasn't a regular pig. It was the king of pigs. It filled the roadway as it settled on his posterior to give Luke more study.

This swine was the size of a handsome cab. It would have fed a regiment for a month. The hairy, floppy triangles that passed for ears were mounted on a massive globular head. Its snout was as large as a dinner plate, and its eyes were suspicious black pinpricks that gazed at Luke. Jowls were thick and rubbery. The pig's shoulders and chest formed one colossal slab of muscle. Patchy hair covered some of the hog's brown and gray stippled skin. It stared at the boy with what appeared to be much satisfaction, sitting there on the road.

Smarting from his tumble from the stage, Luke said, "I don't have time for pigs today, pig." He continued his walk east along the road.

The hog grunted, lifted its grizzled huge self from the roadway, and huffed after Luke, ten feet behind him.

Luke's chin came up. He had never before been followed by a pig. Dogs once in a while but never a pig. When he turned around, the animal stopped.

Luke pointed back down the road. "Go home, pig."

The worthies at the Royal Society—with thousands of dissections among them—would assure Luke that pigs do not have the facial musculature to enable them to smile but this pig appeared to be grinning at Luke.

"Don't follow me, pig," the boy said. "People will think I stole you, and I'll get arrested, and boys are sent across the ocean on a boat for less. You go on back home."

Again, Luke walked eastward, and again the hog followed ten feet behind him, snuffing and blowing, its grand girth shifting left and right as it moved forward. When Luke tested the pig by running a few steps so did the pig, ten feet behind the boy.

Luke spun to the animal. "Go home, you."

No movement from the pig, so Luke stepped up to it and pushed its shoulder. The pig grunted but gave no indication he was going to alter his present inertia in any way. The boy tried again, leaning into the pig, his hands sinking into the pig's wiry hair. He shoved mightily but for all the movement ceded by the pig Luke might as well have been pushing an oak tree.

Then the boy tugged on the rope around the animal's neck. The pig looked at him, but otherwise gave no indication it was inclined to move off his spot on the road. Their eyes met in what might have been an instant of shared understanding.

Luke surveyed the fields on both sides of the road. "Ain't a pig alive that turns down food."

He walked to the side of the road and climbed up a stone wall. He jumped down into an orchard where the tree trunks were gnarled and the boughs bent and spotted with lichen, trees as old as the earth they stood on. He scanned the field. The farmer's house was at the edge of the orchard.

Luke jumped and snagged a branch. He picked off two apples. A turnip wagon passed, the driver cursing the pig for sitting in the road. Up and over the fence Luke went, back to the hog.

He held an apple six inches from the pig's snout. "Do pigs like apples? Why not? They like everything else."

The pig moved toward the apple but Luke sidestepped it.

"Follow me, pig, and I'll give you this nice apple. Yum. I bet it's good."

Luke began walking back the way he had just come. With a grunting, rasping, heaving effort the pig realigned itself to follow the boy. Luke held the apple behind him as he walked, and the big pig moved after him. They came to a gap in the stone fence, and Luke pinched his nose against the inimitable odor of a sty.

Luke gave the hog one of the apples, and its slavering, chomping, and drooling would have been gratifying under many circumstances but rather than appreciate the satisfaction with which the pig consumed the apple, Luke held out another one, and moved toward the sty.

"I'm not going to be arrested and sent far away because of you, pig." He walked around a bramble toward the enclosure.

The sty must have been owned by the same family whose apple crop Luke had just reduced. Their cottage was through the trees, a whitewashed stone building with clay pots of red geraniums near the front door. A cowshed was behind the barn, and beyond that a fenced field, and then marshland to the river.

Luke lured the pig along between pear trees. The grassy field gave way to mud as the boy and the pig approached the sty. Inside the sty three pink sows stood in muck up to their hocks. They stared at the big pig and his human escort. A ramp from the mud led up to a ramshackle pig shed made of unpainted boards. The gate to the sty was open but the sows hadn't availed themselves of the opportunity.

"This is easy." Luke held up the second apple. "Come on in, big boy." He stepped through the gate into the sty, his shoes sinking. He wiggled the apple in the pig's direction. Outsmarting a pig was a sublime moment, to be sure.

Not much good occurs when one gets between pigs and food. Aimed at the boy who held up the apple, the sows rushed across the muck, and the big pig must have spotted the threat to his second apple so it, too, charged. The first sow bumped Luke's hip and the second one knocked him backward, and the big pig brushed him, spinning him around and toppling him to the muck. The apple flew into the air, and which pig managed to catch it would forever remain a mystery to Luke.

But the brown slime on the ground of a pig sty would no longer remain a mystery because Luke landed flat upon it from his toes to his forehead, splashing it up on both sides of him. This was goo in its vilest form. Stinking, slimy, nasty, and nauseating. Luke tried to scramble to his feet but he slipped and landed back down in the muck on his left side. The sludge seeped under his shirt and into his shoes. He lifted his head out of the sludge, it clung to his ear and chin and hair. He manically tried to brush it from his head but that just spread it along his arm and down his neck.

He gasped and spit and wiped his mouth with the back of his hand. He spit again and again. Moving carefully, one limb at a time, he successfully rose to standing and he stepped toward the sty's gate. The muck sucked off his shoes, and he couldn't stand the thought of fishing them out. The huge hog staring at him, Luke pushed through the gate, and crossed the field toward the road. He held his arms away from his body. Clumps of sty slop dropped off him.

So this is how the boy found himself again on the road east. As foul a manifestation may have never before presented itself in Kent. Smeared, smattered, and smudged in pig grime. Every orifice, every surface, every hair, right down to between his toes. His eyes were shiny white orbs in his filthy face.

Luke stunk so badly that a dog that had been minding its own business on the side of the road sprinted away into the bushes. And a horse carrying an officer of the King's Own stopped and would not proceed one more step until the officer directed his horse into a field around the boy.

Luke could have turned back, as he was still closer to the city than he was to his destination, but retreat did not occur to him. Sodden, malodorous, and dripping, he continued his journey east, his mission still desperate.

19

Fagin squinted up at the light. In the Old Bailey courtroom, a mirror hung from the rafters reflecting window light onto the defendant so that jurors could clearly see his face, the better to detect dissimulation. The pickpocket stood at the bar, a hand on the oak rail for support, and a sheriff at his shoulder. A judge in a powdered wig and black robe occupied a horsehair chair so wide that the upholsterer's rows of brass nails could be seen on both sides of him.

"Jurors, you have just heard the crown's case, and though the defendant, this"—the judge glanced down at his documents— "Mr. Fagin did not retain the services of a lawyer he has been allowed to defend himself, and he did so, and a more vaporous skein of half-truths and lies has seldom been heard in this court."

The pickpocket wore jail sackcloth trousers and shirt woven from hemp. "Your worship, are you not prohibited from commenting on the testimony?"

"In your case," the judge replied, "justice requires an exception."

Old Bailey was also called the Sessions House, Justice Hall, and the Central Criminal Court. One wall of the courtroom had until recently been open to the air—no wall at all, the floor above supported by columns—so that the fresh air would prevent jail fever, known outside the confines of the jail as typhus, but winters were bitter and prisoners succumbing to the fever was more reasonable than a judge wearing mittens and an overcoat.

"Were I shorter," the judge said, "I would put your file on my chair to elevate me so I could fully see the courtroom. It is that thick."

Crumbs of humor seldom fell from the bench, and this exception was met with hearty laughter.

The judge sat a good distance from his desk because the size of his belly demanded it. Twice a day he ate in the Lord Mayor's dining room on the ground floor of the Old Bailey, with its Turkish carpet, mosaic fireplace, mahogany dining table, and wine vault. The prisoners' pens below ground were nothing of the kind. Nor was the semi-circular brick bail dock just outside the building where more prisoners waited.

The judge's dewlaps wagged when he spoke. "This is the defendant's fourth time at the dock in the courtroom. Jurors, you have the power to make it his last."

One wall contained windows, and raindrops slid down the glass. The courtroom was a sea of faces: those of turnkeys, sheriffs, bailiffs, proceeding writers, newspaper reporters, prosecutors, defense lawyers, witnesses, jurors, clerks, ushers, and shackled defendants awaiting their turns.

The prosecutor was a smidgeon of a man whose trousers were almost up to his armpits and whose cuffs were rolled back. He jammed a monocle into a socket. A blue ribbon—his only bow to color—connected the eyeglass to his lapel. His face was pinched, lined, and uncharitable.

He said, "My closing statement, your honor." He rose from his chair and pulled out items one at a time from a bag and held them up. "A silver presentation dagger with *Major. A.D. Leffler* engraved on the blade. Three pocket watches, one of them inscribed *To my loving husband John*. Eight silk handkerchiefs, two of them with embroidered initials on them, none of them with an *F* for *Fagin*."

The accused, that very same Fagin, became smaller and smaller as each item was displayed, folding in on himself.

"A silver inkwell, a gold boutonniere pin, six silver watch chain seals, and a belt with a filigreed brass buckle, and how someone can remove a belt from his victim's trousers speaks to Mr. Fagin's artistry. All these expensive objects were found on Mr. Fagin when he was arrested."

Spectators had been admitted to the gallery a story above the courtroom, for which they were each charged a shilling. Many of the gallery attendees lived their lives there, the courtroom more entertaining than the theater because the stakes were higher. The dreadfully solemn moment when an accused heard his fate—to watch the defendant's face when he learned he would soon become acquainted with the afterlife—was worth a shilling. If the defendant were a woman, admission was two shillings. The horror, the sobbing, the wailing from her family, the rending of garments, her collapse, turnkeys carrying the condemned woman from the courtroom to the cell below. It was more than entertainment; it was an edifying display of both the frailty of the human condition and the majesty of the English justice system. And spectators could eat meat pies and boiled eggs in the galley.

The prosecutor said, "Mr. Fagin will steal anything than is shiny or engraved. He is a walking haberdasher of other people's possessions."

This fine phrase from the prosecutor brought laughter from the gallery.

The judge hammered his desk with his gavel and glared at the spectators. "Silence up there."

What this court lacked in jocularity it made up for with alacrity. Fagin had been arrested that very morning.

"The crown rests its case, your honor."

The judge withdrew a piece of hard candy from a drawer and pushed it into his mouth. "It falls upon me now to give you, the jury, your charge, and it is this: if you find that Mr. Fagin owned the items just shown to you, then you should acquit him. If not, then convict him. I now ask you to render a verdict. The court will remain in session while you deliberate."

The Old Bailey did not have a jury room. Still inside the jury box, jurors turned to each other to review evidence among themselves while the judge, defendant, and all others in the room waited. Some thieves were branded after pronouncement of their sentences, and the irons were in a rack near a stone fireplace.

Regarding the pickpocket Fagin, reaching a verdict was a matter of the jury looking at each other and nodding.

Wearing a white cravat above a white waistcoat, the foreman rose to his feet. He regally lifted his chin, and loudly cleared his throat.

"Has the jury reached a verdict?" the judge asked.

"We have, your honor. We find the defendant guilty as charged of all counts, and had the crown brought more counts we would have found him guilty of those, too."

The gallery applauded.

The judge reached for his gavel. "A verdict given with such admirable alacrity deserves a sentence delivered in the same alacritous spirit. This court sentences you to transportation to New Holland on the next available ship."

"New Holland, your honor?" Fagin shook his head. "In the southern hemisphere? When will I be able to return."

"Not in your present corporeal form. The sentence is for your natural lifetime."

Two jailors moved toward Fagin.

"And until the departure date of the next ship to New Holland, you will be kept on a hulk on the Thames because you are an escape risk." The judge's gavel came down sharply. "Case closed."

The jailors led Fagin away.

"Next." The judge pulled a file from his stack. "Cheswood. Larceny and arson. Bring this Martin Cheswood to the bar, sheriff."

* * * *

Luke pumped water, and splashed it onto his hands, brushing them together, trying to rid himself of dibs and dabs of disgusting dross. He dashed water across his face, and was about to try to fit his entire self under the nozzle when he spotted a woman in the window of the cottage. She wore an apron, and she placed a pie on the window ledge, fanning it with a hand. Luke stopped pumping, and slid across the yard toward an ash tree, hoping the lady hadn't seen him.

The woman in the window withdrew into the cottage, leaving the pie on a rack in the window. Luke stunk so badly from his frolic in the pigsty that he held his nose high into the air trying to lift it above the putrid vapors rising from him. He hadn't eaten anything since the day before, and nobody in the city of London would be so careless as to leave a pie in a window and so this was a veritable invitation to partake in it.

Trailing stench, he walked from one tree to another, hiding his approach to the home. Above the stone walls the thatch roof was new and still yellow. Smoke rose from a chimney. To the west were cow pens, and a slat building was in the rear, a mill or plant or warehouse. A chaffinch whistled and chirped in a bush near the house.

Luke hid behind laundry hanging from a line strung between two posts. He sniffed the air, hoping to catch a scent of the pie. Might it be apple or cherry? Or maybe it is a shepherd's pie with meat and potatoes. The boy reeked but even so he could imagine the taste of that pie. As he stared at it from behind damp linens fluttering in an idle breeze, his hunger became profound and desperate, as it is with boys. Sounds came from behind the house. Hammering and scraping. And despite his own overpoweringly foul pig odor, Luke detected another scent when the wind shifted, this one so nasty that it chased away thoughts of the pie. He clenched his entire face against the new smell. It was a chemical odor, sharp and powerful.

But then the breeze turned again, and the new, outrageous smell went away. Luke looked again at the pie. His stomach demanded it. He had to have that pie right now. He crossed the yard toward the window, and a brown rooster with crimson comb and wattle emerged from behind a woodpile to watch him. On his tiptoes, Luke approached the window, and with both hands made to snatch the pie.

And the lady made to stop him. "Get away from that pie, you," she called from inside.

Luke gripped the pie tin and stepped back from the window. The tin was hot but he held it on the tips of his fingers. The rooster dipped its beak, appearing to approve. The boy ran toward the corner of the house in the direction of the road but the woman must have come from a rear door to cut him off.

A broom held in her hands she charged him. "Give me back that pie, you good-for-nothing devil."

Luke sprinted away; the pie held in front of him.

Her apron flapping, the woman ran after him, her broom high over her head, cocked and loaded. "Come here, you."

The boy dodged a mossy tree stump, then ran around a brush pile. The lady could run, make no mistake, and she cut off his retreat to the road. He dashed left.

'I'll get you, you thief." Her voice was piping, and her words delivered between gasps for breath.

Luke ran by a four-wheeled barrel cart with a mule in harness. The mule turned its ears toward Luke but otherwise didn't appear interested. Hoping to find a hiding place, the pie thief sprinted toward the out-building behind the cottage. To his right were racks of cowhide, stretched to dry. Under a shingle roof held up by posts were stacks of hides splattered with dried gore and blood and rabbit pelts hanging from bars.

The woman swung the broom, stirring the air behind Luke's head. He darted left around a goat pen. Three or four men worked in a shed forty yards ahead, hauling skins. For an instant Luke considered dropping the pie to make his escape from the demon lady but he couldn't bear the prospect of not eating so he dashed past a tool shed aiming for the marshland beyond.

He didn't make it. As he changed directions—the woman still behind him—Luke didn't see the hide scraper lying on the ground, and his foot caught under the handle, and he flew sideways into the pond.

But this wasn't a pond. It was a tanning pit. In all the world between the Barents Sea and the Sphinx, between the Canary Islands and Lake Ladoga, the only thing more foul than a pigsty is a tanning pit, where hides are soaked in urine. Cow urine, goat urine, horse urine, lady with the broom urine, all available urine, too precious to waste. Tanning pits are the only item in the landscape that flies will not fly over. Too close, birds will fall from trees. The smell—which would embarrass a corpse and gag a maggot—had been known to start wars.

The pie landed in the pit and then so did Luke, throwing out a wave of urine and sending up drops of the same. He had recent experience with belly flopping into fetid slop, and he managed to keep his eyes and mouth shut.

"My pie," the woman hollered. "Now you are in for it, boy." She circled the pit.

A fellow—perhaps her husband—in a tweed cap had been pushing a wheelbarrow nearby, and he left the barrow and moved to the tanning pit, looking down at Luke.

Her hands on her hips, the woman declared, "Ben, your dinner is in there, along with that thief."

The tanner stared at the boy as he might a page of Newton's calculus.

"You get that boy." The woman ordered Ben, her equine nostrils flaring. "Get that thief. We'll take him to the magistrate."

"He's a boy and it was a pie. It's not the Great Fire of London, Hannah." She narrowed her eyes at the tanner. "I worked all day on that venison pie. He must be brought to justice."

Ben laughed. "I think he already has. Go on with you, boy, and I hope you have somewhere to go."

Urine splashing off him, Luke slid his feet on the pool's bottom so as not to slip, and stepped up to solid ground at the pit edge. He wiped his eyes, and didn't dare look at the pie lady or her husband. Other tanners had lined up to stare at the lad. Luke squinted, trying to keep the fluid out of his eyes. He dripped from every surface.

The goat backed away as Luke rounded the house. Sodden, squishy, and smelly, Luke found the road again, and turned east.

* * * *

"Humbled and humiliated, I stand before you," Inspector Buckle said.

"You look horrible." Miss Havisham held the baby Estella in one arm. Her other arm, the injured one, hung at her side. "Your bruise is an unusual color. Green and yellow. And the swelling under your eye is purple. Your split lip is red. With all your colors you should be displayed on a gallery wall alongside a Gainsborough."

"I am feeling too poorly to be humored, madam." His face had been ill-used. Stitches laced together a wound under an ear. His other ear was swollen, and dark patches colored the skin under his eyes. Scabs had formed along his chin line. Copper buttons lined Bucket's coat. "You hired me to protect and advise you, and I have failed on all counts."

Miss Havisham led the detective along the hallway toward the library. A pink blanket covered Estella. Wispy strands of the baby's hair were adorned with a yellow bow. She was asleep.

"You placed such trust and confidence in me—and paid a goodly fee—that a letter from the city to you would not have sufficed for my declaration so I have traveled here." Bucket stiffly drew himself up. "Madam, I am resigning from your employment."

"You are my articled apprentice." She grinned at him. "You can't resign."

"My face hurts too much to smile, Miss Havisham."

"I have asked that you call me Margaret."

She entered the library. Leather-bound volumes filled a floor-to-ceiling bookcase on the far wall. Sun from a window lit up a mahogany desk with inlaid bands of a darker wood and brass drawer handles. The walls were of dark paneling. A poker, hand broom, and shovel were in a rack next to the tiled fireplace. A fringed purple and crimson Berber carpet covered much of the floor. Against a wall were carved oak chairs resembling thrones.

"Do you read fiction, inspector?"

"I do not."

"Why not?"

"Because it's fiction."

"My fiancé Samuel Compeyson used to read to me under the arbor in the garden outside. Such wonderful stories. And he had a lovely voice." She kissed the baby's forehead. "A voice designed to generate warmth."

"And lull suspicions?"

She said, "Your resignation is not accepted."

"Do you know how many fistfights and brawls I have endured during my police career?"

"How could I possibly know that?"

Estella opened her eyes, yawned, and closed them again. Miss Havisham rocked the baby in her arm.

"Thirty-eight."

"You keep a record?" she asked. "Like a counting house clerk with a quill and a ledger?"

"And that's not counting those involving knives and clubs. Just fists, those thirty-eight." He followed her from the library along the hallway to the stairway,

"I can give a mighty blow and I can take one," Bucket said. "I've learned to be good with my fists. Or thought I was."

"I want to show you a room." She carried Estella up the stairs. "It may make things clearer for you."

He climbed after Miss Havisham, and said, "But I was following Compeyson and I ran into a something new, a fellow who had many times my ability. He was beyond my experience. He was guarding Compeyson."

Window light coming through open doors lit the hallway.

"It was such a mismatch," Bucket said, "that while I was being pummeled, I felt silly. I'm not sure which hurt more; the beating or the embarrassment."

"Judging from your face, the beating hurt more."

"You need a better bodyguard than me. And I have failed at the second part of my charge, which is to give you good advice. Which is to say, advice you will follow."

She walked along the hallway. "Who knows the seamier side of London better than you? When have I ignored your advice?"

"Horseback riding in the park, which resulted in your shoulder injury. I asked that you not go out in public without me accompanying you."

"Hold Estella, will you please?"

Bucket stepped back. "I don't know how to hold a baby."

"I learned and so can you." Miss Havisham leaned toward the policeman. "I can't use my injured arm so you take her. Put her into the crook of your arm."

189

Bucket lifted the bundle and held Estella in both hands. He looked at her and then at his own arm.

Miss Havisham laughed. "She'll fit. Go ahead and try."

Bucket maneuvered the baby onto his arm.

Producing a key from a pocket, Miss Havisham bent over the door's keyhole. She turned the key. "This is my special room." She stepped inside.

Bucket and the baby followed her in, and the detective stopped, and his eyes widened. Drapes covered the windows, and the room was dusky. His gaze swept the room and found the wedding cake that had settled in on itself. Hardened pieces of frosting had dropped from the cake's side onto the table. Air in the room was heavy and musty. Candles on the chimney piece were unlit, and cold cinders filled the fireplace. The cloth on the long table likely had once been brilliantly white but dust had dimmed it. The silver epergne on the table had lost its gleam. The apples and pears inside were shriveled and stinking, as was the fruit on the garlands. A spider web covered a corner of the room near the fireplace. Dried, crumbly flower bouquets occupied many places in the room. A mannequin wore Miss Havisham's fading wedding dress, the shoes on the floor near the hem.

"Do you feel anything in this room, inspector?"

"I feel the urge to flee."

"I mean, does the room speak to you?"

Bucket looked at Miss Havisham. "Is this room talking to you, Margaret?"

Her smile was humorless. "Not in so many words. I wanted you to see what drives me."

"Shouldn't you throw the cake and fruit into the waste bin? What is the purpose of saving them?"

"The fruit is getting nasty, isn't it? And the cake. The nastier they get the nastier I'll get."

"I spend my life around criminals." He smiled. "You aren't nasty like they are."

"You have no idea."

"You and I are working to locate Samuel Compeyson. Nastiness isn't involved. It's my job to arrest him. We'll get him."

"Getting him is only half of his due. Almost everything I learned about my fiancé Samuel was fiction except, I believe, this one thing: he is desperate to join the *beau monde*. Wealthy, fashionable society has an allure for him that is unnatural."

"Compeyson is a sophisticated swindler," Bucket said. "He can't be that shallow."

"Every time he reads of a gala Mayfair ball that he wasn't invited to, he gets smaller. Every time he sees gentlemen leave their Pall Mall clubs, he dies a little. More than anything in life, he wants to get through those closed doors."

"You are planning something other than his arrest?"

"He is going to be humiliated, just as I was. It will be the worst moment of his life."

"Do you have a plan?" Bucket asked. "Do you know how to do it?"

"I know humiliation, yes."

"What about your brother Arthur? He helped Compeyson."

"Arthur is a weakling and a dullard. I'm going to forget about him."

Bucket passed Estella back to Miss Havisham, who kissed the baby's head. The detective worked his hands together.

"You needn't brush your hands, inspector. The baby isn't dusty."

He looked at Miss Havisham. "This room is worrisome, is it not?"

"Not to me." She rocked Estella.

"People have been sent to Dr. Willis in Shillingthorpe for less, haven't they? George III, for one."

"I am perfectly sane, inspector."

"I'm not seeing evidence of sanity here." Bucket spread his hands, encompassing the room. "I try to base my judgments on evidence—on the facts as I discover them, and I try to look at them in an unbiased and charitable eye—but I must tell you, Margaret, this room is unsettling."

"A few keepsakes. What is wrong with that?"

"Perhaps in boxes in a back room or in a wardroom, nothing wrong with that. We all have a few things put away." He turned left and right, his eyes clicking from one item to the next. "But this display—all your wedding items left as they were that day—is a frozen tableau. It is eerie and troubling."

"I'll get around to sorting and cleaning someday," she said. "I have other things to think about now. One of my guests saw Samuel that day, have I told you?"

"At your wedding ceremony?"

"He was hiding in a shed at the far end of the Mulberry Garden behind Satis House, where he could witness my disgrace and agony." Her tone was full and bitter. "And I am in correspondence with a young lady who lives near Bristol in Gloucestershire. He swindled her, too. He didn't appear at the altar for her, either, and she learned later that he was near the back of the church that day, listening and watching. He likes to witness the humiliation."

"One of your maids confided in me a few minutes ago, Margaret, that yesterday you were patently barmy. 'Quite mad,' she put it."

Miss Havisham laughed. "My dalliance with laudanum. I can recall a few moments after I drank the potion, and I shudder with embarrassment. Poor Mr. Jaggers. He fled back to the city, and I can't blame him."

"Can you get along without it, with your shoulder?" Bucket asked.

"Whether I can or cannot, I will."

"I have known people lost to laudanum."

191

She snuggled Estella against her chest. "I have lost much of the Havisham fortune to my fiancé, and yesterday I learned that my so-called business partner Edward Murdstone somehow owns Satis House, my home. The one thing I know I have—without question—is my intellect."

"An estimable resource," Bucket said.

Smiling, Estella waved her pink arms.

"My brain," Miss Havisham said. "It is my parents' gift to me. I have traded on it all my life. At the end of the day that is what I have. It cannot be stolen from me. I'm not going to pickle it in opium again, I don't care how badly my shoulder throbs."

The detective stepped out of the wedding room, and with a gesture invited her to follow.

But she stayed deeply inside the room, baby in her arms, and spoke to Bucket through the doorway. "After I was left at the altar, I spent many days here in this room. My father was terribly worried."

"Let's go downstairs, Margaret."

"But now I've got my ex-fiancé Samuel Compeyson in my sights." Her words gained speed and timber as if she were trying to use them to convince herself. "He will pay for what he did, I will see to it. With your help. And so my wedding dress and cake can't keep me in here in this room, do you see? They do not have a lock on me."

He stared gravely through the doorway at her. "I will not be in the employ of a madwoman, Margaret. Life is too perilous and crazed as it is."

"You have nothing to fear along those lines. A room of wedding knickknacks and mementoes. Nothing more. Watch this." She surveyed the room, inhaled deeply, then with long and exaggerated steps moved toward the door. But then her shoulders heaved as if seized by an unseen force, and she stopped just in front of the sill, still inside the room. Her gaze shot to the wall near the fireplace. "Did you hear that, inspector?"

Bucket stepped back into the room. "What did you hear?"

"Something." She pressed her lips together, as if afraid to reveal more.

"A voice?" he asked.

"A suggestion. A comforting suggestion."

"You hear words?" Bucket's voice was astringent. "Whose voice? What are you talking about?"

"It was inviting. Lovely and comforting and knowing. Did you not hear it?"

"I heard nothing."

Surveying the room, she turned a full circle. "And it doesn't say things in words, more like tones that enter my head but not through my ears."

The skin of the inspector's face had lost a shade. "Come along, Margaret."

"I think I'll stay. Estella and I like this room. We prefer it here."

"Forgive the impertinence." Bucket stepped to Miss Havisham, grasped her shoulder—the uninjured one—and pulled her and the baby through the doorway and into the hall. He pushed her down the hallway.

Her words crackled with indignation. "You had no right to do that. I am an adult, and I own this house, and I take umbrage at you touching me."

His hand on the small of her back, Bucket propelled her farther along the hallway toward the stairs.

Her eyes wide, Miss Havisham shook herself as if emerging from a trance. Bucket stopped pushing her.

"What was I saying?" She chewed on her lower lip. "Inspector, I had a moment back there. It was nothing. A bad bit of mutton, perhaps. My Lord. What next? A vision of one-eyed Woden on this throne?" She laughed, but it was brittle and forced.

Bucket remained behind her as if to block a dash back to the room.

Miss Havisham continued toward the stairs as if nothing peculiar had occurred. "Once I settle my account with Samuel Compeyson," she said, "I'll sweep out the wedding room and be done with it."

"It appears you also have an account with Edward Murdstone," Bucket said.

"I will settle that, too, I assure you."

Piping words came from the floor below. "Miss Havisham. Help."

The policeman glanced at her, and then he rushed after her along the hall and toward the stairs.

Stitched taut and full of disapproval, a maid rushed up the stairs. "You should see him, madam. I didn't let him inside."

Miss Havisham and the detective hurried down the stairs. And there, in the doorway, stood young Luke.

Dappled in filth, drenched in foulness, and stinking beyond measure, he yelled, "Mr. Fagin has been arrested. He's been taken away."

20

Years ago, an admiral's pennant had flown from the *HMS Fallon's* masthead. Nelson, Jervis, and Collingwood had walked the ship's decks. Seventy-four guns had been ranged to port and starboard. The brightwork had gleamed, the rigging had sung, and the sails had been blinding. The ship had brought the king's majesty to ports in every corner of the world.

But the mighty *HMS Fallon* had been brought low. Bare of masts and rigging, and its figurehead, binnacle, bowsprit, and bell removed, it floated in the Thames keeled to starboard five degrees, and lower in the water than during its days of glory. Black rot worked on the hull's oak planks. Many taffrails had fallen off, and some gun port covers were missing. The *Fallon* was bedraggled, and had the appearance of having been ignored, floating out there in the river.

The ship was far from ignored. It was a prison hulk. Iron bars covered the gun ports and guards patrolled the main deck. Moored alongside was a dingy into which two canvas-wrapped corpses were being lowered, prisoners who had cheated the crown of its justice by failing to live out their sentences.

Miss Havisham sat in the bow of a wherry that neared the prison ship. Her frock was a muted yellow with red flowers embroidered on the sleeves. A tweed handbag with a shoulder strap rested on her lap, and it was heavy, pressing onto her legs. She held a linen square to her mouth and nose.

Through the cloth she asked, "Can't we approach from another direction, sir?"

The wherryman's tin license badge decorated his sleeve. "We'll get there as quickly as ever can be, madam."

"It smells like death out here," she said.

"And there's a lot of that particular malady at our destination, and never were words more truly spoken." The fellow pulled at his oars. Calluses made his hands thick. His nose was so long it hung over his lips. "The wind is blowing from the ship, madam. It's a dirty place, and there's no arguing about it."

An unlit lantern hung from a pole at the aft end of the wherry. The boat was lapstrake-sided and the oarlocks were leather, and was fitted with an oiled cloth cover that could be raised to protect passengers from rain, but the cover was stowed. Thin sunlight made it through the clouds, casting the river in gray.

From the aft bench, Inspector Bucket said, "At least you aren't sitting next to a hog haunch wrapped in a newspaper as I am, Margaret."

The package rested on the burden boards next to the policeman's legs. Inspector Bucket was a wide fellow—heavily molded—and he almost filled the stern thwart. His face was so square it might have been plumbed. His forehead, with the sharp angles at the temples, resembled a sledge. He wore a rounded felt hat called a billycock.

Bucket asked, "Are you prepared for this, Margaret?"

"After seeing little Luke covered in muck and mire, not much will be able to perturb me."

"We are speaking of different things. A smelly boy is one thing." Bucket gestured toward the prison ship. "This is another. Steel yourself."

A gentle wind stirred catspaws on the water. The hulk was moored below the pool of London so the river wasn't crowded with ships but the wherryman's gaze swept left and right as he guided his boat through the shipping lanes. Taking advantage of the tide, a bulky collier made its way upriver. A trawler also swept by on its way to the Billingsgate pier. Crewmen sliced open fish on an aft board and threw the guts overboard. A cloud of squawking gulls followed the trawler. A barge came downriver under its topsail, a load of red bricks on the deck, a fellow leaning over the rudder, a pipe in his mouth.

"Where did you purchase the pig haunch?" Miss Havisham's voice was just loud enough to carry over the wherryman's shoulders to the detective.

"At a butcher's shop in Rochester. I told the butcher it was for my dog."

Haze hid the south shore. On the north shore just beyond the prison hulk was a wool exchange building and a shipyard, with derricks high in the sky and a drydock at water's edge. Willows and maple trees lined some of the riverbank.

Miss Havisham had paid the wherryman twice his usual river-crossing fare, which he demanded once he learned of her destination. He had said, "It'll take me half a day to clean my boat's hull if I get close to that hulk." He now looked over his shoulder, judging distances, pulling on one oar, then the other as the wherry approached the prison ship's accommodation ladder. A flintlock under his arm, a guard on the hulk's deck stared down at the wherry. The dingy carrying that day's corpses had disappeared around the other side of the hulk, heading to shore.

In a low voice, Miss Havisham asked, "Do you think this will work, Lewis?"

Bucket tapped the package at his feet. "I've known dozens of jailors. They are all made from the same piece of cloth. Their hands are out, every one of them."

The wherryman shipped his oars just as his boat bumped against the hulk's hull near the ladder. He gripped the ladder to steady the wherry so his passengers could alight.

"State your business," came from the deck above them. An officer of the guard—wearing epaulettes and a leather shoulder band—stared down at the wherry.

Bucket looked up. "London Watchmen Inspector Lewis Bucket. We have business to discuss with the ranking officer on this ship."

"And what sort of business would that be, sir?"

"One that will be to that officer's advantage."

"Come aboard."

Miss Havisham lifted a foot over the rowboat's transom onto the step. She gripped the side ropes, and rose up the hulk's side. The accommodation ladder swayed and creaked but she climbed it rapidly. The handbag hanging from her shoulder chimed as she moved. Then Inspector Bucket climbed the ladder, the package pressed against his chest. A guard leaned over a rail and offered to help with the package but the detective shook his head.

The detective reached the hulk's deck. Miss Havisham had tucked away her linen cloth but as her eyes swept the deck her hand was at her mouth. She backstepped, so close to the rail that the guard captain touched her elbow to warn her away from the ledge. Bucket's face darkened as his gaze went stem to stern.

Some prisoners sat on the deck and others leaned against the rails and the wheel mount and the rudder post. Many lay flat on the deck, their arms spread out as if they might fly away. Most had removed their shirts to expose themselves to the sun. Their beards and hair were oily and tangled. Several sat up and shaded their eyes to look at the newcomers but the effort may have been too much, and they fell back.

Prisoners had lined up at the water butt where a guard dipped a ladle into the water and handed it to a prisoner, who used fingers to swat away green scum on the water. He drank and grimaced, then handed the ladle back. The next prisoner stepped up. Near the aft end of the ship, one inmate threw delousing powder on another, some of it drifting away to stern in the wind.

"May I be of service, madam?" The guard captain shook his head as if in answer to his own question.

"You have an inmate on this ship named Fagin," Miss Havisham said.
"I do not know prisoners' names. Names have no meaning here."
The guard captain snapped his fingers at another guard, who lifted a ledger
from the top of a weapons locker and walked it over to the captain. Eight other
guards were on deck wearing red uniform coats and gray trousers. Some
carried flintlocks and others bird guns. Most had cudgels hanging at their
waists.

The guard captain flipped open his book, his gaze following his finger
down the page. A ribbon was pinned to the captain's chest, and the epaulettes
on his uniform were oversized, covering his shoulders. The coat's brass
buttons shone. His face was pink and peeling. His blue eyes were close to his
nose, and they glanced left and right as if he feared the arrival of a superior
officer. He wore a bicorn hat.

"Number 421, a new arrival," the guard captain said. "Do you have an
order from a king's bench regarding this prisoner?"

Bucket shifted the package. "Not precisely."

The captain said, "Only clothing, a pipe, and a twist of tobacco are allowed
from shore. If personal items for the prisoner are in your package, you must
return them to shore."

The river current shifted with the incoming tide, as the hulk leaned a few
degrees, wood and iron groaning. Miss Havisham shifted a foot to keep her
balance.

"May we speak to you privately, sir?" she asked.

"That, madam, is an extra-judicial suggestion. It cannot be countenanced
in any fashion. I follow court orders and directions from the ship's warden,
and nothing else." The guard then half-stepped closer to Miss Havisham and
the detective. "But unlike my wards on this ship, you are his majesty's free
subjects, and I cannot prevent you from speaking, of course."

Cormorants flew low past the prison ship, their wings tapping the water
with each stroke.

"Your prisoner number 421 has been unfairly arrested, convicted, and
imprisoned," Miss Havisham said.

The captain laughed, a mean grating noise. "A widespread circumstance
here on board the *HMS Fallon*. Most of the convicts are innocent, if you listen
to them."

"Then I will not bandy about my purpose, sir," Miss Havisham said. "I
have made inquiries regarding your living, which is fifty pounds a year."

"Would that be your business, madam?"

"Your prisoner number 421 is worth three years of your wages to you. I
have 150 gold sovereigns in my bag. I'll hand the gold to you when you give
me the prisoner."

197

The guard captain leaned closer. "And what is your proposition? That the prisoner just walks off the ship? What about this evening's count in this ledger, which I must give to the warden tomorrow morning?"

"Nothing could be simpler," Bucket said. "Prisoner 421 jumps overboard, and is shot as he tries to swim to shore. His ruined body floats away downstream, never to be seen again."

"It happens once in a while." The guard glanced at Miss Havisham's handbag. "And it's a tragedy, of course."

"It can happen today," she said. "Order your guards and prisoners to go belowdecks."

The guard captain chewed his lower lip, glanced at the guard at the accommodation ladder than at the guard at the water butt. Then he ordered the prisoners toward the hatches. The prisoners looked at him but were silent. Several guards stared at the captain but said nothing at the unusual order. The prisoners pushed themselves to their feet, some groaning. A few swayed and grabbed a rail or post for support. Their faces were wan and sunken, their ribs showed, and their eyes were lusterless. When in active service the ship's deck had been holystoned every morning—the surgeon could have operated on it—but moss grew between the deck's plank, and rot worked on wood below the rails.

Prisoners shuffled toward the hatches, and the guards hurried them along with shoves, threats, and epithets. When a prisoner near the windlass grumbled, a guard jabbed the stock of a flintlock into his back. The prisoner stumbled forward and said nothing more.

"I want to get prisoner 421 myself," Miss Havisham said.

The guard captain looked again at his book. "Four twenty-one is on the orlop deck. You don't want to go down there, ma'am. It is not a suitable place for you."

"Take me to him," she said. "Wait here, will you please, inspector?"

The deck was almost cleared. The guard captain led her past davits toward an aft hatch. He shouldered his firearm, and descended the ladder. The odor rising through the hatch staggered Miss Havisham. She slapped her hand over her nose and mouth but it made no difference; the stink reached up from below decks and surrounded her. It was a putrid, wicked smell as thick as molasses.

She stepped back and gasped for breath but the stench stalked her, filling her head and lungs. She bit down, gripped the rail, and stepped onto the hatch ladder. She descended into darkness, then stepped onto a gundeck, her handbag rattling against her hip.

"This way, madam," the guard captain said.

"Why are these men confined on this old ship, captain?" she asked. "Instead of a jail?"

"The prisons are full, madam. His majesty's government must find confinement for the iniquitous and depraved, and it has found it on this vessel." From the deck's darkness came shuffling and clanking. A prisoner moaned, and another spit loudly. She could make out white faces, men who stared at her. They wore grayed underdrawers and tattered shirts. More prisoners were farther back on the deck, glimpsed in the gloom. The air was hot and wet, and smelled of corruption.

The guard captain descended through another hatch, and Miss Havisham followed. Her hands gripped the steps because there were no side rails. The lower gun deck was just like the one above: ghostly faces and despairing noises. Several spaces were gloomily lit with kerosene lamps but the darkness had a pervasive weight. Then down another hatch to the orlop, the deck just above the bilge.

The air was viscous, as foul as in a cistern. The ship shifted in the current, and bilge water splashed below. Darkness pressed her down, and only a few patches of frail light from above made it to the orlop deck, which was below the waterline. She glimpsed haunted faces at the edges of the light, bearded and dirty, with eyes far back in dark hollows. Her hand brushed a damp and moldy timber. She swallowed as a defense against the putrid smell of bilge water, filthy bodies, rotten food, and decaying timbers but the odor invaded her, threatening to chase her back up the ladder.

She squeezed her eyes closed and shook her head, bracing herself. Then she followed the guard captain into the deeper darkness. Men who must have been too weak to stand lay in hammocks. Other prisoners sat on the deck, backs against the bulkhead. In the steamy heat of the orlop deck, most were shirtless and barefoot. Some followed Miss Havisham with their gazes but it is likely that curiosity had been starved and bullied from them long ago. She pushed herself through the thick air.

"Let's see," the guard captain called to her. "Four twenty-one." He kicked aside a recumbent prisoner's leg that was in his path. "Four two-one. He is here somewhere."

A beam loomed out of the darkness, and she ducked it just in time. Her hands out in front, she stepped around a chain locker. Her shoe sank into a rotted deck plank. She moved between rows of prisoners.

"You, stand up," the guard captain ordered.

No response from a black corner of the deck where a prisoner leaned against a wood column, surrounded by other begrimed men sitting and lying on the deck.

"You hear me, four twenty-one?" The captain's foot swung at the prisoner.

Miss Havisham roughly shoved aside the captain. She knelt to the prisoner. "Fagin?"

The prisoner's face was grey and slack. Dark red stubble covered his cheeks and chin. His hair was stuck to his skull with dirt. He was spavined and graveyard thin. He did not lift his eyes.

"Fagin, it's me, Margaret."

The pickpocket blinked, then licked his lips, but gave no sign he could see or hear anything.

Miss Havisham put a hand under his shoulder. She told the guard captain, "Help me lift him."

He stepped back. "Madam, I don't touch prisoners unless it's with my boot. It's not healthy. Ringworm, headlice, scabies; it's a long list of torments best avoided."

She bent to put her arms around Fagin. "Try to get your feet under you, Fagin."

As he moved his legs he bit off a moan. His legs shook as he placed the bottom of his feet on the deck.

"Here we go." She clutched him and locked her hands together behind his back. "Lift."

She pulled him. Fagin rose from the deck, his legs trembling. He wheezed as loudly as an axle in want of grease.

"Can you walk?" she asked.

His voice was ragged. "Margaret Havisham?" He blinked.

When she placed one of his arms over her shoulder, he sagged into her. She walked along the deck back toward the hatch, half carrying and half dragging Fagin. The guard captain followed, saying something and perhaps looking for a prisoner to kick.

At the hatch Fagin began to help himself. He lifted a foot onto a step, and gripped the rail. She climbed after him, pressing him into the ladder so he wouldn't fall back. They gained the gun deck, Fagin standing straighter.

He looked at her. "My lord, it is you. I am astonished."

"If you are as astonished as you are smelly, you are agape," she said.

She took his elbow to guide him to the next ladder. Prisoners' gazes followed them. The guard captain went up first, then Fagin and Miss Havisham. She squinted against the daylight, and inhaled hugely as if she had held her breath the entire time below deck. The orlop deck's odor clung to her. She wiped her forehead and cheeks with her sleeve.

The guard captain removed his flintlock from his shoulder, and walked across the deck to Inspector Bucket. A guard was at the hulk's forepeak, and another near the wheel posts. Other guards and all the prisoners were down inside the hulk.

Miss Havisham led the pickpocket to the accommodation ladder at the edge of the deck, and patted his shoulders as if to plant him there. She hurried across the deck to the rail where the detective untied the twine around the package. Inside was a hog haunch and bits of pig gore.

Bucket looked at the guard captain. "Ready?"

The captain nodded. "So are my two men. They will earn a few coins from my pocket."

"This is a transparent charade, captain," Bucket said.

The captain said, "It answers satisfactorily all the questions I may be asked about prisoner 421."

Bucket dumped the package's contents into the river. The pig haunch hit the water and drifted alongside the hull with the current.

The guard captain yelled, "Prisoner overboard." He shouldered the flintlock, aimed along the barrel, and fired at the haunch. The bullet ripped away part of the meat. Then he ran aft along the deck, keeping up with the floating hog haunch as it moved with the current alongside the hull. He pointed at it over the rail.

Another guard rushed to the rail and fired. The haunch split in two, and a portion slipped beneath the surface. The guard captain worked his ramrod, then pulled back the hammer. He fired again. The mangled hog haunch drifted away.

"Prisoner killed while trying escape," called the guard captain. "Is that what you saw, Perkins?"

"Yes, sir."

"You will counter-sign my entry in the ledger? Prisoner four twenty-one was mortally wounded by guard gunfire and slipped beneath the river surface. Will that entry be correct?"

"Aye, sir."

The guard captain leaned his weapon against the rail. "A tragedy, of course. But we cannot allow prisoners to simply swim away from their confinement. English justice must be served." He turned to Miss Havisham. "Madam, your part of our arrangement is at hand."

Miss Havisham removed the handbag from her shoulder and passed it to him. When he shook the bag, the coins jingled, and that appeared to be a sufficient inventory for him.

"Good day to you, then." The guard captain lifted his flintlock, and marched along the deck, and judging by his actions Miss Havisham, the detective, and prisoner four twenty-one had vanished.

Miss Havisham crossed the deck to the pickpocket. "Do you need help down the ladder?"

Fagin stared at her. "I am newly invigorated, madam."

"You look like you've been dragged behind a dust cart," she said.

Bucket joined them at the ladder. "You two can have a nice chat later. Let's go."

FAGIN & MISS HAVISHAM

Miss Havisham went first, climbing down the hull and into the wherryman's boat. Then down went the pickpocket, and finally the detective. Miss Havisham settled in the bow. Bucket removed his coat and draped it over Fagin's shoulders then squeezed in next to Fagin on the stern thwart. The wherryman pushed against the *Fallon's* hull, and lowered his oars.

Prisoner four twenty-one had died in an escape attempt and the body could not be recovered. Entries attesting to these circumstances would be made in the ship's book, the warden's ledger, and in the court's files. It happened frequently.

The wherryman rowed the boat away from the prison ship. The pickpocket Fagin and his rescuers were carried toward the river's south shore, which was still hidden in haze.

21

Even in London at night, among the city's lowest and most despairing, among the exploited and needy, and among predators and prey, metaphor had its uses. There at the bottom, strict language was often deficient, and lacked the clarity to convey meaning with force and precision. Thus, a metaphor had to be offered: if common sense were a louse, then love was a fine-toothed comb.

It would be too much for a reptilian brain to understand such use of the King's English, and so Bill Sikes strolled along Piccadilly unaided by metaphor or, indeed, by thought. With Green Park on his right and closed shops on his left, he found nothing to kick, pummel, steal, or drink, and so he was peevish and out of sorts. Daylight's coal smoke haze had been replaced by nighttime's coal smoke haze, which was the same but darker. A church bell rang, the sound hanging in the air.

Sikes jammed his hands into his pockets, and he scuffed along, still limping from the burns. A wool cap was low over his forehead. His black velveteen coat needed patches at the elbows, and his breeches were frayed at the hems. His scowl was fierce, and he leaned aggressively forward as he walked. Pedestrians allowed him a goodly distance on the sidewalk, perhaps concluding that Sikes's wardrobe should include manacles.

At an intersection Sikes brushed the shoulder of a short red-haired woman who was pulling along her red-haired son, and she said, "Your humble pardon, sir."

A pony-and-trap passed on the street. Sikes stepped around an inebriate sitting on the sidewalk and leaning back against a post, a bottle between his knees.

A voice intruded on his absence of thought. "It's Bill Sikes, sober and upright." A girl's voice. "I never thought I'd live so long as to see him in such a state."

Sikes turned to the words. It was Nancy, the young lady who had been hired to humiliate Jeffrey Beals at his club. A clever riposte as distant from Sikes as was the moon, he asked, "What do you want?"

"I'm walking along, wanting nothing." She smiled at him. "Remember me?"

"If you are selling yourself, I ain't interested." He spoke out of the corner of his mouth.

Nancy laughed, a bright sound on the street. "You have no money; is why you aren't interested."

"Be gone with you." He gestured as if swatting a fly.

When he turned to resume his route, she accompanied him. Her red promenade dress swished with each step. A white wrap covered her shoulders. With red rouge and white powder, her face was made up for evening. She had a narrow nose and enticingly-shaped lips, delicate without being weak.

"Are you going to supper?" she asked.

"I would if I had a farthing to my name."

"The Rose and Feather is serving duck this evening, their board said." She smiled at him again.

A curious disorder was widely dispersed among young people. The affliction had not presented itself for discussion at London's Society of Apothecaries, though it is well-known among the society's members who have children of a certain age. It was the desire among otherwise smart and sensible young people to romantically attach themselves to worthless rapscallions destined for poorhouses or prisons. The ageless question was: why the attraction for someone for whom ambition, rectitude, and a day's work are foreign shores? Nancy suffered from this scourge, which manifested itself in its most severe form in her approach to Bill Sikes.

"If you are hungry, Bill, maybe we can sit down somewhere," she suggested.

Carriages rolled by, and mounted riders passed them. Clouds were low in the sky.

"And whose pocket are we emptying?" Sikes asked.

"I have a few coins, enough for two meals."

"I don't eat unless I can drink."

She put her hand through his arm. "I can take care of that, too."

* * * *

"Father likes to argue." Anna Wilkinson gripped Harry Beecker / Samuel Compeyson's arm, though to her he always presented himself as Ambrose Franks. "Can you be persuasive?"

"I've stolen your heart, my love." Franks kissed her forehead. "And I had to be persuasive to win you."

She giggled, a girlie sound at odds with her age, which was in her middle twenties, desperately late for marriage, with spinsterhood around the next bend. Her hair and eyes were perfectly matched in hue—the color of chocolate in a cup—and her eyes were set in such a way that she always seemed about to laugh. Her mouth was not wide and sensual but that flaw was hardly noticeable because her grin seldom left her face. Her hair was tucked under a green sun bonnet, though a few attractive curls had escaped along the nape of her neck. Yellow ruffles decorated the collar of her high-waisted frock.

"I must speak of business with your father," Franks said. "He would think less of me were I to avoid the subject."

Anna said, "I wish your parents were here to do so."

He put an arm around her hip and squeezed her. "My father's gout in his toes is so painful he can't even put a sheet over himself. He can't travel, and mother remains at home to care for him."

"A dowry is such an odious topic."

He said, "It cannot be helped, I'm afraid."

"But father hasn't even met you yet."

His voice firmed. "I'm too busy to come out here often, Anna. Best to get it over with now."

They moved toward the mansion, gravel crackling under their feet and passing under maple boughs and alongside a topiary statue of a horse. The Wilkinson estate was a hundred miles west of London near the River Severn, across from Wales but that could not be helped. The three-story home was of white stucco with black doors. Wrought iron-wrapped balconies were on east and west ends of the house. Columns held up a grand portico, under which was a polished green Wilkinson carriage without horses in harness, sitting there as a display straight from the Wilkinson carriage works in Lambeth.

"Do you want to set a date, Anna?" Franks asked.

Her eyes filmed with tears. "Should we?"

"Let's have a wedding date that is sooner rather than later. September is a good month. The weather is still fine."

With her fingertip she wiped away tears. "September, it is."

The nearest town was Thornbury, and many of the villagers worked on the estate. Two gardeners replaced faded daisies with fresh blooms along the path, and they touched their hat brims toward Anna. A glass conservatory was north of the home, and on the other side were stables and a hay shed. Also on the grounds were a sculpture park, meditation pond, and three guest houses.

Persian silk trees had been brought from the south of France and planted near the home because Mrs. Wilkinson liked them, and Lombardy poplars from Italy formed quarter mile-long windbreaks to the north and west. Acres of grass comprised the grounds, and sheep roamed the place, keeping the grass down. Starlings stabbed their beaks into the ground and made squeaky calls.

Leaning against each other, Anna Wilkinson and Ambrose Franks walked under the portico. A butler in a black jacket and trousers with red stripes on the side seams smiled at Anna but the grin faltered when his gaze settled on Franks.

"Your mother is in the conservatory, miss," the butler said.

She led Franks through the home. Never were their feet forced to touch upon anything but Tabriz or Kashan carpets, never did their gazes have to settle upon anything but oil paintings, potted palms, and Chinese cloisonné vases. Steering him by an arm, she led him along a hallway, through a parlor, down another hallway, and into a glasshouse that had a pitched roof and columns supporting iron ribs. The air was moist. A Coade stone statue of a lion rested on the tiled pathway, and fan palm branches were overhead. They walked alongside a bed of yellow narcissus, and then Anna pushed aside the boughs of a rubber tree.

"Ambrose, this is my mother, Harriet."

The woman lowered her book and rose from her chair to extend a hand toward Franks, and when her eyes found his face, they locked on it. She shook his hand, and then apparently forgot to release it. She might have been incapable of speech, looking at him. Then her gaze flowed down Franks's form to his feet, then back up to his face, and there it settled. His hand in hers, she was as still as the Coade statue.

Perhaps quite accustomed to a flustered reaction from women, Franks increased the width of his grin.

"Mother?" Anna said. "Will you say 'hello'?"

Color touched Harriet's cheeks. "Yes, of course. How do you do?"

Franks replied, "Very well, and I hope you are, too."

Harriet released him, then glanced at her own hand as if it might have betrayed her, gripping him like that. Her sun hat was made of woven cane, held in place by blue chenille cord tied under her chin. Blue ribbons decorated her muslin morning dress at the wrists and hemline.

Anna's nod toward Franks while looking at Harriet was a silent question: "What do you think?"

Franks's golden curls covered his ears, and his smile seemed to generate light. His chin—with its playful notch—was narrow, as was his nose. Deep dimples at the corners of his mouth and his blue eyes—bordering on violet—made him seem both friendly and amused. Whether Harriet noticed the artfully applied foundation on Franks's forehead that hid a purple bruise—

courtesy of Bill Sikes—is not known. His cravat was the same color as his eyes, and the silver buckles and black patent leather of his shoes were faultless mirrors.

He bowed. "I am entirely persuaded that Anna is your sister rather than your daughter."

Harriet mewled her gratitude for the compliment. Her green eyes were bright with pleasure and perhaps she was overwhelmed by Franks: her mouth was uncouthly open and she baldly stared at him. Harriet's waist was slender but her shoulders and hips were extensive, giving her the figure of an hourglass. A few wrinkles at the corners of her eyes made her appear wise rather than old. Her eyes were not quite brown and not quite green but something in between. Her mouth had retained all her teeth, and she smiled broadly.

"Have a chair, Mr. Franks," she said in a girl's voice. "May I get you anything? Anything at all?"

Pronouncing precisely, Anna said, "Mother, take a few breaths, why don't you?"

"You are here to see your father." Harriet spoke to Anna but her eyes still had not left Ambrose Franks. "He is with the rats. Will you stay for the weekend, Mr. Franks?"

"I'm sure he will." Anna pulled Franks toward the glasshouse's doors.

They stepped into the formal garden where boxwood rows separated flower beds, and they walked by cypress trees and white-blossoming viburnum. They rounded the stables, a hay rick, and a grain bin.

"Father is a sportsman," Anna said.

They walked by a gardener who raked leaves from the gravel walkway, depositing them in a wheelbarrow.

She said, "Horses during the season. And the pit year round, and it's his pit. And he wagers on everything."

Franks lifted his head. "Your father makes a wager now and then?"

"'Now and then' is an inadequate phrase. He will wager on whether a squirrel will go up or down a tree trunk." She shrugged. "He can afford the losses so it's not my place to criticize him."

They left the garden and moved along a dirt path approaching an outbuilding where horses were tied to posts, and gigs and broughams were parked, some with drivers standing by. The horses shivered their skins against the flies. A red phaeton and a black landau were also there, along with a dozen humbler vehicles such as hay wagons and carpenter's van, boards sticking out the back. Cheers came from inside the building.

"Mother thinks the whole thing is disgusting," Anna said. "But I don't mind poppa having an amusement."

The building was of whitewashed lap siding. Franks pulled open the door for her. They stepped into a crowd of twenty-five or thirty people, all men, some wearing foot-high toppers and others with rough wool caps. Some were dressed in pristine silk waistcoats and others in cotton shirts besmudged with evidence of their day's work.

"There's father," Anna said, "near the back."

Talking and laughing, the men were arrayed around an open area, and Anna led Franks toward the rear. Dogs barked, accompanied by an eerie piping and scratching coming from wood boxes.

"Ready, gentlemen?" called a man wearing a double-breasted coat with a fur collar. "Is Bandy Legs ready?"

"Aye, your honor," another fellow answered. "As ready as rain."

Ambrose Franks may have seen money change hands so he abruptly left Anna and worked his way through the crowd toward the center of the room. Frowning, Anna followed him. Spectators surrounded a seven-foot-deep pit lined with wood planks. Franks shouldered his way to the edge, pushing aside a fellow of substance, judging from the pleated frill on his shirt front. Ambrose nodded an apology.

"Are you ready, Mr. Timer?" a fellow in the fur collar asked above the crowd's noise.

Another man at the pit edge held up his hand, displaying a repeater.

"That's father." Anna gestured toward the man with the fur collar. "He is always referee because he owns the place."

Her father called, "Release the rats."

A stout man in a leather apron shoved a wood box to the edge of the pit, slid open a hatch, and tipped the box toward the bottom of the pit. Out spilled ten wharf rats. They landed on the pit floor, and crazily ran to and fro seeking an escape.

There was none to be had. The rats were colored from brown to gray, some spotted in a darker color. They were huge, each a foot long not counting the tails, as disreputable and ugly an appendage as has ever been affixed to animals.

"Release Bandy Legs," Anna's father ordered.

Another man—one with a face resembling a bucket of mud—held up a dog, a twenty-pound terrier whose tail had been lost or chopped off earlier in its life. "Here he is. Our champion." He waved the dog back and forth.

The dog's gaze—which was villainous in the extreme—was on the rats at the bottom of the pit. In his magnum opus, Dr. Johnson defined *affrightful* as *full of affright or terrour*. The good doctor doubtless was contemplating a dog such as Bandy Legs. In addition to having lost its tail the dog was missing an ear, revealing a hole into its skull. His remaining ear looked as if numerous beings had chewed on it. Where its right eye should have been was an empty black socket. The good eye was a narrow slit, and the forehead was flat without much of a rise above the nose. The front of the dog was an orange and brown brindle while the aft end was mottled gray.

Bandy Legs's legs were turned oddly, and the rear ones scrabbled against its owner who held him high for the spectators to see. The dog's dewlaps were drawn up, revealing dagger teeth. The dog whined and barked madly, spit flying from its mouth. Had Lord Byron ever seen this dog, all thought of pulchritude would have been forever extinguished, and *She Walks in Beauty* would never have been penned.

"Here we go," cried Bandy Legs's owner.

The dog was dropped into the pit, and the timer glanced at his watch. Bandy Legs instantly became a whirlwind of carnage. It leaped across the pit floor and seized a brown rat and savagely shook it, killing it in a thrice. He released the corpse, and charged a second rat which tried to dodge but Bandy Legs would not be fooled, and altered its trajectory at the last instant, and gripped the rat's neck to shake it to death in one second. The dog threw this one aside and aimed itself at another rat.

The rats scurried about the ring, some leaping, trying to reach the floor above from which spectators peered down. They shrieked and hissed but there was nothing to be done for them. Bandy Legs made no noise during this deadly business; not a bark, not a howl, not a growl. One rat after another, until the dog was the only animal alive in the pit.

"One minute, twenty-five seconds," the timer announced.

Ten dead rats lay on the pit floor, and Bandy Legs looked up at the mud-faced man, then leaped up the pit side into the arms of his owner, who held the ratter high again to the spectators' applause. Currency and coins changed hands.

The man in the fur collar called, "Next dog is Blackie. Smathers, where are you and your dog? Gentlemen, make your wagers. Rat man, clean the pit and get ready."

Anna said to Franks, "Let's go talk to father."

"Now?" He didn't look at her. His eyes swept the room, and perhaps he was searching for Blackie. "I want to put a little money down on the next dog."

She asked, "Do you know anything about rat baiting? Enough to judge a dog?"

He laughed. "I know rats. And what can be known about this? If a dog looks game, I'll pick a low time. If not, a higher time. Nothing could be simpler."

She tugged his arm. "Father is always in a good mood at the pit. Let's go speak with him rather than letting him become ensconced in the library where his mood will be darker."

209

She pulled at his arm, and only when she did so again more energetically did he step away from the pit.

He followed Anna toward the referee who under the fur-collared coat wore a cloth-of-silver waistcoat embroidered with glittery silver thread, perhaps a reminder to the spectators of their places—below him—in the grand scheme of things. Straw covered the floor, and the place was too warm with all the bodies, and smelled of old sweat and dogs.

"Papa, may we speak with you?"

"Can it wait?" He only turned a fraction from the fellow he was speaking with. "You can see I'm busy here. The next bout is at hand."

She said, "I want to introduce you to Ambrose."

Her father grimaced, then backed away from the rat pit. "Let's go outside."

The crowd closed up to take their places. The timer took over as referee, calling out the number of the rats in the next contest. The rat man carried another box to the pit.

A few steps from the building, Anna said, "Ambrose, this is my father, Elijah."

The two men shook hands, Franks smiling.

"Young man, you have won my daughter's heart," the older man said. "She is the youngest of my four daughters so I have trod this path before."

Elijah Wilkinson's eyes had the dry glitter of a businessman about to strike a deal. His brown hair was artfully combed forward to lessen the acreage of his forehead, and his nose was a map of burst capillaries. His chin was undershot, giving his face the aspect of a weasel. That Anna resembled her mother was great good fortune. He was an older man, but appeared full of vigor.

Elijah's salt-and-pepper corduroy trousers were tucked into calfskin half-boots. "I'm a busy man, Franks, as you can see." He glanced at the door to the rat pit, perhaps wishing he could return straightaway. "I have exchanged letters with your father. Your family is suitably substantial, and you seem to be a proper prospect."

Franks bowed. Anna gripped his sleeve and grinned.

"I should not be speaking about such matters with the groom," Elijah said, "but your father cannot be here, and said in his letter than you can handle yourself."

"He is too complimentary." Franks squeezed Anna's hand.

Applause came from the building. Wilkinson's eye again shot to the doorway, and he rolled back and forth on the balls of his feet, his every move indicating he was desperate to return to the rat pit.

Wilkinson said, "I will not have Anna marrying into penury. Your father instructed his man at the Exchange and his Yorkshire land agent to send me summaries. Everything appears in order."

A gardener drove a cart along a road toward an orchard on the west end of the property. In a buckthorn bush a goldfinch chirruped.

"I knew there were funds in manufacturing my carriages"—Wilkinson spread his hands, encompassing the estate"— but had no idea about shipyards. The boat-building Franks have done well."

"Father, please. You'll embarrass Ambrose, talking about his family like that."

Ambrose Franks said, "Here is another letter from my father, received just yesterday. He asked that I read it, then give it to you."

Wilkinson read the letter. "I do not speak of business in front of women, even my daughter. Will you excuse yourself, Anna?"

"No."

Wilkinson hesitated, then smiled. "There is iron in her, Ambrose." He hooked his thumbs in his waistcoat pockets. "She gets it from me."

"I am happily aware of Anna's iron, sir." Franks beamed at his betrothed.

"You two make me blush," Anna said.

"To business, it is," Wilkinson said. "I will settle upon you a sum of eight thousand pounds upon the day of your marriage to Anna. I will personally give you the check a few minutes before the ceremony." He glanced again at the pit door. "Once the rat match is over, we will go to my study in the house."

"Daddy," Anna exclaimed, rising on her toes. "How could you? You speak of the dowry's sum in front of me?"

Wilkinson looked at her, apparently bemused. "I am a man of commerce, Anna. A negotiator."

Cloud shadows raced across the yard. Another carriage parked alongside the building, three men climbing down, heading for the pit door.

"Forgive me, Mr. Wilkinson," Franks said. "I do not fault your memory or your honesty when I remind you that the agreed upon sum is ten thousand pounds."

"Yes, of course," the older man said. "It is the excitement of the match that has jostled my mind. Ten thousand pounds as your dowry, and that will be enough to get you started in life." He stepped toward the door. "Will you return to the pit with me, Ambrose?"

"I prefer bull baiting, Mr. Wilkinson. Rats are too small for me, and too ratty, if I may be speak the truth."

Wilkinson folded the letter and inserted it into a pocket. "Then I will see you at supper." He dipped his chin at Franks and stepped back through the door toward the pit.

The betrothed couple walked back along the path toward the mansion.

"You father is a fine fellow," Franks said, "and a sensible man."
She pecked him on the cheek.

The reason for Franks's smile at this moment cannot be known with certainty. It might have been how well this meeting at the rat pit with Elijah Wilkinson had gone, and it had indeed gone well. Or it might have been that the letter Franks had handed to Elijah Wilkinson was a forgery, as were other documents sent to Mr. Wilkinson in the past week.

None of them were authentic. They were all exquisite fabrications created by the Old Nichol artisan named Tilley. As he escorted Anna along, Ambrose Franks's grin was indeed wide.

22

"Do you need help with your clothes, Fagin?" Miss Havisham stood in the hallway just outside a Satis House guest room.

"My hands are trembling," Fagin said. "A fine wirer whose hands shake is like a sundial at night: utterly worthless."

"May I come in?" she asked.

"If you don't mind *dishabille*, eh? My hands won't cooperate."

Miss Havisham walked into the guest room where Fagin gripped a bed post with one hand and fiddled with buttons on his linen shirt with the other.

"If I release the post, I'll fall over," he said. "My time in that prison hulk is still with me."

"Let me help." Miss Havisham buttoned his shirt, then lifted the leather braces from the bed to drape them over his shoulder. She affixed the back straps to his trousers, then moved around to secure the front, slipping the braces' holes onto pants buttons.

"These were my father's," she said. "How do they fit?"

"As if bespoke, madam." Fagin sank onto the bed. He wiped his face with his hand. "I am feebler than I care to admit."

The bed's curtains were tied to posts. A pitcher and basin on a stand filled a corner of the room, which looked out onto Satis House's Queen Elizabeth Garden. Under a green gesso-framed mirror on the wall were a dressing table and a padded stool. A finely carved oak commode stood in a corner.

Miss Havisham opened a wardrobe and removed a leather vest. She held it up. "Coconut shell buttons, quite the fashion. Dad favored this vest when in the brewery so it smells of malt."

Fagin wet his lips. He brought up his hands and stared at them. "I must gather myself."

She scooted over the stool so she could sit in front of him. "Was it a guard or a prisoner?"

"Five days in a row this big convict on the orlop deck punched me—smacked me right in the face—and took my bowl. After the first day I held the bowl out to him but he hit me anyway—I suppose for his amusement—then took the food. It was fish stew, or at least that's what it might charitably be called."

The room smelled of roses Miss Havisham had clipped from the garden earlier that morning, crimson and yellow blooms in a blue marble vase on the dressing table.

"You didn't have anything to eat for five days?" She leaned forward, an elbow on a knee.

"Your cook has been bringing up trays of food for me every two hours. I'm regaining my strength."

Fagin still looked ravaged. The skin on his face resembled paper stuck to his skull with paste. A violet bruise ran from his ear to the point of his jaw. His eyes normally glittered with his intelligence but they seemed remote and dull. A barber had been summoned from Rochester, and so Fagin's cheeks and chin had been scraped clean of stubble.

"How was your neck wounded?" She touched his neck. "They are gouges."

He flinched. "Some fellow on the prison ship said I was in his spot, so he grabbed me by the throat to throw me aside, and when I resisted, he raked my throat with his fingers. His fingernails were long and sharp. It smarted; I don't mind admitting." Three lines of scabs crossed the front of his neck in the pattern of hayfork tines. "Your cook, Mrs. Hartley, has been cramming food down my gullet. She is skilled, and could make a pump handle taste like jellied eel. It's kind of her."

"She is otherwise old and cranky, Fagin. You have charmed her."

"That's my particular talent, isn't it?" He laughed in a small way. "Charming people. In truth, not once in my life."

Miss Havisham had just returned from the stables, and wore a fitted riding habit; a blue doublet buttoned to her neck and a long skirt in matching blue. Her head was bare, revealing her hair, an odd silver-white. She was too young to have gray hair, and she had inherited this color from her mother, of which her mother had been inordinately proud. Miss Havisham had not brushed her hair after her ride, and it was windblown, with wild waves and curls, giving her a fetching unmade look. Her eyes were "as gray as a hornet's nest," her father had liked to say.

She studied the pickpocket. "I suppose you've charmed many women."

Fagin smiled warily. "Madam, you seek to embarrass me."

214

"To look at you, you wouldn't think so but you gain on people, particularly women, is my assessment."

Fagin gestured as if discarding her comment. "If you have been assessing my effect on women you do not have enough to think about during your day."

"But is it true? You have much experience charming women, and so you ... have had your way with them."

"My dear, our conversation has taken a desperate turn." Fagin laughed. "At our first meeting in your carriage you asked me to incriminate myself, and you do so again now."

"Someone who knows the streets of London well also knows the world well." She touched her chin. "Among the things you know are women. Is that not true?"

"I know much about a few things, and a little about many things."

On the stool she leaned toward him as if to hear his thoughts. "You duck my question."

Fagin straightened his backbone. "It is not a proper subject."

"I simply want to know more about you." She laced her fingers together. "It is a tame request."

"I've had a few such experiences, and heaven forfend if I have taken your question wrongly." He raised his eyes as if to study the ceiling. "My mother and father were dead, and so I was left on my own. No guidance, no clarity about how to live a life. I fell in with a hard band, older than me, most of them. Young toughs and wastrels, and they introduced me to the young ladies. Bawds, the lot of them. Charm had little to do with it."

Miss Havisham asked, "So did you?"

"My word, that is an impertinent question." He laughed, more a rattle.

"Do you see this home, Fagin?" She held out her arms, encompassing the estate. "The gardens, the brewery?"

"You have already given me an edifying tour of your home and grounds. Does your question have a point?"

"My entire life has been lived here, within the confines of these walls."

"Forgive me for being observant," Fagin said, "but I have seen you in London, and you just returned from a horseback ride through the country. And you spent some time on the continent when you were young. If these walls are a prison, they are porous."

"I am painting with a broad brush, Fagin, and you know it. You are again weaving and ducking, avoiding my question. Tell me how you learned about women."

"About women as a philosophical question?" he asked. "Or something else, eh?"

"Something else. Your first."

"Miss Havisham. Margaret. This is no topic for. . . ."

"For reasons I cannot explain perhaps even to myself it would help me to know."

"I was wild when I was younger, out on the street." Fagin brushed his knee. "I look back now and am embarrassed. My so-called friends passed a hat, and hired a doxy and a room above a public house." He waved a hand as if the memory were a bad smell.

"Did you know what you were doing?"

"Madam, I am blushing. My face has just become as red as my hair."

"We are adults, and can speak frankly of these things, much like a doctor talking with a patient."

Fagin's mouth moved, as if trying to find the right words. Then he said, "I had utterly no idea what was to befall me in front of that woman in that room. And I refuse to re-ignite that memory by discussing it with you." He crossed his arms in front of his chest.

"Was it humiliating?"

"I appear to still be discussing it." Fagin rubbed his scalp as if trying to excise a memory. "After the session with that . . . that votary of love, who scared me to death, I had nothing to do with women for three years."

"And since then?"

"I am working hard at my fetter here, madam."

"My plans depend on knowing you well," she said. "So since then?"

"I have been an orderly, natural human being along those lines."

Miss Havisham rubbed her arm with a hand. She looked out the window, her expression as diffuse as a cloud. "Are you not curious, Fagin?"

"If I see a necklace, I'm curious about it. Same with a silk handkerchief and a pocket watch. But I fear I am not taking your meaning."

"Curious about me."

"In an older brother way, of course," he said. "You have been very kind . . ."

She cut in. "I mean, curious about me as a woman."

"It would be imprudent of me to be curious, would it not?"

"My parents didn't keep me locked in a room but my chances to be alone with young men were few. The word *none* might be more accurate. I was entirely proper. Reticent, ladylike, genteel, just what mother demanded."

Fagin wore the pained expression of one wearing tight shoes. "I have no business knowing what I fear you are about to reveal to me."

Miss Havisham still stared out the window. "And young ladies in society must be presented to their grooms in a certain state."

"Margaret, this is a conversation you will regret tomorrow. Such things shouldn't be confided between close friends, much less to a low Clerkenwell fine wirer you've only been acquainted with for a short time."

"If you don't count my parents and governess, I've been kissed less than twenty times in my life."

"Margaret, please." Fagin looked left and right as if trying to find a place to hide from her words.

"So that was my condition on the day that was to be my wedding." Her voice was light and dry, oddly disconnected to her revelations. She was far away. "I was pristine. Unsullied. White was the color of my wedding gown, and it was the color of my entire existence in terms of men."

"Have you taken a squint at the new Allan Ramsay portrait exhibit at St. Martin's Lane?" Fagin asked. "I've heard it is extraordinary."

She rose from stool. "Will you move over?"

"Pardon me?"

"I want to sit next to you." Her voice had become breathy, like wind through trees.

"Are you not sufficiently close, standing there, eh?"

She sat next to him on the bed, and then shifted so that their legs touched. She knotted her hands together and said nothing, apparently waiting.

Fagin said, "I know how this has happened, Margaret."

"I am simply sitting near you. Nothing else has happened."

"To you I am an exotic species, someone who is strange and not from your everyday world. I'm from the king's zoological garden. Foreignness can be enticing. It is a sailing adventure into the unknown, into unexplored seas, with someone like me."

She turned her head toward him. "We must deal with the circumstances we find ourselves in, don't you think? I find myself on a bed with you."

"Exoticism is not something that . . . ."

She lifted one of his hands in hers. "I don't know how to do this, Fagin."

"Madam, I cannot take advantage of your fragile emotional state. It would be unseemly of me."

"Is this how it is done?" She spread his fingers and placed his hand on her breast, softly at first, and then more firmly. "I don't know about these things."

He swallowed.

She whispered. "Now what do I do? Do you know? Can you help me?"

"I'm in a weakened state, Margaret."

"Then I'd best take care of you."

A loud voice came from the other side of the door. "Mr. Fagin? It's turtle soup time. Served up piping hot and in a mug. And olive bread I made myself."

As if bitten, Miss Havisham leaped up from the bed.

The cook called, "We'll put some meat on those bones of yours, if I know anything about anything."

Fagin exhaled loudly.

"Here I come, then," the cook said through the door.

The latch sounded, and the cook pushed open the door with her posterior. She gripped a silver tray. "And tea, too, for you, sir."

At Satis House this cook ate as much as she cooked, and she was broad-beamed. Her face was pink and merry. She smiled at Miss Havisham. "I'll just set this down on the table."

"Good day, Mrs. Fisher." Miss Havisham's voice was rough, and her cheeks were the color of tomatoes. "Passing the time of day, is all."

"I'll just set this tray up in here." The cook bustled toward the dressing table. "Pour the tea, butter the bread. A minute is all it will take. And you two can go on with whatever it was you were doing."

Miss Havisham said, "Take your time, Mrs. Fisher. I was just leaving."

"Ay," Fagin fairly barked. "She was just on her way out."

To be sure, Miss Havisham's retreat was ignominious and rapid. But at the door, she hesitated, then looked at Fagin over her shoulder, and there was something of a victory in her smile.

* * * *

"I am not of an inclination to be reformed." Carrying a leather folder, Fagin walked along Newgate Street. "There is no profit in becoming a better person. And it is too late for that."

Luke asked, "Are you talking to me, Mr. Fagin?"

"I am speaking with the wind, young man. Let me add, as long as you and the wind are listening, that Miss Havisham does not suffer indolence, and indolence is one of my principal pastimes."

"Watch this, Mr. Fagin." Luke glanced up at Fagin to insure he was watching.

Then the boy quick-stepped sideways, and bumped into a fellow walking along the street reading a newspaper, a folded umbrella hanging from his wrist. The man started, then frowned.

"Forgive me, governor." Luke tipped his cap.

The man's voice was a growl. "Watch where you are going, boy."

"Next time for sure, sir." Luke caught up with Fagin and held up the man's handkerchief, a linen square with letters embroidered at a corner.

"My dear, we are not working today." Fagin took the handkerchief from him and inserted it into a pocket. "Not at picking pockets, in any event. We have an important mission; one we dare not fail."

London's workday was over, and night had come, though a few buggies and wagons still rolled along the street. Fagin and the boy passed a feather dealer's shop, a slop seller's store, a tallow chandlery, and a paper stainer's plant, all closed for the night. Pedestrians moved along the pavement in both directions.

"Oops." Luke pointed theatrically. "My shoelace is undone."

He bent to tie the shoe but the lace was apparently difficult to seize because he took several small steps doubled over before he could tie the lace, and when he sprang aright he bumped into a woman walking arm-in-arm with a gentleman in a top hat.

"Pardon me, madam." Luke bowed. "I didn't see you."

"Go on with you," the woman's escort said in a menacing tone.

"Too right." Luke skipped ahead, and when he reached Fagin he held out the woman's reticule and the scissors with which he had snipped it off its shoulder strap.

Fagin waved his hand. "I won't take my usual eighty percent today, my wee mignonette. I'm too consumed with ponderation."

Luke opened the purse, extracted a gold sovereign, and bit into it. "As real as the pox, Mr. Fagin."

"Kindly do not use any phrases heard from Bill Sikes. They are unseemly, coming from someone of your tender years."

Luke said, "That's what Miss Havisham says about cutting purses and picking pockets. They are unseemly."

"She has many fine qualities, butting into another's business not being among them."

They stepped around a spit-brown dog chewing a shoe.

"Miss Havisham wants me to learn to read," the boy said.

"Nothing good can come from education, Luke. Believe me, I know."

"Maybe it would be fun to read."

"The ability to read will give you insufferable airs. I learned to read when I was young, and haven't made a farthing from it since."

"Do you read now, Mr. Fagin?"

"Not even headstones when strolling through a graveyard."

"Miss Havisham can read," Luke said.

A hackney cab passed them, two passengers waving bottles and singing a foul drinking ditty.

Fagin said, "Don't pattern yourself after Miss Havisham."

"Why not? I like her."

"I like her, too, in an academic, abstract, theoretical, hypothetical, algebraic, astronomic way." Fagin kicked a brickbat on the pavement. "But she might be touched, if you take my meaning, eh?"

A man in gaiters and a gold-colored waistcoat walked his dog toward them, the dog sniffing the ground. Silver brads studded the dog's collar. Its owner wore wire-rimmed spectacles and a soup-strainer mustache.

Luke called out, "Oh, what a pretty doggie." He knelt next to the dog and vigorously petted and scratched it. "I wish I had a dog."

"Someday you might have one, lad," the man said. "Though there are few dogs as fine as this one. His name is Bertie."

"Goodbye, Bertie." Luke rose to rejoin Fagin, passing him the dog's collar.

Fagin pocketed the collar. "Miss Havisham might be addled."

"What does that mean?"

"She has two feet just as do you but neither of hers is adequately affixed to the ground."

They passed a pieman's cart. Luke leaned close to smell the pies but the vendor shooed him away with a curse. When the boy rejoined Fagin, he gave him one of the pudding slices he had just obtained.

Fagin bit into the pudding and said with a full mouth, "Did you buy this with your new sovereign?"

"I never pay for anything." Luke chewed on the pudding. It was spotted dick. "I learned that from you."

Fagin looked over his shoulder. "We are getting close, Luke. Are you ready?"

Another couple walked along the pavement toward them. The man wore the blue jacket of a naval officer, and the lady an azure carriage dress and a fox wrap.

The boy wiped his hands on his pants. "Mr. Fagin, may I borrow the handkerchief I just gave you?"

Fagin handed over the linen handkerchief.

The couple passed them, and Luke turned to follow them. "Ma'am, did you just drop your handkerchief? I just found it on the cobblestones." He waved the cloth at her.

The woman pulled out her own handkerchief. It was red silk with yellow trim, a dear piece of cloth. "Mine is right here." She held it up so he could see it, then tucked it back into the dress. "Why, you are a fine young man, being so honest." She warmly shook Luke's hand. "The very best to you."

The navy officer smiled at Luke, who bobbed his head at him, and shook the woman's hand with vigor.

The boy said, "Bless you."

Luke ran to Fagin who, wary of any uniform, had kept walking. The boy handed him both the linen hankie and the woman's red silk handkerchief. Fagin pushed them into his trousers' pocket.

The boy said, "Miss Havisham always has something to eat for me."

"Miss Havisham's lumber contains many knots," Fagin said, "more than you can see, with you being young and short."

Pulled by two matching white horses and with harness bells ringing, a landau came down Newgate, the driver in blue livery including a tricorn hat, and his four passengers—young, handsome, and judging from the looks of them out for a lively evening—laughed and chatted. Luke stepped around a water trough toward the street.

Fagin might not have seen Luke leaving him, as he said, "There are a few weeds in Miss Havisham's garden, some dregs at the bottom of her wine bottle. Are you following me, Luke?"

When Luke stepped into the path of the landau, the driver called out a warning and yanked the reins. The horses stopped a few feet from the boy, tossing their manes and snorting.

Luke called, "Sorry, sir."

"Get out of the way, you little fool," yelled the driver.

Luke patted the nearest horse. "Ay ay, sir. Here I go." He stepped back to the walkway.

The driver tapped one of the horse's flanks with his whip, and shouted, "Hiyup."

The landau chimed and rattled forward, one of the passengers saluting Luke in a mocking way.

Luke ran up to Fagin and handed him a brass bell from the horse's harness. Fagin shifted the leather folder to his other hand, and the bell disappeared into his pocket.

"With you along I need a coat with more pockets, boy. Here, we are. Do you have the stone?"

Luke patted his trousers. "Right here."

Fagin turned onto Old Bailey Street.

The boy was at his heels. "Do you know where we are, Mr. Fagin?"

"I've been here a few times, usually in irons."

They walked along the wall of the Old Bailey courthouse, which was adjacent to the Newgate jail. St. Paul's quarter-jacks rang, filling the street with their low sound. Carrying his torch, a lamplighter worked his way down the street. Fagin led Luke to a door in a passageway off the street, lit only by starlight and not much of that.

"This is the lawyers' door," Fagin said. "I'm surprised the door is of a normal size, lawyers being low and squat like toads."

Columns framed the door and a portico was overhead. A glass fanlight was above the door.

"Where are the bars?" Luke asked.

"This goes to courthouse offices, not the jail, which is next door. Bewigged and berobed judges and solicitors come and go through here." He lowered the folder to the walkway, and put his hat there, too. "Get the rock out."

"Done and done, sir." Luke held up a stone the size of a chicken egg that had been in his pants pocket. He spread his arms.

Fagin gripped Luke under his arms and lifted him, first up to his chest, then grunted as he pushed him higher so that the boy sat on Fagin's shoulders. "High enough, eh?"

"Let me stand on your shoulders."

Luke climbed up, Fagin holding his legs. The boy tapped the stone against a fanlight pane. Then harder, and the pane cracked. With the rock he cleared glass shards from the pane, then reached through to unhook the window latch.

He gripped the window frame. "Pull me back some."

Fagin backstepped, and the hinges creaked as the boy pulled open the fan window.

"Now closer." Luke put a hand on Fagin's head, and rose on his toes. "I can grab it."

Fagin tottered. "Careful there."

"Here I go." His shoes scuffing Fagin's head, the boy pulled himself through the window frame.

Fagin heard him land on the tiles on the other side of the door, crunching glass. The bolt was thrown from the inside, and Luke opened the door, grinning at Fagin, who lifted his hat and the leather folder from the walkway.

Fagin patted the boy on the head. "You're a fine snakesman, lad. This way."

The two walked on a marble hallway with doors to a courtroom on their right and offices on the left. The hallway was dark, and their footsteps echoed. Fagin hesitated in front of a door, then moved on to the next one.

Luke whispered. "I can't see much."

"Here we are." Fagin pushed open a door and entered a room. "This den of iniquity belongs to the crown prosecutors. Knaves and caitiffs, every one of them."

Street lamplight came through a window, and everything in the room was gray. Half a dozen desks filled the space, each with an oil lamp, ink well, and blotter. An array of open filing shelves lined a wall. Each of the cabinet shelves held wood boxes which contained court records. Fagin rifled through documents, moving left to right along the cabinet, picking papers out of their boxes to squint at them, returning them, and moving again. Peering at the dark corners of the room, Luke followed Fagin along the cabinet.

He came to a cabinet box that appeared to hold his interest. "The files are arranged alphabetically, and here is what we need."

"I need supper, is what I need."

Fagin leafed through several documents in the box, examining them closely, then removed the papers from his leather folder, patted the pages square, and slipped them into the box. He shoved the box back onto the cabinet shelf. "Let's make our retreat."

"Do I have to climb through the window again?"

He put a hand on the boy's shoulder to guide him out of the prosecutor's office into the hallway. "Luke, we'll go out the door like gentlemen."

"Miss Havisham said she is going to make me a gentleman."

Stepping on shattered glass on the floor, Fagin opened the door to Old Bailey Street. "Do not worry, young man. I will work diligently to undo everything she does."

23

Then to business. In a nation of clerks the path to success in business was not difficult but this particular endeavor was disapproved in many quarters, though not by those seeking hurried profits without the irksome intrusions of taxmen, rate-seekers, customs house agents, sheriffs, and other king's men, their postures the same everywhere: one hand open to receive tribute, the other holding iron cuffs in the event the tribute was not forthcoming.

Best to be avoided, the lot of them, and on the ship *Northern Star* they could indeed be avoided thanks to a clever double hull, access to the space between the real hull and the false hull gained through a hidden hatch in the sail locker.

This is where Miss Havisham found herself just as the Greenwich Observatory's red ball dropped on its pole, indicating one o'clock in the afternoon, sailors on vessels clogging the Thames having kept their eyes on the ball to set accurate ships' time.

"I hold you fully responsible for my wound," Murdstone said. "I paid a doctor two sovereigns to clean it and insert stitches, and that money shall be deducted from your share."

"Kindly keep to the subject, sir." Miss Havisham held a kerosene lamp, and she leaned forward to peer into the space between hulls.

Murdstone said, "If there were a way forward in this business without you, I would journey in that direction but your father's contacts and influence seem to have settled on you."

In the dark and dank sail locker Murdstone reached into the space between hulls and produced an item packed in straw and bound with twine. He glanced at her. "May I borrow your blade, the one so recently used on me?"

From the folds of her skirt she produced the dagger and passed it to him, and he cut the twine. He returned the blade to her, then pulled away the straw to reveal a two-foot-tall statue.

In the cramped locker he held it up like a trophy. "This is the Lady Tiye, mother of Akhenaten, and this figurine is more than 3,000 years old, from a tomb near the Nile at Al Wasta."

The figure was carved of stone, and she was lithe though with bounteous curves. She wore a shift that covered her from shoulders to ankles. Her head was outsized, and her features were delicate with a slight and knowing smile. Her hair fell to her shoulders in tight braids. One slender arm hung at her side and the other crossed her body below her breasts. The flickering lamplight seemed to shift her expression and caused her bosom to rise and fall, giving her life. Even in the sail locker's murk this small woman-in-stone was exquisite and powerful.

Miss Havisham asked, "Who does she belong to?"

Murdstone pushed himself back against the hull as if her question had been a blow. "Why, she belongs to you and me. There are two more of these statues hidden in the hull. Sir Jerome Rakely has a passion for ancient Egyptian statues of women, and he will purchase all of them. He is a crazed collector, which is to our benefit."

"I mean, who did they belong to back in Egypt?"

"What does it matter?" He harrumphed unpleasantly. "Possession is nine-tenths of the law. And do not tell me that the daughter of Hugh Havisham is troubled by scruples."

"Not in the least," she said, and then silently mouthed, "as you may learn shortly."

"Jerome Rakely has many of these statues your father and I have sold him over the years." Murdstone laughed in way he may have thought devilish but was a mere dry cackle. "And by the by: Lord only knows what he does when he is in a room alone with them."

"I beg your pardon."

He waved away her comment. "Nothing but fanciful speculation."

Angles in Murdstone's face were hardened in the flickering lamplight, features not quite put together as nature had intended, with cheeks so sunken that his molars were traced on his cheeks, along with that strange misaligned eye which was not on the proper plane: a handsome face at twenty yards, a mysteriously odd face at ten yards, and a disturbing countenance up close, which was Miss Havisham's vantage at the moment. Even a passing glance at his visage indicated he was incapable of laughter, and that if a smile were forthcoming it would be artful or begrudging and would hurt his mouth for lack of practice.

He said, "Your father had agents in Alexandria and Paris, all eager to ship to him whatever our customers wanted. He dealt with procurement and shipping, and my portion of the business was receiving and hiding the goods and distributing them to purchasers. It was a magnificent partnership, each of us tending to our specialty."

Miss Havisham wore a leather apron courtesy of the ship's carpenter. She backed out of the sail locker as Murdstone returned the statue to its space between the hulls. He placed the hatch so that it aligned with the planking, rendering it invisible. The effigies would be removed from the vessel by *Northern Star*'s bosun, whose percentage of the profits would be significant.

Murdstone and Miss Havisham climbed to the deck then walked aft, passing the mainmast and walking under ratlines that ascended toward a yard. The scents were of Stockholm tar and Chian turpentine.

The *Northern Star* was moored at Pettibone's Warehouse on the Thames's north shore just above Greenwich. Longshoremen loaded and unloaded vessels at the warehouse and at a pier extending into the current. Ships' rigging filled the sky. Carts and wagons crowded the dock. A boom with a pulley extended from the peak of the Pettibone Warehouse, and a cotton bail rose up the building headed toward a hatch on an upper floor, pulled up by a mule in harness. Dockside was filled with noise: iron wheel rims on cobblestones, and the shouts and curses of brokers, dock workers, draymen, sailors, and public house touts. A kingfisher dropped into the water off the *Northern Star*'s prow.

Miss Havisham passed the wheel and binnacle, walking along the starboard rail to a hatch where she and Murdstone descended a ladder and moved aft again along the passageway, coming to the master's cabin.

Murdstone stopped. "My informants tell me you have been consorting with a shiftless criminal."

"You have been spying on me?" she asked.

"This Fagin is a notorious pickpocket, and weak in every way except stealing handkerchiefs from doddering old men. How he might help you in any fashion is beyond me, and that you would consort with him—a Clerkenwell thief—is another indication that you are trodding on ground that is foreign to you, and the sooner you abandon the field the better off you will be."

"You have had little experience being rejected by a woman, as I turned you down, and it has made you bitter." Miss Havisham braced herself against the bulkhead as the vessel shifted against the dock in a swell. "You are indulging yourself with whiney accusations."

"Do you have any idea how many hands have handled those Egyptian statues when they were on the way here? And the mules, carts, and ships that brought them here? The borders crossed? All the subrosa payments? All the douceurs? All the officials suborned?"

"If you and my father learned the business so can I."

Murdstone said, "You have no more conception of all this than of the backside of the moon. I am prepared to make you an offer to buy you out of Havisham and Murdstone, to get you out of the business and out of my way. I have prepared documents of sale, and I have them with me."

He opened the hatch and she followed him into the master's cabin. Port-to-starboard windows in an elegant curving frame threw the place into stark relief, and only after a moment could Miss Havisham make out the French-polished desk with its feather pen, ink pot, and seals. A bunk hung from lines, and a set of chart drawers were against a wall. A barometer was on a wall near a set of crossed presentation cutlasses. A silver tea service rested on a round table with wrought iron legs. A tea schooner's bow was visible through the windows.

Murdstone stepped toward the desk. He was wearing a coat made of oiled canvas, and from an inside pocket he pulled a packet of documents. He settled himself into a chair behind the desk and grandly swept invisible dust from the blotter before spreading out the papers. The chair had lion claw arms.

He spoke slowly, emphasizing each word as if addressing a moron. "My offer is eight thousand pounds, and for this you will sign over to me all your interest in Havisham and Murdstone, and . . . ."

The words died in his mouth when the hatch opened and Inspector Bucket walked into the cabin, having to twist sideways so his shoulders had sufficient clearance. He wore black from cap to boots. His mouth turned down and his hands balled at his side. His eyes were on Murdstone. Bucket was huge and fearsome.

He greeted Miss Havisham with, "Servant, madam." He handed her a piece of paper.

"I have brought a document, too." Miss Havisham held up the paper. "And you will sign it now in this cabin."

"Who is this man?" Murdstone's voice had lost its stately cadence.

"I have learned that my father executed a last will and testament dated one day before his death," Miss Havisham said, "a day he spent in a pain-and-opium induced delirium."

Murdstone half rose from his chair but when his eyes again found Inspector Bucket he settled back and made do by pointing at Miss Havisham. "To whom would your father leave Satis House? Your brother Arthur, who has no more spine than a jellyfish? To you, a daughter from whom he had become estranged?"

His words hit her like an errant ship's boom. Her voice rising with each word, she exclaimed, "That is an outrageous lie."

Murdstone smiled. "In his last years your father viewed me as a son, and a worthy beneficiary of his life's work. He willingly signed his latest will, and I brought two witnesses to the signing ceremony."

"In his last days, my father was in extremis. Nothing he signed will be upheld in court."

Murdstone spread his hands. "Perhaps so. I've heard that your lawyer, this Jaggers, is a good one. But a court will now indeed decide whether I have been legitimately bequeathed Satis House, and I anticipate a lengthy legal struggle—years and years—one that will make the fabled case of *Jarndyce and Jarndyce* look evanescent."

Miss Havisham steadied herself by spreading her feet on the deck.

"But perhaps this lengthy legal process to resolve ownership of Satis House can be resolved right now as part of the sale of your share of Havisham and Murdstone. We can rid Satis House of the cloud that regrettably hangs over its title."

She struggled to keep rage from her face. "That is extortion."

Inspector Bucket rose on his toes.

Murdstone said, "I will relinquish my claim to Satis House if the price of Havisham and Murdstone is reasonable, and you sign the sales agreement right now."

"I will sign nothing. But you will, Mr. Murdstone." Miss Havisham held up her piece of paper. "This is a quitclaim deed whereby you transfer to me whatever interest you may have in Satis House."

Glancing again at the detective, Murdstone laughed. "You overestimate your persuasiveness, madam."

"I have observed that you are right-handed," Miss Havisham said.

Murdstone's eyes shifted back and forth between Miss Havisham and the detective.

She said, "We must leave you with the ability to sign this quitclaim."

Bucket was a big man, and had Isaac Newton contemplated the topic he would have correctly concluded that large objects appear to be moving more slowly than they are in fact moving. So it was with Lewis Bucket who before Murdstone could blink had flown across the cabin, seized Murdstone's wrist, and spread his left hand on the desk as flat as a leaf.

Miss Havisham had again produced her dagger, and she viciously swung it downward, sending the blade through Murdstone's hand and deeply into the desktop. He screeched and flung himself up from the chair but he was pinned to the desk, and he collapsed back into the chair. He cried out and may have been trying to form words but nothing came but a falsetto keening. The dagger had skewered his hand. The blotter soaked up his blood.

Miss Havisham said, "You have one remaining hand, and my guess is that you will use it to sign the quitclaim deed to Satis House."

228

* * * *

"I'm going to tell this woman that I am your new father." Fagin held Luke's hand. "Careful, now. She may be espying us out her window."

"Are you my new father?" Luke asked.

"Never in life, my dear. I am merely a beacon on your narrow path, one who is dispensing a rare and singular knowledge to you without fee or begrudgement."

"Who is this lady?" Luke stopped to scratch behind the ears of a stout tabby which had found a spot of sun near a doorway. Then the boy hurried after Fagin.

"At one time, nary half a year ago, she was in possession of the sixteen silver spoons in our bag." When Fagin jiggled the cotton sack the spoons chimed. "The family initial—a garish *Z*—is engraved on each handle."

"How did you get them?"

"The same way I get everything, my sweet: I took them."

"Why haven't you sold them?"

"I should have picked a home where the family's name began with a letter earlier in the alphabet. Not much demand for silverware embossed with the letter *Z.*"

"You could turn the spoon sideways and pretend it's an *N,*" Luke offered.

"It was a bungled affair from the start, and I paid a price." Fagin pulled down the scarf at his neck and along with it the collar of his shirt. He stooped to offer a view of his shoulder. "Do you see this red skin? A bullet creased me."

"Did it hurt?" Luke asked.

"The butler or footman or the gentleman of the house who held the pistol was surely aiming at my heart, and only my dashing about—panicked, I don't mind admitting—saved me. It was pandemonium; a broken lamp, a shattered window, yells and screams, and all because Bill Sikes in the darkness had tripped over a tea service table. Amidst all the commotion, the lady rushed into the room with a lantern but I don't think she got a good look at Bill or me before we fled out the door, me bleeding."

"But you got the spoons," Luke said.

'And just the spoons. We had designs on much more. Here we are." Fagin indicated a gray stone residence fronted by precisely trimmed rows of boxwood. "Now remember, call me father." He turned the bell handle.

The door opened and a butler looked down his nose at them. He wore dark green livery and his head was as hairless as a hammer. His voice oozed with condescension. "May I help you?"

"Madam Zane, if you please," Fagin said.

The butler raised his nose even higher. "And what would your business be with Mrs. Zane?"

Fagin pulled out a spoon and handed it to the butler. "This is my calling card, eh? She will see my son and me, I am sure."

The butler examined the spoon, looked at Fagin as he might an errant cigar butt on a carpet, then said, "One moment. He closed the door and loudly shot the bolt.

It was less than a moment.

Mrs. Ellabeth Zane threw open the door. "My spoons," she exclaimed. "You have all of them?" She gripped Fagin's elbow. "Come in, sir, and bless you."

Judging from appearances, Ellabeth Zane spent her days eating ham. She was wide fore to aft and beam to beam, and her double chin covered a vast expanse between her mouth and her breastbone. The yellow frock draped over her would have shaded a regiment. Her green eyes were bright with pleasure as she guided Fagin and Luke into a parlor, waving the engraved spoon in front of her.

At some point in her life Mrs. Zane had stopped eating long enough to acquire a Russian samovar, which was displayed on a red cherry table. Heavy curtains had been drawn back to let in daylight. Birdcages were all the rage—most often without an occupant—and an empty cage hung from a stand near a window.

Mrs. Zane signaled toward a sofa, and she lowered herself onto a straight-back chair with as much dignity as her size would allow, the chair disappearing under her mass and meeting the challenge with a groan.

She said, "Officer, I am so happy to see this spoon again. You have the others?"

Fagin gave her the cloth bag. "Ay, sixteen spoons in sum, madam, your entire complement, I believe. And kindly do not confuse me with an officer of the law."

"He is my father," Luke said.

"Superintendent Pottinger is such a dear man." She fanned her face with a hand, apparently at the thought of how dear he was. "The superintendent said I deserved the utmost police effort to try to return my spoons, and here they are. Thank you for solving the case, officer. You are not in uniform, sir. Are you one of those detectives I have read about in the newspapers?"

"May I repeat myself?" Fagin asked. "I am not a policeman. Detective or otherwise."

"What a night that was, officer. Utter chaos. The crashing, the gunshot, and me screaming." Then she caught herself. "You aren't a police officer?"

"I am a reformed man, a penitent who humbly presents himself to you in hopes of forgiveness."

"He is my father." Luke's hair had been combed, his face washed, his jacket brushed, and his shoes blackened.

"My beloved sister has gone to her reward," Fagin said, "and as her only bequest to me, she left me her child, young Luke here."

"My heartfelt sympathies to you, sir," Mrs. Zane. "But a fine-looking lad he is."

Fagin said, "I have indeed been blessed by his appearance in my life."

"He is my father," Luke said.

Fagin nudged the boy's knee, then said, "I am attempting to reverse my iniquitous life with such gestures as providence will allow me, and one of them is to return your precious spoons to you in hopes that the boy here will learn from my modest purgation."

Mrs. Zane dropped the spoon into the sack where it joined the others. "Sir, if you aren't a policeman, and you didn't solve the case of burglary of my home, where did you find my spoons?"

"I found them in your silver service cabinet in your dining room."

Mrs. Zane shifted on her chair which squealed like a hog caught in a gate. She shook her head, which roiled her double chin so that it resembled a wave on the sea. "I am not comprehending you, sir?"

"Nothing could be plainer, madam," Fagin said. "I had your spoons because I took your spoons."

She stared at him. "You took them?"

"I confess to the burglary, and I prostrate myself before you, asking for your forgiveness in light of my new life with this young man." He patted Luke's knee.

"He is my father," Luke said.

"Which we have adequately established, Luke," Fagin said.

Mrs. Zane's hand shot to her mouth. "You are the housebreaker?"

"A harsh phrase but accurate in this particular."

"You were here that night? You stole the spoons? You are the burglar? My Lord, what shall I do?"

"I hope you will do nothing but accept my abject apologies and the return of your silverware. My dedication to raising this lad demanded that I give you back your property so that he may learn to lead an exemplary life. He gives an early indication that he may become an ordained man of the cloth."

She looked at the bag of spoons, then at Luke. "Young people need guidance and it is a noble thing you are doing, raising him, I suppose."

"I asked my partner that night to come with me to apologize to you but he refused. He said, 'The old bat doesn't deserve to get back her spoons.'"

Mrs. Zane cried, "He called me an old bat?"

"In the poor light during our wretched burglary that night he may not have seen the charming young lady who sits before me now, and would never have called you an old bat. You must have seen him. He is a head-turner, with hair the color of your frock. Bright yellow."

"Yellow?" she asked. "I glimpsed a swarthy fellow—wide, with a mean scowl—but his hair was brown or black, I can't be sure. My bedside lantern doesn't cast much light, and everyone was rushing about, and with my valet firing his pistol. Such a night."

"A dark-haired fellow? That must have been me." Fagin touched his hair above an ear.

"Yours is red, and a lovely color, if I may say. I know red, and it wasn't you I saw."

"He is my father," Luke announced again.

"Madam, have I the wrong house, eh?" Fagin asked. "With the Z-engraved teaspoons? My partner that night had gold hair, even brighter than gold. A remarkably handsome fellow, younger than me. He has a notch in his chin."

Mrs. Zane pointed at her own chin. "I distinctly recall the cleft in his chin. And his hair might have been yellow, for all I know. It was dark, and everyone was a tumble."

"Yes, that was my partner. You must have seen him as clearly as a bird sees a worm."

"He was handsome, wasn't he?" she asked. "With all that glorious hair."

"And blue eyes." Fagin rose from the sofa. "I'm sure you would recognize him if he knocks on your door to apologize. My son and I are off to our new and reformed lives, halleluiah,"

Mrs. Zane could gain her feet only after rocking several times when finally enough of her weight had shifted, sunk, and lifted again on the rebound so that she could propel herself upward in a manner addressed by Descartes in one of his later essays but understood by few others.

"I certainly forgive you, sir," Mrs. Zane said, guiding Fagin and Luke to the door. "You have expunged the moral record in my regard."

"My foul accomplice—with the blonde hair, blue eyes, and cleft in his chin—should be so lucky as to meet with a compassionate and understanding lovely young woman as yourself." Fagin gripped the door handle. "Good day to you, madam."

"I am leaving with my father." Luke bowed to Mrs. Zane.

"Goodbye, sir," she said, still holding the bag of spoons. "Goodbye, young man."

After the door had closed and they had gained the street, Fagin said to Luke, "Let us hope you are a better thief and pickpocket than an actor, my dear."

* * * *

"I never miss a hanging," Samuel Compeyson said. "They are restorative and bracing."

Magwitch replied, "Not so much for the condemned, eh?"

"These louts are here for entertainment." Compeyson spoke loudly to be heard over the laughter and cheering. "I am here to better myself. It's a grim day for this highwayman Johnny Dodds but a fine one for me."

"What is the fee for a window?" Magwitch asked as he surveyed the buildings across the road from the prison.

"Three guineas for each of us so here we are on the street with the odorous."

Fifteen thousand people filled the streets in front of Newgate Prison. The crowd had come from as far away as Bath, had begun arriving at three in the morning, and had grown so large that spectators were squeezed against buildings and perched on lamp poles. They filled windows and covered rooftops. Vendors sold gin and pies from carts. Newsboys waved papers, and several editions already had lurid accounts of what had yet to occur.

"Get me closer," Compeyson called.

Magwitch nudged aside a lumpy woman who scowled at him, then a fellow who carried a child on his shoulders. Then a man with a red nose who held a beer tankard. Perhaps these onlookers might have objected to being shoved aside but a glance at Magwitch's square and bony face would cork any throat.

Drawing closer to the scaffold, Compeyson followed in Magwitch's wake. Compeyson's long, deep-pocketed brilliant green coat and even brighter green cravat and waistcoat contrasted with most spectators' brown and black raiment. Rain had fallen at dawn, and the smells were of wet wool and rotted dentition.

The crowd was festive, and drink and song ruled the day. Two troops of Life Guards were on duty but they leaned on their muskets on side streets. Spectators broke into the bawdy sailors' song *Meet Me Halfway Down*. A line formed at a barrel of ale on a donkey cart, mugs filled one after another without the tap having to be turned off. A one-legged balladmonger—a knotty man with a close-grained face—sold sheet music for comic songs for a half-penny each. A red feather boa had been snatched from a woman's shoulders, and the crowd batted it above their heads. So thick was the crowd that it leaned left then right as one, resembling waves on the sea.

Magwitch wore a miner's cap, a striped cotton blouse, and corduroy pants: drab to invisibility next to Compeyson. A wilted carnation in her cap, a prostitute squeezed through the crowd to approach Compeyson, smiling with teeth so wrecked her grin resembled a broken fence. Magwitch wagged a finger at her, and she turned away to approach someone else.

Compeyson said, "I come to these hangings for two reasons, Magwitch."

"That's one more reason than the condemned has, now isn't it, sir?"

"The first is to inspire me to work harder," Compeyson said over the noise. "Have you ever been poor, Magwitch?"

"I am poor right now as I stand before you."

"Have you ever been unable to walk because of hunger cramps in your belly?"

"I've never been that helpless, your honor." Magwitch gently pushed aside a fellow who swayed with drink.

"For much of my childhood nothing passed my lips but my breath. Sometimes my father had money for food, most times not. I remember my first full meal, the very first time I wasn't hungry." Compeyson spoke directly into Magwitch's ear. "It was Boxing Day, and I was thirteen years old. I stole a shepherd's pie and a blood pudding from a Southampton inn. I shoved it all down my throat as fast as I could, and have never felt better before or since."

"Shouldn't this confession be between you and a priest?" Magwitch asked.

"I will not be poor and desperate ever again. I am telling you these things so you will understand why I work so hard at my craft."

"I am just your bodyguard, and so I don't need to understand anything."

Magwitch broke through a group of gentlemen wearing top hats and nosegays, pushing closer to the scaffold. Compeyson followed. Magwitch stepped around a man with no legs who was on a wheeled cart but Compeyson put his foot on the cart and shoved the man into the legs of a woman selling cider from a canvas bag, earning imprecations from both. An acrobat in red tights performed a one arm handstand, his other arm out for coins. A craftsman stood on his chair re-caning cart for a better view. Trying to open a view, an old woman swatted spectators with a lacquered fan. Such was the fervor and anticipation that few women's gazes lingered on Samuel Compeyson, a rare state of affairs.

"And the second reason I come to these affairs is to remind me to be careful," Compeyson said into Magwitch's ear. "I was hung once from a tree at the side of a road in Somerset. The bride's three brothers caught me two hours after the wedding was supposed to have taken place, and with a rope pulled me up to an oak bough by my neck."

A squirmy boy tottered on his father's shoulders, then fell back, and might have hit the ground had not Magwitch pushed up the boy so he could regrip his father's head.

Compeyson pulled down the cravat under his ear, revealing a trench of purple and red skin containing ugly folds and striations of skin. "The brothers lifted me up, lowered me to the ground, lifted me up again, and set me down again; I do not know how many times, until I was no more sensate than the bough from which I was suspended. Then they left me naked in a ditch."

"An unpleasant day, all told." Magwitch gave a coin to a vendor, who slid a Yorkshire pudding from a skewer and passed it to him. Magwitch put it into a coat pocket for later.

"I blame myself, not the brothers." Compeyson jabbed Magwitch's chest with a finger. "They found me because I was careless. I have learned from that day."

Magwitch smiled but he gripped Compeyson's finger and turned it aside. "I don't favor being poked, your worship."

"I take my time," Compeyson went on. "I watch things closely. I look over my shoulder, and take small steps. I am never careless. I learned these things hanging from that tree, and the scar around my neck is my permanent reminder."

Newgate Prison was the length of a city block. Time had blackened the building's stone face. Windows were few, small, and barred. A temporary brick scaffold had been built in front of the prison forty years ago but business had been steady so it had never been torn down. Last night the hand-held execution bell had been rung outside Johnny Dodds's cell. And at the moment, if procedures were being strictly followed as is usually the case with English executions, Dodds was in the pinioning room where his arms were being strapped to his sides with leather belts, and where the prison governor would formally release Dodds to the executioner.

"Magwitch, I have been invited to Lady Burke's salon." Compeyson beamed, his expression as close to rapture as allowed on earth. "You have heard of her?"

"Can't say as I have."

"At her home in Mayfair she entertains artists and philosophers and scientists."

"A thrill, I'm sure." Magwitch cracked his knuckles.

"I have been working on this invitation for a year. I had to befriend a writer, for God's sake. He regularly attends Lady Burke's. He arranged the invitation."

"Are you going to find someone in the room to work?" Magwitch asked. "One of your swindles?"

Compeyson's expression suggested Magwitch had stomped on his toes. "All my life I have tried to be introduced into this society. It is the apex of my ambition. These people at Lady Burke's will be my new companions. This will be my new milieu."

Magwitch said, "Roaming with that toff mob will be costly, sir."

"When I'm finished with that twit Anna Wilkinson, I won't need to worry about funds for a long while."

The crowd roared when the executioner rose on the stairway to appear on the scaffold. He held up a white hood and then bowed to the onlookers. Compeyson turned from Magwitch to stare at the gallows.

The crowd took up the chant, "Three cheers for the hangman."

And Philo Spotswood surely deserved the acclaim. He had been London's executioner for eight years, and he earned a guinea a week plus an additional guinea for each convict he sent across the River Styx. He was also entitled by right to the condemned's trousers and stockings, and he always sold four-inch lengths of the rope as remembrances. Spotswood wore a jolly red cap and a tanner's apron, and his teeth were as brown as bark. His nickname was Short Drop.

Another burst of applause and shouts of approval as Johnny Dodds mounted the scaffold. He swayed but managed to grin. His brown hair was matted to his skull, and his arms were tight to his sides. The prison chaplain and two jailors also gained the platform. The chaplain's nose was in the Good Book, and his lips moved steadily. A dull black cassock covered him from neck to feet.

"There he is," Compeyson said. "By God, look at him. His time has come."

The condemned man limped as Spotswood guided him to the trapdoor. The robbery of the royal mail coach hadn't gone as planned when the guard blew off much of Dodds' foot with a blunderbuss. On the gallows, these were Dodds' last steps on this earth so the maimed foot shortly would be of no concern. His half foot and ankle were wrapped in a filthy rag.

His hands deep in his pockets, Compeyson licked his lips. "And those leather straps that bind him. They are perfect, just the thing. They are elegant and lovely. I have some just like them."

Magwitch stood at his shoulder, his eyes going between his employer and the scaffold.

Compeyson said, "What must that poor fellow be thinking? The sheer horror of seeing the noose and the crowd and the hangman."

With a theatrical movement—raising his hands toward the sky then steadily lowering them—Short Drop Spotswood placed the hood over Dodds's head, and the crowd issued full-throated approval.

"Look at that hood," Compeyson exclaimed. "What an adornment. How perfect."

The purpose of the hood was not to hide the doomed man's face from spectators but rather so that the fellow didn't time a jump to the side just as the trapdoor opened. Spotswood fitted the noose to Dodds's neck, the knot under an ear. Dodds's hood ballooned outward as he exhaled.

Compeyson breathed quickly. "Look at him, standing there. My Lord, what ecstasy, to stand next to a hangman on the trap."

Magwitch stared at him.

"I tremble, I just tremble to think of the terror." Compeyson pushed his hands farther into his coat pockets, and rocked back and forth, as much movement as the pressing crowd allowed.

"Are you all right, your lordship?" Magwitch asked.

Noise on the street fell to a whisper. That exquisite instant of magisterial retributive justice was at hand, and breaths were held in chests and mouths were silenced.

Compeyson's face reddened, and his mouth opened, his tongue sliding across his upper lip. "Look at him, about to meet his maker, and he stands on the scaffold and there is nothing he can do. He's a steer at an abattoir. He's helpless. Utterly, completely helpless."

"I'm not fully understanding you, sir," Magwitch said.

"His fate is an inch from him, the eternal unknown a few seconds from resolution."

Magwitch moved away, only a few inches due to the pressing crowd.

Compeyson rocked back and forth, his eyes never leaving the scaffold. "The horror and joy of it, right there, right in front of him."

Short Drop Spotswood stepped to the platform's side near the rail, raised a hand to acknowledge his people, and then jerked back the trapdoor lever.

"My God, hell is at hand. It's coming, you doomed fool," Compeyson barked. "My God." Compeyson shuddered mightily and his inhale was fierce.

Johnny Dodds plummeted downward and disappeared through the trap. The spectators gasped.

Spotswood had earned his nickname Short Drop because he used a two-and-a-half foot drop which mean the condemned's neck was not broken resulting in instant death but rather that he was fated to strangle to death, and indeed, Dodds twitched and kicked at the end of the rope. Some in the crowd moaned and others laughed. This was an edifying spectacle, one to recount at home during the long, listless English winters.

Compeyson wiped a sleeve across his forehead. "The joy of it all." He inhaled mightily and pulled his hands from his pockets. "I'm all right, Magwitch. Nothing to concern you."

Short Drop Spotswood gripped the rope and climbed onto Dodds' shoulders, riding him and bouncing up and down, hastening Dodds' last tortured breaths as the noose cinched up due to the added weight, a kindness for which Dodds had likely paid the hangman a sovereign. Dodds' legs stopped kicking, and he hung there as still as a ham. The crowd sang *Rule, Britania.* St. Sepuchre-without-Newgate's mournful bells rang to mark the execution.

Compeyson again turned to Magwitch. "I attend these affairs to see what might have happened to me had I not struggled to escape this victim's fate.

Without my wits and work, I would doubtless already have been stretched from a rope at Newgate."

"A ghastly spectacle, none to my liking," Magwitch said. "But you were fairly carried away by it, it seems."

When Spotswood climbed off the highwayman's body he was met with more huzzahs. After another bow, he left the platform, followed by the chaplain and jailors. The body would be left to hang for thirty minutes. A coffin was on the cobblestones to one side of the gallows.

Compeyson moved away from the prison. "Strange things have been happening to me, Magwitch. Unusual things, and I don't have an accounting for them. But I'm going to find out who or what is behind them."

Magwitch pushed aside those who dawdled as they left the site.

"A hanging is a lesson regarding what will happen to me if I slip up," Compeyson said. "It makes me careful."

Magwitch nodded pleasantly at an old man before nudging him out of the way.

"Because in my profession," Compeyson said as he followed Magwitch, "there are old men and there are careless men. But there are no old and careless men."

24

"Is it real?" the lawyer asked.

"Truth is your scruple, Mr. Jaggers." Miss Havisham's voice had a teasing lilt. "So how can you ask such a question?"

"Were you in the witness box, madam, I would sternly tell you that I am the one to ask questions, not you." Jaggers scratched his chin, staring at it. "So, I ask again: is it real?"

"'Take nothing on its looks,' you always say. Well, is it a real mermaid?"

"I don't believe in mermaids."

She smiled. "Then what is the creature in front of you?"

Jaggers stood there, his posture full of propriety. His gaze was on a five-foot length of desiccated bone and sinew, all of it brown and corrupt. Ribs were recognizable but where a pelvis would have been on a human skeleton was the ray of a dorsal fin and thin vertebrae ending in fin rays of a tail.

"I put the case that the aft end is a surely a fish," Jaggers said.

"What about the rest of it?"

"Are those human bones, the arms and hands?" Then shifting his gaze to the head, the lawyer inhaled loudly. "A cranium containing holes for ears and eye sockets, and a chin, all of it bone. It's a human skull."

Patches of skin and muscle were attached to some of the bones, so dried and brown they might have been jerked. Tufts of black hair clung to the skull. The eyeball sockets were deep, black, and malevolent. The lipless mouth contained two-inch canine teeth. The forehead was almost flat and slanted back, making the protruding face aggressive and hostile. Bits of flakey skin on the face were purple.

"If it is a true mermaid," Jaggers said, "and if mermaids are this ugly and horrible, the seas would empty. Yet the seas are filled with fish. Ergo, that is not a real mermaid."

Light from the warehouse's grimy window was gray and weak, and the mermaid could not be seen clearly, making her more threatening.

Miss Havisham said, "I purchased this for fifteen pounds from a *Temeraire* sailor. The bridge contractor Hubert Sunderson has offered me five hundred pounds for a mermaid skeleton, and so this is a mermaid skeleton."

The lawyer hesitated. "Is it real?"

"You are charmingly naïve about some things, Mr. Jaggers." She smiled at him. "The sailor sewed the upper half of a dead monkey to the bones of a fish the ship's wardroom had eaten for supper."

Jaggers leaned closer to the creature, which was on a warehouse shelf amid other rarities and exotica.

"If you look carefully under a good light using a glass, you'll see stitching and glue."

"Won't Hubert Sunderson object when he finds it is a fraud?"

"What will he do?" She laughed. "Complain that he was foolish enough to buy a faux mermaid? He'd be a laughingstock at his club."

"Is that how you are now earning your provender? Selling forgeries?"

She stepped along the shelf to place a hand on a lumpy canvas bag. "This is a half bushel of cinchona tree bark imported from the South Seas. Sailors chew on pieces of the bark to relieve malaria symptoms. Some call it quinine. Much of what I sell is authentic."

"Why the need to smuggle in quinine?"

"The customs house would want its share."

"You are learning quickly, madam." He started toward the warehouse door. "My advice is now, and has always been, to divest yourself of your father's importing business. Your brewery is sufficient, is it not?"

They passed a stack of Flemish carpets.

Miss Havisham said, "I sent a messenger to your office with a quitclaim deed."

"I received it, and have already filed it with the court." Jaggers walked with his hands locked behind his back. His voice was orotund. "I was confident your father's deathbed will that Murdstone produced could be defeated but it would've taken many months, maybe years."

"And so that worry is at an end?"

"Satis House is yours entirely and irrevocably. How in the world did you obtain Murdstone's signature on the quitclaim?"

She laughed again. "I had no idea I could be so persuasive."

"What are those?" Jaggers gestured toward square bales.

"American tobacco headed to a snuff factory in the east end. Imported at Portsmouth and brought here overland under loads of cabbages. No customs house involved in that transaction, either."

Jaggers pointed in the direction of the warehouse's double door. "Who is that fellow?"

"He says his name is Emmanuel and he says he is French. He used to work for Murdstone but now he works for me as a guard. I haven't had any trouble since I hired him."

The lawyer stopped to stare at the man who wore his cap low over his eyes and a long canvas coat. "He is missing an ear, isn't he? His name is Emmanuel LaLonde. He has never been able to afford me as his defense counsel but I've seen him in court a number of times. He has spent half his life at Newgate or the King's Bench Prison. He is nasty with a knife."

"Who isn't?" Her eyes widened and she covered her mouth with a hand.

Jaggers looked at her. "Pardon me?"

"He seems like a fine fellow. And I think he fancies me. I'm perfectly safe around him."

As they moved closer to the door, Emmanuel LaLonde tipped his hat and offered his wrecked smile. She returned a grin. He opened a door for them and Miss Havisham and Jaggers stepped into an alley opposite another warehouse. Workmen unloaded lathed chair legs from a wagon and carried them into the other warehouse.

She asked, "Have you ever had a moment's fun, Mr. Jaggers?"

"Fun?"

She smiled. "The concept of fun just stopped you on the cobblestones as if you were yanked by a rope."

"I am having fun right now in this alleyway speaking with you, for which you are being charged by the hour. What could be more fun than that?"

"You know what I mean." She touched his arm. "Have you ever had a frolic, once in your life?"

"I have not, madam."

"Never danced in a field of daisies?"

"Where did that appalling image come from?" His black coat was held around his waist with a leather belt. His top hat sat too high on his remarkably large head, and it is unlikely he could find a hat that fit him well. "Are your feet on the ground, madam?"

"Call me Margaret."

"My hourly fee is the same irrespective of whether I address you by your first name or more formally."

"Are you smiling?" she asked. "I didn't think you were capable of it."

As they left the alleyway, he asked, "Will you have a glass of punch with me? Right here at the Rose and Thorn?"

"A public house?" She narrowed her eyes. "The patrons are rowdy, are they not? Will we be killed?"

"If I am killed, who will defend the villain at the trial for my murder?"

241

A sign draped in garlands hung from a pole attached to the building. He opened the door for her. Sitting on benches and chairs, imbibers glanced at Miss Havisham, then turned back to their mugs. A deer stag's head was mounted on a wall above three barrels of ale. The barkeeper wiped mugs with a rag, setting them on the counter. Miss Havisham was the only woman in the room. Her crimson frock was a striking dash of color in the drab place. They found a table and chairs next to the front window.

She settled into a chair. "Have I ever told you that I ran away from home once?"

Jaggers ordered punch from the barkeeper, then said, "You have never told me anything about yourself. Were you to reveal you are one of a set of triplets, it would be news to me."

"I was sixteen years old, and desperately wanted to be an actress, and to see a world where everything didn't smell like malted barley."

Jaggers histrionically used the chain across his belly to pull out his repeater. He opened and stared at the dial. "If this conversation is going to be about personal things, I suppose I must turn off my billing clock."

"When I told my mother I wanted to be an actress she became dyspeptic and went to her bed for a week. Dad didn't think I would do anything about it."

The bartender placed mugs of punch on the table. He eyed Miss Havisham, a woman in his establishment being as foreign as a kangaroo.

She said, "I filled a carpet bag with a few things and ran away."

"I sit here before you astonished." The lawyer sipped the punch. "I had thought you to be domiciliary. When I visited Satis House, you were always playing the pianoforte or brushing your horse or out in gardens with a basket. A smiling, happy youngster."

"I was." She grimaced when she tasted the punch. "And then one day I wasn't so I left. I was gone a year, and it remains the most fun I ever had."

"There is no profit in fun, madam." Jaggers tugged at his waistcoat, an action which punctuated the probity of his words.

"I didn't go far, at least at first." She stared at the far wall. "I walked to Rochester, and I found myself outside a small theater, one of those places that is a dry goods emporium one day and a theater the next. To get out of the rain I walked inside. The troupe was rehearsing, and the manager yelled at me, 'Can you play an oak tree?' I found myself on a stage holding two artificial tree boughs."

"Even the English Sappho Mary Robinson probably started her stage career holding tree branches."

She looked at him. "I'm trying to be serious."

Jaggers mopped his mouth with his palm. "Running away from home to join the theater is a topic outside my experience."

"And at the end of the tree bough rehearsal, no one asked me to leave so I stayed. And when the troupe moved to Margate, I went with them. Then to Ramsgate, then Deal." She laughed. "Whenever the production called for someone awkward and gangly, I'd be cast."

"You never beg for compliments, Margaret, and you are not doing so now so let me volunteer that you today are anything but awkward and gangly. You move with grace and you fill out your clothing in a pleasing way, if I may put too fine a point on it."

She swirled the punch in the glass. "Dad found out I was safe and was with an acting ensemble, and so didn't try to retrieve me at first. He came to get me after a year, when the troupe was in Salisbury. He later said it was cheaper to have me run away with actors than to send me on a grand tour of the continent."

"And what about your mother?"

"The strangest thing, Mr. Jaggers. When I arrived home, she gave me this bracelet." She held up her wrist and jangled the bracelet. "Just handed it to me. The diamonds are huge. And she never once mentioned my year with the actors."

"She didn't talk about it with you, your reason for running away?"

"Not once, not ever." A wistful note in her voice, she added, "I suppose I was ready to go home when dad found me. But I loved those people, the actors and the manager and the sceneshifters, all of them. They took me in and taught me a lot. It was the best time of my life." Her face cleared. "Except for Samuel's courtship of me which until the very morning of the wedding was wonderful."

Jaggers leaned back in his chair. "You must put that in the past, Margaret."

"It will never be in the past,"—her face became stone—"though Samuel Compeyson is going to wish it were. He is going to be ground upon his own beef bones. You have my bond on that."

* * * *

"How much is this peach?" Bill Sikes picked one up and held it up to the fruit lady's nose.

"Tuppence, sir." The lady pointed at her artfully arranged stack of peaches. "Fresh from a Wiltshire orchard to you with nary a day between the picking of it and your holding of it."

"Tuppence is too much." Sikes squeezed the peach so that pulp and juice squirted from it, specks landing on the woman's cheek. He tossed the mangled peach onto the street, and lifted another from her pile. He held it up. "And how much is this one?"

She wore a stained apron and a faded blue bonnet. She licked her lips. "One pence, sir?"

243

He said, "It's a fine specimen but a penny is still too much." He squeezed the peach so that, crushed and ruined, it extruded through his fingers, the mush dripping from his hand to the street.

"Sir, that's not . . . ."

Sikes lifted a third peach. "And how much is this one?"

The woman gestured despairingly. "You may have that peach, sir."

"That's obliging of you, missy." He jauntily tossed the peach into the air and caught it. "A fine and generous lady you are, and that's certain." He stepped away from her fruit stand.

"Bill, that's mean." Nancy put her arm through his. "You shouldn't do things like that."

"And have my girl go wanting for a peach?" he asked. "Not when she's with Bill Sikes."

When, with a grand sweep of his hand he presented the peach to her, she dropped it into a cloth bag she carried as a purse. They walked near St. Paul's on the west side of Covent Garden market, which was loud and busy, filled with produce and flowers and those who made their livings in those trades. Porters carried wicker baskets on their heads while salesmen and brokers haggled. Horses and carts jammed the area. Wickerwork crates were stacked twenty-feet high. Flower girls filled their hampers and laborers unloaded apples and carrots just in from the country, hard workers, surely, but a petition signed by nearby residents said the square was also frequented by "a great number of profligate and disorderly people." Bill Sikes would have been counted among them.

"And I'll drape you in flowers, madam." Sikes rose to his toes to snatch a fistful of carnations from a basket balanced on top of a woman's head.

The flower lady might have felt a disturbance, and she turned toward Sikes, who grinned tauntingly at her. Gripping her basket with both hands she moved rapidly away from him.

Sikes wore a tarpaulin hat he had found somewhere. His linen shirt hung outside his trousers, and the hemline was tattered and soiled. His blue scarf was wrapped around his neck. "A gin palace is around the corner. Let's go there to cool off."

"It's not hot out here, is it Bill?" The hem of Nancy's frock swished along the ground, stirring discarded carrot leaves and mushroom stems. "I'm fine."

"But I'm parched, honeydew. Have you got a bob on you?"

Golden gray coal smoke was wrapped around the market. A breeze carried scents of roses and ground horseradish. Horseshoes clicked on the cobblestones, and wagon axles squeaked. A gray dog the size of a bread tin charged from under a table of apricots, barked ferociously at Sikes's ankles, then just as abruptly retreated under the table. An open-air iron and brick hallway had been proposed for the market but construction had not begun, and the place was still filled with canvas tents and knock-down sheds.

"Can we wait until noon?" Nancy smiled up at him, her mouth generous and her eyes the color of the sky in places other than London. "We'll have lunch."

"Thirst knows no time of day, my dear. It doesn't wait for the bell tower to ring and it doesn't wait for the tide to turn."

She found the coin in a pocket.

He scratched his chest. "And you can do a little work this evening."

"I thought maybe . . . ."

"No thinking needed on your part, dearie." He tapped his temple. "That's why you've got me beside you."

Nancy knew little of her father other than that he had abandoned his family to dire poverty. He may have been an indolent drunk, more intent on finding his next bottle than on putting food on the table, and one day he likely just wandered off looking for that bottle, never to return. But even this worthless father would have been alarmed at the spectacle of his daughter falling for Bill Sikes. And it is a timeless puzzle for fathers. A daughter's good sense can somehow be suspended by a benighted lout, by a worthless crust, by a ne'er-do-well who has no more ambition than a stone and no more wisdom than a wart. A millennium of fathers has watched with stupefaction as their daughters entered these trances. There is no remedy, and so none can be provided for Nancy.

Sikes hummed several measures of *Old Clem*, then said, "You told me this Miss Havisham has invited you to her house."

"Not really." Nancy smiled at the memory. "She gave me her card and said maybe we'll meet again someday."

"That's as good as an invitation to dinner, isn't it?"

"Her home is a long way from here."

"I know exactly where it is because I've been there, and I'm still limping from it. Fagin tells me she has a diamond bracelet."

She looked up at him. "Mr. Fagin would tell you that? Why would he do that? He regards Miss Havisham with much approval, I think."

Sikes chopped the air with his hand. "That fool Fagin thinks I'm his lickspittle. But I'm done truckling to him. He don't think I can do anything on my own, and I'm about to prove him wrong with that bracelet. He don't plan to take that bracelet because he has a liking for that high-and-mighty lady."

"So do I," Nancy said.

"You are going to help me get that bracelet, missy. I got just the plan."

She stopped in front of a beet cart. "And she likes me. I'm not going to steal a bracelet from Miss Havisham."

Bill Sikes grabbed her bicep and pinched it so hard she yelped. She tried to pull away but he yanked her close and stuck his rutted face right into hers.

"That's where you're wrong, little missy," he said. "I've got a plan, and you are going to go to Satis House and get that diamond bracelet for me."

"I won't," she yelled.

Vendors turned their direction.

This time he squeezed her arm so hard she cried out.

"I believe you will, and I knows my girl."

* * * *

"In you go, you brat," the Bow Street Runner said. "No impudence from you, and don't give me a pathetic story about your situation. Hunger and beating and all the rest. I hear them every day."

The runner—one of the policemen, the taller one, who had thrown Fagin into Miss Havisham's carriage—propelled the boy through the door at 4 Bow Street.

"But, sir, I was just minding my own business standing there on the corner." The boy tried to shake off the policeman's grip but he was well-seized.

The runner's name was Charlie Dunstable, and he was as honest as Bow Street Runner's came, which was honest seventy-five percent of the time, give or take. His badly reset nose made one side of his face appear too busy.

"Save it for the magistrate." Dunstable adjusted his oilskin cape. "He won't believe you either."

He hauled the boy to a wall under a pendulum clock. The room was filled with Bow Street Runners and arrestees. Chandeliers hung from the ceiling. Windows allowed an anemic light that apparently did nothing to brighten the moods of the felons visiting the room against their wills. In cuffs and fetters and sitting on benches they were a grim lot.

Inspector Bucket appeared at the runner's shoulder. "I know this boy, Charlie. Let me take over."

Dunstable tapped a finger on his own forehead, a salute. "Certainly, inspector. Less paperwork for me, and so it's a service you're doing." He biffed the back of the boy's head, then moved toward the door to the street.

"Your name is Luke, isn't it?" Bucket asked. "Fagin's apprentice? Who came from the city out to Satis House?"

"That'd be me, sir." Luke smiled, perhaps sensing a reprieve.

"Empty your pockets, boy." Bucket indicated a table against the wall. "Let's see what you've filched."

"My pockets are empty, sir, except for a few small things that my mum gave me."

"I am in no mood for humor. Empty them. And any more prevarications from you, and you'll be wondering what happened when you rise from the floor with a blackening eye." Bucket's tone was light, inferring that the threat was well-worn and hollow. He was a large and square man, muscled and formidable with a rugged face but an aura of cruelty did not surround him. He gestured at the table. "Put it all there and be double-quick about it."

Luke's black wool coat was so large he was fairly hidden in it. The sleeves hung past his hands, and pockets were loose and bulging. The collar was turned up, covering the back of his neck. A sailor's straw hat with a black ribbon around the crown was on his head. He was clearly a child of the streets but he appeared well-fed, with full cheeks and a spark in his eyes.

From a pocket he pulled out a silver scoop spoon with *BR* engraved on the handle.

Inspector Bucket took it from him and held up the spoon to his eyes. "Are your initials BR?"

"I don't know my letters, sir."

"And you don't know anybody with those initials, either, those folks who'll be missing their spoon next time they want chestnut bisque." He motioned with his finger. "Unburden yourself, boy."

From the pocket out came a filigreed silver needle case with an amethyst mounted on its side, then a gold wedding napkin ring, and a slotted silver pie server.

Luke said, "That's all, sir."

"That's all from that pocket." Bucket smiled. "But I'm noticing other pockets."

The boy produced a gold pocket watch still attached to its chain, and then a silver lemon strainer. Then a porcelain string holder with a miniature of King George painted on it and then a glass perfume bottle. Next came a silver wine bottle stopper. And a silver bonnet brush.

The detective asked, "Is there nothing you won't lift?"

Luke continued to dig. From an inside pocket came a silver locket and a pewter ink bottle. Then a brass letter opener, four silk handkerchiefs, an ivory mustache comb, then a half a dozen hair pins, some brass and some silver. And a pair of tailor's scissors and a surgeon's sterling tonsil guillotine.

The boy said, "That's all, sir."

"You sure? No saddles or lampposts?"

The youngster pulled his coat pockets inside out.

A raised voice came from half the room away. "Mr. Bucket, may I have a word with you?"

Bucket pointed. "You sit on that bench under the calendar, boy. I don't need to put irons on you, do I? Don't you move from that bench."

The detective waited until the young pickpocket had settled onto the bench as far as possible from a fellow without a shirt but with leg fetters. Bucket crossed the room toward Sir Daniel Pottinger, superintendent of the Bow Street Runners, none of whom favored being called a *runner*. They were policemen, and they called themselves London Watchmen. There was some talk by the home secretary of consolidating police jurisdictions into a London metropolitan force, an outrageous notion that Sir Daniel could not speak of without balling his fists.

Bucket crossed the room, a combination police station and courtroom termed a police court. At the far end of the room a magistrate in a white wig speedily tried and sentenced malefactors. This particular judge—Horace Farmont—was guided by the principle that the defendants would not have been arrested had they not been guilty. A line of bailiffs waited to take the defendants from the courtroom to jail. Few arrestees exited the room through the front doors to Bow Street and freedom. With their stove-pipe top hats and gilded buttons, Bow Street Runners waited to testify.

Sir Daniel Pottinger signaled for Bucket to follow him to a desk behind which Sir Daniel remained standing as straight as a shinbone with his hands behind his back, suggesting the impending deliverance of bad news. On Fridays Sir Daniel was usually puddled by drink but this was not a Friday. Despite his grand paunch and wagging wattles, he was leather tough on days that weren't Friday. His small eyes were sunken deeply in a perfectly round head topped with a few strands of white hair combed to starboard in an attempt to hide an otherwise shiny head. The wiry brown wig he wore whenever he left the building was on his desk, alongside a stack of documents and a pen stand holding six feather pens in perfect alignment. Pushed by his belly, buttons on his blue waistcoat seemed about to pop off.

"Mr. Buckle, I have heard you are attending to business other than that of this station." Sir Daniel's voice was high and piping, at odds with his bulk.

"Adding a few quid to my living is all, sir." Bucket knew to stand at a reasonable facsimile of attention, Sir Daniel having served with the Green Howards, and despite his ridiculous belly he was not to be frittered with.

Sir Daniel pursed his lips, apparently considering the comment. "And how many hours this past week were you adding a few quid to your living?"

"Perhaps too many, sir."

"I have gathered as much. You have been engaged in private work for that Rochester family, the Havishams?"

"Yes, sir."

"Henceforth you will faithfully attend to this station's business," Sir Daniel said. "Your obligation is to the people of this city not to a Kent brewing family."

"Of course, sir."

"Allow me to add, Inspector Bucket, that you are good at your profession." Sir Daniel generated half a smile. "I need you working in Covent Garden, not Kent. Who is that boy whose pockets you just cleaned out?"

"A tooler Charlie Dunstable pinched outside Hummums Hotel."

"Recommend to the magistrate two years at the Cornhill Reformatory. One way or another I am going to rid Covent Gardens of pickpockets." Sir Daniel lowered himself to his chair and lifted a pen and dipped it into an inkwell. "That's all, inspector."

Passing a woman hawking ploughman's lunches from a handcart, Bucket crossed the room to the boy. "Stand up."

"What's the judge going to do?" Luke asked. "Is he going to send me away?"

"As astonishing as it is, you are a friend of Miss Havisham. And she is a friend of mine."

Luke grinned. "I had meat and potatoes at her house out in the country just the other day. She wants me to learn letters and figures."

Bucket glanced over his shoulder at Sir Daniel, then at the magistrate. Neither seemed to be watching him and Luke. "You beat it, boy. I'm done with you."

"Leave? Through the door, sir? I can go?"

"Try to spend more time with Miss Havisham than with Fagin, you hear me?"

Luke pointed at the table, at the pocket watch and the surgeon's instrument and all the rest. "Can I take my stuff?"

"Don't push your luck, lad. Go."

Luke scrambled away, and within seconds was out the door and onto the street. Inspector Bucket again looked at Sir Daniel, whose head was down and whose pen was moving across a piece of paper. And no one else in the room seemed to have noticed the boy's departure.

Reaching into a pocket for a coin, the detective stepped toward the lunch lady. Then he stopped. He stared at Sir Daniel Pottinger at his desk, then at the door through which the boy Luke had just fled. Bucket rubbed his chin, deep in thought. Then he left the police court building without his lunch.

25

Lady Abigail Burke's salon at her home on Grosvenor Square was the aspiration of many but the attainment of few.

Men of accomplishment were invited to the salon, there to discuss topics of the day. In any given session an astronomer and a coal mine magnate might converse in front of the fireplace while a poet, a biologist, and a mathematician exchanged views by the stairway. The writer Walter Scott, architect John Nash, painter Thomas Lawrence, and the physician James Blundell were often in attendance. The landscape painter Hiram Olden once exclaimed that he would rather be invited to Lady Burke's salon than receive a knighthood, a fine sentiment, but it was widely believed that whatever chance Olden had of bending a knee before the monarch was thus forever extinguished.

In her younger years Lady Burke had been a notorious beauty, the subject of wild gossip and course longing. Whether Lord Byron was one of her paramours was discussed more often in certain circles than was the weather. At age twenty-six she had married above her station though certainly not her intellect. Her husband, the Baron Farleigh, spent his time hunting at their country home in Wiltshire, and had no more interest in intellectual pursuits than he did in Irish jigs.

Lady Burke was widely read, urbane, and clever. Her bi-monthly salon was the pinnacle of London's intellectual society. To enter through her door with the red iron hinges and the brass lion knocker was an acknowledgment second only to an invitation to Kensington Palace. And it was a chance to gaze at Lady Burke, a preposterously lovely balm for the eyes.

"You stay out here," Samuel Compeyson said. "Is my cravat square?"

"I'm your bodyguard, not your valet," Magwitch said. "And I've never worn a cravat. How would I know?"

"Appearances are everything, Magwitch. If the surface is fine, what lies beneath is of little consequence."

The surface was indeed fine. Compeyson's tailcoat was of beryl blue with fashionably deep notches in the lapels. His linen shirt was crisp and white, and gilt buttons adorned his waistcoat which was the same blue as his eyes. Two red medallions hung from a gold fob that crossed his waist. His knee-high boots were tight to his calves. Compeyson removed his silk top hat, closely examined it, then returned it to his head.

He pulled out a pewter-framed pocket mirror, and examined his reflection. He smiled at himself. "I am ready."

Magwitch's clothing was gray and dull. They approached Lady Burke's home, passing between iron railings on one side of the walkway and carriages on the other. On the pavement drivers and footmen spoke with each other in low tones. Horses jangled in their traces. The moon was a low smear in a hazy purple sky.

The front of Lady Burke's terrace home was white stucco crossed with lines that made it resemble marble. Compeyson surveyed the building, inhaled deeply, and climbed the steps to the door where he pulled the cord. An iron boot-scrape was near the door. Lace curtains behind sash windows framed the entryway. Compeyson removed his hat.

Yellow light spilled onto the steps when the door opened. Compeyson announced himself to the butler who took his hat and led him through a hallway into a drawing room filled with the city's intellectual might.

Cigar and pipe smoke hung from the ceiling. Gentlemen filled the room, about twenty of them. They were dressed for the evening in tailcoats and bright cravats, and they held crystal cordial glasses. Conversation was lively, with abundant laughter, and with many sly and admiring glances at the hostess, Abigail Burke, who stepped away from two men near the fireplace to greet the new arrival, Samuel Compeyson.

Such was her grace that she glided rather than walked, and she seemed magically suspended just above the floor as she approached him. Her hair was the color of a new penny, and was short and layered—a style made acceptable by Lady Carolyn Lamb—and her head was bare, without a turban or bonnet, which would have been shocking in some quarters. She was in half dress, a fine, flowing white muslin that made her resemble a statue. Woven into the fabric were green lace stripes that descended to the hemline. A gold cord cinched the frock. Between her magnificent breasts was a thumb-sized emerald which drew envious glances from the gentlemen not because of the gem's worth but because of its location.

"We have not met." Lady Burke smiled and held out her hand.

Compeyson said, "Nicholas Partheny, madam, a friend of Mr. Grantham's, who was kind enough to secure an invitation on my behalf."

FAGIN & MISS HAVISHAM

"We call Ollie Grantham *Double Grantham* because he often finds someone to invite to my home, and I have met the most interesting people courtesy of Ollie, and you are most welcome here, Mr. Partheny."

Compeyson lowered his head to acknowledge her graciousness. Lady Burke's neck was long and elegant, and her chin line was sharp, contrasting with her full mouth. Her nose might have been considered too large on others, but on her it lent dignity to her face. Her eyes were the color of fog, a light gray, and her brows were arced in a way that made her seem intensely fascinated with whomever was in front of her. And instead of the bored and haughty expression common among Mayfair hostesses, Lady Burke seemed to focus her entire attention on the new arrival, an alluring woman's full attention being a heady moment, and a significant draw to her household. If only for a moment she closely gathered in a guest, a virtual embrace of felicity and beauty, leaving the object of her attention giddy and grateful.

Whether she had this effect on the confidence man Samuel Compeyson, who this evening presented himself as Nicholas Partheny, is unknown, a man who could readily summon documents identifying himself as Samuel Compeyson, Ambrose Franks, Ronald Farquhar, Cecil Anton, Giles Stoddard, and Harry Beecker, but the disaster about to befall Nicholas Partheny—Miss Havisham's onetime fiancé Samuel Compeyson, of course—would be observed by everyone in Lady Burke's parlor, and would in the days ahead become even more exquisitely painful in its retelling in Mayfair parlors and dining rooms. Ah, how wonderfully excruciating it was to be. The abject down-to-the-bone humiliation soon to be visited upon Partheny-Compeyson-Franks-Farquar-Anton-Beecker-Stoddard and witnessed by Lady Burke's guests was to be both deeply shocking and brilliantly entertaining.

"I read your poem *The Gallant* in *The Quarterly,*" Lady Burke said to her new guest Nicholas Partheny. "I was moved and impressed."

Partheny smiled. "You have made my day, madam."

"I have tried writing poetry," Lady Burke said, "but I do not have the gift."

Partheny-Compeyson-Franks-Farquar-Anton-Beecker-Stoddard didn't have the gift, either. He had purchased a poem from a shabby underfed scribe on Beak Street near Golden Square, and had covertly paid the editor of *The Quarterly* five pounds to publish it, sufficient to establish Partheny as a rising literary light.

She said, "Let me introduce you to the novelist Levi Silas."

"Novelists bore me," Partheny said. "I'd rather spend the evening with you."

"Now, now." She laughed. "I'm the hostess and must divide my time."

She led him past a burled wood side table on which was an ivory cribbage board, then between several men near a fireplace that was trimmed in brass. The mantle held crystal candelabras and a gilded Swiss clock.

A beefy fellow rose from a chaise lounge. He pulled spectacles from a pocket, wrapped them around his face, then rudely pointed. "Say, aren't you the fellow at the racetrack table? The one who had extra cards in his clothing?"

Partheny-Compeyson-Franks-Farquar-Anton-Beecker-Stoddard stopped as if he'd run into a wall. "I beg your pardon, sir."

"Sure, it's you." The fellow bounced on his toes, and his voice rose. "You were playing with my friend Lawrence Alder and a couple of others, and some cards were in your hands and a few more were in your clothing."

The guests stopped conversing and looked at the accuser and his subject.

Partheny's face reddened so deeply it might have been dipped in paint. "You are mistaken, sir."

Another guest, a man holding himself up with a silver-tipped cane and whose waistcoat was a lively yellow silk, said, "And you were challenged to a duel by a navy captain at the table at the racetrack."

"You, sir, did not appear for the duel." This from a young man near the fireplace whose dark hair was in Beau Brummel's Brutus style. "Captain Dalton waited half an hour, but you were absent from the field."

The room was as silent as a cemetery.

Partheny-Compeyson-Franks-Farquar-Anton-Beecker-Stoddard said, "I was waylaid by a thug. He struck me, and I was rendered unconscious."

The young man laughed. "And then did Old Scratch with his horn and tail spring up from the ground and hang you from a tree?"

Another guest joined in. "Hard to appear at a duel when Old Scratch has you, isn't it? Did he poke you with his spear?"

He snickered and so did others.

Partheny yelled, "I was approaching Captain Dalton on the green when I was assaulted. I was laid low on the path, senseless."

Under a powdered wig, an old gentleman near a bowl of candied fruit on a side table said, "The stories of faeries and goblins I hear from my granddaughters have more credence."

"I am telling you the truth." Partheny's voice filled the parlor to every corner. "I was attacked by a villain and beaten unconscious just steps from the duel. I would have shown up and. . . ."

Laughter cut him off. Lady Burke held up a hand. She moved her lips but made no sound.

Then a guest called, "How can you show your face in society?"

Then the old man with the silver cane again. "Be gone, you shameless coward."

Lady Burke chewed on her lip, then said, "Perhaps it is best if you excused yourself, Mr. Partheny."

"An Englishman cowering at the prospect of a duel," Beau Brummel-hair called. "Running and hiding. I cringe for our country."

The confidence man was shrill. "You will regret this, all of you." He spun on his heels and retreated across the parlor.

Someone shouted, "Go join the French army."

More laughter.

Another: "Craven and cowardly. Hide yourself from children and dogs."

The doorman was too slow. Partheny pushed himself through the door, out onto the porch without his hat and then down the steps. By the time he reached Magwitch, Partheny was running. Away from Lady Burke's salon. Away from the rarified society. Away from his fiery lifelong ambition to be accepted by the toffs.

"What's the difficulty, your honor?" Magwitch called.

The confidence man loosed an unintelligible shriek, and fled north on foot, perhaps blindly. Frowning, Magwitch followed him.

* * * *

As Compeyson sped past, Miss Havisham pulled back the carriage's curtain to look at him. Both Compeyson's hands were on his head as if to ward off a pummeling. He emitted a soprano wail, an unearthly yowl that out in the home counties would have set the dogs on him.

Inspector Bucket leaned forward in the carriage seat to glance out. "How did you do it?"

"From my time with Samuel Compeyson—when he was bringing me flowers and smiling at me in that way he has—I learned that society meant more to him than anything else."

"Except you." Bucket's hat was on his lap.

She grimaced. "He couldn't keep his other aspiration away from me. He was desperate to get past the guards, footmen, and butlers who keep out the unwashed and unpedigreed. He wanted to be admitted into society's parlors so he could bow before the great and noble and shake hands with the titled and renown. His passion for this was genuine, and his passion for me was a fraud."

A carriage blanket was on Miss Havisham's lap. She wore white gloves and a light blue frock with white lace ruffles along the neckline.

"How did you serve him out?" Bucket asked.

She smiled without humor. "Fagin arranged for him to be accused of cheating at a loo table at a racetrack in a room filled with the affluent. Compeyson has a terrible temper, and what happened next was predictable. He struck one of the men at the table, a Navy captain, who then of course demanded satisfaction."

"I have advised against working with this Fagin. He is a schemer who has no one's interest at heart but his own."

This time her smile held warmth. "He is indeed a schemer, and so am I. Lady Burke was a friend of my mother and father, and is too strong to turn away from our family because of my wedding disaster. I asked her to invite Samuel, who was posing as a poet named Partheny."

"How did you know he was calling himself Partheny?"

"Fagin has been checking around."

Bucket looked at her but didn't ask more about this, perhaps because he didn't want to know. Instead, his eyes returned to the window, and he asked, "Who is that fellow following Compeyson? Running right after him?"

She shook her head. "Maybe he's a valet carrying his umbrella and hat. He has always liked servants."

Bucket's eyes followed the man. His eyes narrowed. "No, it's his big bodyguard, the one who left me lying on the pavement."

She opened the ceiling hatch to address the driver. "The Pulteney, please."

The driver clicked his tongue at the horses, and the carriage pulled out onto the street, rattling and bouncing. A cool breeze came through the carriage window. A cat yowled from out in the darkness.

The detective settled back into the seat. "And Compeyson didn't appear at the duel?"

"Mr. Fagin took care of it. He knows someone who was big and burly who would stop Samuel, just hold him up for a while to keep him from arriving at the dueling commons."

Bucket drew wind through his teeth. "You aren't talking about a knee-walking drunk and house-breaker named Sikes, are you?"

She shrugged. "That's his name. Sikes."

"I've arrested Bill Sikes half a dozen times. He is a reprobate, and anything he touches is fouled and corrupted."

"What if I have a use for somebody of his ilk?"

"I must warn you in the strictest terms." Bucket held up his hands, his fingers wide, encompassing everything. "No good can come from dealing with Bill Sikes."

She looked out the window at a lamplighter carrying his torch over his shoulder. A bone cart passed, going in the other direction.

Inspector Bucket said, "My superior has learned I have been working on the side for you, and he has asked that I attend my regular police work. Your ex-fiancé has been soundly humiliated. It would be a good time for my employ with you to be at an end."

"Can you continue with me for a short while?"

"Compeyson just ran down the street, defeated and disgraced." Bucket's brow was drawn. "You have returned humiliation for humiliation. Aren't you finished with him?"

Miss Havisham's mouth peeled back into a snarl. "I have just begun with Samuel Compeyson."

FAGIN & MISS HAVISHAM

* * * *

"Yow, that hurts." Nancy Argyle gripped the sides of the tub. "My hair isn't a rug to be beaten, ma'am."

"I've never had my hands in anything worse," the maid said as she sank her hands into Nancy's hair again. "Feels like a basket of nettles."

From a chair just outside the room, Miss Havisham said, "Ladies, calm yourselves."

Mary Halsted was Satis House's first floor maid, a thick, cheery woman whose cross words were always accompanied by a grin. She wore a blue apron over a dark blue work dress. She squeezed the soap suds from Nancy's hair, and they spilled off her bare shoulders into the bathwater.

The maid laughed. "This bathwater is so dirty, if I throw it into the river the river will throw it back."

From behind the door, Miss Havisham said, "I've gone through my dressers, and have found just the thing, several things. You'll look less like a doxy. I've asked a gardener to burn your old clothes."

Mary lifted a bucket from the floor. "Here's the rinse."

She poured water over Nancy, who gasped and burbled. Soap suds swirled around her knees, and drops splashed onto the floor. Nancy shook her head, then wiped water from her eyes. The tub was half of a fermenting barrel from the Havisham Brothers Brewery. Water had been warmed on the kitchen stove. Mary lowered the bucket toward the floor.

From outside the room, Miss Havisham called, "I'll come in after a while."

Mary's hand stopped, the bucket still hanging from it. She looked up. "Pardon me, Miss Havisham?"

From the other side of the door came, "I'll be there, and I'll bring Estella. Don't worry. I'll be quick. I miss you, too."

Nancy's brows knitted together, and her gaze found Mary.

"Are you speaking to me, Miss Havisham?" Mary called.

Several seconds passed.

Her voice diminished, Miss Havisham replied, "I'm not speaking with anyone, Mary."

Mary asked, "Is someone out there in the hall?"

"No one but me." Miss Havisham added, "I'm alright. Don't pay me attention. It's nothing."

"If you say so, madam." The maid plucked a towel from a hat stand. "Up you go, clean as a tooth."

As Nancy rose from the tub Mary draped the towel over her, then used another towel to wick water from her hair. An oak commode was in a corner, along with a washstand on which were a Dresden pitcher and wash basin. The room's window looked out onto the back garden.

"Being this clean isn't healthy, is it?" The towel hugged tightly to herself, Nancy stepped over tub's rim and onto the wood floor. "When I was little, I stood at the well, and momma poured ladles of water over me, and that was clean enough."

"Out you go then," Mary said. "Miss Havisham is waiting."

Nancy stepped into the other room, where Miss Havisham, cradling the baby Estella, rose from her chair and smiled. "You look new and twice as pretty. Come over here. I've selected something for you."

Miss Havisham carried the baby across the room toward a chest of drawers, and Nancy padded after her, dripping water. Estella wore a pink ribbon attached to the gossamer strands of her hair. A bed with curtains folded back to the posts was along one wall near a Stubbs painting of a prancing horse. Between two windows was a dressing table which held an oil lamp, a mirror, and a jewelry box.

An hour earlier Nancy Argyle had simply appeared at Satis House. At the door the old butler Tavers had inquired of her purpose, and Nancy had replied, "I was asked to come here. I'm Nancy." Tavers had surveyed her up and down, and then had said, "And I'm the Duke of York. Pleased to meet you." He had made to close the door but Miss Havisham had been in the parlor, and had overheard the exchange, and so rushed to the door, fairly pushed Tavers aside, took Nancy by the arm, and escorted her inside. Tavers's scowl had been as black as the bottom of a well.

Miss Havisham pulled out a sprigged muslin day dress from an armoire. The flowing dress was of a light green color with tiny yellow flowers. She held it out.

"It's lovely, ma'am." Nancy said. "And very fine. Nothing like I've ever worn."

Miss Havisham rocked the baby in her arm. "Try it on. There's a chemise in the top dresser drawer you can wear under it. You have I have the same size feet, more or less, so find a pair of slippers in the drawer at the bottom of the wardrobe. Then come downstairs. I have a position to offer you."

Estella was asleep as Miss Havisham kissed the baby's beribboned head, which she did every two minutes, and closed the bedroom door so that Nancy could dress.

Nancy threw the shift and then the dress over herself, her eyes on the dressing table and its jewelry box. She glanced over her shoulder at the door, then, still barefoot, stepped to the dressing table, which held tiny corked bottles of perfume, a powder puff, bottles of Lacey's Bloom of Ninion, and Seraph's Milk of Roses, along with a cloisonné powder box. The jewelry box was made of lacquered maple inlaid with Italian coral.

Nancy looked again at the bedroom door, then slid open the top drawer, which was lined with black velvet. Seven rings were displayed there, one a diamond ring, another with an amethyst stone, and the rest were small and modest rings likely given to Miss Havisham when she was a girl. Nancy opened the second drawer, which contained three cream-colored silk pouches. She plucked open the draw string on one of them, and pulled out an ornate repousse gold bracelet that had no stones. She returned the bracelet to the pouch and the pouch to the drawer. She lifted the bracelet from the second silk bag and held it up to the window light.

Here it was, the diamond and silver bracelet Bill Sikes had demanded. The bracelet was twice the weight of the gold one, and the diamonds were the size of peas. Remarkably intricate silver work surrounded the diamonds which threw off light from the windows.

She wasn't a thief, not really. After all, she was going to leave everything else in the jewelry case, not even looking into the lower two drawers. Just this one thing, and it was so very important. Miss Havisham had much other jewelry, and this huge house and stables and gardens. Maybe she wouldn't even miss the bracelet, surrounded by all this extravagance.

Nancy turned to the bedroom door, looking for a place to conceal the bracelet in her new clothing. Two taps came from the door. Nancy gasped, and was startled to stillness.

Miss Havisham pushed open the door, smiling, still carrying Estella. "Nancy, there's also a scarf that . . . ." Her gaze found the diamond bracelet.

Nancy made no more sound than a stone.

"My bracelet?" Miss Havisham asked. "Is that my bracelet?"

Nancy's face colored deeply. "I . . . I'm sorry, ma'am."

Miss Havisham closed her eyes, defeat written on her face. "There's a strange fellow in front of the brewery with a gig. He's been there since you arrived. A big, rough looking fellow. Does he know anything about this?"

"He's my friend. My boyfriend. I'm sorry, Miss Havisham. I couldn't help it."

"You come with me."

She took the bracelet from Nancy and tossed it onto the bed, then fiercely gripped her wrist and led her out of the room, along the hallway, and down the front stairs to the door, Nancy whimpering the entire way, the baby in the crook of Miss Havisham's arm. Miss Havisham waved away Old Travers, opened the door, and pulled Nancy out onto the walkway.

"That's him, am I right? Down there with the gig and gray horse? What's his name?"

"Bill, ma'am."

Rooks cawed in an alder tree. The breeze carried the perpetual scent of malt. A white cloud moved overhead, its shadow racing across the road toward the river.

"You wouldn't do something so outrageous unless you were in love with him, and he ordered you to steal from me." Miss Havisham's voice was as tight as a wire. "I'm correct here, too, am I not?"

"Madam, please. You have been so kind and . . . ."

"My one act of charity in my life, the one time I did something kind, was to try to help you." Miss Havisham drew her hand across her forehead. "I don't want it to go to waste. The lord only knows when such an impulse might strike again. You aren't wicked, not in your bones."

Nancy looked down the roadway at Bill Sikes, still in front of the brewery, his hand on the horse's harness. Sikes beckoned her.

"Nancy, I'll offer you a choice," Miss Havisham said. "You can go to him, or you can step back through Satis House's door with me, and never see him again. I'll do my best to make your life worth living."

Nancy veiled her eyes and turned away. Several heartbeats passed. She half-stepped in Sikes's direction, then pulled her foot back. She exhaled and shuddered. Then she said, "I'm so sorry, Miss Havisham." She left Miss Havisham, rushed along the walkway to the road, then hurried toward Sikes.

Hugh Havisham had once told his daughter that she had no tear ducts, that he had never seen her weep, not since she was a toddler. Tears were foreign to Margaret Havisham. Still, she touched the corner of her eye where a tear perhaps should have been as she watched Nancy reach Bill Sikes.

Miss Havisham whispered, "I'm sorry, too."

26

Morning mists had lifted from the St. Mary of the Woods chapel, and fewer clouds were rolling in over the southern hills, and so lovely weather was promised for Anna Wilkinson's wedding to Ambrose Franks. The chapel was three miles from the Wilkinson estate, alongside the Green River—more a brook—which was lined with alder and buckthorn. Lilacs and rhododendrons surrounded the chapel, and in the little distance were weeping willows and silver birch.

All this foliage hid Detective Bucket, his superior Sir Daniel Pottinger, fifteen policemen, and a prisoner wagon. The policemen carried flintlock pistols and Brown Bess muskets, and fetlocks and handcuffs hung from their belts. Some wore their city blue coats but others had found leather hunting jackets and canvas pants. Standing behind a yew tree here, crouched behind a buckthorn bush there, two kneeling behind a mossy fallen tree, another by the stone bridge over the brook; all could see St. Mary's of the Woods but none could be seen from the chapel.

The chapel was of whitewashed stone, a friendly edifice. A portico fronted the building. The white steeple had no bell, as they were costly, and the narrow windows were of simple glass. Thatch covered the roof. Lavender bloomed in purple along on both sides of the front door. A bed of forget-me-nots was under a side window.

Behind the chapel were a storage shed and a privy. A half-acre pasture was to the west of the chapel, with cherry trees and hornbeams at the edges of the field. A belled black goat grazed in the grass, and a thrush in an oak tree repeated its song again and again.

"Do you think we have found him, Bucket?" Sir Daniel's coat of worsted wool with green and maroon stripes resembled a tartan. He had left his wig at the station but he carried a flintlock, and he appeared comfortable doing so.

Bucket had never seen Sir Daniel outside the Bow Street Runner's office. That he had traveled into the country west of London was evidence of his superior's enthusiasm for the case.

"I won't count on him appearing until he appears. He is shrewd and careful." Bucket carried a collapsible brass telescope. A flintlock pistol was a bulge in his oil-skin coat pocket.

Sir Daniel hitched his belly back above his belt. "He hasn't been given the dowry yet. The prospect of ten thousand pounds would impinge on anyone's caution."

At his club earlier in the week Sir Daniel had mentioned Inspector Bucket's work for the Havisham heir to Adam Owens, publisher of *The Gentleman's Magazine.* Owens had heard rumors of another jilted fiancé, the daughter of the wealthy Manchester canal contractor Timothy Jasper. The Jasper family had desperately tried to suppress reports of the humiliating event but news this delectable could not be constrained. Sir Daniel had no doubt a substantial amount had been settled upon the suitor, and that the confidence man was the same one who had swindled the Havishams. Here was a criminal worth catching, the arrest of whom would nicely answer the home secretary's notion to rework the police jurisdictions to eliminate the Bow Street Runners. So Sir Daniel had come west to the Wilkinson wedding with Inspector Bucket.

Sir Daniel tugged a chain to pull out his repeater. He asked Bucket, "It's time, isn't it?"

It was. The rattle of a vehicle came from the forest, and then a phaeton pulled by two auburn horses emerged from the woods on the road. The carriage was painted with red lacquer, and a brass headlamp was next to the driver. Another phaeton was close behind, with matching blue roans in harness, and it was followed by several young men on horses weaving in their saddles, likely having imbibed in refreshments early. The carriages stopped near the chapel, and the riders tied their horses to a hitching rail. Wearing a double-breasted black cassock, the minister came out of the chapel to smile at the guests.

Sir Daniel said, "Not many guests for a society wedding."

"I suspect the swindler manages it that way," Bucket said. "Fewer people to elude, fewer who'll recognize him next time."

A gust of wind shook loose dew from overhead leaves, sending the droplets onto Bucket and Sir Daniel. Robins and the black goat worked the grass near the chapel.

The bride's father and brother posted themselves at the phaeton's door, and they held out their arms to help Anna Wilkinson step down from the phaeton. Her white gown trailed behind her—her brother holding up the train—as her father escorted her across the gravel toward the chapel. Her brown hair was up in pins under a cap adorned with flowers. In a magenta walking dress, Anna's mother stepped down from a carriage. Guests gathered at the chapel entrance.

The bride's father, Elijah Wilkinson, walked a few paces to stare down the road, then spun on his heels, and walked back. He wore a black coat with tails, a white waistcoat, and a top hat. The other guests were dressed in colorful finery that contrasted with the humble chapel and the muted greenery of the woods, except for Anna's governess, wearing a dark green smock and a matching Saragossa mantle. Her face was as adversarial as always, apparently unaffected by the day's happy prospects.

A gig pulled by a bay horse appeared from the woods, rolling toward the chapel. The driver was twice as wide as the passenger. The road was still muddy from the night's rain, and the gig's wheels splashed mud aside.

Bucket opened the spyglass and put it to his eye. "That's him, the slender fellow with all the yellow hair and the big smile. Next to him is his bodyguard, with the reins in his hands."

Sir David said, "The bodyguard looks solid and dangerous."

"I owe that fellow a lesson, and I hope I can deliver it today." The inspector swept the field and woods with the glass. "I can't see any of the other watchmen."

"Just as we want it."

The confidence man—on this day posing as Ambrose Franks, of course—leaped down from the carriage to shake hands all around. The bride, who would enter the chapel last on her father's arm, stood apart, smiling shyly, her governess nearby. The guests numbered no more than a dozen.

"There he goes," Inspector Bucket said.

Smile still in place, Ambrose Franks walked across the gravel to Elijah Wilkinson. Business was at hand, and the other guests stayed away from them. Elijah Wilkinson turned his back to the guests and pulled out an envelope. The gig's driver—Abel Magwitch—stayed back, still with the horse that had pulled them there, scratching the animal behind its ears. Then he stepped to the hitching rail.

Pottinger said, "My experience—and it is first-hand experience—is that a lecture always accompanies these transactions. I laid down the law to the grooms of both my daughters."

"Wait another moment," the inspector said. "His fraud will be complete when he takes the envelope. Only then has he committed the crime."

"How is he planning to escape?" Sir Danniel asked. "He won't actually take the marriage vows, will he?"

Bucket replied, "I don't know what his plan is. He'll somehow take the money and run."

While the guests waited, Elijah Wilkinson made a show of lecturing Ambrose Franks, and while Inspector Bucket could not hear the words,

Wilkinson's cutting gestures made clear that he expected Ambrose Franks to be dutiful and caring, and perhaps that—again judging from the hand motions—the groom's potential philandering would be handled with a fowling piece. Wilkinson waved the envelope in front of Franks's nose. With his hand and fingers open to receive it, Franks nodded again and again, the expression on his face one of a dog about to receive dinner.

Bucket said, "Another few seconds."

Elijah Wilkinson finally placed the envelope in Franks's hand, and Franks slipped it into an inside pocket, still nodding at the marital law as laid down by his impending father-in-law. Then they turned toward the chapel door.

"It's time." Sir Daniel lifted the flintlock, aimed it at overhead leaves, and pulled the trigger.

The flint sparked and the gun gouted flame. The report shivered nearby leaves and fled rapidly. Detective Bucket pulled out his pistol and ran toward Franks.

As Bow Street Runners emerged from the woods the pastoral wedding became an ambush.

Constables came from the trees and the bridge and outbuildings, and hurried across the grass toward the wedding party, their weapons in front of them. As the lawmen hurried in, their boots sank into the grass and splashed in the mud.

"Halt in the name of the crown," Sir Daniel called. Impeded by his girth, his age, and the long flintlock, he rushed after Bucket.

Several in the wedding party dashed into the chapel, others held up their hands. The governess pushed Anna Wilkinson against the chapel's wall, then stood in front of her, protecting her from whatever was to come. His mouth pulled back and glancing all around, Elijah Wilkinson joined them at the wall. Two guests ran toward the trees, passing between the policemen, who let them flee. The pastor dashed into the chapel and the goat vanished into the tree glade.

After an instant's hesitation Ambrose Franks sprinted toward the forest but then must have seen the policemen charging from that direction so turned toward the shed but Bow Street Runners were coming from there, too. He ran back, his head swiveling left and right as he sought an escape.

"Compeyson, stop." Bucket pulled back the hammer on his piece. "You are under arrest."

The confidence man angled himself so that he might have a chance to slip between two policemen, and his legs churned. Bucket fired his pistol at Compeyson but missed.

Compeyson's bodyguard, Abel Magwitch, un-tethered a guest's horse, put his foot in the stirrup, and lifted himself into the saddle.

"You, Broderick." Bucket pointed at a nearby policeman who carried a bird gun. "Bring him down."

Broderick yanked back the hammer, put the barrel to his eye, and fired. Shot tore into Compeyson's leg, spinning him around and throwing him to the grass. He scrambled up, his pantleg torn open. Blood poured onto the ragged cloth. He tried to resume his sprint but it was a hobble. He yelped in pain. Bucket and three policemen closed in on him.

They must not have seen Abel Magwitch. He was on a grey horse, and the hooves pounded the gravel and then the grass, throwing up clods of dirt. He was not a skilled rider, and he bounced uncharitably on the saddle.

"Compeyson," Magwitch yelled, then perhaps to make sure he called, "Franks. Beecker."

On this day he was Franks, and he turned toward the approaching mount. He grimaced as he limped toward the Magwitch and the horse and held up his arms to be lifted.

The horse brushed a policeman, then its shoulder rammed Inspector Bucket, throwing him to the ground. One of the horse's rear hoofs jammed into Bucket's calf, and he grunted. He rolled, and sat up, and winced with the pain. The inspector tried to rise but it was slow and accompanied by a groan.

Magwitch leaned low over the horse's shoulder and grabbed the confidence man's arm.

"Jump," Magwitch said. "I'll haul you up the rest of the way."

But instead of leaping Compeyson planted his good leg on the ground then yanked Magwitch's arm. Magwitch started to topple from the saddle, and Compeyson assisted the process by seizing the back of Magwitch's collar to pull him free of the horse. Magwitch thudded on the grass.

Compeyson good foot was in the stirrup, and he was on the horse's back before his bodyguard could rise to his knees. The confidence man took the reins and dug at the horse's flank with his good leg.

His face a mask of rage, Magwitch climbed to his feet and lunged for Compeyson but he was too late. The horse shot forward, and Compeyson guided it toward the road to the west. He bent low over the saddle as if expecting to be fired upon. One of the constables obliged, but he was a policeman not an infantry skirmisher, and his ball went wide. Compeyson and his new horse disappeared into the wood on the road.

When Magwitch looked up, six muskets were pointed at him. He rose to his feet, and put his hands over his head.

Inspector Bucket said to Magwitch, "Remember me? Out at the West India docks? You left me on the pavement in an alley." Bucket kidney punched Magwitch, a fierce chop from one who knew how to do it.

Magwitch grunted and dropped to his knees, then sideways to the ground, his eyes rolled back in his head. Several policemen laughed.

"Put him in irons," Bucket said. "And throw him into the van."

* * * *

"I simply will not play a willow tree." Thomas Lenville's face was streaked with stage paint. He stood among stage screens and paint pots. "Trees do not speak, and I must have a speaking role." He wiped his chin with a rag.

Vincent Crummles held up the script, one he had written himself as the troupe still had no writer. "But this tree speaks. It has eight lines where it tries to dissuade the dog from lifting its leg."

"Is your plan to shred my dignity even farther? This evening I played a mute who could only communicate with gestures. And now a tree?"

The show earlier that evening, *The Feather and the Lint,* had been sparsely attended—twelve paying customers and four children who had snuck in—and Crummles intended to stage a new play the following night with a rehearsal in the afternoon. West End theaters were lit with gas but the Crummles troupe made do with candle chandeliers and candle boxes on the stage. The candles had not yet been extinguished, which was Lenville's task once he finished arguing about his next role.

"The Infant Phenomenon will play the dog." Crummles voice was more hoarse than usual, sounding like wood file at work at work on chair leg. "It's a comedic masterpiece. And you are the only member of the troupe slender enough to get into the tree costume. Your arms will be graceful boughs, and your high-pitched voice has always impressed me as willowy."

"It's Margaret," Mrs. Crummles called from stage right as she peered into the darkness of beyond the stage lights. Delight was manifested in her tone. "Margaret is here."

Vincent Crummles was in a red and yellow harlequin costume. He smiled from his cheekbones and put his hand to his brow to look out into the darkness. "Margaret, will you play a tree tomorrow?" He laughed and rushed to the edge of the stage to give Miss Havisham a hand up the steps.

Not known for smiling, Thomas Lenville grinned, as did Mrs. Snevellicci. Miss Gazingi flicked the ends of her imitation ermine boa, her elucidation of happiness.

Miss Havisham said, "You were magnificent when Samuel was here, every one of you."

Crummles theatrically cleared his throat. "The part was challenging but I brought years of experience to it and, I must add, I've never had a more edifying role, insuring that Compeyson tried to snare Anna Wilkinson."

Miss Havisham laughed. "You played Falstaff when I was with the troupe. More challenging than that?"

Crummles enveloped Miss Havisham in his arms. "The challenge was not to strike down Compeyson with my fist as he wooed Anna in my theater. I had to put a stopper onto my best inclinations. I almost served him out, right in front of our audience."

Vincent Crummles' wife, the praiseworthy Nina Crummles, came from behind a curtain. She smiled all over her pink face, and she, too, hugged Margaret Havisham.

Nina Crummles said, "We still miss you, Margaret. You were our ray of sunshine."

Miss Havisham carried a leather bag over the shoulder of her pale green frock. She stepped to prompter Mrs. Gruden and the set-painter Miss Gazingi. Miss Havisham found embraces with them, as well.

She asked Crummles' wife, "And you, Nina, how did you keep the scowl on your joyful face? It must have been dreadfully hard."

Nina Crummles replied, "My face was meant to eat apple tarts, not scowl."

"Nina, I hear you were imposing and magnificent as Anna's busy-body governess," Miss Havisham said.

"What about me?" came a voice from the stage door. "I had most of the lines." Anna Wilkinson came onto the stage. At least, that was the name Ambrose Franks had known her by. She had been a member of the Crummles Family Troupe since the age of fourteen, and her true name was Juliet Dolanger.

By consensus—if Thomas Lenville were not included in the vote—Juliet was the finest actress in the company, surely headed for Covent Garden. She wore a yellow chiffon broadcloth dress with blue embroidery at the neckline and cuffs. Her smile was wide and enticing. Unlike when on the stage, she was wearing only a hint of makeup which colored her lips and accented her eyes. Her walking dress was high-waisted: deep blue above the cinch and pearl below.

Juliet said, "Had I not known he was so corrupt, I might have fallen in love with Ambrose."

"You wouldn't have been the first," Miss Havisham said.

It had been a trap for Ambrose Franks, otherwise known as whatever name he was using that day. When Miss Havisham had run away from home at age sixteen, it had been the Crummles Family Troupe she had found. Her bright spirit—an infectious laugh and easy smile—had made her popular among the players, and she was loved by Mr. and Mrs. Crummles, and it was a dark day for the troupe when Hugh Havisham appeared at the stage door to take her home.

In her distress at being deserted on her wedding day, Miss Havisham had contacted Vincent Crummles, asking for the company's help. They were eager to oblige. Mrs. Crummles' role had been that of the governess Mrs. Truly.

Vincent Crummles, that of a helpful if dimwitted stage manager. The troupe might not have been ready for Drury Lane but they were utterly convincing for their audience of one, Ambrose Franks, known to others as Samuel Compeyson and yet to others by more names than in Boyle's Court Guide.

Miss Havisham's wealthy uncle Felix—at one time half of the firm of Havisham Brothers Brewery—had played Anna Wilkinson's father Elijah at the estate and at the chapel. His wife—Miss Havisham's beloved Aunt Nell—had been Anna's mother, and Thomas Lenville and their adult children—all heavily made up—had played the brothers at the chapel. Felix and Nell's estate near the River Severn had been used as the Wilkinson estate, Felix and Nell only too happy to go along with their niece's plan. Their Gloucestershire friends were the rat pit enthusiasts. Uncle Felix and Aunt Nell had been at Satis House that terrible wedding day, waiting for the groom to appear, and that day they had sworn vengeance on Samuel Compeyson. Felix had in mind a noose but his niece Margaret had convinced him her way would be more satisfying.

The authentic carriage manufacturing family, the Wilkinsons, knew nothing of the ruse.

Miss Havisham slipped the leather bag's straps from her shoulder. "I want to give you all little gifts." From the bag she pulled out linen handkerchiefs tied into pouches with lengths of red ribbon. Each had a name tag. The pouches jingled with guineas inside, and quite a few in each.

She gave one to Mr. Crummles, who took the pouch but said, "There is no need to pay us, Margaret."

Mrs. Crummles received her pouch. "We would have done it for free."

"This isn't payment." Miss Havisham smiled. "It's a gift, a remembrance of my wonderful year with you."

She passed out the wrapped coins to each person in the troupe, including the Infant Phenomenon. When the Crummles' sons Charles and Percy appeared through the street door, they also received coin packages. The sum of the coins Miss Havisham had brought to the theater was more than the troupe would otherwise earn in a year.

"I'm sorry it didn't work, Margaret," Vincent Crummles said. "We tried so hard."

"You and the troupe played your parts perfectly. That the arrest failed at the last minute was not your doing."

Crummles pushed his packet of coins into a pocket. The Infant Phenomenon arrayed her guineas on the stage floor to count them on her fingers.

Miss Havisham closed the leather bag, and returned it to her shoulder. She stepped down from the stage, then said to the troupe, "I may not be done with him. I have another chance."

FAGIN & MISS HAVISHAM

* * * *

Miss Havisham said, "You will not touch me again."

Murdstone held up his hand that was heavily wrapped in a bandage. "And how about you? I should have the same assurances. The doctor said I might never be able to move two fingers."

The warehouse was lit only by thin daylight making its way through fly-specked windows on the south wall. Miss Havisham and Murdstone stood next to bushel baskets of tulip bulbs the firm of Havisham and Murdstone had smuggled from Holland.

"I understand now that you bring certain talents to the business," Miss Havisham said. "And I need you as a partner."

Murdstone's face was cast in a pale green color by the window light. His eye, with its odd angle, prevented his visage from ever coming together entirely pleasingly. His blue greatcoat was belted at his midriff.

Miss Havisham said, "We are bound together by necessity. And to keep you from amorous advances and to keep you from cheating me I have hired an assistant."

"That policeman you have been consorting with?" Murdstone laughed in a brittle way. "You would trust an officer of the law in our unlawful business?"

Miss Havisham's pewter-colored bonnet and jacket matched the warehouse's dim illumination. She blended in with the shelves and walls, giving her the aspect of an apparition. "Inspector Bucket no longer works for me. His superior has told him to withdraw from side engagements. So I hired someone else." She looked to her left, and called, "Emmanuel."

The little Frenchman stepped from behind a stack of shelves. The brim of his hat hid his eyes. His hands were deep in the pockets of his canvas coat. His teeth were still wrecked and his left ear was still missing. The smile slid off his face as his gaze found Murdstone.

Murdstone pointed with his bandaged hand. "That frog works for me."

"No longer," Miss Havisham said. "And when I asked him in French if he would kill someone who touched me or cheated me, he replied 'With pleasure.'"

Murdstone stepped back.

She said, "So this is the new basis of our partnership, Mr. Murdstone; civility and honesty or I send Emmanuel to you. Are we agreed?"

He fairly yelled, "Yes, of course."

27

Compeyson-Franks-Farquhar-Anton-Stoddard-Beecker-Partheny   hid
behind a yellow post chaise across the street from the Ludgate Bank, a smaller
building than the Bank of England on Threadneedle Street, but still stout, with
four stone Corinthian columns supporting a triangular pediment depicting
Greek soldiers carrying bows and swords.   Groups of men in top hats
conversed on the steps up to the bank's entrance, and more were in the shadow
thrown by the pediment near the bank's front doors.

The confidence man's gaze swept the street again. He bit his lower lip.
Two young women under a parasol stared at him as they passed but he didn't
look their way. A blue-coated policeman was down the block near Stonecutter
Street standing next to a crossing sweeper. A linen draper's delivery wagon
rolled by, and the horse's shoes clopped hollowly on the granite pavers. At a
cabstand six hackney coaches were lined up in single file along the street.

The older bankers, merchants, and brokers wore breeches and powdered
wigs while the younger ones had on trousers and had foregone the wigs, as had
Compeyson. His navy-blue coat was over a white linen waistcoat.

With another glance up and down the street, Compeyson centered his top
hat on his head, inhaled deeply, then limped across Farringdon Street toward
the Ludgate Bank. Bandages made his pant legs bulge, and he winced with
each step. He maneuvered between carriages and carts, then reached the
sidewalk in front of the building. Here, too, he surveyed the street. To the
west St. Paul's dome was shrouded in brown haze. Down Farringdon,
carriages moved into and out of the coal smoke, eerily vanishing and
appearing.

He climbed the marble steps to the portico, stepping around groups of
businessmen who may have preferred the airy portico to their offices for
negotiations. Pairs of men spoke earnestly, gesturing, and occasionally

shaking hands. An attendant pulled open the massive bronze door, and Compeyson stepped into the lobby and onto white marble with bright green veins. He removed his hat and walked confidently toward the teller's cage. High windows allowed dull daylight into the huge room, where patrons sat at long tables filling out forms. Mounted on a wall was a display of heavy cavalry swords once used by the Royal Horse Guards and the Dragoon Guards.

The swindler had reason for confidence. The check Elijah Wilkinson had given him fulfilling the dowry obligation was a banker's draft, meaning that the funds had already been deducted from the Wilkinson account and were being held by the bank until the payee withdrew the money. So without doubt the money was in the bank and ready to be disbursed.

But there was a profound dilemma in front of Compeyson. The ten thousand pounds was so close, right behind the brass bars that separated the tellers from customers. But the police at the sanctuary had detected his scheme, had located him, and he had almost been caught, and his bodyguard Magwitch had been seized. The confidence man had not had time to determine how he had been set up at his wedding to Anna Wilkinson. Something had gone horribly wrong.

And what of the other recent disasters: being accused of cheating at cards, and then being prevented from appearing at a duel? Being laughed out of Lady Burke's salon? He normally was in strict control of every moment of his day, presenting himself as he wished to be presented, manipulating those around him, profiting from it all. But his life had soured this past two months. Dreadful things had happened to him he didn't understand. For the first time in his life he seemed cursed.

But even so he had the check in his pocket. This vast sum would right the ship. He would go to France or Italy or America, beyond the curse and beyond the law. He never doubted his talent. He would begin anew, and he would succeed wherever he landed.

The prospect was dazzling, and it was so close, just on the other side of the bank lobby. He weighed the risk against the reward. At what point was he willing to take the risk of cashing the check? Certainly not for fifty pounds, nor a hundred. But this document in his pocket was worth 10,000 pounds sterling. And the money the check represented was right there, forty yards away. He turned a full circle, eyeing everyone in the room. Nothing seemed unusual. No one seemed interested. It was another day at the Ludgate Bank.

Compeyson pulled out the envelope that contained the check, and stepped to the counter. "I'd like to cash this. Twenty Bank of England 500-pound notes, if you please."

The teller had a high forehead and a snaggle tooth. When he looked at the check his eyebrows rose. "I'm embarrassed to say that I am too junior to cash a check of this amount. Please see the gentleman at the end of the cage, the older fellow. You have identification forms, I presume."

"Of course," Compeyson replied.

"Then he'll be able assist you."

Compeyson took back the check, and stepped around two customers waiting in line, and walked to the end of the counter where an older teller dipped a pen into an inkpot, and entered sums into a ledger. From his coat pocket Compeyson removed a passport signed by the secretary of state. It was of course a forgery, as was another document he carried, a certified copy of his baptismal record from the Parish of St. John in Dorset. With the check and these documents in hand, Compeyson cleared his throat to gain the attention of the senior clerk.

The fellow looked up. His eyes were remarkably small and suspicious, and his head was so large it might have been about to topple off his neck. A blue wool scarf circled his neck.

"Sir, I was told that you were the person to speak with to cash this check." Compeyson passed the check to the elder clerk. "I have brought documents of identification with me."

"They won't be necessary." The senior clerk grinned. "I know who you are."

The old fellow was Sir Daniel Pottinger, superintendent of the London Watchmen, and he lifted a horse pistol from his lap and pointed it through the brass bars at Compeyson's midsection. "In the name of the crown, you are under arrest."

Compeyson gasped and his fist crushed the forged documents.

"If you move I'll send a bullet through you." Sir Daniel smiled evilly.

In that instant the prospect of prison must have flashed before Compeyson because even with the huge bore of the pistol aimed at his belly he turned to run, to make a mad dash toward the door.

He made three steps. Inspector Bucket sent a lead-filled sap into Compeyson's temple, and the confidence man dropped to the floor like a steer at the slaughterhouse.

* * * *

"You will like it here, Luke," Miss Havisham said. "Pronson Academy is the finest school in Westminster. You'll make a lot of friends, and most of them will be honest." She raised an eyebrow at Fagin.

"Will they give me food here?" The boy's new blue jacket and matching pants still held creases from the tailor's box.

"Three meals a day plus a biscuit at bedtime."

"Do I really need to learn to read?" Luke asked. "I'm doing good already."

"And you'll learn your figures. You don't want to be an ignoramus, nor do you want their company." She taunted Fagin with a grin.

"We will take good care of the lad," Rupert Belvedere said in a stentorian voice that filled the room. The school master sat behind his desk, his hands folded over his belly as he nodded sagely. "Turn him into a right scholar. Nobody from the Pronson Academy goes on the parish."

Under a window was a low bookcase that contained worn volumes. A soiled wool rug covered some of the floor. Two bentwood chairs were alongside the desk but everyone in the room was standing save the master.

"Here is this term's tuition." Miss Havisham placed a linen pouch on the master's desk.

"We brook no foolishness or insolence," Master Belvedere said. "Up at six in the morning and to bed at half seven in the evening. There is much to gain from adherence to a strict schedule. A disciplined compassion is what we practice here, madam." He lifted the pouch, hefted it a few times, then returned it to the desk.

Luke frowned and glanced at Fagin who nudged the boy closer to the master's desk. A kerosene lamp, a sterling letter opener, and a brass-and-glass hourglass were on the desk next to three primers in a stack.

A silver broach of six pearls was pinned to Miss Havisham's lilac spencer jacket. She wore white kid gloves, and the color of her silk bandeaux matched the jacket.

"I will come to the city five days before Christmas to take you to Satis House," Miss Havisham said. "You'll spend Christmas with me and baby Estella. We'll have a grand time."

"I suppose," Luke said.

"I'll say goodbye to you, Luke." She bent to hug the boy. "The term will pass quickly, and then we'll see each other again."

The boy returned the hug, then stepped back. "Goodbye, misses."

Master Belvedere rose from his chair and stepped around the desk to place his hand on Luke's shoulder, then guided him toward a door behind the desk. "He is in excellent hands," he said over his shoulder as he led the boy into a hallway.

Miss Havisham shook her head. "I didn't know if I'd be able to say goodbye to Luke without weeping. I just barely made it."

"Ay, it appears to have been close." Fagin's tweed jacket had patches over the elbows.

She put her hand on Fagin's arm, and they stepped from Pronson Academy out onto the pavement. "I must say goodbye to you, too, Fagin. I'll miss you." She laughed lightly. "I don't know why but I will."

"You have been a tonic, madam, and I don't mean simply because you have paid me handsomely."

She put both her hands in his, smiling at him, then she put her arm around his neck and kissed his cheek.

Fagin said, "My last advice is to not let your guard down."

"I won't."

"You already have, eh?" He retrieved her pearl broach from his pocket and handed it to her.

She laughed again as she pinned the broach back onto her spencer. "You know where Satis House is, Fagin. Maybe you could call someday."

"I will."

"You won't. But I want you to know you are welcome, and that I would love to see you." She left him in front of the academy's door, and crossed the street toward her carriage. The footman jumped down to open the door for her.

* * * *

Fagin leaned against a lamppost on the pavement next to the Pronson Academy. From his jacket he pulled out a silver watch that until that morning had belonged to a Gray's Inn barrister. He opened the case to check the time.

Miss Havisham's carriage had departed ten minutes ago. He returned the watch to his vest pocket, then shined one of his half boots without taking it off by rubbing it on the backside of his pant leg. The sun was a milky wafer overhead. Across the street was a stocking weaver's shop next to a whalebone merchant's office. Fagin picked at a tooth with a fingernail. He shook his head at a lady offering pickles from a bucket.

He turned to the sound of a window opening twenty yards farther along the academy building. He hurried to help Luke raise the window, then he pulled the boy through and lowered him to the pavement. Fagin closed the window.

"I hope Miss Havisham won't be mad," Luke said, passing Fagin the linen pouch containing the academy's tuition.

"For one who is so vengeful she impresses me as also understanding." Fagin dropped the pouch into his pocket. "She would not argue against a young man fulfilling his destiny out here on the streets."

Luke handed Fagin the hourglass from Master Belvedere's desk. "Maybe I should learn to read someday."

Fagin lifted a housebreaker's tool from a pocket. "You need more practice with my picklock, my dear. I have just the place in mind."

"I did good last time." He gave Fagin the silver letter opener that had been on Belvedere's desk, and then had to move his legs quickly to keep pace with Fagin.

"It took you two minutes to spring the haberdasher's lock yesterday, and a ship's bell makes less sound than you did."

273

"I'll get better."

Fagin grinned down at the boy. "I'm sure of it, Luke."

* * * *

Mrs. Ellabeth Zane pointed a sausage-shaped finger at Compeyson. "That is the man who was in my home, who stole my silver spoons. I would recognize him anywhere, with that yellow hair and the notch in his chin."

"I have never seen this woman before," Compeyson shouted, "and I have never been in her home."

"Silence, you," said the judge under his powdered wig at the Old Bailey.

At Compeyson's left shoulder was a jailor from whose belt hung an iron ring holding dozens of keys. On Compeyson's right was a lawyer, the finest the Middle Temple could produce who, suspecting his client's proclivity for shiftiness, had received his substantial fee in advance, and who did not ask from which of Beecker's-Compeyson's-Franks's victims the money had come from. The lawyer's wig was thickly powdered, some of which had fallen onto his gown's sleeves, speckling them.

The judge said, "Mrs. Zane, thank you for your testimony, and you are dismissed."

The crown prosecutor—a wiry little man not much higher than the table he stood behind—said, "The crown rests its case, your honor."

Compeyson stood under the mirror that hung from the courtroom's rafters. His remarkably handsome face was lit by a beam of reflected daylight which made his hair appear gray and dispirited. The prisoner's sackcloth trousers and hemp shirt were half-again as large as his slender frame required, and he resembled a rag hung from a hook.

The judge addressed the jurors. "Will you need time to deliberate, good sirs?"

The twelve jurors turned in their chairs to glance at each other, some shaking their heads.

Then a juror in a dark blue waistcoat under a suede jacket rose from his chair and said, "We are unanimous, your honor. The defendant—a loathsome felon to whom we jurors gladly deliver justice—is guilty of all charges."

"What is happening to me?" Compeyson yelled. "That woman I've never seen before, spoons I know nothing about. I demand . . . ."

A burly bailiff squeezed Compeyson's arm with such vigor that Compeyson yelped.

The judge said, "This court has determined that your name at birth was Harold Beecker, which is the name under which your sentence will be passed." His dewlaps waggled with each word. "The surnames Compeyson, Franks, Giles, and a number of others are your inventions. The jury has found you guilty of personation, fraud, and breaking and entering. Do you have anything to say before sentence is passed?"

Compeyson's voice was dark with sorrow and resentment. "I protest my innocence of all charges, your honor."

"Protest all you like after you have been taken away. The jailors will be much amused." The judge placed a piece of hard candy into his mouth. It may have been peppermint, as he pursed his lips and inhaled air.

The crowd in the upstairs gallery had fallen silent because a sentencing was a highlight. Slices of meat pies were set aside, and knitting needles were lowered. English justice in all its dignity and grandeur was about to send some fellow to hard and miserable punishment, and there could be no finer entertainment.

The crown prosecutor pushed his notes into a briefcase on his table. The trial had taken one hour, and Inspector Bucket was a witness called by the prosecution. The defendant had testified on his own behalf but his entire adult life had been as vaporous as a cloud, and he had few solid facts on which to cling, and Compeyson—so convincing in other situations—had been hesitant, evasive, and implausible.

Standing in the dock, the defendant said, "I hope you, sir, will take into account that this is the first time I've been brought before this honorable court or any other court."

The judge slid a file from the side of his desk to place it in front of him. He unfolded a pair of spectacles then wrapped them around his face.

"I've never been arrested before," Beecker-Compeyson-Franks said. "And I hope your honor will consider my earlier blameless life when rendering the sentence."

The judge lifted a page from the file. "It says here that one Harold Beecker . . . that is you, is it not?"

"On occasion, yes, sir."

"It says here you were convicted of embezzlement two years ago in front of Judge Artismus, stealing a Bath woman's inheritance with a false will and testament."

The defendant stepped back so abruptly he might have been slapped. "Embezzlement? Me? I've never been convicted of embezzlement or anything else. I've never even been arrested before."

The jailor shoved Compeyson back to the bar. His lawyer stared at the defendant, a look of silent reproach for having hidden his past.

The bejowled judge brought up another document. "And here is a conviction for selling shares in a sugar cane plantation in a West Indies nation called Poypai. The planation didn't exist and neither did the nation. You spent four years at Fleet for the crime."

Compeyson eyebrows had crawled up his forehead. "Sir, I have never been convicted of such a crime and I have never set foot in the Fleet Prison."

The judge pulled another candy out of his sack. "This trial over which I have just presided established that you are a convincing liar, Mr. Beecker or Compeyson or Franks. And that is what I'm hearing now. Lies." He held up the document. "Here is your prison record from the Fleet. It lists your date of internment, date of release, and three punishments for rules violations, right here in Warden Batterson's handwriting, which I recognize well enough."

"Sir, that document is a forgery. I've never . . . ."

"And you were convicted by this very court, the late Judge Collins presiding, nine years ago of burglary, spending two months at Coldbath, a light sentence due to your youth."

"Burglary?" Compeyson exclaimed, a glow coming to his cheeks. "I would never stoop to burgling, not back then nor today with silver spoons. It is the profession of morons."

The judge held up the documents and shook them. "You stand there arguing against your own history, which you know better than anyone, but which these records give a sordid if only partial account."

These documents were the same ones Fagin and Luke had smuggled into the Old Bailey's records room a few weeks before. They were forgeries, every one of them. They reflected a low criminal past but a fictional one, and while Samuel Compeyson's life was doubtless a little more than a compilation of crimes, his crimes weren't the ones portrayed in the papers the judge wagged at the defendant.

"You, sir," the judge said, "are a lifelong criminal for whom prison has failed to teach you the errors of your way. Prison is clearly not enough."

This was the delectable moment. Spectators in the gallery leaned forward. Lawyers and clerks fell silent. The room was as quiet as a closet.

Until Compeyson yelled, "I did not do those crimes and I have never been in prison."

The jailor gripped Compeyson's arm.

The judge lifted a feather pen from an inkwell. "I hereby sentence you to fifteen years in the custody of the crown."

Compeyson gasped and staggered.

The judged added, "And I deem you, with your apparently born and incurable deviousness, an escape risk, and so the sentence will be served aboard a prison ship." He scratched the verdict and sentence onto a sheet of paper. "I bind you over to the prison transport service for shipment to your place of incarceration."

A frisson of pleasure swept through the room, and a burst of applause came from the gallery. The spectators called out their approval. Harsh crime deserved harsh sentences. This is what separated England from France and other anarchistic places such as Belgium: sure and severe punishment. The streets of Paris and whatever was the capital of Belgium were filled with toughs, malcontents, and criminals because they were never dealt with severely. In a blink the felons were back on those foreign streets where they just accumulated like maggots on a carcass. Not here in England. Ah, the glory of it, the splendor and justice of it, England forever, and God save the king. The gallery's clapping lasted a full minute.

Compeyson yelled at the judge when the jailor pushed him toward the door to the cells. Then the swindler charged the judge, pointing at him with one hand, his other hand a fist. He shrieked something unintelligible, and he almost reached the bench.

The jailor tackled him, and both landed on the floor. Compeyson kneed the jailor, who snorted with pain, both scrambling on the floor. A sheriff joined the pile, and placed Compeyson in a headlock. A bailiff grabbed Compeyson by the shirt, and then pinned his arms to his sides. Compeyson was lifted to his feet, and the sheriff sent his fist into Compeyson's belly with such ferocity that Compeyson folded like a fan. The gallery applauded.

The three men carried the newly-convicted felon—who was gasping and groaning—toward the door, and he was handled roughly. They disappeared into the darkness of a hallway.

The judge reached for yet another document. "Next case, number 586. Mr. Bailiff, bring the prisoner Abel Magwitch to the dock."

Inspector Bucket had observed the trial and sentencing from near a column below the gallery. He said to the fellow next to him, "You must do nice work, Tilley."

The forger replied in his high voice, "I would agree but it would incriminate me."

Tilley was wearing his Newmarket coat. His face was narrow and pallid. He was the Old Nichol forger who Samuel Compeyson had hired to create several documents for the Wilkinson swindle. Inspector Bucket had known Tilley for ten years, since Bucket had testified against him at a trial. Though the testimony had sent Tilley to Newgate for two years, Bucket had liked the fellow and had admired his skill, and had maintained contact with him, once in a while venturing into Old Nichol. Tilley had been a source of tips, too. Tilley burying himself deep within Old Nichol had helped him avoid another arrest but so too had the friendship of Lewis Bucket.

Compeyson had hired Tilley but then so had Miss Havisham, and the forger had created for her the sentencing reports regarding Harold Beecker that the judge had just referred to before sentencing Compeyson to fifteen years, which were those same documents Fagin and Luke had snuck into the court's files. Tilley had also created the banker's check that Compeyson had tried to cash at the Ludgate Bank.

The forger said, "I don't like being in the city, Bucket. Too many dangers."

"You mean too many policemen." Bucket smiled. "I'll walk you some of the way back."

They stepped from the courtyard to the street.

"I'll inform Miss Havisham of the success of your work for her," Bucket said. "And it'll be a pleasure."

28

The prison van was an iron box on iron-rimmed wheels. Padlocks on the doors weighed five pounds each. Windows were the size of mail slots. The van was black fore to aft, top to bottom, even the driver's coat was black. Four horses pulled the van, and four soldiers in red coats and shakos followed on horseback. The procession kicked up mud as it travelled on the moor road. The river was just to the north, and the van turned toward a plank dock at the edge of the water.

Clouds lay low over the Thames, the rain was more a mist, falling lightly but still making the horizon close. The far riverbank was hidden, as was anything more than three hundred yards distant. The mist appeared to have pressed the river flat as there were no waves or even catspaws, and the river surface shone dully. A twenty-foot rowboat was tied to the dock, two pairs of oars shipped on the benches.

When the driver hauled back on the reins, the prison van stopped near the dock. Out in the river the hulk ship was an ethereal presence as the mist revealed it then closed over it again. The hulk's masts and yards had been removed long ago, and the navy's checkerboard black and white pattern along its gunwales had faded to insignificance. Wood rot blackened the hull near the waterline.

The soldiers drew muskets from scabbards and dismounted, gathering around the prison van's door. They fixed their bayonets into the barrel slots. The driver jumped down, his keys jangling.

Another vehicle was near the dock, this one a Berlin with a driver on the box who wore a Petersham coat. A footman in green livery stood by the carriage's door.

The driver opened the prison van's door. Two redcoats emerged from the van, put on their shakos, and joined the others. Then Samuel Compeyson struggled to climb down from the van because his ankles wore iron fetters. Manacles held his hands close together. He looked around, squinting against the gray light. His blond hair was stuck against his skull. Grime covered his convict pants and shirt. The jailor shoved him from the door so a second prisoner could come out of the van.

Abel Magwitch emerged from the van, and he too moved awkwardly due to leg irons. His face was twisted with wrath. He shuffled toward the river between the soldiers. Two soldiers walked onto the dock, then boarded the rowboat.

Moving as quickly as hobbles allowed Magwitch lurched forward and brought his arms down over Compeyson's head, yanking back his hands so that the handcuff chain throttled Compeyson.

Compeyson gagged and reeled backwards against Magwitch's chest.

"Pull me off the horse and leave me out there?" Magwitch yelled into Magwitch's ear. "When I was rescuing you?"

Compeyson scraped feebly at his chain around his neck. He sank toward the ground.

A soldier viciously jabbed Magwitch's head with the butt of his musket. Magwitch toppled, dragging Compeyson down to the dirt. The soldier grabbed Compeyson's arms to unhook him from Magwitch, then lifted Compeyson to his feet by the cuff chain. Compeyson leaned on his knees, and his inhalations sounded in his throat. Another soldier shoved him toward the dock.

Magwitch gripped his head with both hands, then rolled to his side. He groaned. A soldier prodded his back with the tip of a bayonet. Magwitch tried to rise to his feet but the ankle shackles hampered his movements. Two redcoats lifted him by his arms. When he swayed one of the soldiers shoved him forward. Two gulls at the end of the dock cried out, rose in the air, and flew upstream.

The Berlin's footman placed a stool on the ground and opened the door. Miss Havisham emerged from the carriage, and held the footman's arm as she stepped to the ground. Her gray jacket was the color of the river. She was forty yards from the prison van. Soldiers glanced at her but may have seen no threat so they escorted the prisoners toward the dock.

Perhaps Compeyson sensed her presence. He turned toward her, and his gaze found her. A few seconds passed, and then his face slackened. He slumped, and a rough sound escaped him. He appeared to become smaller as if the mist squeezed him. When he raised his shackled hands toward her, a redcoat jabbed his back with a fist, and the confidence man stumbled toward the dock.

Miss Havisham's expression betrayed nothing but her gloved hands were knotted together. Mist droplets gathered on her shoulders. When the prisoners reached the dock, she said, "I'm ready to go, William."

The footman gave her his arm, and she stepped up, and after she entered the Berlin's cab he climbed to his seat at the back. The driver clicked the horses forward.

The carriage turned back toward Satis House. She kept her gaze straight ahead, at the cab's front wall, and didn't look again at Samuel Compeyson.

* * * *

"Now I ask you, clean out this room, Margaret." The lawyer Jaggers spread his arms to encompass the place. "Toss out all these unwelcome things, all these cruel reminders."

Miss Havisham kissed the baby Estella's forehead. "I'm not in a hurry."

"But you should be," Jaggers said. "This room—with all the memories of your bitter day—now has no purpose, if it ever did. This room and the molding cake and flowers and gift boxes apparently inspired you to vengeance and kept you to your purpose."

"They did, yes."

"But now your account with Compeyson has been settled." Jaggers thick black eyebrows rose. "He is on a prison ship on the Thames."

"So I saw."

"He is a clever fellow, and he has surely determined you were the cause of all his misfortune, of his shaming and his imprisonment."

"I hope he does."

"You and he are quits."

Estella was wrapped in a red merino wool blanket with the initials EH embroidered repeatedly at the edges, a little something Miss Havisham had ordered for the baby in the city. Estella held Miss Havisham's finger and grinned up at her. The baby was perfectly proportioned, with luminous green eyes, and she would smile with the least provocation. That she was the loveliest baby in Kent was firmly believed among the Satis House staff and the brewery workers.

Jaggers said, "Ask your housemaids to clean out this room. They can do it today, while I'm still here. I'll help, and won't charge you for my time."

Miss Havisham surveyed the room. Decay and dust increased daily. The garlands drooped more and more, and leaves were becoming brittle. Flowers in their vases yellowed and crumbled. A pair of shoes on the dressing table was turning from white to yellow. The wedding dress on the mannequin had sagged, and the beading had lost its luster. Curtains were drawn, and only mantle candles lit the room.

"I'm going to keep the room as it is." Miss Havisham rocked the baby in her arms. "It will be a reminder of my foolishness."

"You are anything but a fool, Margaret."

"This room has been a forge. It has hardened me."

"You are paying me for the most candid advice I can offer, advice based upon my years in the courts."

"Sometimes you are too candid." Miss Havisham smiled at him. She was wearing a cream frock.

The lawyer said, "Some people are tossed off their horses, and they never get back on. Many of my clients are like that, as is my maid Molly, whom you have met. I take everything on evidence, Margaret, and I fear for you."

"I'm stronger than that." She crossed the room to the wedding dress and fiddled with the pearling.

"It has nothing to do with strength. It has to do with madness."

"Am I a lunatic?"

"The force and focus with which you went after Samuel Compeyson is not normal. You were an angry wasp." Jaggers turned a circle, his hands out. "I take everything on evidence. Here is this room that you won't clean up. And there is a clock that stopped that you refuse to wind. Open the drapes and let the light in."

"They are just old wedding things."

"Allow me to recommend someone for you, a physician in the city. I have sent several clients to him. He has medicines and he talks to you. He can help you find your way."

"Mr. Jaggers, I know you speak from friendship but I would like you to attend to my businesses and not to me. I am an adult and can make my way without a male governess." She placed her hand on his arm. "Good day to you now."

"Keep my offer of an introduction to this physician in mind, Margaret." Jaggers bowed and left the room. His footsteps faded down the hallway.

Miss Havisham looked down at the baby. "What do you think, Estella? Shall we clean up this room?" She touched Estella's cheek then sat in a leather chair near the wedding dress. "And shall I wind the clock? Shall I open the curtains to let the light in?"

The baby happily gurgled.

"I will do no such things, my beautiful little Estella." She looked at the wall above the fireplace, and she addressed that wall. "There is much wisdom in what you say." She looked down at the baby. "Did you hear that, Estella? The room doesn't want me to wind the clock or open the curtains. It wants me to stay here for a while."

She cradled Estella in her arms, tucking the blanket more tightly around the baby. Estella grinned, a first tooth showing.

"I have much to teach you about handsome young men," Miss Havisham said, "and we can begin this very day."

The End

JAMES THAYER

FROM THE AUTHOR

I have loved Charles Dickens's novels since I was fourteen years old and I have often wondered, "Where did these wonderful characters come from? What are their stories? How did the pickpocket Fagin become Fagin? How about the wretched bruiser Bill Sikes? And the madwoman Miss Havisham? David Copperfield's evil stepfather Murdstone? And the convict on the moor, Abel Magwitch?" Dickens created these unforgettable characters but left us few clues as to their origins.

In *Fagin & Miss Havisham* I have attempted to recreate Dickens's characters when they were young, during the actions and intrigues that shaped them. My novel mixes these characters together and sets them on their paths. I hope you have enjoyed it as much as I enjoyed writing it. I had terrific fun inventing their stories, knocking around the loathsome Sikes, helping Miss Havisham in her distress, and aiding Fagin as he lifts pocket watches. At the end of *Fagin & Miss Havisham* these folks are where they are at the beginning of Charles Dickens's novels. My hope was to represent the characters honestly and authentically in a way to make Dickens and his fans proud. I welcome your feedback on your favorite bookseller's website. And I'd enjoy hearing from you through my website or social media pages.

James Thayer
January 2024

ACKNOWLEDGEMENTS

Charles Dickens's stories have inspired and entertained readers for more than 150 years. Fagin & Miss Havisham pays homage to him. And thank you to Dan Chosich for his design work.

ABOUT THE AUTHOR

James Thayer is the author of fourteen critically acclaimed novels. The New York Times Book Review said his "writing is smooth and clear. Deceptively simple, it wastes no words, and it has a rhythm that only confident stylists achieve." And Kirkus Reviews said he a "reputation as an elegant stylist and presents complex issues with haunting lucidity." His popular podcast, The Essential Guide to Writing a Novel, is available at Google, Apple, and Spotify. He graduated from Washington State University and the University of Chicago Law School, and he lives in Seattle.

ABOUT THE PUBLISHER

Creative Texts is a boutique independent publishing house devoted to high quality content that readers enjoy. We publish best-selling authors such as Jerry D. Young, N.C. Reed, Sean Liscom, Jared McVay, Laurence Dahners, and many more. Our audiobook performers are among the best in the business including Hollywood legends like Barry Corbin and top talent like Christopher Lane, Alyssa Bresnaham, Erin Moon and Graham Hallstead.

Whether its post-apocalyptic or dystopian fiction, biography, history, true crime science fiction, thrillers, or even classic westerns, our goal is to produce highly rated customer preferred content. If there is anything we can do to enhance your reader experience, please contact us directly at info@creativetexts.com. As always, we do appreciate your reviews on your book seller's website.

Finally, if you would like to find more great books like this one, please search for us by name in your favorite search engine or on your bookseller's website to see books by all Creative Texts authors. Thank you for reading.

Made in the USA
Coppell, TX
20 March 2024

30353954R00162